THE HAWK
AND THE RAVEN

STACEY DIGHTON

CRANTHORPE
— MILLNER —
PUBLISHERS

First published by Cranthorpe Millner Publishers (2021)

ISBN 978-1-912964-89-5 (Paperback)

www.cranthorpemillner.com

Cranthorpe Millner Publishers

About the Author

Stacey Dighton is an author of horror, crime, fantasy and science fiction. He lives in the south-east of England with his wife, Jo, and their two children, as well as their elderly Bassett Hound, Lily, and their geriatric tortoise, Nelly. He enjoys live music and can often be seen plucking on a battered guitar or yelling something resembling a tune into an old microphone.

www.staceydightonstoryteller.com

To my wife, Jo, and our wonderful children, Jayden and
Harley.
Love you always.

Prologue

'Is it done?'

He shook his head, the ice cold water gently lapping into his eyes and in his mouth. He gagged and spat the salty, frothy liquid out. He looked up.

'Is it…? I don't understand.'

Again the soft, female voice whispered with gentle urgency.

'Is it done?'

'I don't know. What do you mean?'

His vision was blurred and from his prone position it was hard to picture a form, face or any other details of significance. The visage that swam in front of him flitted in and out of focus like a badly filmed montage. He could barely make out blonde hair, pale complexion and what appeared to be a loose fitting vest top and denim shorts.

A man joined her. Despite Raven's semi consciousness he could see that the male was tall; around six feet, dark hair, short beard, some sort of rock band T-shirt and combat shorts. The man bent down and looked at him solemnly.

'She's asking if it is done.' He ran his hands through the woman's hair. 'Is it finished? Can we be set free?'

Raven tried to sit up but a hot shard of pain fizzed across his temples. He winced and uttered a gruff *'ugh!'* He couldn't move his hands and his legs felt like jelly mixture that hadn't yet quite solidified. He was wet and freezing cold.

'Look mate, I dun know what yo are gorn orn about,' his mouth was moving in slow motion and his words would not form correctly. He blinked and tried to move his leaden head but each time he was hit with a bolt of hot pain like dipping his scalp in molten lava.

The open space was black apart from the luminescent figures in front of him. A third character joined. An older man in swimming shorts.

'We need to be released, young man. It has been far too long.'

The middle aged gentleman stood next to his younger companion and they nodded at each other. The young woman smiled with longing, tinged with a despairing regret.

Raven looked beyond the man into the beckoning blackness. There was a sound like a constant hiss or a hum, a white noise that seeped into his skin and bones, washed over his consciousness and impregnated his thoughts. He pushed himself back towards a damp wall with his rubbery, gelatinous legs and tried to right himself. The water had soaked his clothes through to the skin and he shivered.

'I dorn know how… or what.'

A fourth character, an older woman in filthy, bedraggled clothes, and a fifth, rotund man with a walking stick, joined the three.

They spoke in unison: 'Is it done?'

'I…'

'Tell us it's done!'

Raven pulled at the binds around his wrists and rubbed against the jagged wall behind him. He had no strength in his muscles and he was so, so cold. He pleaded with them.

'Look, people…'

A sixth and seventh character. An eighth. They moved towards him, their feet gliding through the water without creating a ripple or a sound. They loomed over him. He was being set upon by a desperate mob and he had no way of escape. He cried out.

'Help!'

The figures bore down on him, their arms reaching for him, their eyes imploring him, their very essence soaking into him. The large man waved his stick at him. The elderly lady shook a fist at him. Swim shorts man angrily kicked out a leg. He screamed.

His binds tore apart and he gripped the wall, desperately pulling himself upwards, his fingers sticking to the wall like octopus tentacles. He was desperately trying to keep himself as far away as possible from the angry, ghostly mob …

The mob that had …

Disappeared.

The room was black and eerily silent aside from the constant hiss. He took in a large gulp of cold and salty breath.

The water was rising and was now halfway between his ankles and his knees. He moved his feet and kicked a rock. He reached a tentative and unsteady hand to his head and felt a stickiness. And pain. There was a pop and suddenly memories came flooding back to him as if a dam of recollection had suddenly split in two.

He remembered. He remembered it all. Every last damn second of it. An ominous dread poured over him like a tepid, odorous liquid. He had to get out. He turned towards the tunnel only to see a shape, an object, a sudden movement and then ...

    A loud bang.

Act 1:
Dark Times

Go ye not by Gallowa
Come bide a while, my frein
I'll tell ye o the dangers there.

Chapter 1:
The Killing

Lizzy was drunk. She knew it. She shouldn't have had that last black Sambuca but her friends had egged her on and she had always been a sucker for a free drink. Of course, the several rum and cokes beforehand hadn't helped either. Or the Coronas before that. She hadn't felt the effects of the alcohol until she had left the club and then the cold, sea air had hit her. She had done well not to throw up on her way there but she was pretty sure she had kept her nausea from him. She hoped so anyway. He was really cute.

Dan looked at her and couldn't hide how attracted he was. She was stunning. Long blond hair, tanned skin, beauty spot high up on her right cheek, piercing green eyes. She wore bangles on both wrists, a light green vest top and tight shorts. She was carrying her flat shoes in her hand and her painted toenails looked adorable as they pressed into the sand.

He had spotted her immediately in the pub and he and his mate, Chris, had made a bee-line for Lizzy and her tall friend Donna. Chris was useless with girls and it quickly became obvious that Donna didn't find him attractive at all. Chris had tried his usual chat up lines – 'are you Google? Because you're everything I've been searching for'; 'if you were words on a page, you'd be fine print' – that kind of cheesy and tacky thing, but Donna just looked bored. By about the third drink Donna left and Chris went back out onto the dancefloor to lick his wounds. Lizzy on the other hand…

They had slow danced and shared a kiss. Her lips were soft and sugary, her hands caressing and tender and he knew then that he'd be going home with her. Maybe she could heal the heartache he felt after … well after Cheryl abandoned him. It had been so long.

'Come on, Dan, let's see how fast you are.'

Lizzy teasingly looked back over her shoulder and laughed. She kicked sand up into his chest and face and then turned and ran. He laughed back and set off after her.

'Hang on, hang on. That's not fair! You had a head start!'

'I'll race you to Bishop's Crag. Last one there has to skinny dip.' Her legs were pounding hard on the sand and the wind was shrieking through her blond curls. She glanced behind her and could see Dan's long legs striding with purpose. She pounded her arms, set her jaw firm and doubled her efforts. She was desperate to see him in the buff and knee deep in the ice cold West Solent.

Dan was giggling as he sprinted after her. She really was quick and he was having to put in some real lung bursting effort to keep up, but he knew it was all just a prick tease. They both wanted each other, that was obvious from the start, and this was simply Lizzy's way of stretching out the inevitable. They were going back to his place tonight and if it meant he had to walk out there in the ocean with nothing on but his birthday suit and a smile, then so be it.

The beach grew a lot darker further away from the town

and the glow from the streetlights faded to a dull ember just past the point where the dunes grew to a little over seven metres in height. The large, three storey detached homes on the Palisades looked down on them from their lofty perch as the road that ran parallel to the beach, Sunnyview, stretched up into the hills and out of sight. It was two o' clock in the morning and Dan knew that the good people of the Palisades, mainly bankers, stockbrokers and the assorted staff of various Premier League clubs, would be nestled into their duvets and dreaming of the size of their next bonus, premiership points' advantage or FTSE five hundred windfall. Lizzy was some ten metres away and, while Dan was steadily closing in on her, the darkness was enveloping them and he could barely make out the shape of her supple legs or her beautifully rounded posterior.

'Lizzy,' he breathed in the cold night air and bellowed, 'wait! It's getting dark out here!'

He stopped and placed his hands on his hips. The condensation from his hot breath formed a mystic halo around his head and he sucked in the sea air.

'Lizzy?'

He looked out at the sea, the white swell of the tide lapping at the shoreline. He could make out the lights from tankers making their slow, cumbersome path across the south of England towards the US and the blinking red beacons from the wind farm a few miles further south. He turned and looked behind him, the Westhampton seafront with its pubs, restaurants and souvenir trinket shops seemingly a million miles away. The dunes and rocks to his left looked dark and menacing; the black and gnarly marram and couch grass reached out to him like the withering hands of some wicked

15

old witch. He ran a hand through his hair and called out again.

'Lizzy, stop messing around!'

He peered into the darkness in front of him but all he could see was Lizzy's footprints in the sand and then, a few metres out, nothing but black. He walked further up the beach and followed her trail.

'This is starting to piss me off now, Lizzy. Come on!'

He reached into his pocket, pulled out his phone and looked at the battery level.

'*Shit*,' he cursed. Two percent.

He swiped down and searched for the torch icon. After a moment to see whether he'd had any Instagram updates (none, which he found mildly disappointing) he found it, touched the picture with his forefinger and then, almost instantly, the area before him erupted in bright, blue-grey light.

Lizzy was lying on the ground about five metres in front of him, her arms above her head, hair all over her face, her legs bent and crossed at the knees and her eyes closed. She didn't appear to be breathing.

'Shit!' Dan ran over and bent down beside her. He put his phone on the floor so that the light irradiated the area and leaned over to check Lizzie's pulse. He placed a hand on her chest, feeling for a heartbeat or any sign of her breathing.

'Lizzy, Lizzy, don't do this, don't…' he was panicking. His mind was racing. What had they had to drink? Had Chris spiked her rum and coke (lord knows, they'd done it before)? After the incident with the girl at the swimming pool he couldn't afford another rumour-fuelling disaster. He ran a hand across his forehead. He was sweating despite the cold.

'Get your hand off my tits.' Dan snapped out of his daze

and looked down at Lizzy. She was looking up at him in amusement and smiling inanely. 'Don't you think that's a little forward?'

'You...' he grabbed her arms and leaned over her, 'you bloody ...' he bent down to kiss her and she turned her head away. 'You cow.' He leaned forward and she turned to him. Their eyes met and their lips touched. She put her arms around him as their mouths joined as one and he reached a hand behind her back and pulled her towards him.

'Well, isn't this lovely.'

A voice from above them. Dan broke away and looked up, only to see a hazy silhouette of a stranger on the empty beach. He turned and got to his knees. 'Who the fuck ...'

'I am the Hawk.'

Dan looked down at Lizzy who was visibly shaken. Her eyes implored him to do something.

'You're the what?'

'I am the Hawk.' There was a sound like metal on leather. 'And this is how you die.'

The silhouette extended its arm and with a swift movement cut a gaping wound across Dan's jugular vein. Blood sprayed in a fierce jet across the golden sand of Westhampton beach and down Dan's chest and shirt. His mouth fell open in shocked bewilderment and he reached up with a shaking hand to try to prevent the lifeblood seeping from his leaking throat. He attempted to speak but blood bubbles formed on his lips and all he could manage was a desperate hiss.

It took a moment for Lizzy to react, the scene in front of her playing out as if in slow motion. She tried to scream but no sound came out. She thought of her parents and her

17

younger brother, Tom. She couldn't let this maniac take her from them. Dan was a goner, she couldn't do anything for him, but she could do something for herself. Damn right she could.

As Dan fell forward into the cold, damp sand, she leapt up and sprinted back towards town. She knew she was quick, she was her secondary school two hundred metres sprint champion after all, but she intended to be much quicker than she had ever been before. The adrenalin would see to that.

Five metres became ten metres became fifteen metres and she was crying and laughing at the same time. She was getting away; there was no way this goon was going to keep up with her. Whatever that creep wanted, he wasn't getting it today.

And that's when someone pounced on her from the right hand side, knocking her headlong into the sea, and plunging her face first into its murky depths. She thrashed around and gasped for breath but the more she fought, the more the freezing, salty liquid entered her mouth and throat. She coughed and spluttered and tried to scream for help, but she was drowning and silt and seaweed filled her lungs as her thoughts turned into a fuzzy mulch. She was crying but her desperate tears dissipated into the watery vastness of the ocean.

Her last thought was for her mum. She would miss her.

Chapter 2:
The Assignment

The bird of prey sat silently and gracefully on a mossy overhang at the top of the cliff. Its hooked beak was turned down in a sneer, its black, marble eyes stared emotionlessly out towards the horizon. It idly scratched its throat with its razor sharp talon and peered down at him. Its coffee brown and off-white plume ruffled gently in the swirling wind as the clouds swept by overhead. He glimpsed the milky moon between jagged breaks in the overcast sky and it appeared to smile smugly at him with a hint of morbid curiosity. He felt afraid.

He saw the couple as they kissed on the sand. She had her arms around him in a gentle embrace, he had his face nuzzled into the crook of her neck. They were laughing.

The young boy with the short brown hair ran along the sea front, his shorts flapping loosely, just past his knees, his T-shirt hanging from his body like it was three or four sizes too big. He stopped and looked down at the young lovers. He appeared amused but lost, like a child who had misplaced his parents. He walked over to them, his hands hanging by his side, chewing gum. He stared down at the pair with disinterest, ran a dirty hand through his shaggy hair and drooled. His spittle hung, swayed in the breeze and dropped, landing with a soft plop on the back of the young man's head. The man raised his hand and wiped it away, his face never leaving the soft skin of his beau's tanned neck.

The girl looked up at the boy from her horizontal position and smiled.

'Hi, stranger. What ya doing?'

More drool fell from the boy's pooched bottom lip and it ran down the man's back and onto the sand.

'You hungry, kid?'

The boy looked up at the cliff. The bird of prey seemed to nod and then spread its wings as it launched itself into the strong headwind. It plummeted down towards them in tight arcs. The boy started to laugh.

Raven looked down at the girl and her mouth drew down in a terrified scowl.

'*No!*'

The man pulled his busy lips away from her tender throat and turned to face Raven. His own throat was cut from ear to ear and seaweed spewed from the wound like bloody tendrils. He smiled gleefully back at him and black and sticky blood hung from his lips like treacle.

The girl turned to the boy.

'You bastard!'

The boy wiped the spittle from his lip and without another word he turned on his heels and ran. He galloped into the sea, the waves crashing around him with a furious and infinite energy. He laughed like a naughty schoolchild.

The hawk, its talons thrust out in front like deadly spears, lunged at the girl's face, its claws penetrating her smooth, supple skin with ease and tearing chunks of raw flesh from her cheeks and forehead. She leapt up and tried to shake it off, her face a mask of feathers, blood and loose skin. Her arms flailed side to side like the wings of a downed plane, her shrieks of agony echoing off the cliff tops and drifting out to sea.

Raven cried out, 'No!' He sat bolt upright and hit his head hard. 'Shit, shit, *shit*!'

He raised his hand briskly and pushed the dresser drawer closed, wondering to himself how he had managed to end up on his bedroom floor. His soiled underwear hung from the drawer handle and gently caressed the bump on his forehead. Sunlight spilled in through the bedroom window and he raised a shaky arm to his face to check his watch. Through his hazy vision he was dismayed to learn it was already eleven-thirty in the morning.

'Bugger.'

He had an appointment at mid-day and it was going to take him at least twenty minutes to get across town. He rummaged around on the floor, pushing aside empty packets of nachos, spent beer bottles and a half drunk bottle of scotch and eventually hit on his phone. He furiously rubbed the sleep from his bloodshot eyes, raised the battered keypad to his face and found his contacts. After much pressing of the wrong keys and cursing he eventually found Wesley; his round, freckly face peered up at him from the phone's scratched LCD screen like one of those black and white portraits on a lost child poster.

He hit dial, and after four rings Wesley picked up.

'Hi, Luke.' The kid's voice was riddled with the sweet essence of youth and naivety.

'Hey, Wes. You up?'

'Sure. I was just filling the bike.' Wesley drove a battered moped and he was constantly letting it run too low on fuel, despite Raven's protestations. 'I should be at the Cooper place in around ten minutes.'

Raven smiled. The kid was reliable.

'Well that's why I'm calling, Wes. I might be a little late.' He grimaced as the sour taste of single malt flavoured bile rose in his hoarse throat. 'I'll be there when I can, but in the meantime take the details, get her to sign the disclaimer and quote her the usual.'

'Is this another one of those cheating husband cases, boss?' Raven could hear Wesley sigh ruefully down the phone line. 'Cos they're getting kind of boring. And dangerous. Last time, when I was spotted up that ladder, taking photos of old man Wellard and that male prostitute, I nearly fell and broke my bloody neck.'

Raven laughed to himself. He remembered that. The kid almost went through the skylight in the dirty old bugger's kitchen extension.

'No, no. This one's a fraud case of sorts.' He casually pulled on his three day old socks with his spare hand, his phone tucked into the crook of his neck. 'Ms Cooper thinks her boyfriend, Benny something or other, is taking money from her mother's pension fund and using it for some private interest of his.' He gazed out of the window, regretting the night where he had lost all self-control and given that bitch Deveraux a tattered old rope to hang him with. 'Something like that anyway. I'm sure she'll give you the lowdown when you get there.'

'OK, boss. No problem. Same split as usual?'

Raven sighed. The kid was barely worth his thirty percent; he was clumsy, dim witted and more than a little annoying, but for some reason Raven liked having him around and he certainly needed the company. Especially after …

He shook it off.

'Yeah, same split. And make sure she knows its cash in hand. None of that PayPal or bank transfer bullshit.'

'Sure thing.' Raven could hear Wesley placing the pump nozzle back haphazardly. He imagined him spilling unleaded fuel all over the petrol station's forecourt. 'Will I see you later?'

'Yeah, yeah,' Raven wiped a calloused thumb across his dry mouth, 'I've gotta deal with a couple of things and then I'll come over. You can brief me on the assignment.'

'Sounds great. I … I've got a pack of the alcohol free Bud in if you fancy a beer and a pizza.'

Raven pulled on his jeans and winced as he felt black shards of shame flash across his consciousness. The kid really was naïve.

'Yeah, sure.' He looked at himself in the mirror, unshaven, in need of a hair-cut and a good wash, his paunch hanging over his belt buckle like an old shopping bag. 'Why not? I'll …' he ran a hand through his short beard and checked his nose hair in the mirror, 'I'll give you a call.'

With that he hung up and tossed his phone onto the bed.

He thought of Lisa, how her red hair glistened in the morning sun, how her sweet, musty scent reminded him of good times and laughter. He saw his son's face smiling up at him from his cot as he bent down to collect him, cradling him in his arms and kissing his forehead. He smiled warmly as he recalled sunny days in the park, he and Lisa pushing little

Harry along in his pram and talking about what they wanted for their son, what they planned for his future, for *their* future. The memory faded like an old photograph and all that was left was the tragic image of a middle aged, overweight, sad and lonely excuse of a man glaring at himself in the bedroom mirror and ruminating on the past. The past where he still had his DI badge and a paying job that he loved. The past that he had destroyed. He sneered, picked up his bottle of scotch, took a heavy swig and threw it furiously at the glass.

His image shattered.

Chapter 3:
Molly

It's not as if she was born nasty. She didn't pop out with a sense of fierce self-loathing and hatred for all those around her. No, she was an energetic, smiling baby. All tight curls, big dark eyes and a laugh that could melt the hardest of hearts. Her mother called her Molly after her own grandmother and it suited her.

Of course, she was lucky to be alive. Born a little under three months early and weighing just over three pounds she spent her first months of existence in a Perspex case in the intensive care ward of Westhampton central, tubes in her nose and stomach and looking like she was some kind of semi-artificial octopus. It affected her.

Her mother told her that she and her father had spent hours every day just watching her through the clear plastic, praying she would be saved – but Molly doubted that very much. Her father was a wealthy, successful and very busy man and her mother was a spoilt, privileged lush. How on earth would they have found the time?

Little by little the machine providing her with nutrition fattened her up like a pitiful little Christmas turkey and she popped out of the hospital in time for her mother's thirtieth birthday.

They say there was a big party at the manor. Scores of well to do guests, buckets of lobster ravioli, crates of moules marinière, endless trays of coronation chicken and lashings of filet mignon. They had a swing band – the best in town – and the Mayor gave a speech about how he had almost swept her mother off her feet, way before her father had had the good grace to make an honest woman of her. It was quite the spectacle by all accounts. And little Molly was collected from her plastic prison by the hired help and taken to her nursery in the east wing of the house, away from the bustle, carousing and alcohol fuelled orgy continuing in the great hall.

Molly was an only child. Complications in childbirth meant her mother was left as barren as the Mojave Desert. That suited Molly – she would have hated a little brother and would have resented a little sister. It was for the best. Really.

Her nanny was an elderly lady with long, white hair called Gretchen. Gretchen was from the Bavarian region of southern Germany and had broad shoulders and even larger hands. She sang Germanic folk songs to Molly to get her to sleep and fed her powdered milk from a plastic bottle with a rubber teat. She embroidered Molly's very first blanket with a scene showing a Vorderwald cow with little calves suckling on their mother's udders. In the background was a snow-capped mountain range and swathes of lush foliage. The mid-day sun shone down on the little cow family and they looked wonderfully happy. There was a young, blonde girl in the background carrying two large milk churns that hung from a wooden pole that sat across her shoulders. She was dressed in a brilliant white dress with puffed sleeves and bright blue stitching and she wore moccasins that curled at the toes. Her eyes were big and sparkling and she had the look of someone who was really alive. Molly found the scene enchanting and full of hope – everything was so cheery. One of the little calves even looked like it was smiling although every now and again Molly would get the feeling it was mocking her.

She still had that blanket although now it looked a little worse for wear. It had … been through a lot after all.

Molly's mother would come to the east wing to visit, mostly in the afternoons and never after dark. She would saunter in, smelling of perfume and cigarettes and kiss little Molly on the forehead. Molly would have been too young to remember many of those encounters with any great clarity but she did recall the last.

'Hello, my little orchid. What a beautiful smile and sunny disposition you have today.' Her mother was wearing a bright green button down dress and three inch, black heels. She had a lavish pearl necklace around her neck and gold, colourfully bejewelled bracelets alongside a Cartier watch adorning her left wrist. She was a tall, slender woman with long, ebony hair. She was beautiful but there was always a distant emptiness in her topaz blue eyes. 'Your mother is in a good mood, my little munchkin.' She pinched Molly's freckled cheek tenderly. 'Your father is taking me on a holiday to a wonderful place. Very far away from here in a distant land full of history, mystery and elegance.' She stood and looked out of the large window overlooking the ornate and spacious grounds. 'We will be meeting royalty, my dear, keeping the company of lords and ladies. People with real class and pedigree. Can you believe that? The little girl in dirty clothes from the damp and dilapidated water mill rubbing shoulders with that kind of company.'

Molly doesn't remember whether she reacted – it was before she could form words in any discernible way – but she does remember how happy her mother looked. She had never seen her that way before.

'Your father has promised to mend his ways, you know how he can be, and whilst I'm not sure whether I believe him entirely he has never taken me on one of his business trips before and … well,' she looked at Molly and it was at this point that she knew her mother was never coming back, 'this could be the trip that changes our destiny.'

Although her mother was smiling, there were tears rolling down her cheeks. They trickled off the tip of her pointed chin. 'I haven't been a very good mother to you so far, my little orchid, I know that, but Gretchen is going to take very, *very* good care of you. We paid for the best and she is the best and I hope, someday, you will remember and appreciate what your father and I have done for you.' She bent down and kissed Molly on her forehead. Her lips were cold. 'You will never go wanting. That I can promise you,' she looked down at the floor, 'your father has seen to that.'

And with that her mother stood, smoothed down her dress, furiously wiped the tears from her cheeks and nodded at Gretchen who had entered from the doorway to the adjoining room. 'I will see you in this life or the next.'

She didn't turn back to Molly who was still standing and clutching one of her dolls to her chest, her big eyes peering at her mother through a single lock of dark, curly hair. Instead she spoke to her as she exited the room like a zephyr

28

might silently whisper across an empty plain.

'God will decide.'

Chapter 4:
My Bloody Valentine

It wasn't my idea. Definitely not my idea. You think I could come up with a plan like that? No that little credit would have to go to Ronny Valentine. The big V. Yeah, that's right. Old Ron had someone on the inside.

To be honest, I didn't even need the money. You know that. The business has been going well despite all of the bad press and you and I have been getting on like a house on fire recently. I reckon you see me as your knight in shining armour after I interjected that time and knocked that jumped up prick to the ground. No? That's a bit extreme, you say? Well, pop my little fantasy bubble why don't you. Jeez!

Anyway, Ronny had been a friend of my old man's. You know? On the inside. They'd spent three years together in the clink. They'd even shared a cell for six months, worked in the kitchens together and ran their own little poker syndicate on the side. So yeah, they were pretty close. Ronny had even visited him in hospital before he passed with the cancer, read to him and made sure the prison nurses took good care of him, so I'd always had a certain respect for the man. He knew all about loyalty, looking after your friends and putting yourself out for those in need. The bloke's got real class despite what you may think.

I was on a job actually, sorting out the wiring in Ronny's mother's house out on the old London Road when he dropped in.

'Well if it isn't little chubby William.' He grabbed me from behind. I was on a step ladder with my head poking between two overhead joists when he pinched his fingers into my waist. He hit a nerve and I jolted as if being struck by lightning and nearly fell off.

'Jesus Christ, who the fu-' I turned and saw the six and a half foot boar of a man behind me, greying hair slicked back with Brylcreem, white stubble on an iron cast jaw, fists the size of bowling balls. 'Ronny fucking Valentine, as I live and breathe!' I jumped down off the ladder and shook his hand vigorously. 'When the hell did you get out?'

Ronny clasped my shoulders in his vice like grip and beamed down at me. 'Oh, earlier this week but I've been busy sorting out my affairs. I thought I'd pop round and see if you were taking good care of my mother.'

I set down my screwdriver and pliers. 'Of course, Ron. Only the best for old Mrs V.'

He pointed a gnarly, cow prod of a finger at me. 'Not so much of the old now, William.' He always called me that; he knew it wound me up something chronic. 'My mum's young for her ninety years. Doesn't look a day over sixty if you ask me.'

I had to agree. The old girl had always looked good for her age although her film-star looks had long since departed. 'Well,' I wiped dust and soot from my nose and eyes, 'she's in the front room if you want to pop in and see her. I'm sure you're desperate to say hi after all this time.'

Ronny shook his head. 'All in good time, William my boy.' He unbuttoned his suit jacket which was cream with a pastel blue handkerchief tucked in the breast pocket, and withdrew a scrap of paper from his beige slacks. As hard as Ronny 'Bloody' Valentine was, he had always been a snappy dresser. 'I've got a proposition for you.'

I turned and picked up my flask. I was gasping for a coffee. I poured one into the lid and offered it to Ron. He declined politely and so I took a big sip of the hot, bitter liquid. 'A proposition?'

'Yep, an attractive proposition at that.' He put a hand on my shoulder. 'One that could be very profitable for all those involved.'

I'll admit I was curious, but I was also cautious. My dad had told me all about the notorious Ronny Valentine: his fierce temper, his tenacious attitude and his thirst for a good punch up.

'Well ...' I took another sip from the cheap, instant coffee, 'let's take a look.'

He held out the scrap of wrinkled and torn note-paper. I had to take off my spectacles, rub the crap off them with the bottom of my CCR T-shirt and place them back on the tip of my nose. I squinted. It was a maze of lines, interjected with slashes, vertical squiggles and box shapes. A circuit diagram.

'What's this about Ron? It looks pretty complicated.'

Ronny let out a rip-roaring boom of a laugh. 'It's an alarm system, William. I thought you of all people would know that.' He tipped his head to one side. 'Well?'

I shrugged.

Ron shook his head and huffed. 'Do you think you could

32

do it?'

I frowned. 'Do ... do what, Ron?'

'Do what you do, William my dear boy. Shut that thing down.'

I didn't want to ask but I just had to. 'Why would you want me to shut down an alarm system, Ronny? You've just got out of the nick.'

Ronny stooped over me and whispered. 'Because this little haul is worth the risk. It's life changing.'

I gulped. 'But I don't do that kind of thing anymore. I went legit years ago. I've been on the straight and narrow since Dad died.'

Ronny Valentine loomed over me and I suddenly felt like a little stray puppy dog. 'You'll do this one. You'll do it for your dad.'

I admit it, I was scared but also a little excited. I've often looked back on that day and pored over my decision while downing a pint or three. The only conclusion I can reach is that I felt something akin to what a recovering heroin addict might feel when he sees a friend heating the devil's syrup in a rusty spoon. All those old feelings came rushing back to me like the scent of an old lover and I felt aroused. I nodded and the atmosphere instantly lifted.

'Ha ha! Excellent, my boy. Just excellent.' Ron clapped me hard on the shoulders with his pallet sized hands and then whispered, 'I'll be in touch.'

I smiled and turned to pick up my tools. 'Okay. Sounds good.' I was salivating at the thought of a job. 'Just let me know when you need me.'

'Will do, Billy West, my son. Now where's that mother of mine. I could murder a brew.'

Chapter 5:
Sole Custody

'So when do I get to see him, then?' Luke Raven was getting agitated and it had less to do with the modest amount of liquor he'd consumed in the last hour and more to do with the immovable negotiating position of his ex.

'When you get your act together, Luke, which is what I've been telling you for the last month.' Lisa Clancy was more than able to hold her own against Raven and then some. 'You heard the judge. Sole custody!'

Raven slammed his hand on the white, pebble-dashed exterior wall of his local pub, the Golden Swan. The sharp stones buried within the rough and cracked render left red, painful dents in his palm. 'I know that's what the judge said, Lisa, but I'm not asking for joint custody.' He cast a cautious glance along the High Street as if fearful of curious eavesdroppers. 'I just want to see my son!'

'And you will, Luke.' She sighed. It sounded like a deflating balloon whistling out of the tinny mobile phone speaker. 'When you've got your shit together.'

'And what exactly does that entail, Lisa?' He pinched the bridge of his nose between his thumb and forefinger. His vision was swimming. 'I mean, I've set up my own business, I'm earning a steady wage and I've even taken on an employee.' He chuckled sarcastically under his breath. 'If that's not being a model citizen then what is?'

It was Lisa's turn to laugh. 'Oh come on, Luke. Since you were put on permanent garden leave from the force without pay, something that was solely down to you and no one else, may I remind you,' Raven almost uttered a *no you can't, thank you very much,* but thought better of it, 'you've been barely earning enough to keep yourself in clothing and lodgings, let alone feeding another small, dependant human being.'

He groaned inwardly. She was right. Being a private dick didn't exactly pay well and he had only taken on young Wesley to fill the diary gaps when he was otherwise indisposed.

'Come on, Lis. You know DCS Deveraux has had it in for me over the Richards thing since the day she joined the department, and my friendship with Dave didn't help either.' Dave Simmons was Raven's ex-boss, mentor, friend and the local constabulary's DCI prior to the consumption of the Westhampton police force into the Hampshire county HQ. The arrival of the caustic and ever so slightly malicious Christy Deveraux was just the icing on the cake.

'That may be true Luke but beating the crap out of that nightclub bouncer while pissed didn't do you any favours either.'

He nodded in reluctant defeat. She was right. 'But I'm up for review in the next three months and as long as I keep my nose clean and say all of the right things to the panel, I'll have my DI badge back in no time.'

'Well then, that's when you can see Harry.' She sounded regretful but Raven knew Lisa well enough to know when she considered a debate closed.

'Okay, okay.' He glanced at his watch and swore under his breath. 'Look, I've got to go but just promise me one thing, Lis.'

He could hear her stirring her tea and his heart skipped a little. He wanted to be there with her. 'What's that, Luke? And don't try your luck.'

'Just promise me you'll finish with that loser Lonny.'

'That's rich!' she hissed. 'God, you're so bitter!'

'He's no good.'

'He's been good to us, Raven! Not that it's any of your business. He put a roof over our heads and food in our mouths after you ...' an accusatory pause, 'did what you did.'

'He's got a record, Lisa.'

'Well we've all done things we regret, Luke.' He could practically smell her venom down the phone line. 'You of all people should know that.'

Chapter 6:
Mother's Ruin

Raven pulled up outside the Butler residence and wiped greasy cheeseburger from his stubble. He burped loudly, swigged down his coke (mixed with more than a tot of single malt scotch), picked up his phone from the passenger seat and clumsily exited the vehicle. He looked up.

Mrs Chelsea Butler lived in a four bedroom, semi-detached place in West Street; what his father would call the middling side of town. Certainly not upmarket but most definitely not as run down as some of the old, terraced houses in the 'stockades' as they were known. No, those properties were old, two bedroom buildings thrown together to house the many thousands of dock workers that would unload the ships that brought in coal and other much needed consumable imports from around the globe during the post war era. Those golden days were long gone but the houses remained. The Butler residence, however, was much nicer. A large, block paved driveway, neatly trimmed hedgerows, big bay windows with leaded panes, nice 2018 plate Range Rover out front.

She had called Wesley early the day prior as he was

finishing up with their previous case with Mrs Cooper - an encounter that hadn't gone well. Apparently, as soon as Wesley arrived, in his shabby tracksuit and on his rundown moped, the suspicious old bag had started accusing him of eyeing up her jewellery like some cheap crook, then suggested he had pocketed some cubic zirconia earrings with sentimental value, and had promptly thrown him out into the street.

Raven shrugged it off but he was pretty pissed that they'd lost a paying job. Wesley had promised to make it up to him but, really, was it his fault? The Cooper woman sounded a little unhinged and, in the long run, Wesley had probably done them a favour. If she was that touchy after one meeting, he could only imagine how difficult she would have been when Raven began digging around in her private life. No, he didn't need any of that drama, not for the pittance she was prepared to pay them.

The Butler woman on the other hand ... he suspected she had a little more capital and was therefore more likely to negotiate a higher price point.

He strode up the long driveway and pressed the doorbell. After a few moments, a tall, slender woman came to the door. She had long, blonde hair, slightly greying at the sides, full lips, attractive laughter lines in the corners of her eyes, long legs and an enticing scent of cherry blossom. She was dressed in casual slacks and a beige sweater. She was maybe late forties, no older than fifty, and she oozed a relaxed elegance. Raven smiled and held out a hand.

'Mrs Butler?'

She nodded and took his hand in hers. Her expression gave away a nervous uncertainty and her eyes were darting up and down the street, as if she was looking for something.

'Luke Raven at your service.' Her hand was soft and as she pulled it away, he could feel her long nails delicately brush the inside of his palm. 'You called my colleague yesterday. Something about a …' he took a notepad from his jacket and flipped through several pages until he found the entry he was looking for, 'a missing person?'

'Yes … something like that.' She ushered him in. 'Please come through. I'd rather not speak about this in the street.'

'Of course, Mrs Butler,' he said, following her into the house and closing the door behind him.

'Please, call me Chelsea.'

'Chelsea … yes, of course.'

She swept down the hallway. 'Can I offer you a drink?'

He wiped the back of his hand across his dry and greedy mouth.

'Tea? Coffee?'

He shook it off. 'Coffee would be great, thanks. Black, no sugar.'

'Of course. Please,' she ushered him into her home, 'follow me.'

They walked past a curved stairway. On his right was a living room furnished with large cream sofas and a cast iron log burner, on his left a downstairs bathroom that smelled of pineapple and was decorated with gleaming tiles that looked clean enough to eat from. Next to that was a small study, and at the end of the hallway, a large, modern and well equipped kitchen-diner. The room opened out onto a decked patio area complete with rattan sofas, a round, well used firepit, LED lights inset into the composite decking board and a four-burner gas barbeque with wood smoker. The well-tended garden showcased a neatly trimmed lawn, hot tub and rose covered pergola.

Chelsea inserted a pod into the coffee maker and the machine whirred into life. In less than a minute she handed Raven a lightly frothed americano in a burgundy mug. He thanked her and took a sip. The coffee was extremely good. Barista good.

'It's my daughter,' she said.

He swallowed his coffee and he felt it mix happily with the Glenfiddich in his belly.

'Sorry?'

Chelsea turned and inserted another pod. 'I believe you know her.'

Raven frowned. 'I don't know. Maybe. What's her name?'

'She was with that lunatic. The one that blew his own good for nothing brains out after submitting my daughter to years of idle selfishness and cruel torment.'

Something clicked in Raven's subconscious. A swirling mass, long claws, red, soulless eyes. And a black presence. He glanced at the corners of the room to satisfy himself that the darkness hadn't returned.

'*Anthony Richards*,' they both said in unison.

Anthony Richards had been a deluded young man who had believed that summoning a mythical beast would help him win back the heart of this woman's young daughter. It had been DI Luke Raven's last big case.

'Your daughter … is Jane Butler?' Raven recalled how Jane had recoiled in horror as Richards turned the gun on himself. 'She's missing?'

Chelsea sighed. 'Yes, for around ten days.'

'Around ten days? You're not sure?'

She looked away. 'I … I've been away, you see. On a spa holiday with some friends and I hadn't contacted her for a while. But when I texted her to say I was coming home I didn't get an answer. She's always really good at texting back and so I thought it was a little odd.'

Raven pulled his notebook from his pocket and started to scrawl. Part of him thought it all sounded like a waste of time but he was more than happy to spend the afternoon in such good company and nice surroundings.

'I told myself it was nothing, but when I returned, she wasn't here – she's been living with me ever since, well, you know. And the kitchen was left in a mess. She'd never do that, she's so tidy. To a fault.' She fought to suppress the tears.

'And this was?'

'Three days ago.'

Raven stopped scribbling. 'But I thought you said she had been missing for around ten days?'

Chelsea took a sip from her latte. The froth on her upper lip reminded him of delicate icing on a red velvet cupcake.

'Bob, my neighbour, he said that she had gone out for a run not long after I'd left for my trip and he hadn't seen her since. He had assumed she had stayed with a friend.'

'And she hadn't?'

Chelsea pulled a tissue from a box on the kitchen counter and blotted her eyes. 'I've called all of her friends, her work colleagues and all of our family.' She lifted a trembling cup to her lips and took a small sip. 'No-one has seen or heard from her.'

'And your husband?'

Chelsea took a sharp intake of breath. 'My husband has been dead for fifteen years, Mr Raven. I hardly think he had anything to do with this.'

Raven pulled his size nines out of his mouth and answered sheepishly. 'Look, I'm sorry. That was crass of me, but I obviously need to understand all of the details, no matter how small. Family members are always number one on the list when it comes to this type of thing I'm afraid.'

She lowered her head. 'I'm sorry. I truly am. I've been snapping at everyone. I just don't know what to do. The police don't seem to be doing anything. They think she's just run off – she would *never!* I'm just so alone. I do nothing but stare at the door waiting for her to walk in and say hi. She has such a warming welcome, you know. So kind and full of heart. But the door remains closed, the house remains silent and I feel so desperately useless.' She looked up at him, her waterproof mascara damp at the corners of her eyes but her make up still impeccable. 'I don't know what to do, Mr Raven.'

Raven sighed and held out a hand to her which she took. He had a feeling he was going to regret it but what the hell. He liked her. 'I'm deeply sorry for what you're going through. I can assure you that I will do everything I can to find your daughter and bring her home. I promise.' He clasped his free hand over hers. 'And please,' he smiled, 'call me Luke.'

Chapter 7:
The D.I.

Detective Inspector Randall Kipruto was a tall man; dark skin, neatly trimmed black goatee, short, black hair. He liked to look after himself and it showed. His suit was well pressed, his shoes a glossy black leather, his scent a heady mixture of Christian Dior and Ted Baker.

His parents were second generation African immigrants; his grandparents migrated to England during the sixties in an attempt to escape the political oppression of their homeland, Kenya. They had settled in London and his grandfather found work on the docks, a job that paid just enough for them to afford their own home; a modest two up, two down in the east end. Before long his grandmother had given birth to twin daughters and a son – his father, Joseph. Joseph was a strapping, strong-willed young man and he tore through the education system with gusto, earning himself a place at the University of London where he obtained his business degree and his MBA and, before long, had set up his own white goods retail business. Trade was good but Joseph did not like the crowded streets of the capital and so he relocated to the south west, meeting Randall's mother, Celine, in the process and soon after two little boys arrived: Randall and his younger brother Felix. Felix was an artistic character who had all the flair and less of Randall's solid sense of direction.

On this overcast Tuesday, Randall Kipruto wished that he was anywhere else. The last place he wanted to be was in front of these two distraught parents, talking to them about their son. He had been missing for over a week now and items of his clothing had been found alongside those of a young girl, Lizzy Easter, on the beach by Bishop's Crag.

He exhaled slowly.

'You say the last time you saw your son was late afternoon on the 6th July?'

Daniel Riley's mother, Karen, answered, 'Yes. We had all sat down for dinner. I'd cooked us sausage and mash,' she dabbed at her eyes with a handkerchief, 'Dan's favourite. He and his sister – Amber – were at home which was unusual, so the four of us sat up the table and ate together as a family.' She paused to regain her composure. Her husband, Peter, gripped her hand tightly. 'It's so rare for us all to be together at the same time now they're older. It was a really lovely dinner wasn't it, Pete?'

Peter put his arm around Karen's slumped shoulders and hugged her. 'Yes, dear. Yes, it was. A really lovely dinner, you put on a good spread, my love.'

Randall scribbled some notes. 'And it's rare for Daniel to be away for so long without making contact?'

Karen answered, 'He's a good son, Inspector. He never goes a day without at least messaging us on the family group chat.'

Randall inwardly smiled. His family had the same check in system.

'Have you ever met the young girl that he was last seen with? Elisabeth, or Lizzy, Easter?' Randall hated the stock questions that he was forced to ask but he really needed to build a picture of Dan's last few hours before his disappearance. He could see the incessant probing was upsetting Peter and Karen and he hated that. Sometimes he hated his job. He certainly hated the pressure that Deveraux was putting him under to put this case to bed without causing a commotion in the media. She seemed to have already reached a foregone and, in his opinion, misguided conclusion that what they were dealing with here was a case of two young lovers off on a secret triste. He wasn't convinced in the least. There had appeared to be small spatters of blood on the clothing.

Peter shook his head. 'No, never.' He sipped his tea 'Do you … do you think she had something to do with whatever has happened to our son?'

Randall set down his notepad. 'At this stage, Mr Riley, it would be foolish for us to rule anything out. However, I can assure you that we will gather all of the facts from both yourselves and the Easter family and share as much as we can as and when we find anything.' He hated the next question but had to ask. 'Do you know if Daniel was in any kind of trouble?'

Peter grunted. The question clearly upset him. 'My wife has already told you. Our son is a good boy. He's never caused us any problems, not at school, not at home, *never*. We couldn't ask for a more perfect son. He works hard and, yes, he goes out in town and has a few drinks and gets into a few scrapes but who didn't at his age?'

Randall didn't. He was never a drinker and not into the

46

night-clubbing scene. That was the sense of purpose he got from his father. Some called him boring but he didn't care. He had a nice car, a nice flat, a good wage and a decent lifestyle.

'I understand, Mr Riley, but something has obviously happened here and I need to ascertain all of the facts.'

Karen started sobbing and she tucked her face into the crook of her husband's arm. He hated seeing how distraught they were. His mother always told him he was a sentimental boy and she was right. He often wondered whether he was in the wrong profession.

'I think we'll leave it there for the time being.' Randall collected his notebook and pen. 'When your daughter is home it would be good if you could let me know. I'd like to collect some details from her also.'

Peter didn't look up. He just nodded.

DI Kipruto showed himself out, leaving the parents to their own personal torment. He had a date with forensics. Hopefully they'd have something positive for him, some evidence he could actually take to the Super.

This was no jolly holiday for young Dan Riley and Lizzy Easter. The Hampshire constabulary had a double murder on their hands. He was sure of it.

Chapter 8:
Daddy's Little Girl

Molly was nine years old when her father first took her shooting. She was far too little to hold the rifle but her dad, a hunting nut with the means to fund his hobby with only the best equipment, wanted her to experience the great outdoors, the thrill of the chase and the excitement of the kill.

Her dad was a very fit man. He was just over six foot five inches in height, broad shoulders, heavy set neck, clean shaven, neatly trimmed brown hair and dark eyes. Even at her young age she knew that her dad was an important and successful man. A man of great standing and stature. She was proud to be his daughter, despite only having fleeting moments of private time with him. He was extremely busy and she was so lucky to have Gretchen. Gretchen took good care of her.

Since her mother left, her father had brought home many women, some of whom had hung around longer than others. Some that she had secretly hoped would become her new mother and some that she desperately hoped would not, but one by one they all disappeared only for a new one to arrive not long after. Gretchen treated them all with the same due respect and hospitality and Molly did the same. She learned a lot from her nanny, not least that you should be nice to people until you needed not to be.

'Now, Molly my dear. This is an important day for you in your young life.'

Molly, dressed in waterproof clothing, mittens and a deer stalker hat looked up at her dad through the inquisitive eyes of one so young and naïve. 'What do you mean, Daddy?' The ground was sodden and the grass very long but she was determined to keep pace.

'This is the day where you hunt your very first deer.'

Molly was shocked. 'But I don't want to kill a deer. They're so beautiful.'

'Of course you do, my darling. It is a wonderful experience.'

Molly stopped and stomped her feet into the mulchy earth. 'I don't!'

Bernie Staker sighed, stopped and bent down. 'They may be beautiful, but here's the thing,' her father peered into her eyes with a look that sought to impart an earnest wisdom, 'sometimes beautiful things die. Not because they are mean or nasty, but because everything has a purpose. We, for example, have a purpose to grow and blossom, like the flowers, and to fulfil our real potential.' He pinched Molly's cheek softly. 'You have real potential. I can see it in your beautiful eyes and in your smile.' He pointed upwards at two buzzards circling overhead. 'The buzzards, their purpose is to kill the rodents, keep the population down so that they don't infest our homes.'

Molly could see the birds swooping and gliding and she wondered what it would be like to be able to swoop and glide like them.

Her father pointed to the beehives in the field to the south of them. 'The bees' purpose is to pollinate the flowers so that they grow and spread and give us all of the wonderful colours that we see in our garden. And they give us beautifully sweet and sticky honey that we have on our toast in the morning.'

Molly laughed. She loved the toast that nanny Gretchen made her. She sometimes had honey, sometimes jam and sometimes peanut butter although she wasn't supposed to let her daddy know about that.

'And when the plants grow, the deer eat the plants, and they in turn grow and have baby deer, and those deer eat more plants and grow and so on and so on.'

Molly listened to her dad intensely and his gruff but soothing voice intoxicated her.

'And when those deer are big and strong and run around in our forests, we hunt them. You see,' he brushed a curl from Molly's eyes, 'they enjoy the hunt just as much as we do. It's all part of life's big game. The hunter and the hunted, the prey and the predator. You will learn this, Molly my darling. You never want to be the prey. A Staker is never the prey.' Her father's stare hardened and his voice deepened in tone. 'Stakers are leaders.' He stood and ran a hand down the barrel of his rifle. 'If you remember one thing I've taught you remember this,' he gritted his teeth, '*never be a victim.*'

A tear rolled down Molly's cheek and she wiped it away quickly. She didn't want her daddy to see her cry. He hated weakness and she didn't want to be weak. It was just that sometimes, when he spoke like that, it frightened her. Gretchen told her that her daddy could be a hard man but that he still loved her dearly. She wanted to love him back and she tried every day to do so, despite some of the things she saw her daddy do. Like killing beautiful animals. And hurting people.

It took them all morning to get their first sighting, by which time Molly was bitterly cold and hungry. She hadn't eaten since Gretchen had woken her in the early hours, when it was still dark outside, and her little belly was rumbling. She held a hand over it while they ducked down behind a fallen tree so as to dampen the sound and not scare off the deer. She knew her daddy would be furious if that happened.

Her father whispered to her, 'Now, we have to remain very still and very quiet if we are to snag this beautiful beast. Do you understand?'

Molly nodded.

'I want you to watch and learn and be mindful of the rifle. When I pull the trigger the stock of the gun will kick back and I don't want you getting hurt.'

Again, she nodded but didn't really understand.

Her father cocked the rifle and rested the barrel on the fallen tree. She watched him close one eye and place the other to the rifle sight. The deer was stooped, eating some leaves from a shrub on the ground, and it looked up, glancing left and right while chewing gently on the foliage. Molly was mesmerised by it; its wonderfully brown sheen, its taught leg muscles, the slight, white plume on its long, thick neck, its tiny ears that flapped to ward off flies, its little brown and white tail that swept from side to side. She wondered if it was a mother and, if so, where its children might be. Was the deer collecting food for its family? Were they expecting her home soon? She thought how wonderful it would be to have the freedom of the forest, allowed to roam as you please without any walls or doors. She envied the deer.

Her father looked back and nodded at her and she smiled feebly at him. She wanted him to miss so badly.

She started to back away from the fallen tree, behind her father so that she wouldn't see the bullet striking the beautiful animal. Again, a tear slowly rolled down her cheek. She forgot what her daddy had told her about the rifle's kick. She didn't see her dad pull the trigger, didn't hear the loud bang as the bullet left the barrel, didn't hear the deer grunt as it was struck in the neck and barely saw the blood as it spurted from the wound in a thick, red and gloopy jet.

All she heard was a loud crunch and her own piercing scream as the rifle stock flew backwards and struck her hard in her cheekbone.

And then darkness.

Chapter 9:
Christy

Christy Deveraux was forty-two years old when she was elevated to the rank of Detective Chief Superintendent for the Western District of the Hampshire Constabulary, responsible for the region stretching from Westhampton to the western border of Dorset and as far north as Romsey. She was the first woman to achieve such a rank in the area and she had not achieved such success through luck or good favour. No, she had had to fight for every inch of progress, every word of faint praise and for the crown on the epaulette that sat atop her treasured bath star. She had dealt with her own insecurities and hardly buried inner demons while working her way through the ranks; from her graduation from Portsmouth Polytechnic through to passing her sergeants' exam, and she had struggled daily to suppress her anxieties and feelings of isolation and despondency. Her therapist had helped her with tools and techniques to understand where it all emanated from – of course, her time at the foster home had been the topic of much discussion – and to react positively to it before it became a 'thing'. She loved Ivan. He had enabled her hard exterior and even tougher resilience.

She was taller than most of her female peers at five foot eleven inches, her platinum hair was always tied back in a tight, neat bun, her sharp jaw line and piercing green eyes were strikingly memorable and her razor wit was more than a match for any adversary. DCS Christy Deveraux did not suffer fools. She knew that in life you were your own best advocate and own worst enemy and were therefore wholly responsible for your own actions. She quickly identified the bad eggs when she took the position and had acted both swiftly and decisively in removing the 'retired on the job' DCI that presided over the department in the old, out of date structure. More than a handful had felt her unsympathetic wrath and she didn't mind the bad headlines – if anything they just helped feed the myth, a myth that she was more than willing to cultivate. It kept the wolves from the door.

'So forensics confirmed the blood traces.' Randall Kipruto was resting on a pedestal and sipping from a Styrofoam cup. 'It belongs to the boy, Daniel. There were also some skin fragments from both Daniel and Elizabeth, traces of spilt alcohol, food crumbs – the usual noise. Plus some very interesting skin cells that have no direct match.'

Deveraux was reclining in a leather backed chair, one hand on her chin, the other twirling a fountain pen on the hardwood desk. Her eyes were transfixed on those of her DI.

'Which means?'

Randall plucked a stray hair from his lapel. 'Well, it's my opinion that this is either a violent abduction, in which case we have a case for unlawful imprisonment, or it's a murder enquiry.'

Deveraux crossed her legs and chuckled under her breath.

54

'I think that's a rather hasty conclusion, Kipruto, based on the very limited evidence at hand.'

The office was large and housed a wide, oak desk and filing cabinet, various reference books from esteemed and well renowned experts, two large PC monitors, a forty inch LCD TV screen mounted on the wall to Deveraux's right, various awards and commendations and a well-used Tassimo coffee machine. Out of the window behind the reclining DCS was a panoramic view across the West Solent and a landscape that showcased the green and brown hills of the Isle of Wight. The day was slightly overcast but the air was warm and the wind slight. She could see the ferries and hoverspeeds traversing to and from Portsmouth and Southampton, the water glassy and blue. The tranquillity was suffocating to her.

'What about the blood, ma'am?'

'For Christ's sake Randall.' Deveraux set down her pen and folded her hands on the desk. Her jaw was set firm and her eyes steadfast. 'The boy could have had a nosebleed, popped a spot or cut himself shaving. There's not enough blood in that sample to cause us to suspect any foul play.' Her face was passive, unmoving. 'If we chased every lead down where young lovers mysteriously disappeared without leaving a note, we would have scores of officers tied up for months on end. No,' she stood up and smoothed down her skirt, 'we will file this one under the 'watching brief' category until some other piece of evidence comes to light. If the couple have not returned or made contact within a week, we will apply some additional manpower.' She walked purposefully towards Randall and forced a half smile. 'In the meantime, keep your ear to the ground and,' she placed a hand on the door and opened it, 'if you hear anything be sure to let me know.'

Randall sighed but she ignored it. The conversation was over. She'd made a reputation out of being steadfast in her views and firm with those who disobeyed her. She'd already suspended one other DI who some considered to be a local hero and she wouldn't think twice about doing the same thing to this young upstart, despite his perfect record and obvious potential.

Randall was barely two steps from the office when Deveraux had a thought and called him back.

'One more thing, Kipruto.'

He turned to face her. 'Yes, ma'am?'

'I've heard rumours that Luke Raven is moonlighting as some sort of private investigator. Have you heard the same thing?' It was a rhetorical question. She'd overheard him talking about it with one of the other officers over coffee.

He shrugged. 'No.'

Deveraux eyed him with suspicion. Why would he lie? Why protect Raven? He had no loyalty to him. They had barely crossed each other's paths before she had cut Raven out of her department like a cancerous tumour.

'Well, do me favour and dig into it for me would you? It worries me that he's out there on the streets, potentially screwing up ongoing cases. Or, worse still, causing trouble where there is no trouble to be had.'

Randall gritted his teeth. She could see that he wasn't keen on the idea of spying on a fellow police officer, but knew that he would comply with her wishes nonetheless. 'Sure thing, boss.'

'And let me know what you find. I'd like to deal with it

personally if something comes up.'

She watched as the DI turned and strode sheepishly out of her office and she closed the door behind him. Whatever Raven was up to, she was going to find out and put a stop to it. And if she had to sacrifice Kipruto in the process, then so be it. She had bigger fish to fry.

Chapter 10:
Ronny and the Dreamers

The moon was high and bright in the sky; a sky that was speckled with trillions of stars, their reflections glistening off the ripples in the ocean like sparkling diamonds. The soft hiss of the low waves played the evening's easy listening soundtrack. The space was peaceful, the empty beach a haven of serenity and calm. Raven felt a deep inner peace as he sat on the sand, his legs folded underneath him. He turned to his left and saw nothing but a long, dark coastline running away into the distance like an empty highway. He turned right and saw the sleeping seafront, the shops with their shutters down, the streetlights switched off, the amusement rides idle and ghostly.

The man emerged from the water like a mighty kraken. Raven hadn't seen him swimming back towards the shore and the sight of his head, adorned with goggles and a dark blue swim-cap, rising from the foamy water like a sea beast startled him. The man was in his fifties, rakish with dark hair, a hairy torso and a green and blue tattoo on his forearm. His body glistened with the slightly eerie concoction of sea water and moonlight.

The man grabbed a towel from behind a low dune and dried himself vigorously. Even though it was early summer the air was chilly and Raven thought the water must have been freezing. He shouted out a 'hiya' to the guy but he didn't appear to hear him.

The man set down his towel and grabbed his rucksack which Raven assumed contained his clothing. Raven closed his eyes and turned away, not wanting to embarrass the guy by watching him get undressed.

As he opened his eyes, he saw the tree and on top of the tree a bird of prey. A hawk, he thought. Or maybe a buzzard. It was the same type of raptor from his dream a few nights prior.

He heard the man from behind him.

'What are you doing out here this late in the evening, young man? Are you lost?'

Raven turned and saw the moonlight swimmer, still in his swim shorts but now wearing a hooded sweatshirt and flip flops. There was a young boy standing in front of him, the gentle waves lapping at his bare feet. The boy wiped his muddy hands downs his Nike T-shirt and laughed, pointing at the man's skinny legs.

'Now look here, young man ...'

Raven had a terrible feeling something bad was about to happen. He looked to his right at the bird which was peering across the sandy expanse towards the young boy. He turned back to the man and screamed, '*Get the hell out of here!*'

The man looked in Raven's direction as if he had heard a noise but seemed to shake it off. Raven shouted again: '*It's coming for you! You need to leave, now!*' Raven tried to stand but he suddenly realised that he was submerged in sand from the waist down, his upper body writhing around furiously but unable to wrestle his bottom and his legs from their burial mound. He pushed down with his hands but he wasn't budging. He looked back at the bird of prey. It seemed to be smiling at him.

The young boy continued to laugh at the swim shorts guy, an annoying, snorting giggle. He was almost doubled over with the hilarity of it all, the water splashing around his ankles and drenching the bottom of his shorts, his hands on his stomach, his belly trembling in hysteric convulsions.

'What is up with you, boy?'

In an instant, the laughter stopped and the boy looked across at the hawk. He winked at it.

The bird immediately launched itself from its lofty perch, and soared into the night sky, climbing up and up and beyond Raven's field of vision. He peered upwards towards the mottled patchwork of The Milky Way looking for a small, winged shape with a hooked beak. The swim shorts man was gazing upwards also, his lips pulled back in a sneer of disgust and his eyes wide with morbid curiosity. He tried to move but his feet seemed glued to the ground. The young boy huffed a final chuckle, turned on his heels and ran, flipping the guy the bird as he sloshed through the shallow water.

Raven heard a whoosh and a high pitched caw and he glimpsed the hawk slashing through the darkness like a mortar shell. It dug its talons into swim shorts man's cheeks and plunged its beak into one of his eyeballs, the gelatinous orb popping like a chunk of sinewy gristle, his nose ripping from his face like the skin from a cooked chicken. The man yelled in agony, his arms thrashing around and his hands clawing at the bird's feathers and animated wings. Blood poured down the man's cheeks and neck and he fell backwards into the swell of the ocean, his body and face fully submerged, the bird barely visible above the waves. Raven tried to drag himself across the sand towards him but his legs would barely move and when he tried to usher a call, he found his mouth was full of sand. He gagged on it and couldn't seem to catch his breath. He wretched and bile and sharp sand filled his throat and mouth. He turned his head, spat out what he could and then descended into a choking fit. His vision swam as the energy drained from his body.

He collapsed.

****

Raven awoke and wondered what on earth he was looking at. A small crawl space was ahead of him, a thin veil covering what appeared to be an exit some five or six feet away. He felt the floor and ran his hands across the rough material covering what appeared to be a firm base. His legs were above him as his top half hung upside down as if he had been inverted and suspended in some type of warm and sunlit cave. He looked left and right and saw clothing and empty bottles and looked behind him at the large, bright source of light.

He groaned as he pulled himself back onto the bed and searched frantically for his phone. His weird dreams had been going on for well over two years now and frankly they were tiring. But he had to admit there had been times they had been useful.

He couldn't explain them. Were they messages from his subconscious dream state, only to be unlocked when his mind was relaxed and free from all conscious thought, or were they other-worldly scenes being played out in some far-away place or some other dimension? He didn't know, he didn't care. What he couldn't dispute was that on more than one occasion they'd made him look at things differently, take on a different perspective and hunt for clues in places he previously had not considered. 'Psychic ability' was a strong term and not one he subscribed to but he was becoming more accustomed to the idea that he *saw* things. Things that no one else could see and things that were relevant and personal to him.

A loud rat-tat-tat on his front door shook him from his rumination.

He jumped out of bed and quickly pulled on his jeans and a faded Metallica t-shirt. He checked himself quickly in the mirror, ran a hand through his hair and then crossed the hallway into the lounge and to the door of his flat. He took a quick look through the peep hole, uttered a 'fucking hell' and slid the chain from the catch.

'Good morning Raven, you fucking bent old copper. Or should I say … ex-copper?'

'Hi Ronny.' Raven held the heavy fire door in one hand and the wooden frame in the other. He was ready to slam the door shut in an instant. 'When … when did you get out?'

'Couple of days ago,' Ronny Valentine was in a tartan jacket with a cream shirt and tan trousers. He wore a tartan trilby atop his huge mound of a head. He looked down at Raven and laughed. 'Oh come on, Raven! If I was after revenge, I would have kicked the door in.'

Raven relaxed a little at that but he wasn't foolish enough to open the door too wide just yet. 'I know, Ron. You're much smarter than that. And anyway,' Raven smiled, 'domestic violence just isn't your style.'

Ronny let out a huge, booming laugh at that and patted Raven on the shoulder with a dinner plate sized hand. 'Too right, my son. I'd much rather have it out in the middle of the street with a crowd cheering us on and the old bill breaking us up.' He held his arms open, 'I'm too much of a showman to beat you up in private.' He winked. 'That would be a waste.'

Raven gripped the door handle hard. 'So …what do you want?'

Ronny Valentine bent down and peered into Raven's face, close enough that Raven could smell the cigar tobacco and scotch on his breath.

'Raven, my boy. What I really want is a nice cup of tea.'

Chapter 11:
Swim Shorts Man

Randall Kipruto stood on Westhampton beach and looked out to sea. His view took in the Isle of Wight, the town of Gosport across the estuary a few miles east and dozens of pleasure boats sailing along the slip of water between Yarmouth and Keyhaven. There was a peace out there that he yearned for but not one that was in his immediate timeline. He knew that and resigned himself to it. There were murders there in Westhampton and he not only had to prove it to the courts – he had to prove it to his boss.

'The wife says Simon Farrington was out here last night for his weekly midnight swim,' the young PC, Ruby Cropper, standing next to Randall said. Ruby had graduated from desk duties earlier that year. She lifted a hand and tucked her long, unruly hair behind her ear. 'Apparently it's a habit he's had since university. He swims two miles out and two miles back every Tuesday night.' She looked across the wide expanse of water with a mild look of astonishment on her face. 'I mean, it's fine when the weather's like this but what about when the wind's up and the waves are ten feet high?'

Randall looked up and down the long, golden beach. A thirty foot section around Simon Farrington's abandoned rucksack and swim shorts, an area that stretched from the shoreline to the gnarly sand-dunes behind them, was cordoned off from the general public. 'And he hasn't made any contact?'

Ruby, or Tuesday as she was known to her colleagues, shook her head. 'Nope, not a peep, boss.' She checked her notebook. 'Mrs Farrington says that her husband is normally in constant communication with her, and when he's not at work he's normally at home working on his trainset or on his vintage BMW sports car.'

Randall shook his head and sighed. Three disappearances in less than a week and not a lead to speak of. And *him*, in the job less than six months, still looking for his one big success story and now with a side-job of keeping watch on some has-been, washed up DI. Although, he mused, at least Raven had enough about him to nail Anthony Richards.

'Get those items of clothing to forensics as quickly as you can, Ruby, and tell them I asked for them to be put to the top of the priority list. I can't imagine there's much else happening in this fine town that warrants the same privilege.' He checked his watch and swore under his breath. He was supposed to be keeping an eye on Raven's apartment every day from eleven in the morning until one in the afternoon, that being Raven's usual window of departure time. The Chief had demanded that she know where Raven was going each day and what he was up to. Randall thought it was a huge waste of his time but she was very insistent. 'I've got an appointment but let me know when you find anything. Make sure you check in on Mrs Farrington later today to see if she has heard anything and,' he looked down at the young PC, 'see if you can get a trace on Mr Farrington's cell phone.'

Ruby sighed. 'No point, boss.' She pointed over at the rucksack lying idly in the sand like an empty husk. 'We checked. It's in there.'

Shit, Randall thought. Either their guy was carrying out some real Reginald Perrin crap or they really did have a murder on their hands. And that would make this a serial killer case. He could feel his skin grow clammy in the hot sun and a sheen of sweat start to form on his forehead and cheeks.

'Ruby, get hold of Lola and see if there's any word on the street. I can't believe that no one knows what's been going on down here. We either have a very sick individual on our hands or there's gangs involved.' He scowled as he recalled his first big case involving the Medics, a violent group of local hoodlums and drug dealers. 'And I want to know which it is.'

'Will do.' She scrawled some more notes in her pad. She stopped abruptly and idly pushed the tip of the parker pen into the corner of her mouth. 'Just ... just one other thing.'

Randall pinched the bridge of his nose. He was getting a headache. 'Yes?'

'When we got here, you know, first thing before the tide came in? Well, we noticed marks in the wet sand. Two deep troughs as if someone had been dragged from the spot where the clothes were left abandoned.'

Randall turned to face her. 'You have a trail of where the body, assuming there is a body, was taken to?' He shook his head in disbelief. 'Why didn't you say this before?'

Ruby paused before she spoke, considering her next words very carefully. 'Well, because the troughs went out around fifty or sixty feet into the mud flats and then …' the corner of her mouth turned up as she played the sentence over in her mind. She looked more than a little perplexed.

'Well? Spit it out.' Randall was getting frustrated with the young but very capable PC, compounded by the need to get to his next pressing engagement.

'They just vanished.'

Chapter 12:
The Meet

What a lot of people don't know, or care to remember, is that Raven put Ronny away. It was one of his first big arrests and oh what a big fish he caught. Ronny 'Bloody' Valentine, one of the biggest crime bosses this area has ever seen and one that almost every copper since the late sixties has pursued with a rabid, almost blood-thirsty interest.

That morning when Ronny came to see him, Raven was obviously more than a little anxious. But Ronny laid it on thick, spelled it out bit by bit, and gradually Raven could see the logic in the plan. The risks were low and the stakes were high and Raven, being on his extra-long, unpaid holiday from the old bill and with no guarantee of re-instatement, needed the dosh. And Ronny needed Raven's experience of police procedure, insights into how thieves typically made mistakes, what the first responders would be on the lookout for, how the CSI guys collected their evidence – that kind of thing. And from me, of course, Ronny needed my electrical skills.

Since that day, when I've been sitting there quietly supping a pint or watching the telly, I've often thought that

Ronny took a hell of a risk going round there and coercing Raven into signing up. There was no guarantee that Raven wasn't going to just take Ronny's plan straight to the Chief Super's office and use his inside knowledge to get his badge back. That would have been game set and match for old Ron, alright. However, as you and I know, Luke Raven is a complex character and, as I learned later, Ronny knew how to play on Raven's hatred for Deveraux and his disgust at the way he had been treated, especially after what had happened with the Richards thing. Little did I know back then how things would pan out.

It wasn't long before Ronny set up the meet.

'I know you, don't I?' Raven was sitting at the end of a long coffee table towards the back of Gino's Café. He was wearing a button down, dark checked shirt and dark blue jeans. There was a hint of brandy on him and a musty body odour.

I took a big swig of my cappuccino, the chocolate dusting peppering my nose and moustache and smiled. 'Yeah, we met a couple of times round my place. After the incident with the mayor and all that other stuff.'

Raven stirred a teaspoon in his Americano thoughtfully for a moment, and then: 'West!' He looked me up and down, 'Billy West, Richards' next door neighbour!'

'For my sins.' I reached across and shook his hand. 'That was a terrible business. One that Sally and I still live with every day.' If only he knew the half of it, eh? How we'd argued about it, how we'd blamed each other, how we'd played back every conversation, every situation. Could we have done anything … different? Tony was my friend, one of my *best* friends, but if I'd known what was going to eventually unfold, I would have gone to the authorities immediately. The guy had completely lost all his senses and yet somehow had managed to pull the wool over my eyes. Over both our eyes. I'll never be as trusting again.

'Yeah, I can imagine. It's not something you forget in a hurry.' By the look of Raven he was still living with the fallout and probably not comprehending the effect it had had on him.

We sat there silently for what seemed like an eternity but in reality it was probably no more than ten or fifteen seconds.

'Alright then boys, I see you've met!' Ronny heaved himself onto a stool, its legs creaking painfully as he settled his full weight onto the three legged construction. 'I assume you've exchanged the usual pleasantries and how do you dos.' He slurped on his coffee and wiped whipped cream from his upper lip. 'So shall we get right down to it? My girl's Lulu and she has the inside track. She's given me full shop layout; all three storeys, key code to both the basement door and the vault, shift patterns of all the staff and, here's the beauty of it, an escape route that leads us all the way out to the coast without ever having to run the risk of being picked up by CCTV.' Ronny held out his hands, seemingly for applause, and then crossed his arms, a huge, cigar of a smile spread widely across his granite features.

Raven leaned back on the well-worn sofa. 'So why do we need the electrician?' He looked up at me. 'No offence, Billy.'

I held my hands up. 'None taken.'

Ronny took a bite from a large biscotti and then sprayed crumbs all over the table as he spoke. 'Because the only people who have the door code to the shop are the proprietors of the establishment, Mr and Mrs Greenbaum, an odd couple if you ask me. He's Jewish and she's Hawaiian,' he scratched the top of his head, 'very bizarre.'

I had to ask, 'And what's the approximate value in the vault at any one time?'

'Well here's the kick, William my old son,' he slapped me on the shoulder hard, 'the vault gets cleared out twice a week, once on a Monday and once on a Thursday.' He took off a beige shoe, uncovering a white and black speckled sock, and rubbed the sole of his foot. I grimaced. 'The particular week that we are planning to hit it, the week of the August bank holiday, there's only one collection – on the Monday prior. The vault doesn't get opened again until the day after the bank holiday, which means ...'

'Double the takings.' Raven looked mildly disinterested but at least he was paying attention.

I'll be honest with you, I was salivating a little at the anticipation.

'Well, chaps. The Greenbaums, being the good businesspeople that they are, have decided to open on both the Saturday and the Sunday of that week, so they will have a full six days of trading in a very busy period. That's a lot of cash, gold and jewels holed up in that vault for an extra extended period of time. My estimation,' he was grinning like a Cheshire cat, 'and I've had Lulu check this with the accounts from the same period last year...'

My heart was pounding in my chest and my ears were ringing. I'd already been warned about my ever-rising blood pressure; the doc was always telling me to lay off the cakes and beer, and I could feel my arteries at bursting point.

'...is that there will be approximately 1.5 to 1.8 million

71

of Her Majesty's Great British Pounds slowly baking in number 82 High Street, just waiting for someone with light fingers and even lighter toes to scoop it up and whisk it away.'

I gulped. Raven's eyes twitched. There was a silence as Ronny looked from me to Raven and back again. He blinked but the grin never left his leather skinned cheeks. 'Well?'

Raven leaned forward and spoke in a hushed monotone. 'Tell me about this escape route.'

'Well, I told you about Del, right? How I met him inside, what his professional skills are?'

'You did, but I still don't see why we need another pair of hands.' Raven was eyeing Ronny curiously and I had the distinct feeling that he was about two wrong words from getting up and walking out.

'Well, Raven, my old son, for those of us that have been around this town for a bit, and I've been around these parts more than most ...' He glanced around him at the half empty coffee bar, looked up and nodded at the young, pretty waitress, and stared half dreamily out the shopfront window towards the quiet street outside. 'Well, us old timers know the old smuggling stories. Tales of sailors in the eighteenth century smuggling tea, wine and spirits into the country from overseas. They would sail up the channel from Spain, moor the ship out to sea and bring in row boats when there was no moonlight to illuminate them. They'd come up the southern coast, along this shore from south wales to the west or from Dover to the east, and bring their goods onto dry land, normally stashing it in wooden shacks or roughly hewn out caves.'

Raven was shaking his head. 'Thanks for the history

lesson but I've got an appointment to get to. Can we hurry this up?'

Ronny leaned over and grabbed hold of Raven's leg in his vice-like grip. Raven jumped, startled.

'If you would listen you might learn something and then we can all get out of here.' I eyed Raven and Ronny, half expecting a fight to break out. I knew Raven was volatile at the best of times and Ronny was never one to back down from a dust up. 'Those smugglers used to bring their wares into Westhampton from the coast on a regular basis. This area was well known as being a prime location for smuggling liquor and, being so close to the forest, the smugglers could get it ashore quickly and then whisk it away under tree cover and out onto the highways and byways that criss-crossed this whole country at that time. From there it would make its way into the city or up north to fill the shelves of every inn and tavern across the land.' He grabbed his coffee in his other hand and took a very large, greedy slurp. 'And how do you think they got it ashore without being noticed?'

Ronny looked at me and I shrugged.

'*Tunnels*!' He slammed a hand down on the table and both Raven and I jumped in our seats. 'Tunnels that led from the cliffs at Annie's Cove, all the way under the heathland at Wildberry's, across town under the industrial estate, beneath All Saints Primary and up the hill into the centre of Westhampton.' He looked across at Raven and me as if he had just revealed the world's biggest conspiracy theory. 'Of course those tunnels have long been blocked up with concrete as they're not reinforced inside and there's always been a danger of rockfall; a few kids were buried alive in one of those tunnels after the second world war … tragic circumstances those…' I looked over at Ron, who had lost his train of thought, but then he juddered back into life. 'But Del says that won't be a problem. Not a problem at all.'

I was intrigued and confused at the same time. 'I don't get it, Ron.'

'Del's into demolition, William, my boy. Worked twenty-two years at the chalk quarry up near Portsmouth. He knows his way around a stick of dynamite and a splodge of Semtex, I can tell you.' He chuckled, reached out his arms, grabbed both Raven and me by our necks and pulled us into a huddle. 'You see, lads, one of those smugglers' tunnels leads right the way from Annie's cove, all the way up to the basement of none other than ...' He dragged us in close and whispered, 'the Greenbaums.' He kissed us both on the cheeks and I could smell his cheap brut aftershave and Havana cigars. 'Just a bang and a poof and we'll have disappeared like ghosts.'

Chapter 13:
The Missing

Chelsea Butler was reclining in a tangerine coloured sun lounger and sipping on an iced tea. She was wearing an all in one, floral patterned, fifties style bathing suit and round, dark brown sunglasses. Raven sat across from her in his jeans and shirt, slowly cooking in the mid-day heat and wishing he had accepted her offer of a drink. He had decided to bring young Wesley with him for moral support but the boy looked less than professional in his tight fitting jean shorts and bright red, vest top. At least, he thought, he'd removed the snapback.

'So we've done some digging, Mrs Butler …'

'Chelsea.'

'Apologies, yes…' he could feel his cheeks flush with colour, 'Chelsea.'

Wesley smiled cheekily and gave him a wink of approval. 'As I say, we've done some digging and we've managed to ascertain that your daughter was last seen buying a bottle of mineral water in the newsagents off Shepherd's Avenue.'

Chelsea set down her glass and removed her sunglasses, revealing her pastel blue eyes. 'The little shop on the corner.

Run by the Eastern European family.'

'The Borkowskis. Yes, that's right.' Raven was sweating under his shirt and he hoped the swipe of Lynx that he'd rolled on before he came over was man enough for the job.

'They sell that … odd food.'

'Well I can't speak for that, Mrs … Chelsea, but that's the place.'

'They do a lovely line in wraps in there, Mrs B.' Wesley was stretched out on a rattan chair under the parasol, his pale skin far too delicate for the intense sunshine. He clinked the ice in his glass and sipped his drink through a lime green straw. He looked as pleased as punch to be there and was clearly revelling in the plush, comfortable surroundings. 'I've been in there loads of times. Cheap too. You can get a meal deal for less than three quid.'

Chelsea replaced her sunglasses and glared at the kid. 'Well I'm not particularly interested in the price or quality of the meal deals served by the Borkowskis, Mr Pollock, but what I do know is that my daughter would never visit such a place.' The sun was glistening off her lightly tanned skin upon which she had obviously carefully applied sun cream before they had arrived, and there was a scent of coconut and lemonade in the air. 'And, in any case, my refrigerator is constantly stocked with bottles of water and ice cubes because I know Jane enjoys her exercise and needs to hydrate regularly.' She looked over at Raven and shrugged.

Raven leaned forward. 'Well, I can only tell you what we've found, Chelsea. We have CCTV footage of her there. Both Wesley and I sat with the owner of the shop just yesterday afternoon and watched as your daughter…' he glanced at Wesley for confirmation, who was nodding along agreeably while sucking on his straw, 'left the shop, a bottle of water in hand and dressed in her yellow and blue running top and shorts. She then turned and started up the hill as if she was headed back this way.'

'Is she very fit, your daughter, Chelsea?' Wesley had stood up and was looking at the hanging baskets that were strewn across the rear of the Butler residence.

'She is, yes. Since she got into fitness classes after work.'

'Have any admirers?'

'Well … no, not really. Not since that terrible thing happened with …'

'Yes, yes, we know about that. But,' Wesley took two steps towards the older woman, his thin arms reddening in the sunshine and his bony knees protruding awkwardly from his shorts, 'with a body like hers, surely she had men flocking for her attention day in, day out.'

Chelsea gasped in astonishment and Raven stood up. He'd had enough.

'Wesley, do me a favour and go wait in the car would you.' He glanced over at Chelsea who was glugging on her iced tea. 'I'd like a quiet word with Mrs Butler.'

Wesley looked from Raven to Chelsea and then back again. His eyes narrowed, his lips thinned and then he smiled. 'Okay, I'll be out front. But think about it, Chelsea. It could be important.' And with that he turned and exited through the open French doors.

Raven walked across the garden decking and took the sun lounger next to Chelsea. He leaned forward in the chair, his elbows on his knees.

'I'm sorry about him. He's a good help to me but he often forgets to think before he speaks.'

77

'It's fine. It really is. I guess … I guess he has a point. Jane is a very pretty young lady with a wonderfully kind personality. I would be foolish to think she didn't have any male companions. It's just that …' she stifled a tear and Raven put a hand on her arm to comfort her. 'I would have thought she'd tell me. Since she's moved back home, we've become so close. Like sisters really.' She leaned closer to Raven and he felt his pulse skip at her sweet scent. 'Do you think something terrible has happened to her, Luke?'

He looked away. 'I don't know. I don't think you should dwell on those kinds of thoughts. But there is something else that I need to ask you.'

Raven took a folded piece of A4 paper from his back pocket and opened it. On its crumpled surface was a colour print of Jane Butler leaving the newsagents, fully dressed in her running gear and purple running shoes and swigging from a bottle of water. Raven pointed to the grainy image of a man standing on the street corner some twenty feet or so behind Jane and just out of her view. The man was wearing dark trousers and a plain, dark T shirt. He had neatly trimmed, black hair, a ruggedly handsome face and was sporting what looked like a short beard. He appeared to be following the path of the young woman with keen interest.

Raven looked up at Chelsea who was staring at the slightly blurred image.

'Do you know this man?'

Chapter 14:
Molly's Place

Molly was just twelve years old and starting to feel the first signs of pre-pubescent anxiety when she caught her father in the act.

She had been playing with her dogs in the back garden, two black and tan Bassett Hounds called Bert and Ernie, when Gretchen had called her in for her supper. She was happy and sad in equal measure. Sad because she only had an hour of play time with the dogs each day and she so loved hugging them and chasing after them as they sniffed every blade of grass and every mulchy pile of leaves that littered the edge of the grounds, and happy because her stomach was rumbling and she had been looking forward to Gretchen's beef lasagne all day. She kissed both dogs tenderly on the snout, waved them adieu and headed back inside, taking a seat at the large dining room table which was set for one.

'Where's Daddy, Gretchen?' Her voice had just started to show the tonal shifts of a girl approaching her teenage years. She absent-mindedly stroked a finger along the mottled two inch scar that ran along the right hand side of her face – all that remained of the accident that had shattered her cheekbone and very nearly blinded her in one eye. The boys at her school called her 'the Terminator' after the movie about the killer droid that lost half of its synthetic face in a battle with another killer bot. She didn't care. She knew that she was developing other things that the boys would find much more interesting.

'Your father's busy, Molly.' Gretchen was scooping a big slab of cheesy and meaty pasta onto Molly's plate, coupled with a side salad and a chunk of garlic bread.

Molly's stomach growled loudly and her mouth was salivating from the delicious scent of tomato and oregano. Gretchen set the plate down on Molly's placemat and Molly hastily picked up her knife and fork.

'Aren't you having any?' Molly hated eating alone, but it was becoming more and more the norm as she grew older. She couldn't help but feel a little lonely.

'No, I'll take my supper later after you've gone off to bed. I've got a lot to do before I turn in for the night. This place doesn't just look after itself, you know.'

Molly sighed and resigned herself to a lonesome albeit tasty meal. She idly made humming noises as she cut into the lasagne, heaving in large forkfuls and then biting down on the opulently oily garlic baguette. It took her less than fifteen minutes to devour the lot and wash it down with a large glass of blackcurrant juice. She leaned back in the chair, looked sheepishly around her to ensure no one was within earshot, and let out a mighty burp. The crescendo ricocheted off the wood panelled walls and large, stucco ceiling.

After the meal had settled nicely in her stomach and her appetite had been satisfactorily appeased, she decided to look for her TV remote. She had lost it a week prior and, no matter how hard she and Gretchen had looked for it, from the loft room at the top of the house to the farthest reaches of the utility room at the rear, they just couldn't find it.

She mentally crossed off the places they had searched and made a short list of potential locations. Her father was always complaining at Molly for holding the remote in her hand when she was doing other things, like making a peanut butter sandwich in the kitchen or doing her homework on the coffee table in the lounge, but she had searched all of her usual hangouts. No, she thought, one of the dogs must have done something with it, in the curious way that dogs do. She came to the conclusion that she would have to look in rooms that she did not usually frequent. One of those rooms being her father's bedroom.

Safe in the knowledge that her father was busy with work, probably in the study or outside in the garage, she pushed her chair back quietly and swiftly exited the dining room.

Her father's bedroom was on the first floor, in the south-eastern corner of the large, Victorian house.

The house was starting to get dark; the long shadows being cast by the slowly setting sun threw weird and unsettling shapes across the walls, floor and ceiling. Molly considered flicking on some lights but then thought better of it. She didn't want to cast any unwanted attention on herself. She was, after all, going to be prying in her father's private quarters.

The stairs creaked and groaned as she climbed them and she tried to place her feet on the firmest section of each step, treading as lightly and delicately as she could. If she could have done so she would have floated up the staircase like a ghost.

When she reached the first floor landing she gazed longingly down the long hallway to the closed door of her bedroom. The white and pink sign hung in the centre of the door, upon which, in tall and exquisitely crafted italic script was scrawled the words *'Molly's Place'*. She thought about giving up on her treasure hunt, the TV remote suddenly seeming inconsequential to her, but she shook it off. This was her home and she was damned if she was going to let some ridiculous superstitious notion or her own innate fear prevent her from feeling free to roam as she pleased.

She took a right-hand turn, rounded the corner that led to the southerly, first floor hallway and headed for her father's room. There were no lights on in this part of the house either and as she glanced out of the large south wall window, she glimpsed the sun slowly disappearing behind a copse of tall oak trees. She could see the garden below and the grassy area where she had tickled Ernie's tummy less than an hour earlier. She couldn't wait to see her dogs again.

She reached her father's door and placed her hand on the metallic handle. It was cold in her grasp. She shivered.

She bit down on her lower lip and cursed herself. She was being such a child. What did her father always say to her? *'Courage, Molly, is resistance to fear. Not the absence of fear.'* She had once said that to her home tutor, only to learn that her father's supposed wisdom was actually a quote from an author from long ago; Mark Twang or something like that. In any case, it seemed appropriate at that very moment so she repeated the motto under her breath and turned the door handle.

What she saw on the other side changed her life forever.

On the bed was a woman. She was face down, naked

except for a pair of leather boots and with what looked like thick straps on both wrists and ankles. Her arms were spread wide and tied to the uppermost corners of the bed and her ankles, blood trickling from the binds which were clearly tied way too tight, were likewise bound to the bottom corners. Molly could see that the woman's mouth was gagged. Her eyes were wide like a terrified, cornered animal and she was uttering low, guttural grunts. There were large red welts across her back and Molly thought she could see a tear rolling down her cheek.

Standing behind the woman, with his back to Molly, was her father. He was dressed in running shorts and black socks and he was holding a pair of thin, black canes. His back was bare and sweat was pouring from his slick hair and rolling down his slim torso. He looked out of breath but exhilarated. Molly stood there, her mouth agape, watching the scene with morbid curiosity.

'You have been a naughty girl, Bethany. A very naughty girl.' Her father's voice was different; deeper and with a stern authority that was completely alien to Molly. It wasn't the kind, soothing but firm voice that her father used with her. She wondered whether her father had been possessed in some way by a strange, malevolent force. 'You really must be punished, if not for me, for your parents. You don't realise the torment and the upset that you have been putting them through. You must learn how a lady behaves, for your own good.'

Molly couldn't tear herself away. She felt something inside of her click, like someone had flicked a switch and turned something on that previously had been sitting idle, silently crouching in a dark corner like a fearful but wanton creature. She felt a fascination and … an excitement. She ran a trembling finger down her scar which suddenly felt warm to the touch. Her father raised the canes high above his head and Molly felt the thrill inside of her migrate to her temples and pulse with a fierce energy. 'I will teach you that disobedience, impudence and insolence cannot remain … *unpunished*!'

Her father's shoulder and back muscles rippled as he sliced the canes through the air with a whoosh, bringing them down hard on the woman's taut and scarred back. There was a loud crack, the sound of the thin wood striking soft flesh, a muffled shriek of terrible pain and a visceral grunt from her father.

Molly gasped, swiftly placing a hand over her mouth to stifle the sound, then turned and ran down the hallway as if the devil was fast at her heels.

Chapter 15:
Wise Counsel

Raven held out his mug as Dave Simmons poured thick black coffee from his red, tartan thermos. His two black Labradors, a pair of middle aged sisters, Venus and Serena, ran around them eagerly, their tongues hanging out of their gaping mouths and dripping large blobs of saliva as they hoped in vain that their owner was about to bring out the doggy treats.

'So, long time, no see my friend.' Simmons was leaning against his shed and smiling at Raven like the sympathetic and concerned father figure that he was. 'I think the last time we talked, you were still on the force and keeping your life in order.' His smile faltered and he peered at Raven over the top of his spectacles. 'What the hell's been going on with you?'

Raven sipped his coffee and took in a sharp intake of breath as the boiling liquid burned the tip of his tongue. 'Shit, that's *hot,* Dave!'

Simmons let out a belly laugh. 'Well it came from a hot place. What did you expect?' He grabbed a rag hanging from a nail protruding from the shed roof and threw it across at

Raven. Raven caught it in his left hand and rapidly wiped the spilled coffee from his chin and T shirt.

He returned the rag, smiled warmly and then looked down at the sodden earth. He had to admit, he was more than a little ashamed. A part of him felt that he had let his ex-chief down – the one guy that had been around to mop up after him every time Raven had made one of his now legendary cock-ups. 'I messed up, Dave, I really did. I had a great thing with Lisa, with Harry and with life in general and I took it all for granted.' Raven looked up at Stuart, Dave's partner, who was at the north side of the allotment working over a rather stubborn patch of soil. He raised a hand in greeting and Stuart smiled and waved back. 'I got bored. I mean, I probably didn't think in those terms at the time, but looking back I think that's exactly how I felt. Maybe I wasn't ready to settle down or maybe I had some misguided delusion of myself, one that still craved the excitement of flitting from relationship to relationship, maintaining a detachment from any type of commitment or responsibility. And the drink, Dave. It still has a grip on me and – *my god* – I fight it every day, I really do, and it takes all of the meagre strength that I have, but,' he shook his head, 'I'm human and I'm weak and, more often than not, it beats me into submission like some shot, journeyman fighter. I just don't have the chin anymore.'

He wiped his bottom lip with the back of his hand but refused to meet Dave Simmons' gaze. He continued, 'And the *dreams*. The dreams are still haunting me. Two, maybe three times a week I wake up in a cold sweat and screaming. It's like they're mocking me, taunting me … *accusing* me.'

'Raven, you can't keep thinking like that. As the police

psychologist said to you at the time, these dreams are just manifestations of your own inner fears and insecurities. If the dreams are accusing you it's because, deep down inside, you are accusing yourself. You feel guilty. Maybe for the Richards thing, maybe for Lisa and Harry, maybe for the way your career went. But you need to stop thinking about what these dreams, these *fantasies* mean and start focusing on what you are doing with your life. Your *real* life.'

'Was it real, Dave?'

'Was what real?'

'What we saw? At the mayor's house that night with Richards and Damo? That … thing?'

Simmons stepped closer to Raven and bent down to whisper in his ear, casting a wary glance at Stuart to make sure he wasn't listening. 'You know what that was. They *told* us. Communal hallucination, nothing more. And … *that's what we stick to.*'

'Do you still think about it?'

'I don't.' Simmons gave him a somewhat tight, strained smile. 'And neither should you.' He tipped the dregs of his coffee onto the garlic patch and turned to set the cup back down on the makeshift shelf of his shed. 'It's in the past, where it belongs.'

'Jane Butler's missing.'

Simmons turned back to Raven with a start. 'Richard's ex-partner?'

Raven grimaced. 'The very same.'

Simmons paused, rubbed a hand across his unshaven chin as if concentrating, chuckled to himself and bent down to pick a dandelion from the claggy soil. 'It means nothing, Raven. That case was solved and Richards is in the ground.'

87

'Maybe.' Raven handed Simmons his empty cup. 'But maybe not.' He took his phone from his pocket and scrolled through his messages to the last one he had received from Chelsea Butler. He held it up to show Simmons. 'Her mum has hired me in a private capacity to see whether I can help locate her. She's very worried.'

'Then she should call the police.'

'She did, but you know as well as I do that all that cold, venomous bitch Deveraux is interested in is popularity contests and rapid career progression.' He fought to bury his bitterness. 'The last thing she wants is another spate of bad press and national, red top headlines.'

'You're playing with fire here, you know that right?'

'I'm helping a friend.'

'You're out for revenge. Do not underestimate Deveraux. She's proven herself to be a very capable adversary.' Simmons knew that all too well. He had the scars to prove it and as a result had reluctantly learned to keep his powerful enemies close. As close as was comfortably possible.

'I won't. This isn't about that.' Raven turned and looked across the wide expanse of allotments, all being tended lovingly by dozens of retirees, men and women, their heads protected from the sun in wide brimmed, straw hats, their boots covered with dirt and weeds, their backs bent over from day after day of physical exertion. But despite all of that, he jealously observed, their faces were filled with the glow of relaxation, personal pride and an almost complete absence of stress.

'I hope not, Luke. For your sake.'

'You okay, guys?' Stuart said, coming over. He was a greying, slightly overweight man with bright red cheeks and a hearty persona. His face was red and blotchy from hours in the sun but his smile was unyielding. He set down his fork against the low fence and shook Raven's hand energetically. 'Enjoying this glorious weather?'

Raven looked over at Simmons and smiled. 'Yes, it's great. You're doing a good job with the veggie patch.'

'Oh, we think so, don't we, Dave? We just love it out here, and so do the dogs.' He beamed at Raven. 'Can't get enough of it really. Now Davey here is retired we can come here just as much as we like.'

Raven grinned. 'I bet. And I'm jealous as hell.' He and Simmons shared a knowing glance. They knew they'd said all there was to say. For now. 'Well, I best be off. We don't all have calendars as empty as you two, you know.'

Stuart laughed warmly. 'I bet you don't.' He clapped Raven on the back. 'But don't worry, it comes to us all, eventually.'

Behind him, fifty metres or so east along the sheltered country lane and sitting in a silver Mercedes C class saloon, Detective Inspector Randall Kipruto frantically scrawled some notes, started his engine and slowly followed.

Chapter 16:
The Big Bang

Now, I don't know whether you've met Derek Luscombe? Well, for your personal benefit let me warn you that Del is a certifiable lunatic who should not be let anywhere near the general public without a health warning sticker splattered all over his body. The bloke is a nut job.

Ronny had suggested that he and I go over and meet with Del at his farmhouse in Hilltop, a little hamlet near the village of Beaulieu. Raven couldn't make it as he had another appointment but he gave us his blessing so off we went. I drove, of course, as Ronny hadn't yet managed to acquire himself some wheels.

'So what do you think of Raven? Do you think he's in?' Ronny was sitting in the passenger seat and sucking on a huge Cuban cigar. I don't normally allow smoking in my van but Ronny was Ronny and I was still half in awe of him.

'Yeah, I think so. Based on what he told us, and what you told me about his personal situation, I don't think he can afford not to be.' And, deep down, I was hoping that Raven was dedicated to the job. After all, what better protection could you ask for? A bloody copper on your heist team.

'I'm not so sure' Ronny dragged on his cigar and blew a thick plume out of the window. 'He doesn't seem like he's fully committed.' He pointed the cigar in my general direction. 'You keep an eye on him for me. He likes you.'

I didn't know whether to be flattered or afraid but I settled on the former.

Ronny pointed his large finger down a dark dirt track on my right and I pulled my van in, its suspension crying out in agony as the van bounced and hopped down the roughly marked out terrain for three quarters of a mile. Del's farmhouse sat at the end of the track, a small bungalow style cottage surrounded by a large meadow, a small group of trees to the north and what looked like a herd of highland cows to the south. Ronny informed me that Del's place wasn't really a working farm. Just a property that he had inherited from his wife's deceased parents that he was able to live in mortgage free. And, more importantly, a place where he could focus on his one true vocation. Namely, blowing shit up.

Del came hurtling out of his house just as soon as my van touched down.

'Hello, boys! Hello! *Hello*!'

Del was wearing camo combat shorts and a khaki T shirt. Around his swollen waist he wore an ammunition belt containing various tools and assorted gadgets and his boots were standard issue territorial army. He had a military style tattoo on his right forearm, some kind of shield with wings, and large gold sovereign rings on every finger. As he approached us, he spat out a large gloop of brown chewing tobacco.

'Derek, my man. May I introduce you to William West. I

knew his father very well. We were in Dartmoor together.'

Del launched himself at me and grabbed me in a tight, slightly suffocating bear hug. 'Any friend of Ronny's is a friend of mine.'

I respectfully retracted myself from his embrace and offered my hand. 'Please, Derek,' he looked me up and down as if offended, 'call me Billy.'

His hard expression cracked with a huge moustachioed smile and he shook my hand vigorously. 'Only if you call me Del.'

'So,' Ronny strolled out into the meadow, 'Derek my son,' Ronny turned and faced the two of us. 'Show us what you've got!'

****

If you haven't been up close and personal with the types of explosives a man like Del Luscombe is used to dealing with then you won't really understand what I'm about to tell you. All I can say is this: take what comes next, sprinkle it with a little bit of that magical dust of imagination and then swirl into it a great, big spoonful of '*fucking hell!*'

Del had what can only be described as a battleground laid out in a huge expanse of barren land set out behind his farmhouse. The pitch was around an acre and a half and was completely secluded from prying eyes by large pine trees, beeches and oaks of various sizes. Littered around the ground were mock brick buildings, wood and metal shacks, block walls, sections of concrete slabs and battered vehicles. Almost all the structures on show had large chunks missing and great swathes of soot and mud smearing their outer façades.

'Welcome to the showground, gents.' Del splayed his chunky but remarkably short arms out as if leading us into a fairground. The beige and brown of the scene behind him was somewhat underwhelming to say the least. 'Now, what I've set up over here,' he spoke with confidence and bravado as we weaved through the chunks of rubble and oddly unsettling architecture, 'is as much of a replica as I could fashion from what little I know of the target area.' We rounded what looked like a mock World War Two gun emplacement and were confronted by a large concrete wall, within which was set an oval doorway which itself was filled with a three foot deep concrete and steel bar reinforcement.

'This here is the entrance to our getaway tunnel.'

I gulped. The bloody thing was around ten feet tall and six feet wide and was as thick as your arm was long. 'Do you … do you have the equipment to blast a hole through that?'

Ronny put an elephant leg sized arm around me and laughed. '*Haha*! What do you say, Del? Do you want to show him?'

'I can't believe he doubts me, Ron. And *me*,' he walked around the other side of the wall and I could hear him rummaging around, 'with my reputation to uphold. Does this young man think that a measly obstacle such as this would defeat the great Dynamite Del?'

I hadn't heard that nickname before but it sure suited him. I paced up and down the wall to get the lie of the land. I considered the number of drill-bits, top of the range ones too, that I had shattered trying to bore my way through such concrete structures when re-wiring houses. The stuff was just impenetrable.

Del re-appeared and threw Ronny and me a set of ear defenders and eye protectors each. 'You're gonna need these, chaps. There's going to be a big bang and a lot of shit flying around.'

Ronny grinned at me like an excited schoolchild and mock covered his ears.

'Now a lot of these new guys like to use expansive grout when taking out a concrete chunk such as this,' he said as he withdrew a large Makita battery powered drill and inserted a diamond tipped masonry head. 'But frankly, that takes far too long and the results are a lot less satisfying.' He slipped on his ear defenders and the drill roared into life. Concrete dust flew into the air and soon we were covered in a large grey cloud that coated my lungs and stung my nostrils. One by one Del drilled a half dozen holes in the oval doorway, each about the diameter of a small tomato.

'There, all ready for my little babies.'

With that Del picked up a duffle bag and threw it on the floor in front of him with reckless abandon. He slipped on a pair of workman's gloves and, one by one, he withdrew long, slender cylinders of what I can only assume was nitro-glycerine.

Gradually he inserted the cylinders into the snug holes, slotting them inside their dark, musty coffins like test tubes in a dry nitrogen storage container, and attached the wires to an electrical box on the ground. A small antenna stuck out from this grey, brick shaped piece of equipment and in Del's right hand was the trigger switch.

'Now, probably a couple of sticks of that stuff would create enough of an explosion to crack open that cavity but,' he winked at Ronny, 'we don't take any chances, do we

Ron?'

'No we don't, Del.' Ronny looked over at me, practically jumping up and down with anticipation.

'And, given that I'm not entirely sure how thick the tunnel plug is, my idea is better to be safe than sorry.'

'Sounds like a good plan. We don't want to be caught down that basement with our trousers around our ankles.'

'So, with that, my little hoodlum chums, I suggest we *give it a blast* as they say.' Del roared with laughter and Ronny followed suit. I giggled with nervous energy.

We walked back to the edge of the next building, putting on our ear defenders as we went. Del handed me the trigger, smiling encouragingly. 'Do you want to do the honours Billy? Seeing as it's your first time?'

I took the trigger switch into my hand reluctantly, its solid weight feeling reassuring but terrifying at the same time. I swallowed my cloying saliva, wiping the sweat from my moustache as I did so.

I counted down in my head: three … two … one …

Chapter 17:
The Village Idiot

Raven sat at the bar in the Golden Swan, supping on a Rusty Nail and mulling over his conversation with his old boss.

He was right, he knew it. What was he looking for with the Butler case? Closure? An explanation? Something to silence the nightmares? He couldn't justify it. He was just chasing shadows and expecting to find the darkness, skulking around somewhere, just out of reach but close enough for him to feel its cold breath on the nape of his neck.

He looked up at the red headed waitress standing with her arms folded behind the bar and chewing gum, some other university student cycling through the staff rota in an effort to boost her social fund. It seemed like every time he was in there someone new was serving him drinks. He missed Daisy. He thought about her every single day; the guilt buried like a tic just under his skin, eating away at his raw, tender flesh. It would never leave him. Sometimes he would glance up and see her standing there, unloading the dishwasher or pouring one of her many admirers their daily intake of intoxicants. She would smile at him and he would smile back, they would share a moment of knowing, he would feel some sort of relief from the ice picks of pain that were permanently embedded in his soul, and then she would evaporate like smoke in the breeze.

He heard someone come in through the door and it jolted him from his daydream. He smelt her before the hand touched his shoulder and he smiled. He turned to face Chelsea Butler, dressed in casual slacks, cream blouse and a beige jacket. She oozed class.

'Chelsea, hi. Thanks for coming.' He pulled over a bar stool and she looked down at it like it was the strangest thing she had ever seen. 'Sorry, let's er … let's grab a booth.' He stood up, grabbed his jacket and drink and gestured towards one of the tables by the window at the front of the pub. 'Can I get you a drink?'

Chelsea looked at the glass in his hand, the brown, acidic liquid swirling around the half melted ice cubes, glanced at her watch and smiled. 'I guess it's almost noon. I'll take a dry white wine, thank you.'

Raven ordered her drink, tapped his card on the payment machine – inwardly cursing at the cost of the sauvignon blanc he'd just purchased – and sat down opposite his elegant client. He could smell her perfume, something that reminded him of fresh meadows and time spent out with friends when he was younger; it eased his spirits. He slurped from his drink.

'I … I wanted to talk about our arrangement.'

Chelsea sipped from her wine and brushed her hair from her eyes. 'Our arrangement?'

'I don't think I can continue with this case. It … it's really a matter for the police. I just don't have the resources.'

Chelsea's jaw dropped and she placed both of her hands

on the edge of the table. She looked as though she had just been insulted. 'But you're making progress. *Good* progress, which is much more than I can say about those belligerent oafs at the police station. I haven't heard a thing from them in days.'

'All we've really done is trace your daughter's last steps.' He leaned forward with a determined sincerity. 'I'm sure the police have already done everything that Wesley and I have done but have probably not communicated it in the way that we have. I'm sure they're ahead of us, even.'

She reached into her handbag for a tissue and dabbed her eyes. 'Do you know what I am going through here? Do you?'

He thought that there would be tears, had braced himself for it. But now that he was in the moment, he instantly regretted committing himself to this conversation. He needed another drink. 'I can only imagine, Chelsea. Truly. And I am terribly sorry, but I really think this is for the best.'

Chelsea spoke through gritted teeth and refused to meet his gaze. 'I'm sure you do.'

There was a silence between them. A long one. The pub was almost empty, aside from the waitress and an elderly couple finishing the last of their greasy bacon and egg brunch. He could hear the old building groaning as if uncomfortable at the awkwardness it was harbouring within its brick and mortar shell.

Raven spoke first. 'Look, I know a guy. A *good guy*.'

She was looking out of the window and sipping very small mouthfuls of wine. He could see she was trying to hold herself together.

'Randall Kipruto. He's a very competent DI and I can put in a good word, try to move you up the priority list.'

'You are part of this, Raven, whether you like it or not.'

Raven set down his glass. 'Chelsea, I don't think you're...'

'Listen to me!' Chelsea slammed her hand on the table. The waitress looked up and the elderly man dropped his fork. 'Do you think I haven't connected the dots? That I haven't put everything together? Do you think I'm the village idiot?'

'Chelsea, Mrs Butler, I ...'

'Everything that's happened to my Jane was avoidable. *Everything!*'

'I'm sure that's true, but don't you see that a private investigator cannot *possibly* be the best way to resolve it. It really can't.'

'Maybe not any normal investigator, Raven. I'm sure on that point you are right.' She leaned across the table and grabbed his hand. Her skin was soft like newly washed linen, but her grip was firm. 'But you? Yes you, the guy that put that murderous bastard in the ground. As true as that may be, you still failed my daughter. You allowed her torment to go on for *far too long*.' He recoiled like he had been slapped. 'You have skin in this game, Raven. And you have a responsibility – to my daughter, to *me*!' She stopped and took a deep breath. Her calm, collected demeanour returned. She placed a gentle hand on his cheek and he felt goose-bumps form on his arms. 'You will continue with the work I am paying you for, and you will bring my daughter home. That's non-negotiable.'

He was completely lost for words. He looked over at the bar and the salvation that lurked within the bottle of Glenfiddich. The barmaid was leaning on the counter and smiling smugly at him.

Chelsea stood and kissed him on the cheek. He could feel her hair caress his face, her warm lips on his skin, her scent in his nostrils. She looked down at him. 'And Raven, I know exactly who that man was standing on the street corner. You know? The one in the picture?' She leant closer. His mouth was dry. 'And so … do … *you.*'

With that she exited and all the tension in the room evaporated. He slumped on the table. What did she mean?

His phone rang and he leapt in his seat. He rummaged in his pocket and pulled it out. Lisa's picture glared back at him: her short red hair, her silver hooped lip piercing, dark eyes. He answered.

'Lisa?'

'Luke, it's me.' She sounded agitated.

'What's up?' He could feel himself immediately deflating and he sighed.

'You need to get round here. *Now*!'

He cursed under his breath. 'Lis, I'm right in the middle of …'

'It's … it's Harry.'

Chapter 18:
Felix the Indestructible

Another day, another missing person. This time a homeless woman whom he had seen many times before with her sleeping bag, cup of change and an old mongrel of a dog in the doorway of various High Street shops. A fellow street dweller hadn't seen her in three days and had asked one of the staff to call the station. Randall was getting tired of no leads and umpteen wild goose chases, including tailing Luke Raven from one end of town to the other and watching him wash his life away with liquor and regrets. When he had joined the force he had imagined breaking up major international drug trafficking rings or bringing the boss of an organised crime syndicate in. He was starting to question his own commitment.

Despite all of that, he sat on the bench in the middle of the High Street, acted as professionally as he could and interviewed the ratty old fella; no more than three teeth in his mouth, skin like dried leather, old and tattered blue beanie hat covering his grey and matted hair and a raincoat that was at least three sizes too big and wrapped around his tinder wood frame of a body.

'I seen 'er. Seen 'er three nights ago sitting right 'ere, right by this ole bench. 'Er and Terry 'er mutt.' The old guy was gesticulating like a crazy person and his eyes were whirling around in his head like loose change in a money box. 'She said ole Terry was getting fed up just sitting around all day waiting for scraps. Not that we ever get given anything by the shop keepers.' He shook his head and sighed. 'All capitalist money grabbers the lot of 'em.'

Randall scratched at an itch on his cheek and rolled his eyes. He was almost certain that this was just a waste of his time and he should be pursuing more leads associated with the disappearance of Lizzy Easter, Daniel Riley and Simon Farrington. Ruby had the lab analyse the ruck sack left by Farrington on the beach and they had found an unknown hair caught in one of the zips. The lab was running it through NDNAD, the UK's national DNA database, at that very second and Randall was praying for at least a partial hit. They didn't have a hair root so the hair itself wasn't exactly ideal, but one of the things Randall remembered from his college course in basic forensics, one of the many courses he had undertaken during his initial training period, was that MDNA, or mitochondrial DNA to be precise, was passed down through family members and therefore anyone on file with the same MDNA as their perp would at least give them a lead to follow, if not the exact match. He was thankful that his mother had taught him to be studious and listen in class.

'Are you listening to me, fella?' The old guy was still rambling on and getting frustrated at Kipruto's apparent lack of interest.

'Of course, sir. You were saying that Maggie …?'

'Maggie Humphries. I call her Mystic Mags because

she's always seeing things. *Weird* things.'

'Yes, you said that earlier.'

'Yeah, she was there when that guy killed that girl, over in that warehouse.'

Randall looked up, suddenly very interested.

'Yeah, that creepy guy, the one that killed he's self. Hung 'er up like a piece of meat. Like something hanging over in ole Jon Hunter's butcher's shop across the street.'

Randall followed the line of the old guy's arm and his eyes settled on the slabs of beef and pork carcass hanging in the window like cadavers waiting for the vultures to descend.

'Ole Mags said the bloke was like a ghost, all white and spindly, like that thing in that painting, you know? *The Scream.*'

Randall shivered.

'Yeah, I heard about that. A couple of years ago. The so called 'Pale Faced' killer.' He noted it down in his pad. 'So, Ms Humphries was there when he killed one of those poor girls, was she?'

The old guy smiled eagerly. 'Yeah, for what good it did her. She's been having nightmares ever since; something about a monster rising up from a crack in the earth or summit. She said it had red eyes, a thorny spine and tail and a long black tongue.' His eyes turned into slits as he recalled the details. 'Sharp claws and teeth and fire for breath. Like summit's gonna shoot out of a hole in the ground and gobble us all up.' He laughed at that, a real cackle of a laugh that caused him to double up and break out in a retching, hacking cough.

'Well, I'm sure it was very disturbing, if she really saw what she said she saw.'

'Oh, she did all right. She was in the paper and everything.'

Randall made a mental note to check it out. 'So, you were saying? About the dog?'

The old guy smacked himself on the head. 'Of course, yeah. The dog.' He laughed again. 'I forget my own mind sometimes. Yeah, well, Terry wanted a walk so she said she was gonna wander down to the front, you know? Check out what was going on along the beach. There's always stuff left over down there, chips and crispy bits of fish and stuff like that.' His eyes lit up. 'Got myself a whole whelk the other day. Only half chewed as well.'

Randall screwed up his nose. 'And what time was this?'

'Oh, around nine at night I'd say. It was just starting to get colder and I was laying my box out on the floor to keep my back warm.'

'And in which direction would you say she walked?' Randall was starting to wonder whether there was something to this after all.

The old guy pointed west. 'That way, down towards the fairground and the pier'

'The area down there? The promenade that borders the beach by...'

'Yep, Bishops Crag.'

Randall nodded, placed his pen back into his breast pocket and tucked his notebook in his jacket. 'Thank you very much Mister...?'

'Just Felix to you sir, I don't got no second name.'

'Well then, Felix. Thank you very much. You have been a tremendous help.'

'And ole Mags and Terry?'

Randall sighed wearily. 'I'm sure they're fine, but they will be all the better for the information you've given us.' He paused and smiled. 'I'll be sure to be in touch. Now,' Randall opened his wallet and gave the man a fiver, 'you get yourself a warm drink and sandwich and take good care of yourself.'

Felix took the money and licked his lips. 'Don't you worry about ole Felix, sir. I'm as indestructible as they come. I keep out of danger like a tabby keeps out of the sea.'

'That's good,' he stood and shook Felix's hand, 'I'll be seeing you now. Have yourself a good day.'

Felix turned on his heels and half skipped down the street towards the Starlight café. 'Oh, I sure will …*now*.'

As Randall watched him go, he felt his phone vibrate in his pocket. He picked it up. It was Ruby.

'It's the hair, boss. We've got a match!'

Chapter 19:
The Crack in the Wall

Molly liked catching things. She didn't know why but it gave her a thrill, like the thrill that some people get watching football or winning ten pounds on the lottery. Yes, since hitting her teenage years - she was fourteen now and having her monthly times like Gretchen said she would - she had taken to setting traps and catching stuff.

Ants, bees and butterflies at first, nothing too serious, but she would leave out boxes or jars with honey or sugar in and wait for the little critters to wander in, completely oblivious of the fact that she had lured them there under false and deadly pretences. The ants got boring pretty quickly and the bees weren't much fun at all – she had gotten stung once on the skin between her thumb and forefinger and it had hurt like a motherfucker – but she liked the butterflies. They were so pretty, their wings colourful and patterned like the blankets that Gretchen knitted for her, but their faces were so ugly. All eyes, hair and pincers. They were a real dichotomy and Molly loved them for it. She especially loved their wings and she found it interesting that they needed two wings to take flight. With just one they simply flopped around on the floor and into the walls until they ran out of energy and died from the exertion. Not that it stopped her from … well, from what she did.

Her father was home less and less now that she was older and she could pretty much take care of herself. She spent her days wandering around the big house and causing her own private mischief. Even Gretchen had started leaving her to her own devices. She herself was getting older; Molly thought she was probably seventy or so and she didn't have the energy to follow her around like she used to. And now that she only had one dog – Bert had died when she was thirteen, something that still hung heavily on her heart, especially as she was the one that found him, all lifeless, googly eyed and tongue lolling out of his mouth like a black, oozing slug – she didn't enjoy dog time nearly as much.

The house was old and musty in places and one afternoon, about an hour after she had returned home from school at the end of what could only be described as an awful day, Molly was excited to find out that they had a mouse problem. A *mice* problem in fact. And quite a big one.

She had been sitting on the step of the back door, smoking a Benson and Hedges cigarette that she had found in Gretchen's dressing table and enjoying it immensely despite the awful taste, when in the corner of her eye she spotted a little brown object moving speedily across the tiled floor. She jumped up, tossed her half smoked fag out onto the patio and followed the little creature back to a little crack between the skirting board and the corner of a kitchen cabinet. She lay down, stomach first, on the cold ceramic surface and peered through the crack with one beady, curious eye. She was young and her eyes were still good, despite the near miss she had when she was much younger, and she could make out two thin hairs protruding from the hole and jittering nervously. Her hearing was also excellent and she could hear a tinny, squeaky sound like something small and delicate in a terrible fit of panic.

She sat up and placed a hand on her chin, running a finger down her scar which she was now taking to applying makeup to. She could feel a sense of excitement and desire mixed with trepidation and shame. She knew what she wanted to do but felt bad for even thinking it. She pushed a hand through her dark, curly, shoulder length hair, weighed up the pros and cons and resigned herself to doing the right thing.

That night she went to bed still thinking about the crack in the wall. She slept a little and thought a lot.

When she awoke early the next morning she leapt out of bed, showered in a hurry, hastily dressed herself in jeans and a hooded sweatshirt and went out to her father's garage to fetch his tools. She was going to build a mouse trap.

It took her about two hours and gained her one blister and three sore fingers – she had whacked them with the hammer, causing such profanity to come out of her mouth that even Gretchen would have been shocked – but she was proud of her efforts. The plywood box was around twenty-five by twenty centimetres. She had taken woodwork at school and she knew her way around a hand-saw and a hammer and nails and the box was tidily constructed with a little hole at the front to get in and out of.

Molly tucked the box under one arm, threw her father's tools back in his toolbox and ran through the house to the kitchen. She placed the box on the worktop, bent down and lay on her stomach again, peering with one eye into the crack. This time she couldn't see anything at all but she was thrilled to learn that she could still hear the little squeaks. It sounded like there were several mice in there.

She jumped up and went to the refrigerator. Gretchen always kept it well stocked and she was sure she would find what she was looking for. She was not disappointed. There, in the clear, plastic shelf at the top of the refrigerator door lay a big block of bright orange, mature cheese. She grabbed it in her hands, pulled open the cutlery drawer and carefully extracted a large, sharp carving knife. She gazed at the blade as the morning sun caught the edge of the steel and reflected into her eyes like a bright flare. She smiled and started humming a song, as she lopped a little block from the corner of the cheese. Furrowing her brow in stern concentration, she manipulated the small morsel of soft dairy. She was still humming as she rubbed it around the edge of the box and then pushed it into the hole. Her heart was pounding in her chest and she could feel the steady thump of her pulse in the tips of her fingers and along the length of her scar.

She placed the box about two centimetres away from the crack in the wall and pulled up a kitchen chair. It was still early and she was starting to feel tired – she had hardly slept after all – and she leaned back on the cushioned surface and closed her eyes.

She dreamed of dead Bert lying in a pool of his own urine, an enormous hammer crashing through the walls and down onto the naked buttocks of an unknown woman who was bound face first on the dining room table, giant butterfly wings covering her bedroom window like organic curtains and her mother's soothing voice singing to her through the speakers of her tiny, battery powered stereo.

When she awoke her stomach was grumbling. It was noon.

She leapt from the chair and lay back down on the floor next to her box. She could still hear squeaking from inside the crack in the wall but none from her trap. Her heart sank. Perhaps the mice had gone into the box but got back out again without touching the cheese. Perhaps she hadn't left it long enough and the cheese was still lying there like a delicious cordon bleu meal. Either way, she shouldn't have fallen asleep. She cursed her tardiness. Her father would have chastised her for it.

She grabbed the little rectangular box in a fit of rage and went to throw it into the garden like a broken toy but the box was heavier than she remembered and something was sliding around in there. She grabbed the container in both hands and raised the hole up to her right eye. She smiled. There, inside the box, lying on their sides, their tales wrapped in little coils, their black eyes like little seeds, their mouths open, their little teeth protruding like tiny razors and their titchy little tongues hanging awkwardly out of their small mouths, were two, full sized adult mice. Around their little, delicate lips were the remnants of the cheese. And the chocolate. The chocolate that she had carefully pushed inside the soft texture of the dairy treat. Chocolate that she knew, from the research that she had undertaken at two am that morning, was deadly to mice.

She placed the box back on the floor, ran to her father's garage, grabbed his claw hammer from his toolbox and hastily returned to the kitchen. She put her feet either side of the box and held it tightly there, tucked the claw of the hammer under the lid of the box and yanked. At first the lid didn't move and she was sure that she had hammered the long nails in to the ply too hard and the bloody thing was going to have to be broken open like an easter egg. Then, with one final yank, the top popped off like the lid of a jack-in-a-box. Molly grinned as she looked at her motionless pets. They were amusing to her. She recalled the excitement she felt as the gooey jet of blood erupted from the neck of the deer, remembered the hard and painful slam of the rifle stock into her cheek and once again smelled the salty scent of death.

She reached into the box slowly and grabbed the tails of each of the deceased rodents, one in each hand, and lifted their inverted forms to her face. She put her nose up close to them and inhaled their stench. They were already starting to rot from the inside. She licked the face of the mouse closest to her and she could taste the cheesy chocolate and musty flavour of its fur and faeces. She felt a chill race through her veins like liquid nitrogen.

She walked out the back door in a zombie-like state, her mind completely entranced by the dead animals in her hands. She perceived nothing else around her. Without thinking, and with very little emotion, she placed the both of them on the patio slab side by side, their little forms cold and starting to stiffen, lifted her size four bare foot and stood down on them firmly. She giggled as their bones crunched, their fur and skin split and the blood oozed between her toes like warm tea. She smiled as a cold tear escaped from the corner of her eye, rolled silently across the delicate skin that stretched across her mottled scar and trickled down her flushed cheek.

Behind her, Gretchen stood with her hands on her hips

and shook her head slowly and with a sad resignation. She picked up the box and broken lid from the floor, threw it in the waste bin and returned to her cleaning duties. She swore to herself, as god was her witness, that her days as Molly's nanny were coming to an end. She was not going to go through that again. She simply didn't have the strength.

Chapter 20
The Sea Snake

Westhampton beach was full of sun worshippers. The balmy twenty-eight degree heat on that Saturday afternoon in early August had drawn thousands of locals to the shore. All along the golden sands were families decked out with all varieties of colourful windbreaks, beach towels adorned with pictures of palm trees and scenic views of exotic locations, plastic buckets in the shape of medieval castles and foot long spades meant for excavating large swathes of wet sand, only for the water to come in and fill the large sinkholes to the brim at high tide.

There was a cacophony of joyful and symphonic exaltation; children screaming with excitement and shock as they ran into the cold water, teenagers hollering at each other as they threw volleyballs across a makeshift court or played beach tennis with wooden paddles and ping pong balls, and parents yelling at their kids to be careful and to not stray too far along the beach. The beach side bars were heaving with bare backed holidaymakers supping their favourite warm weather tipple; amber pints of cold lager, rainbow coloured iced cocktails, fizzy glasses of prosecco or such like, getting more inebriated by the hour, and the cafes and restaurants were overflowing with partakers of such coastal delights as cockles and muscles doused in copious amounts of malt vinegar and black pepper, large fillets of cod with crispy, golden batter and greasy burgers in toasted buns and chips the girth of your thumb.

The atmosphere, as they say, was buzzing.

Little Rebecca Worthing was having a great time. She was eight years old, a little older than the other kids she was with – Charlie was only six and his sister, Serena, wasn't much older at seven and a half – and they were having fun, tearing up and down the golden sand like whirling dervishes on caffeine, throwing sand bombs at each other and kicking cold, frothy water in each other's faces. Rebecca, or Bex as her family called her, had a stitch in her side from all the running, laughing and play-fighting. It was one of her most favourite days of the holiday so far, although she really didn't like the sun cream her mum had smeared all over her face, arms and torso. It was all sticky and gooey, it smelled of sickly coconut milk and when she tripped and fell over she got covered in sand. She looked like a donut.

Otherwise, though, she was having a great time.

'You want a drink, Bex?' It was Charlie. He was sucking on a carton of orange juice and he had another one in his left hand. He offered it to her and she took it gratefully. She was gasping.

She ripped open the straw from its wrapper and plunged it into the foil covered hole on the top of the little juice box. She sucked the sweet, cold liquid down into her hoarse and dry throat. It was wonderful.

'Oh come on guys, I want to go in the water with the

Lilo!' Serena, her friend with little black pigtails and a polka dot swimsuit, was dragging a pink and white, inflatable bed along the sand. 'We can pretend we're sailing to an island to find buried treasure.' She smiled and winked at Bex. 'And I can be the ship's captain.'

'Oi!' Charlie finished his juice and threw the carton on his dad's beach towel. 'I want to be the captain!' He pointed a finger at himself. 'I'm a boy and all captains are boys,' he turned to face his father, 'isn't that right, Dad?'

His dad, a slightly overweight, balding thirty-something in unflattering blue and white swim shorts and a sun blushed face shrugged his shoulders. 'Ask your mother.'

'*Mum*?'

'Oh, shut up Charlie! You're being a sexist pig!' Serena shouted at her younger brother. Their mother, who was reclining elegantly on a plastic, orange sunbed that had seen better days, pulled down her sunglasses, looked at them over the top of her rom-com paperback and shook her head.

'A what?' Charlie looked shocked and slightly bemused.

Serena shrugged her shoulders. 'That's what Mum calls dad when he says something nasty about girls.' She looked over at Rebecca. 'So, Bex. Are you coming?'

Rebecca slurped her remaining juice, brushed her mousey fringe out of her eyes and threw out her arms. 'Of course I am.' She grabbed the other end of the Lilo, blew a raspberry at Charlie and they all laughed and skipped towards the water. 'Aye, aye captain!'

They swerved in between the various clusters of beach goers, kicking dry sand over half-sleeping sunbathers and demolishing sandcastles with their inflatable battering ram. They laughed and giggled at each other and barrelled towards the ocean like a marauding gang of cut-throats.

As they approached the water something bobbed to the surface and caught Rebecca's eye.

'Look, Serena, Charlie!' The tide caught the object and she watched as it rolled towards them. 'It's a fish!' She dropped her end of the Lilo, causing Serena to tumble over the suddenly static back end and she collapsed in a heap, rolling over onto her back.

'Bex! Look what you did!' Serena was lying in the sand and crying with laughter.

'No, look. Serena. It's a big fish!'

Charlie helped Serena up and walked towards the edge of the water. All three of them stood in a line and watched the large, pale object roll in on the tide.

'What type of fish is it?' Charlie made loops with his forefingers and thumbs and put them to his eyes, using his make believe binoculars to get a better look at the mysterious creature.

'Could be a shark.' Serena had stopped laughing and was now intrigued by the thing that was now bobbing slowly towards them.

'It's not a shark, Serena. I think it could be a dolphin.' They all jumped up and down and shrieked at the thought of a dolphin frolicking around in the shallow water with them.

Just then, a wave caught the back of the creature and it gathered pace on the top of the swell.

Rebecca spotted something odd and she frowned, her gaze suddenly very curious. 'Wait a minute.' She stepped towards the water as the wave turned into a frothy foam and splashed her face and neck. The thing approached. 'That's not a fish.'

116

The long shape started spinning in the water, plunging down into the depths and then coming back suddenly to the surface as the under-current manipulated its unusual shape in its delicate grasp.

Rebecca noticed the crimson scales – *all five of them*. 'It looks more like a sea snake or something.'

'Er, *a snake*!' Serena jumped behind Charlie and pushed him forwards with both hands.

Charlie's eyes were beaming. '*Awesome*!'

Rebecca bent down as the creature bobbed to the surface once more. She saw the five digits, the rounded curve at the base, the bony features jutting out either side of the head, the widening, thick torso and the large, round bulge at the back that looked like it had been ripped from something. Red and sinewy tendrils hung from its rear like terrible and bloody dreadlocks. Her mind raced, struggling to put the pieces of the visual jigsaw together in any sensible order, but when it did her thoughts went into overdrive, her vision swam and her skin turned prickly and cold. She felt the terror welling up inside of her, commencing from her feet and building in force as it crawled up her shaking legs, into her suddenly unsettled tummy, across her pulsating chest and into her throat.

The three of them screamed and screamed, as if Poseidon himself had risen from the ocean, turned on their heels and ran for their lives as the leg, severed at the knee and with painted toenails still intact, came to rest on the shore.

Act 2:
The Legion

There's nae body kens that he bides there
For his face is seldom seen
But tae meet his eye is tae meet your fate

Chapter 21:
Interiors

Raven's battered Mondeo skidded to a halt outside Lisa's apartment building and he launched himself from the driver's seat with such velocity that he felt the vertebrae in his spine crack and his knees cry out in anguish. He ignored the pain as he swung the car door open, almost catching a hapless cyclist who swerved and gave him an angry finger, and rushed out into the street, circling behind the car and leaping up the apartment steps two at a time. He reached the top, panting and sweating hard, and slammed his hand on the intercom. Within a couple of seconds he heard the magnets in the door latch release and he pushed his way through.

Lisa's apartment was on the second floor so he ignored the elevator and bounded up the stairway. His heart was pounding in his chest like a double bass drum in some hard-core metal band and the blood rushing to his head was giving him a throbbing headache. He thought of his young son, all blond hair and pale skin, tiny hands and feet and a contagious giggle that just infected his aching soul.

He hammered on the door, hard enough for it to shake in its frame. When it finally opened, the large silhouette of

Lonny Sutcliffe – muscular arms, thick neck and chest, grey hair meticulously smoothed to the right with the other side shaved almost to the skin – loomed over him.

'Where is he?'

'Good morning Luke, lovely to see you Luke, how you been Luke?' Sutcliffe's lop-sided smile made Raven's blood spit and boil.

'Get the fuck out of my way, Lonny!' Raven pushed him aside, grabbing the man's stone-like exterior in his clammy hands and grunting as he squeezed past him. He knew it was a fight he couldn't win but he was prepared to go toe to toe with the big muscle-bound imbecile if it came to that. A small, pointy eared, energy drink of a dog ran to him, panting heavily through its nose, its tongue hanging out as if semi-exhausted and entangling its solid torso between Raven's legs. He fought the urge to kick it out of the way as Lonny shuffled the dog into the kitchen.

Lisa was in the front room nursing a cup of tea while Harry played with his toy cars. Despite the veritable fear in her eyes and the tremor in her lips she looked radiant and he felt his face flush with adrenaline. He wanted to go to her and hold her but he needed to see his son. He raced over to him.

'How you doing kiddo? I've missed you.' He grabbed a hold of Harry who looked up in excitable surprise, a huge grin spreading across his face. He had a miniature yellow Mustang in one hand and a red Ferrari in the other. He held them out to Raven and told him all about them in a language only toddlers can understand.

'Ook, ook. Broom brooms. Ook addy!' Harry's soft blond hair was neatly brushed and parted on the side and his cheeks were sensitive and pink from the freshly growing baby teeth inside his little mouth. Raven hugged him tightly.

'I know, Harry. I can see. Look at those cars, I bet they can go really, *really* fast can't they?' He kissed him on his forehead, inhaled the fresh scent of shampoo and soap and placed him back down on the carpet to play with his toys. He ruffled his hair affectionately. 'What the hell happened, Lis?'

She took a large swig of her tea and looked over at Lonny. Raven peered over his shoulder at him as he nodded back to her from the open doorway and reluctantly exited the room. Lisa half smiled but Raven could see the tears welling in her eyes. He knew the dam was about to bust open.

'Oh, Luke!' She leapt up and threw her arms around his shoulders, burying her face in the crook of his neck. He could feel her red hair, her soft skin on his cheek and he willingly allowed himself to become intoxicated by the sweet scent of her perfume. 'I was so terrified, Luke, I thought we'd lost him!'

'What happened?'

'I don't know what I would have done. I just don't know what …'

He hugged her tightly as the tears flowed and her body trembled, Harry swooshing toy cars around their feet as they both stood motionless in the centre of the room and embracing. He wished that he could pause his life right there and hold it that way for eternity. Everyone that was important to him, everything that mattered to him, had *ever* mattered to him, was in that space, in that moment.

After a while he placed his hands on her shoulders and looked into her eyes. 'Tell me what happened. I need to know.'

Lisa stepped backwards, brushed her hair from her eyes and perched herself on the edge of the sofa. Raven took the recliner.

'We were out walking in the park. Me, Harry and Lonny. Lonny wanted to walk Sly and Harry needed some fresh air.' Sly was Lonny's french bulldog, the beast that had confronted Raven in the doorway to the apartment and the most annoying animal Raven had ever had the misfortune of meeting. And he was usually a dog person.

'The little park over the way, in the middle of the square?'

'No … no, the common. We drove there.'

Raven remembered his last trip to Westhampton common. With a shiver he recalled the naked girl he'd found there, discarded at the base of the tree like some empty refuse sack. He could feel the cold memory of that fateful October morning rise like bile in his throat and a darkness descended upon him. He shook it off.

Lisa continued. 'It was busy, there were a lot of dog walkers and families and the sun was out,' she smiled and ran a hand through Harry's hair. 'It was a lovely day, wasn't it Harry?'

He looked up at her, his luminous blue eyes gazing at them both with the beautifully naïve wonder of adolescence. 'Maan? Sor maaan.'

Lisa picked up her cup and her hands trembled once more. 'Yes, yes Harry, I'm coming to that.'

Raven frowned. 'What does he mean?'

'Lonny and I had a fight. Not a big one. Not as big as they can be anyway, but we got into it and, well, you know how I can get.'

Raven knew only too well, having been on the wrong end of Lisa Clancy's infamous flame haired temper on more than one occasion. He nodded.

'We got distracted and Sly ran off. He took off round the pond like he was chasing something and Lonny was terrified he was going to fall in and drown.'

Raven tittered to himself, 'I bet he was.'

Lisa glared at him. 'So Lonny ran after him and I started to run with him, but then I realised. I realised, Luke, that I didn't know where Harry was.'

Raven's demeanour immediately shifted and he shook his head in disbelief. 'What …how did you not know where he was? *He's your son?*'

'Don't say it like that! It's not like I abandoned him. I just,' a tear rolled down her cheek, 'I just took my eyes off him for a second.'

'For a second? Are you kidding me? I know exactly what happened and so do you because it's happened a million times before. You get so caught up in these little *lovers' tiffs* of yours, that you forget everything else!'

She stood up. 'Don't you dare accuse me of neglecting my child, Luke! Don't you *dare*! I'm here every second of every of minute of every day, looking after him, caring for him, feeding and cleaning him!' Her face was bright red and her glare was venomous. 'Which is much more than I can say for *you*!'

'Because you won't let me anywhere *near him*!' It was Raven's turn to stand.

'Because you're no good for him!'

'Oh, and that *thug in the next room is*?'

The room fell silent and they glared across the empty

space at each other, both furiously panting with the exertion.

Harry tugged at Raven's trouser leg and he looked down. Harry held his arms out and Raven's temper melted away. He smiled and bent down to scoop him up.

Lisa sat back down. Her voice dropped an octave and she continued. 'As soon as I realised, I went into a panic, screaming his name and running around the park looking for him, asking all the parents whether they'd seen him. I ... I was terrified Luke.'

Raven kissed Harry on the cheek, just thankful that he was back home with them. 'And?'

'It felt like a lifetime. I thought that he'd gone forever. My world ... my world would have just fallen apart right there at that exact moment. Everything ...*gone*. I collapsed on the grass and I just sobbed. I couldn't stop.' Raven sat down and Harry sat on his lap, bashing his cars together and making extravagant spaceship noises.

'But he's here now, Lis.' Raven kissed Harry on the cheek. 'Somebody must have found him.' He gritted his teeth. 'Was it Lonny?'

Lisa looked up at him. 'What? No.' She ran a hand down her skirt. 'No, he was still off chasing after his dog. The bloody thing had got stuck in some mud and he'd fallen in trying to pull it out.' Her hard exterior cracked and she started laughing. 'He was covered in shit and all sorts when he came back - he'd gone in face first.'

Raven laughed with her and they sat there for a while. Raven missed it; missed all the happy times, all of the laughs, all of the tender moments. They both had their issues, he knew it, both of them with difficult upbringings and with their own personal demons to control minute by minute, day

126

by day, but why did it all have to come to this?

'A stranger brought him back. A man.'

'A man?'

'Yes, a guy in his early sixties, grey hair, short beard. I didn't know him but I could have married him right there. He had Harry in his arms.' Lisa was smiling.

Raven was confused. 'But how did he know that you were Harry's mum?'

'I don't know,' Lisa was shaking her head, 'I have no idea. He just … did.'

'Did he say anything?'

'He said … well, he said one thing that struck me as odd.'

Raven placed Harry back on the floor. 'Odd?'

'Yeah, it was something like … here's *our* little boy.'

'Our?'

Lisa nodded. 'Yep. That's what he said. And he seemed to know you, Luke.' She leaned over to the coffee table and picked up a small, grey piece of card. 'He asked me to give you this.'

She passed the card to him. It had large, blue, italic lettering printed on it with a sketch of a large Tudor house in the background. He held it at arm's length so that he could read the text. As he silently mouthed the words all his worst memories came flooding back in a torrent of emotions. His face went cold and his skin prickled and tingled.

Raven's Interiors
For the county's best quality home furnishings
Call Sam Raven

It was the business card of someone he knew very well.

127

Too well in fact. Someone he had buried long ago, along with his own inferiority complex and deep sense of abandonment.

His father.

Chapter 22:
The Little Bloke

Not long after seeing crazy Dynamite Del and his monumental firework display our preparations hit a snag. Well, a mighty big, eye watering, heart rending, ulcer causing, tyre busting hole in the road actually.

Ronny's girl on the inside, Lulu, no longer had access to the vault.

'Well that's it then.' I didn't know whether I was massively disappointed or just relieved. 'Game over.'

Ronny Valentine was leaning against the waterfront car park barrier and puffing on a cigar. He was wearing a light blue, crushed velvet blazer, cream slacks and a purple silk scarf. I often thought if Ronny wasn't as big as he was and as well respected by the local hoodlums, he would have had his head kicked in long ago. It was almost as if he dressed the way he did because he knew he could.

'Well, let's think this through, William my boy.' He gazed out to sea, blowing large smoke rings and clicking his tongue on the inside of his teeth. 'There's more than one way to skin a cat. We just need to come up with an alternative solution to our little … problem.'

I swigged on my can of lager and adjusted my glasses. I was wearing shorts and an Anthrax T-shirt but it was a hot day and I could feel the sweat trickling down my cheek. 'But what's the point? I can get us in the front door and shut down the alarm system but, unless we're thinking of boosting the empty display cabinets or raiding any cash remaining in the tills, that's where our little adventure ends. If we can't get in the basement we can't get in the vault. Even if we could get in the basement, we don't have access to the vault.' I crushed my empty can. 'It's checkmate, no way out.'

Ronny stubbed out his cigar on the underside of his loafers and tossed it, then reached into the inside pocket of his jacket and pulled out a large roll of paper. It was early in the day and the carpark was empty aside from my van and Ronny's brand new, ludicrously small Fiat 500. He unrolled the manuscript and laid it out on the large, flat display plaque next to him. I stooped over it with him and peered down at what appeared to be the blueprint for the jewellers.

He withdrew his glasses from a pocket and put them on. Somehow, with their thick lenses and antique frame, they made him look ten years older. 'It would have been sweet, just walking in as if we owned the place, but *c'est la vie*.' He traced a finger along the walls of the building's ground floor, under the staircase, along the side and front window, across the entrance-way to the left and around the large arc of the display cases. 'We can't go down, that's for sure. Not without a large explosion courtesy of our mate, Del, but that would attract way too much attention and, before we know it, we'd be back in the Klink.'

I was gazing longingly at the basement plan. It was a large open space, the basement staircase leading out into a small reception area, which in turn led to the vault door. Beyond that was steel-encased Aladdin's cave. There were no markings for the concrete blocked tunnel entranceway that Ronny had told us about but then why would there be? It wasn't part of the building after all and I'm sure the Greenbaums were blissfully unaware of its existence. As I half daydreamed about diamonds as big as your thumbnail and rubies the colour of good red wine, I spotted something.

'What's this, Ron?'

Inside the vault, to the left hand side of the door and against the wall, was a protrusion. A rectangular feature within the vault that didn't look like it belonged. Two parallel dotted lines emanated from the rectangle, back out into the basement reception area, took a right angled turn towards the stairway, continued up past the ground floor and onto the first floor, took a left hand turn through a small room at the rear of the building and then up again and out onto the building's flat roof.

Ronny adjusted his spectacles and bore down over the plan like a large, voracious grizzly bear. For a few moments he stood there, unmoving, making that clicking noise from the inside of his mouth. He traced a thick finger along the parallel dotted lines multiple times, each time gradually increasing the speed of his hand and his quickening breath.

'My boy, I think you're onto something,' he whispered to me as if we were surrounded by hundreds of eavesdroppers. I looked around me with caution, only to find that there was no one else there.

'You … you think so, Ron?'

'Climate control, William.' He stood up and placed his large hands on my broad shoulders. 'Climate *fucking* control! Every vault has it. You can't have your jewels, gold and money getting damp and sweaty can you? Getting all tarnished and mouldy and the bank notes wasting away with the moisture and heat. No, no of course you bloody can't. But these Greenbaums, these beautiful, gorgeous, bloody Jews have gone old school. They probably wanted to save a few bob and didn't reckon on anyone finding out. No internal system for these guys, they've got the dehumidifier and cooling tower on the roof leading right down into the money pot.' He bent down again and beckoned me to look. 'Ventilator ducts leading from the top of the building, all the way down through three storeys and,' he laughed as he bellowed, *'right ...into ... the ... bloody ... vault!'*

I started to laugh along with him. It seemed too simple to be true, but the best plans always were, weren't they?

He took out a pack of cigars from his pocket and offered me one. I declined, remembering something from earlier that day, and pulled out a tin case containing three large joints and offered him one of those. I'd been gradually reducing my intake since the shit went down with Tony but I give myself the odd treat once in a while when things go my way. You know that, right? I've never lied to you about it. Anyway, this seemed like an appropriate occasion. A big, cheeky grin spread across Ronny's face, he winked at me and plucked a spliff from the container. We both lit up and inhaled. The feeling of relaxation and exaltation hit my brain almost instantly and I started to giggle.

'The only problem is,' I pointed at the plan, 'that conduit only looks about two feet by two feet. How are we going to get through it?'

Ronny took a large drag from his joint and laughed.

132

'William, my old son,' he blew out a large plume of yellow smoke, 'we're gonna need a little bloke.'

That was when Wes joined the crew.

Chapter 23:
Teddy

After Molly completed her GCSEs – faring pretty well despite her withering attention span and her ever intensifying interest in the darkness that seemed to slip out from under her nightgown when she wasn't concentrating – her father decided to ship her off to boarding school.

Elderflower Heights was an old Tudor building that had previously belonged to a wealthy landowner in the mid-1800s. Its newly painted, brightly coloured façade and smooth, rounded features set it apart from other stately homes in the county and lent it a relaxed and easy feel. Regardless, it was rumoured amongst the locals that its previous owner had practised black magic there from time to time and there were even stories of gruesome murders and of bodies buried under the trimmed hedgerows and ornamental rose bushes.

The property was nestled in large, neatly lawned grounds which were themselves located squarely in the middle of hundreds of acres of Hampshire farm and woodland, away from the bustle of the towns and the sinful temptations of the seafront. In recent times, as a very selective boarding school, it housed two hundred or so adolescent teenagers, most of whom had been sent there by their very rich and very busy parents in a blatant attempt to get them out from under their own feet and to hopefully provide them with an education that would set them on the way to becoming millionaires in their own right, no longer dependent upon their parents' wealth. Molly had no such desire and hated the idea.

Her room was a decent size, overlooking the forest at the rear of the property and with a double bed, dressing table with a folding mirror, large pinewood wardrobe, a desk upon which to carry out her studies and a bathroom to every three residents. She shared hers with a red headed, lanky streak of a girl named Delilah and a stocky, dark haired young man called Teddy.

Molly barely paid them any mind and spent her spare time wandering around the grounds, looking for small animals to trap and dissect. She'd taken a liking to squirrels and had set up boxes on a number of tall trees and had soaked some acorns and cob nuts in a mixture she'd concocted from starch, glycerine and baking soda. She was yet to have a full blown success but she felt confident that she was getting close.

It was on one of these reconnaissance missions, out in the forest by the old water well, that she spotted the boy from her dorm, Teddy, with one of the girls from their class, Cindy Parsons. Cindy was a tall, athletic blond with a loud mouth and a body to boot and it seemed to Molly that she was never without a young man on her arm. Molly wasn't envious as such – just a little curious. As she'd struck out again in her squirrel hunt, she decided to stay and eavesdrop, and crouched down behind a large holly bush at the eastern side of the clearing.

'Don't tell me this is your first time, Teddy?'

Teddy Palmer, his large shoulders rippling under his black T shirt, was holding Cindy in his arms as she reclined casually against the thick trunk of an oak tree.

'No way. What are you talking about, Cind? I've been with lots of girls, ask anyone.'

'Then get on with it. It's getting cold and we have to be at dinner in just over half an hour.'

'Alright, alright. You don't have to ask me twice.'

Molly watched as Cindy took off her pale green sweatshirt, exposing her cream bra, her toned abs and her firm arms and breasts underneath. Molly let out a soft gasp and placed a hand over her mouth

'Oh Cindy, you look beautiful.' Teddy took off his T shirt and dramatically tossed it on the ground. He grabbed a hold of Cindy like he might grab a pal in a wrestling contest and leaned in to kiss her somewhat awkwardly, bashing his forehead against hers with a loud crack.

'Ow! Careful, you idiot!'

'I'm sorry, I'm sorry. It's just that you're so gorgeous. I just want to…'

'Yeah, yeah.' Cindy looked around to be sure no one was watching. 'Just get your trousers off, won't you?'

Teddy fumbled at his belt buckle and pulled down his jeans, awkwardly yanking each leg out of his tight fitting Levis while carefully maintaining his balance before throwing them into the bushes. Molly could see his dark blue boxer shorts and she supressed a giggle.

'Do you have one?' Cindy pulled down her short, black skirt, exposing her cream knickers and toned legs.

'Do I have what?' Teddy was standing with his back to Molly, his boxers and white sports socks the only things protecting his lightly suntanned, goosebump laden skin from the cool, late afternoon air.

'A condom, dummy.'

'Oh, yeah, yeah. Of course. It's in my pocket.'

'Then go get it you imbecile.'

Teddy brushed a hand through his dark, floppy hair and raced over to where his discarded clothes lay, catching his toe on a tree root, uttering a lough '*Ugh!*' and tumbling theatrically onto the ground. He rolled onto his back and looked over at his beleaguered young beau. Molly caught a laugh in the back of her throat and bit down on her hand to prevent it from escaping.

'I've had enough of this, Teddy.' Cindy pulled up her skirt and collected her sweatshirt. 'Come back to me when your balls have dropped.' She shook her head and laughed cruelly. 'And gained some experience with the opposite sex.'

Teddy sat up and held out his arms, imploring. Although he looked pathetic and vulnerable, Molly couldn't take her eyes off his muscular physique and the outline of a slight bulge in his underpants. She could feel a warmth inside of her that was new and invigorating. She found it almost as exciting as when she found a live, captive animal inside one of her traps. She wiped moisture from her bottom lip and smiled.

'But we were just getting started…' he muttered almost pathetically.

'And now we're just getting finished.' Cindy spun round and walked away with determination, past the old well with its crumbling outer wall, rotting wooden pulley and overgrown border and threw her arms out in disgust. 'I knew I should have come here with Pip Harrison instead. Delilah told me you were weird!'

Teddy watched her leave from his prone position in the dirt and hung his head, muttering something under his breath. Molly thought he looked like an abandoned puppy, a little lost soul searching for some comfort in this cold, desolate world. She wanted to reach out to him, to put her arms around him and tell him it was okay. She could still feel the excitement inside of her but she also felt something she hadn't felt for such a long time. What was it her sociology lecturer called it? Something that she didn't think she had the ability to feel any more. Something she thought she had lost long ago.

Empathy.

She stood up and slowly walked out into the clearing. Teddy was still on the floor pulling one dirty leg into his recovered jeans. She cleared her throat loudly and he looked up with a start.

'Whoa, *whoa*, just a minute there, Moll ...' He leapt up with one leg still in his jeans and went sprawling backwards into the nettles. He yelled as his left arm went in first, followed by the left side of his face and the upper part of his neck and chest. '*Shit, shit, shit!*'

Molly rushed over and put her arms around his body and pulled, her heart skipping several beats at the warmth of his skin against hers and the firmness of his chest muscles in her hands. He jumped up swiftly, the left side of his body reddening with the rash caused by the acidic bite of the nettles, one leg still in his jeans up to the knee and the rest of his body exposed. Molly blushed as they stood there, her arms around his muscular torso and her upper thigh nestled against the bulge of his underpants.

'Did you see any of that?' Teddy was looking down at her, his face red from much more than just the nettle stings.

Molly looked up at him, her dark curly hair framing her face, hiding the remnants of her scar and shrouding her large, dark eyes. She nodded silently.

'All of it?'

She smiled and nodded again. She could feel a heat in her lower stomach, rising into her chest and across her face and neck. Her heart was pounding like a sledgehammer.

'It's not what it looked like.'

She shook her head.

Teddy gulped. 'Really, it wasn't.'

Molly moved her hands slowly over Teddy's back; his muscles tensed as the tips of her fingers traced the valley of his spine, sliding onto the small of his back and finally coming to rest on his buttocks. She could feel sweat form on her forearms and cheeks.

Teddy looked down at her in surprise and gasped. He was confused, she could see it. He didn't know what to think or what to do, but his body did. She could feel that too. Could feel it prodding at her thigh.

'You don't have to be embarrassed, Teddy.'

'I don't?' His mouth was open and his eyes were furtive. She suddenly felt a deep love for him – and a desire. A strong and intoxicating desire mixed with excitement and fear.

'You don't.'

His voice was trembling. 'I don't understa…'

She gazed into his brown eyes and she could see all that she needed to see within their dark chocolate solitude. He

139

needed her. 'We can learn together.'

'We can learn?'

Molly hooked her thumb in the waste-band of his boxers and gradually pulled downwards.

'Together.'

Chapter 24:
The Ice Queen

The little boy was laughing so hard that tears were rolling down his cheeks and elastic snot was streaming from his nose and into his mouth. He was on his side in the sand and holding his tummy like it was about to split open. He could barely catch his breath.

The hawk sat next to him, tearing chunks of flesh from a nameless and shapeless limb that was gripped in one of its hooked talons. Every now and then it looked up, fixing its beady eyes on something in the distance, out there in the darkness and just out of reach. It had a calmness about it, as if there was nothing on this earth that could trouble it. It was as though it was from another time, another space, another world even.

Raven sat in the dunes and looked out to sea. The water was calmly rolling into the shore on a gentle tide. If he wanted to escape, that was the way to go. Over the water like a gull, out into the vast nothingness of the ocean.

'I'm lost young man, can you help me?'

It was a rotund gentleman, maybe mid-fifties in cargo shorts, polo top and a trilby. He was limping along the sand with the aid of an ornate walking cane. Raven wondered why he was out there in the middle of the night and on his own.

'I say … I could use some assistance here.'

The man staggered to his left and then regained his balance. It all became clear to Raven. He was pissed.

The boy sat bolt upright and the laughing immediately stopped. He ran the back of his hand across his top lip; a long string of snot attached itself to his arm, stretching like rubber as he pulled his hand away from his face. He sniffed the length of gooey slime back into his nose and stood up.

'I … I really am lost, little fellow. You have nothing to fear from me. I'm just a weary wanderer looking for his way back to a friendly watering hole. Do you know of one?'

The boy looked down at the hawk which was still chewing greedily on a chunk of flesh and loose skin. He pointed at the flabby frame of the older gentleman and smiled.

Raven knew instantly what was about to happen and started screaming at the man, begging him to turn and run for his life. He went to stand but the dunes suddenly turned into mush and he found himself being eaten alive by bracken and dirt.

The man took a hip flask from the pocket of his shorts, unscrewed the lid and drew a large slurp of liquid into his gullet. He looked down at the boy and smiled, his cheeks flushed crimson and his warm eyes red and bleary.

'Now, that hits the spot, it really does. Not that I condone the young partaking in the woeful habit of intoxication. No, not at all, I am not that sort of a gentleman.' He paused and smirked as a thought occurred to him. 'However,' the man bent down and looked at the boy who was still smiling and pointing at him as if he were the world's most amusing chubby chap, 'if you were to help out a tired and thirsty old boy then, well then perhaps I could spare you a little nip.'

The boy clicked his fingers and it happened. Raven watched helplessly, waist deep in sand and muck, unable to move or make himself heard.

The hawk soared upwards and out of sight, its soundless motion going completely unnoticed by the oblivious older gentleman.

'No? Not interested? Not at all?' He stood up and shook his head. 'Can't you speak, little man? Lost your tongue?' He sighed wearily. 'The youth of today, can't even help out a fellow in desperate need. What is the world coming to? I say that to my old mum all the time. It wouldn't have happened in her day, you know? They all looked out for each other back the-'

The hawk swept downwards in a furious arc like a silent and deadly ninja, digging its talons into the fat man's forehead, its sharp beak plunging into his mouth and tearing out his tongue in one, smooth and terrifying motion. Blood sprayed from the man's jaw and into his throat, the gurgling sound of blood filling his oesophagus and lungs drowning out the man's screams for help. He fell awkwardly backwards onto the sand, the yellow ground beneath him turning red as blood poured from his head and mouth. The hawk reared up, its face covered in blood and goo, and dug its beak and talons into the man's throat, its claw tearing at the jugular vein and a thick jet of warm, crimson liquid spurted upwards in a large fountain. The man grabbed for the ravenous raptor but it was too quick and it moved for the large, exposed stomach, the flabby flesh tearing open easily

143

as the hawk furiously dug its beak into its welcoming opulence.

The boy looked over at Raven and started to laugh, pointing at him and grinning as snot started to stream from his nose again and tears started to roll down his face. He sat down on the ground as the water gently lapped over his legs and bum, and he giggled incessantly. Raven looked over at the blood soaked carcass of the fat man, his body motionless and lifeless as the hawk devoured him piece by piece, chunk by chunk, and he screamed.

****

'NOOO!'

Raven opened his eyes, the sweat pouring down his forehead and cheeks, his own body odour seeping from his pores and into his nostrils. He swung his arms out to grab for the sand but all he could feel was the worn fabric of his sofa and a TV remote. He shook off the sea air and realised he was in his flat, perched in front of the television which was still silently showing the late night movie he'd been watching as he fell asleep. He grabbed the remote and hit standby.

No, this had gone on too long now. He needed to act. The dreams had returned and, whilst it wasn't his problem anymore – he had more than enough shit to deal with, what with the Butler woman and the return of a familial ghost from his past – he couldn't help but feel that he needed to share what he had seen. What he was being *shown*.

As much as he hated Devereux, he knew he wouldn't be able to live with himself if he learned something terrible was going down in the town and he had information that could have stopped it. He'd made that mistake before and it still haunted him. Every single day.

He reached for his mobile phone and scrolled through his numbers. He wiped the sleep from his eyes and the bracken and sand from his waking thoughts and after a moment he found the name of the contact that he was looking for.

The Ice Queen.

Chapter 25:
Applewood House

Randall pulled his car into the narrow entranceway of the care home. Ruby was sitting in the passenger seat and scrolling through her notepad.

'This is the place. Applewood House. Apparently Miss Hanscombe has been here since May of 2002.' Exhaling loudly, she looked up at the grey, breeze block and plaster building with its old, aluminium window frames, dirty wooden fascias and faded paint work and shuddered. 'Jesus, that's a long time. There's no way I could stand being in one of these places for as long as that. I'd go mad.'

Randall took a sip from his hot, black coffee. 'That's the whole point. They're all mad. That's why she's in here, to help her get better.' He leaned back in his seat. 'But clearly she has one or two sandwiches missing from her picnic basket and is still looking for the butter knife..'

He placed his thermos cup – upon which was emblazoned the Arthur Conan Doyle quote 'There is nothing more deceptive than an obvious fact' – back into the cup holder, pushed his pen into his crisply pressed, Hugo Boss jacket pocket, adjusted his designer sunglasses and hauled himself out of his car.

'But it's like,' Ruby held out her fingers and counted, 'eighteen years. She's been in here for most of my life.'

'And a large portion of her own, Rube, so I wouldn't expect her to be too compos mentis. Let's take it slow, ease her into the conversation, listen to what she has to say and,' he mentally crossed his fingers, 'hope beyond hope that she has a gem or two for us in amongst all of the confusion and craziness.'

Ruby nodded and they both strode up the paved pathway towards the building's glass double doors. Randall entered, withdrew his badge and flashed it at the elderly lady propped up behind the reception desk.

'Detective Inspector Randall Kipruto from the West Hampshire police department. I'm here with my partner, Police Officer Ruby Cropper, to visit a Miss Lorna Hanscombe.'

The old lady, her short white hair, short stature and rosy cheeks reminding Randall of a slightly older and rounder Dame Jude Dench, flipped through her visitors' sheet and found them.

'Aah, here you are. Yes, right there under Mr Norris, the man who just came in to see his young son.' She shook her head gravely. 'A terrible business that one,' she turned and grabbed her phone, 'just awful. The poor kid tried to kill himself. Hung himself from a door frame but luckily the timber gave in before his neck did. Severe anxiety they said,' she dialled a number on the keypad, 'that poor man looked ashen. Such a terrible business.'

Randall looked down at Ruby who was biting her nails. She looked a little flustered and he had to admit, the place was more than a little unsettling.

'Janet? Yes, yes. The Detective Inspector is here to see old Lorna. Yes …yes, I'll tell him to meet you at your office. Okay…yes, that's fine. I'll see you at lunchtime. Thanks Janet. Ta ta.'

Randall raised an eyebrow as the old lady looked up from the phone.

'That was Janet.'

'I see.'

'She'll meet you in her office. Through the swing doors, fourth door on your left. You can't miss her. Her name's on the door. Doctor Janet Weir. Lovely lady, big smile and an even bigger heart.'

Randall wrote the doctor's name down in his notebook, placed it in his pocket and gave the receptionist his best, winning smile. 'Good to know. Thank you so much for your help Miss…?'

'Mrs Grover. Betsy Grover. I'm a staple of this place. Been here most of my working life and I love every minute of it. My old fella, Albert, tells me that I must be bonkers myself to have been holed up in here for so long.' She smiled heartily but Randall saw something in her face that was a bit off. Just a little tic in her right eye and a twitch in her cheek as if there was a bug on her skin that was irritating her. It made him more than a little uneasy. He looked over at his partner for confirmation but she appeared to be unaware.

Ruby laughed and took the old lady's hand. 'Lovely to meet you Betsy. It's been a pleasure.'

'Not at all my darling, not at all. It's my job after all. Now,' she pointed to her right and suddenly her smile evaporated, 'don't forget. Through the double doors and

148

fourth door on the left.'

Randall raised a hand and strode down the corridor, Ruby three or four steps behind him and racing to keep up. He urgently needed to get away from the reception area and the old lady with the saccharine smile.

The corridor was brightly lit by overhead panel lighting. The walls were a bright white emulsion and the floor was cream linoleum. Randall was instantly glad he was wearing his sunnies. The first door they passed on the right appeared to be a medical storage cupboard, stocked full of gowns, face masks, gloves and cleaning equipment.

'She was nice.' Ruby's demeanour had changed. She seemed to have settled her nerves and recaptured her ever buoyant spirit. 'Reminded me of my nanna.'

'Yes, a nice lady. Very welcoming,' Randall shuddered as they passed a door on their left, with a nameplate that read: 'Doctor Arthur Snitchell'.

Up ahead, where the corridor met a T junction, a squat man of around fifty years of age pushed a squeaky wheeled trolley towards them.

'It's quite nice here, boss. Not as bad as I expected.' Ruby was almost skipping behind him.

'Mmm … I guess so. Seems friendly enough.'

The next door on their right was some kind of treatment room and Randall caught the whiff of antiseptic cream and saw the prone form of an elderly man, his bare feet hanging over the edge of the cot, his torso exposed and a gowned and masked nurse leaning over him with a pair of scissors in her right hand. The man looked almost catatonic.

The squeaky trolley trundled towards them, behind which was the portly middle aged gentleman. Randall noticed he had a limp in his left leg.

'Betsy said fourth door on the left, boss.'

Randall sighed wearily but he could feel his heart pounding in his chest. He didn't like it. Didn't like it at all.

The third door on their left was occupied by two young nurses, one male one female. The shorter of which, a pretty female with short blond hair, appeared to be washing blood off her hands while the young man stood behind her grinning inanely, as if something had amused him. The sound of the squeaky wheel continued to burrow into his ear like a worm.

Finally they came to door number four which was wide open and welcoming. In the office sat a very large, forty something lady with wild, curly brown hair. She had bright blue eyes, lips that were smothered in bright red lipstick, long, shiny red nails and a bosom you could raise the titanic with.

She stood up and opened her arms out wide. 'Welcome!' she hollered in a thick Glaswegian accent, 'to Applewood House, the place where we give care to those that need the most tender love, a place where gentle souls can come to ease their troubled minds.'

Randall took her hand and shook it. Her grip was firm but a little moist. When their hands released, he had to fight the urge to wipe his palm on his trouser leg.

'It's lovely to meet you, Doctor Weir.'

'Please,' the doctor shook Ruby's hand and then offered them both seats, 'call me Janet. We are not formal at Applewood House.'

Randall settled himself in an overly low chair and smiled. 'Okay. Okay Janet it is. Do you mind if we ask you some questions? Informally of course.'

'Of course, Detective.' She leaned back and smiled vivaciously. 'We are completely at your disposal.'

Ruby spoke up. 'As you know, Janet, we are here to ask you a few questions about Miss Lorna Hanscombe, a lady that has been a resident in your facility for almost two decades.'

The doctor sighed. 'Aah yes …poor Lornie. She is one of the most troubled souls that we have residing here. A very sad lady indeed.'

Randall leaned forward. 'Can you tell us more? Start from the beginning.'

'I can tell you what I know but even I haven't been here as long as Lornie. I joined in 2008, by which time she had been a resident for some six years or so. Would you both like a coffee? Tea?'

Randall shook his head and was surprised when he heard a cheerful, 'Oh yes please, that would be great. White coffee, two sugars,' from his partner.

'Cecil! CECIL!' The doctor's booming voice echoed down the halls like an air raid siren. Within seconds the squeaky wheel returned.

'Yes, Doctor Weir?' The short, portly gentleman appeared at the doorway in his oversized gown, his thinning dark hair slicked to one side as if by glue, his thin moustache smeared down his cheeks like oil.

'White coffee, two sugars please. In fact,' she smiled at Ruby, 'make that two.'

'Yes, Doctor Weir.'

'Now,' the doctor ran her hands down her white coat, 'where were we?'

'Lorna Hanscombe.'

'Ah yes. Well,' the doctor wiped a finger along her lipstick and looked at it absentmindedly, 'as I said, that poor lady has been here some time. From what I gather she was delivered here by two gentleman who claimed she had been found roaming the streets of Westhampton in her underwear, like she had left the house after forgetting to get herself dressed. The poor girl.'

'Seems a little odd.' Randall made a note.

'Odd indeed, Detective Inspector. But true, nevertheless. Tragically so, I'm afraid.'

'And do you have any contact details for these two good Samaritans?'

'Not that I'm aware of. If we do it will be somewhere in the archives of course, but it was such a long time ago. No, as far as I know they were simply two kind strangers doing a good deed for some poor soul in desperate need.' The doctor shot them a sympathetic smile and yet Randall had a feeling that there was something she wasn't telling them.

'But why here, Doctor… Janet? Why Applewood House and not the local police station?' Ruby was leaning forward in her chair. She jumped with a start when Cecil tapped her lightly on the shoulder.

'Is this for you, young lady?' He smiled at Ruby revealing four crooked teeth.

'Er…. yes. Thank you.' She took the mug of coffee from him and smiled. He smiled back and winked, a small amount of spittle leaking from the corner of his mouth.

'Cecil … dear,' Janet reached over and took her mug from him, 'that will be all. I'll call you if I need anything else.' She ran a hand down his arm, her long red nails leaving trace marks in his blue gown.

Cecil afforded another glance at Ruby and wiped a hand across his cheek. 'Yes, Doctor Weir.'

'We look after everyone here, Detective Inspector, no matter how odd they may at first appear. Now,' the doctor sipped the warm liquid, her lipstick leaving thick red marks around the edge of the mug, 'to the officer's question. It wasn't how Lornie appeared that led the two gentlemen to bring her here rather than to the local police station. It was what she was saying.'

Randall removed his sunglasses and hooked them into the breast pocket of his jacket. 'And what was that?'

'Essentially it was complete gibberish. They couldn't get head nor tail out of her, thought maybe she was intoxicated. But, from what I gather, when she got here and blew into a breathalyser, she didn't have an ounce of alcohol in her body.'

'Did they manage to remember any of this ... gibberish? Did the head doctor at the time record any of it in their notes?'

'Well, the resident doctor back then was an elderly man, a lovely fellow but long since passed. Doctor Forster. Very old school but caring nonetheless. It is worth saying that the old boy was somewhat hard of hearing so I would take some of what he wrote with a pinch of salt. Let's just say ... things have improved significantly here since I joined. We have,' she winked at Ruby who smiled back, 'modernised.'

Randall shrugged it off. 'Can we see those notes?'

The doctor answered him without shifting her ruby red smile or switching her empathetic gaze from his young partner.

'It would be my pleasure. As I said, we are at your

153

disposal. But,' the doctor stood and smoothed down her gown, 'before we go rummaging around in the musty old filing room for scraps of paper from eons ago might I suggest that we go and see Lornie herself? You might discover that you'll find everything you need,' she pushed a carefully manicured finger into her left temple, 'right there in her little old head.'

Ruby jumped up as if on a string. 'That sounds perfect. We would love to meet her.'

Randall glanced up at Ruby and raised an eyebrow.

The doctor led them to the left, down the hallway and then took another left at the T junction. They passed Cecil who was cleaning the visitors' toilets. He glanced over his shoulder and smiled at Ruby as she raised her hand to him. The corridor was long and the lights in that part of the building were noticeably less bright, the soft shadows thrown by the dim bulbs as they passed underneath them were tall and misshapen. Randall Kipruto's lanky frame became almost insect like, Ruby's shape stretched and pulled and the doctor's silhouette was an ominous and looming presence that floated ahead of them like a giant zeppelin.

'This is B wing and it contains some of our more passive patients – the depressed, the anxious, those with addictive behaviours – that kind of thing.' The doctor waved a hello as a nurse pushed a blond-haired young man with a saline drip in his arm down the corridor in a wheelchair. Randall noticed that the nurse, a young woman in her early twenties, kept her eyes firmly fixed on the corridor ahead. 'Most of our inmates … *patients* in this part of Applewood House are with us for no more than a few months and many, I'm happy to say, never return.' She turned to face them, her broad smile revealing pearly white teeth smeared with the oily crimson of her excess lipstick. It gave the doctor the appearance of someone who has just devoured a delicious but very rare beef steak. 'And that's just the way we like it around here. Meet them, fix them, bid them farewell.' She turned and continued. 'It's the Applewood way.'

'Is Lorna a resident of B wing, Janet?' Ruby was slightly ahead of Randall and was hanging on the charismatic doctor's every word.

'I'm afraid not, Officer Cropper.'

'Please, Janet. Call me Ruby.'

The doctor stopped and turned to face her as Randall silently groaned. 'What a lovely name for a lovely young person. Ruby red, my favourite of all the colours.' The doctor placed her pudgy, lightly tanned and expertly manicured hands upon the entranced officer's shoulders and gave her a winning smile. 'As we are both now on first name terms, Ruby, I believe that makes us firm friends. And you, Detective Inspector?'

Randall cleared his throat, caught off guard. He composed himself, took a breath and attempted to speak with the assured tone of a man in a position of authority. 'It's Randall,' the doctor opened her mouth as if ready to swallow him whole but he held up a hand, 'but you can call me Detective Inspector Kipruto.'

The doctor paused, nodded her head and her fixed smile returned. 'I see.' She glanced at Ruby and winked. 'Of course Detective Inspector, if that's the way of it then that's the way it shall be.' She turned and beckoned them onward. 'In any case, Miss Hanscombe is a resident of A wing and has been for as long as I can remember. For as long as I have been running this fine establishment, as a matter of fact.'

'And what kind of patients qualify for A wing?' Randall asked.

'The most severe kind. Personality disorders, bipolar disorders, psychosis, schizophrenia, schizoaffective disorders. Many of our … patients suffer distortions of perception, delusions, hallucinations and a loss of contact with reality.' She turned down a corridor to their left and then immediately turned right into an adjoining building. She withdrew a key card from her breast pocket and swiped it against the scanner. The doors ahead of them immediately slid open like the jaws of a mighty beast and Randall caught the scent of death.

She urged them to follow and they walked down a dimly lit corridor with reinforced glass windows cut out of the walls either side of them – spy holes into the bedrooms and personal spaces beyond.

Randall shuddered as he watched an elderly man who was sitting on the edge of his bed gently rock back and forth, a long line of spittle hanging from his lower lip. On the other side of the corridor, in a room with blue and pink Peppa Pig curtains, a slim, middle aged lady was drawing rudimentary pictures of zoo animals on the walls with thick, coloured crayons. Further ahead on their left hand side a young man was standing up against the window and facing them, his hands planted firmly on the glass above him and his lips pressed against the windowpane, his tongue creating a figure of eight pattern in his saliva. Ruby gasped.

'That's Peter.' The doctor slammed her soft hand hard against the glass and the young man recoiled in horror, scurrying under his bed and curling up in a tight, defensive

156

ball. She turned and faced them. 'My apologies. Sometimes tough love is the only love.'

She beckoned them on and they continued, passing a man with a mouthful of chewed fruit, the juice and skin running down his chin and neck, a young lady seemingly holding an animated conversation with an invisible companion, her hands gesticulating as if to chastise the unseen character and an elderly man standing completely naked in the centre of his room, his genitalia exposed and flaccid, and clapping his hands together to the beat of a silent rhythm.

'You will see some things that you might not usually see I'm afraid but you need to understand that these individuals are not very well and their perception of decent, civilised behaviour is not the same as yours or indeed mine.' She glanced over her shoulder and chuckled. 'Although, who's to know what goes on behind our own doors when our friends and family aren't there to judge us?'

Ruby laughed and Randall grunted. He could only imagine what the loud and brash Doctor Janet Weir did in her own spare time.

'Is it possible that Miss Hanscombe could have left Applewood House unnoticed at any time over the past four to six weeks, Doctor?' He was fighting to hide his impatience. They had been too long at Applewood already. He was supposed to be keeping an eye on Raven for at least a couple of hours a day and Deveraux was expecting an update. He was even starting to admit to himself that something fishy was going on with his predecessor – he didn't think it had any bearing on his case but he couldn't rule it out.

'Quite impossible, Detective Inspector.'

'You're sure of that.'

'Absolutely.'

'There is no possible way that Miss Hanscombe couldn't have slipped a key card from one of the orderlies and used it on occasion without arousing suspicion.'

The doctor turned to face him. 'Never on my watch have we had a patient leave these premises without our knowing about it.' She rubbed her hands together in agitation, her face set firm and her lips pursed tightly in a slick, red welt. '*Never*!'

'There's always a first time.'

'Maybe if you can elaborate further Janet? So that,' Ruby was frantically trying to defuse the conversational tension, 'Detective Inspector Kipruto and I can better understand.'

The doctor's smile returned. 'Of course, Ruby,' she glanced at Randall, her cheerful demeanour momentarily diminished, 'it would be my pleasure. You see, aside from the key card access to every door in and out of the building, my card being the master card and the only card that can open every single door in the facility, we have CCTV and motion sensors in every room and along every corridor.' She pointed above them and Randall eyed a plastic dome in the low ceiling, behind which he was sure was a camera watching his every move. 'The screens on which these images are displayed are manned twenty four seven and our server backs up footage for the last twelve months and is then archived on an external server which holds the footage for five years. Inspector,' her broad smile returned and once again Randall found himself wanting to clean the smeared lipstick from her incisors, 'if one our patients gets out of bed, scratches their ear, picks their nose or takes a shit,' she turned to Ruby, 'sorry, my love,' Ruby held up her hand and smiled, 'then we would know about it.'

'I'm sure. But still ... if we could take a look at that footage ...'

'There's no need. You won't see anything untoward.'

'I think we should be the judge of that.' He gave the doctor his best authoritative stare, the one he practised in front of his bathroom mirror every morning. He wasn't prepared to back down from this woman. It wasn't that he disliked her – he just didn't trust her.

The doctor sighed. 'Let me show you something.' She motioned them to a door further up ahead on their right. She pulled out her key card again and held it up to the sensor. There was a hum of magnets releasing and she pushed the door inward. Behind the door was a bedroom painted in lilac with cream curtains that hung from the windows and around the metal framed hospital bed. To the right was a dressing table, upon which was a notepad with scrawled handwriting and rough sketches in crayon. There was a purple felt covered ottoman, on top of which was a collection of cuddly toys – bears, dogs, elephants and the like, many of which had seen better days. A thin layer of dust seemed to lie on every surface and the room smelled of peppermint and vomit. There was a wheelchair at the foot of the bed. 'Detective Inspector, may I introduce you to Applewood's longest serving resident.' The doctor stood to one side and held out her hand, her crimson claws pointing towards the room's single occupant. 'Miss Lorna Hanscombe.'

Perched on the bed, her hair dyed bright red to the scalp and shaved completely bald down one side, was a lady in her early fifties. Her eyes were a dulled blue and her lips were thin and dry. Her tongue occasionally licked at them, protruding from a mouth that was full of perfectly shaped but slightly yellowed teeth. Her cheeks were mottled with ruptured veins that were too close to the surface and her dark eyebrows contrasted vividly against her pale skin and ferociously red hair. She was thin, almost stick thin; her arms were seemingly bone with loose, flaccid skin hanging from them like an old blouse hanging on a rusty and crooked clothesline, and her breasts were empty vessels that sagged under her thin bed gown. The sheets were pulled up to her waist as if for comfort and she looked sad and desperate, like something that she held dear had been taken from her long ago. But most of all, she looked exhausted, like she hadn't had a good night's sleep since she had been admitted to Applewood.

'Hello Lornie, my dear. How are you feeling today?'

Lorna didn't look up. 'I have a black soul,' she said in a mumble, her tone low and subtle but clear.

'Yes, I know dear. You've told me.' The doctor turned and smiled at Ruby. 'Now, these two nice police officers are here to speak with you Lornie, my love. Will you speak with them?'

'I have a black soul and I deserve to die.'

The doctor rolled her eyes at Randall. 'We know, my love, we know. You say that a lot but here you are. Still with us, alive and kicking.'

Randall stepped forward. 'Miss Hanscombe, we wanted to speak with you about some recent events in the town of Westhampton, at the seafront.' He withdrew his notepad and pen. 'Have you ever been to the beach at Westhampton, specifically the beach overlooked by the Palisades, near

Bishop's Crag?'

Doctor Weir cleared her throat. 'Detective Inspector, I have already told you Lornie hasn't left this facility in eighteen years.'

'Miss Hanscombe, we have found traces of your DNA, or genetically linked DNA, on some evidence found near the scene and we urgently need to talk to you about what you might know about it.' Randall was intent on pushing the point, despite the increasingly obstructive doctor.

Lorna Hanscombe lifted her head and looked at Randall. He was struck by the beauty in her eyes, a deep swimming blue that spoke of a time long ago when everything in her world was where she wanted it to be and the people she loved were close to her heart. For a moment he was sure that she saw him, *truly* saw him, and then she blinked and her vacant stare returned.

'I have a black soul.'

Ruby stepped around Doctor Weir and placed her hand on Lorna's.

'Lorna, my name is Ruby Cropper and I work for the West Hampshire police department. There is nothing to be concerned about, nothing at all. We're here to help, we truly are.'

There was no reaction.

The young officer persisted. 'Is there any way at all that you may have left this facility in the last two months? Perhaps you wandered off without realising where you were going, or maybe you were taken out for the day by a sympathetic orderly who didn't remember to tell anyone else in Applewood what he or she was doing?'

Doctor Weir audibly gasped but Ruby continued.

'You really must tell us. It may be that somehow you touched the evidence and if so it would be perfectly understandable that we found DNA linked to yours on the item in question.'

Lorna grumbled under her breath and scratched at an itch on the shaved half of her scalp. 'He is death, I have a black soul and I deserve to die.'

The doctor huffed and pushed past Randall and his partner.

'I really must bring an end to this.'

Randall scowled. 'Doctor, we are investigating the disappearance of four individuals from the beach front, one of which we now know has been brutally murdered.' He grimaced at the memory of the severed and bloodied leg that was discovered by the children on the beach. 'And this woman has been traced through DNA that we found at the scene. If she was anywhere near the seafront during the time of the disappearances then we need to know about it.'

'Well, I have never been so insulted in all my years in the medical profession and I will not stand for it now. You have upset me and you have upset my patient and both of those things are completely and utterly unacceptable!'

'Janet, I…' Ruby attempted to intervene.

'It's Doctor Weir to you, Officer Cropper, and don't you forget it!' Ruby gasped and her cheeks turned a deep pink. 'I can see that your offer of friendship was all just a thinly veiled, disingenuous plot to obtain my hard earned trust and may I tell you that I am extremely,' the doctor was shaking with rage, '*extremely disappointed!* What you and the Detective Inspector have failed to detect is one glaringly obvious problem with your working hypothesis!' The doctor's lipstick had smeared onto her cheek and she now looked like an enraged, overweight circus clown. 'For respected members of our local law enforcement I must say that your powers of observation are somewhat amateur in nature.'

Randall took a breath and attempted to take control. 'Doctor Weir, I must inform you...'

She raised a short but determined finger to him. 'This,' the doctor pointed to the foot of the bed, 'is a wheelchair.' She glared at both Randall and Ruby in turn. 'And why on god's blessed earth would you think that little old Lornie here needs a wheelchair in her room?' She pulled back the bedsheets and revealed Lorna's lower half. Her waist was thin as expected, her gown hanging lazily around the shallow enclave of her empty stomach, but to Randall's stunned amazement he saw that her legs ended abruptly around nine inches from her groin, the conclusion of both limbs completed with rounded off nubbins, the red and blotched grafts of skin stretched over her stumps like tightly fitted membranes. 'You see Lornie here doesn't have any legs. Hasn't had since she arrived at Applewood House, all bundled up and helpless in the arms of the two good Samaritans all those years ago.'

DI Kipruto's mouth fell open and Ruby gasped in shock.

Doctor Janet Weir folder her arms and shot them both a wide crimson smile of indiscrete satisfaction. 'I would say that's case closed, wouldn't you?'

Chapter 26:
Silverbacks

Of course we had to have a trial run. It didn't matter how small Wesley Pollock was, and as you know, that fella was a tiny son of a bitch, or how sure Ronny was that the whole thing was a slam dunk – rapturous in his praise of my brilliant idea and telling me time and time again how much I reminded him of my dad – I insisted. There was no point going through all of the aggravation and stress, taking on all the risk, spending weeks of our own time meticulously planning and re-planning and finding out where the kinks in our little escapade were if, when we got to the rooftop of Greenbaums, we shoved Wes down the air conditioning shaft and he got jammed three quarters of the way in. Not only would we be nicked for attempted robbery but we would also very likely get convicted for the poor bloke's murder. Of course, things might have turned out quite differently if that had happened but ...you know.

Raven helped with the gear. He had a mate who ran a company that fitted out climate control systems for warehousing – you know, those big hangars that have sprouted up all over the country to hub food and consumable goods for the big supermarket chains? Anyway, Raven vouched for him. He said the guy would be discrete, as long as we paid cash and guaranteed he couldn't be traced.

'I spared the guy from the nick,' Raven told me one night over at the Golden Swan, still Raven's favourite boozer despite all that had gone on. 'I caught him selling knock off Rolex watches down near the arcade a few years ago but he was in a right state back then. He'd lost his flat and broken up with his fiancé – she'd done the dirty on him with his best mate and he'd walked in on them while they were in the act – so, you know, I took pity on him.'

'Oof,' I almost choked on my pint, 'the poor guy. That's got to leave an impression.'

'I think he left an impression or two on his mate. From what I hear, the guy still has an imprint from Jonjo's sovereign ring in the middle of his forehead.'

I cracked up, spitting remnants of my pork scratchings all over the table that we were suspiciously hunched over.

'Anyway, Jonjo's your guy when it comes to air-con ducting. He's got an endless supply of the stuff and the big stainless extrusions that we're after, the old school stuff that the Jews have in their shop, he says he can get that no problem, but at a cost.'

Ronny leaned over the table, swept a large handful of dry roasted peanuts into his mouth, and peered at Raven over his glasses.

'How much?'

'He says three-fifty a length.'

Ronny washed his peanuts down with a double gin and tonic and laughed. 'Is he having a bubble, Raven? Three fifty a length. That's going to cost us …' I could hear the wheels turning as he thought it through.

'About two and a half, Ron.' I was always pretty good at maths despite flunking school. My years of being self-employed as an electrician, working out quotes for customers and then figuring out how much I could save on costs in order to maximise my revenue have done wonders for my mental arithmetic. It's amazing how fast you learn when it's your bank account at stake.

'Two and a half? Two and a half! That's a big cost on top of all the other costs I've accrued so far.' He shook his head. 'Del's little firework display cost me enough.'

Raven smiled knowingly. 'It's far less than it'll cost you if little Wesley gets himself jammed in an angular section of ducting and can't get himself either up or down. Not only will you not get your hands on the treasure trove of jewels and bank notes that you've convinced us all will be lying in the Greenbaums' vault, you'll also have a dead guy to contend with.' Raven took a sip of his Rusty Nail cocktail and I could sense the relief as the alcohol hit his stomach and gradually worked its way throughout his nervous system. I've been an addict myself and I can tell you, it's no fun. 'And it won't take too long for the Jew and his wealthy customers to realise that that's not chicken they can smell.'

Ronny paused and I could almost hear him thinking it over. After what felt like an age, he clicked his tongue on the inside of his teeth. One thing I'll tell you about Ronny Valentine – if you play cards with him and Ronny makes that noise you fold. Do not play that hand. Do not even think about putting your chips on the table. Not one. Not even if you have two pair and a high spare. Don't do it. Because Ronny only ever makes that sound when his mind's set on something. It's his tell. Don't let him know I told you that, but it is.'

'Okay, let's do it.' He downed his gin. 'How soon can he get it?'

'The next couple of days, he says. We can set it up and trial it out by the weekend.'

'Excellent – now, what about your lacky?' Ronny had removed his glasses and was glaring across the table at Raven.

'What, Wes?'

'Yeah. What do you know about him?'

Raven took a couple of peanuts from the tray in the centre of the table and crunched them between his teeth. 'We've been over this. He's a good lad. A bit simple but reliable.'

'Reliable's good. Reliable's fine,' Ronny looked at me and I shrugged, 'but *reliable* doesn't get you rich. *Reliable* doesn't mean you get to have a nice dinner, maybe a glass of Dom Perignon and a toot or two and then bang the beautiful girl at the end of the evening. And *reliable* certainly doesn't guarantee that you won't have the plod banging on your door at six thirty in the morning while you're lying in bed and thinking about what you're going to spend your share of the loot on. Reliable is like flatulence.' Raven and I looked at each other, puzzled. 'It's a blessed relief but boy does it stink.'

I laughed loud enough to make the young couple on the table next to us look up. 'What the fuck are you going on about, Ron?'

'I've been in this game long enough to know that when someone says they are *reliable* they are just telling you that they will do what you are asking them to do at the time and the date that you have asked them to do it, which, as far as I am concerned, is the *bare minimum* you should expect from any geezer who has agreed to do a job for you, particularly,' he looked over his shoulder, 'particularly in our line of work.'

'This isn't *my* line of work, Ron. I'm doing you a favour, remember.'

'A favour that's going to earn you a very large pay day, might I remind you, Raven. One that will help you sort out that little mess you've gotten yourself into with your ex and the little boy.'

I could see Raven clench his hand around his glass and bite his tongue. He knew what Ron meant but that didn't mean he had to like it.

'Look, he's a good kid which is usually enough for me. But, if you want to know the ins and outs, for what they're worth, here they are. I met him at the nightclub, Gold Diggers, after I'd got suspended from the force by that bitch Deveraux. I was at the bar having a drink...'

'Surprise, surprise,' Ronny chuckled.

Raven glared across the table and continued. 'The kid was trying to chat up some girl, and her boyfriend unsurprisingly took a dislike to him. I intervened, managed to get the guy to back down. Wes bought me a drink to say thanks and we struck up a conversation. He needed some work, I was looking to set up my PI gig and needed a partner and he seemed a good fit. I saw an opportunity for some cheap labour if I'm truthful but it worked out well. He does as he's told, he turns up on time, he doesn't do drugs or drink, and, aside from an on again, off again girlfriend, he doesn't have any dependants and not many friends.' Raven cracked his knuckles. 'He's also been a good mate to me, he listens to all my shit and doesn't judge and …' he paused, 'he makes me laugh.'

'Sounds like marriage material,' I laughed.

Ronny ignored me and turned to Raven. 'All of that sounds just fine and fucking dandy but can the kid be trusted?'

'Of course.'

'With your life, Raven? Because if all of this goes well and we walk away with over three hundred grand each in our sexy little wallets, I intend to spend the rest of my years basking in the sunshine on a golden beach, enjoying a margarita or three, eating rib eye with garlic prawns and wilted spinach and watching the sun set over the Mediterranean sea. I do not intend to see the inside of a prison cell ever again and woe betide anyone that sees fit to try to put me there'

Raven leaned forward. 'The kid can be trusted, Ron. I'll vouch for him.'

The two glared at each other and I could sense the tension building. The two silverbacks were chest beating and I was caught in the middle of it. Luckily, angels come in all shapes and guises.

'Hello all!'

I turned my gaze from the testosterone fuelled dual going down before me and looked up to see a short, skinny guy in a baggy T shirt and shin length shorts. His hair was spiked up like a young Billy Idol and he had two earrings in his right ear. He held out his hand and pushed it towards my face.

'Wesley Pollock's the name, squeezing into tight spots is the game!'

169

Chapter 27:
The Beastie

From that point onwards Molly and Teddy were inseparable. Delilah, of course, was intensely jealous of their intimacy and made no secret of it, glaring at them as they jointly exited the shared bathroom after she had waited with increasing impatience to take a shower. And she was constantly banging on the thin, stud partition wall that separated their rooms when Molly and Teddy were in the throes of their wild, youthful passion.

Molly found the sex interesting but not essential – she enjoyed the closeness, the warmth and the control she could exert over Teddy when he was desperate for more, but it left her unfulfilled. After she had climaxed it almost felt to her as if she had come to the end of a good book but the finale was disappointing or misjudged. She would lie awake afterwards, while her young, sweat covered beau snored loudly on the pillow next to her, and think of things – odd things.

They shared secrets with each other and she liked that. One night, as they ate burgers and coleslaw while sitting on her bed, Teddy told her of his upbringing.

'My dad is an arsehole, a truly big one at that.'

Molly raised her eyebrows while she chewed on a mouthful of cheeseburger, the ketchup trickling out of the corner of her mouth like blood from a bite.

'He's hit my mum a few times and she just takes it. He comes in agitated from work, I can see it in his eyes, and I just know it's gonna kick off. He's constantly stressed and worried about money and he takes it out on her. I mean...'

Molly placed her hand on his and her tiny fingers looked miniscule in comparison to his long chunky digits.

'There's nothing of her, Moll. Nothing. He could just snap her like a twig and there isn't anything she could do about it.'

'Did you ever stand up to him?'

Teddy shook his head and Molly could see the hurt and shame in his eyes. 'No, never. He ... he terrifies me.'

Molly leaned over and kissed him tenderly on the forehead. 'So you came here to get away?'

'My mum sent me here. I didn't want to come, but...' He fell silent.

Molly knew instantly what he was going to say. 'She sent you here to save you didn't she.'

Teddy nodded slowly but could not meet her eyes.

'She knew that pretty soon your dad was going to turn his attention to you and she couldn't bear to see you get hurt the way that he had hurt her.'

Teddy grunted and she put a hand on his arm.

'It's okay, Teddy. It's okay. It sounds to me that no matter what you did you were in a no win situation. If you'd have stood up to your dad, he would have either taken it out on you or her.'

'Or my brother.'

'You have a brother?'

'Yeah, a younger one.'

Teddy paused for a moment, his breathing slowed and she could see the tempo of the soft pulse in his neck begin to abate. At was as if the relief of getting it off his chest had sated the intense pressure that had been building in his muscular frame. After what seemed like an eternity, he looked up at her and the fire had returned to his dark eyes.

'Anyway, fuck 'em! What will be, will be. There's nothing I can do about it from here.'

Molly sat silently watching the mood shift in Teddy's face. She found it fascinating. She knew he was hiding something but she filed it in the box in the back of her mind marked: Things to Return to Later.

'How'd you get that?' He was pointing at the fading remnants of her scar. She could feel her cheeks flush pink. She steadied her beating heart and smiled at him.

'Same story as yours.'

'As mine?'

'Yep,' she took a large bite from her burger. 'Dad hit me. Hit me very bloody hard actually.'

'What? And caused...' He pulled Molly's dark curls up from her cheek so he could reveal the full length of her wound. 'Caused that? Jesus, Moll, he must have hit you with a hammer.'

'Rolling pin actually but whatever.' She was eyeing Teddy curiously for his reaction.

'Rolling pin? Fuck me!' The room went silent between them and she could see Teddy's anger build in his throbbing neck and temples. 'I'll kill him!'

173

She recalled the retort of the rifle, its fearsome kick shattering her cheek bone as the stricken deer slumped to the forest floor.

'Don't worry. I've got it all planned. The assassination I mean.' She winked at him and grinned. 'House fire. I'm going to graduate from this shithole and then go home, douse the place in petrol, lock the doors from the outside, put a match to my graduation certificate, drop it through the letter box and turn the whole place into a bloody inferno.' She swallowed her burger and wiped sauce from her chin, 'I'm going to cook the old boy like a slab of roast beef.'

Teddy gulped and once again the room fell silent. Molly watched him with a smouldering intensity. After a moment he smiled.

'You're taking the piss!'

Molly's face cracked into a grin. 'Maybe I am, maybe I'm not.' They both laughed. Big belly laughs that had them rolling on the bed, their hands on their sides and their feet knocking their plates over and spilling burger remnants and coleslaw all over her bed sheets. She loved how they could laugh together like that and she knew that he was falling for her hard. Maybe she was falling for him too but not in the same way. After their laughter had subsided, she turned to him. 'All I'll say is this, Teddy Palmer.'

'What's that, Molly Staker?'

'Just watch yourself around me. *I'm deadly.*'

****

'I've got one!'

'You've got what?'

'A beastie.'

Molly ran over to the tree, climbed halfway up the trunk, her foot on a lower, crooked limb, her hand on a branch above her, and she peered curiously into the trap. She could see the soft, fluffy grey and white end of a tail hanging out of the entrance of her little plywood box.

'A beastie? What's a … oh.'

Molly pulled the dead squirrel out of the trap backwards by its tail and held it out in her right hand as if showing it at a county fair. The creature dangled like a fish from a hook. Molly looked at it, her pride obvious in her animated eyes, and smiled. She held it up to her nose and sniffed. It smelt fresh, like pine needles and fresh grass mingled with the scent of meat that had been left out all day.

'What killed it, Moll?'

She jumped down from the tree and rushed over to Teddy. She held the squirrel up for him to peruse, its little legs dangling limply at its side, its black eyes frozen open in a grisly death stare and its lower jaw hanging loose, exposing its tiny teeth and tongue.

'I did.' She was beaming.

He looked confused. 'Why?'

Molly paused and considered her response. 'The sport.'

'The sport?'

She nodded. 'Yes.' She sniffed the squirrel again. 'And food.'

Teddy looked at her and screwed up his nose. 'What … you're going to eat it?'

Molly nodded. She sniffed the squirrel again and fought the urge to lick its face. 'Have you ever eaten squirrel?'

Teddy shook his head violently. 'No, never. Why would

I?'

'Me neither but,' she looked up at him and put a hand on his broad chest, 'don't you wonder?'

'Wonder what?'

'What it tastes like?'

'I … I guess, but …' he looked at the squirrel, 'is it poisonous?'

Molly held it up in both hands, examined its lifeless form and then rested her cheek on its soft underbelly. 'I don't think so.' She turned, placed the squirrel in her rucksack and grabbed Teddy's hand. 'Let's find out.'

Chapter 28:
The Power

'Why am I here, Raven?' Christy Deveraux was dressed in an ash grey trouser suit, gleaming black flat heels and a cream blouse. She looked sharp and she knew it.

'I said it all in my voicemail.' Raven sat in the coffee shop nursing a black Americano and a hangover.

'Well, if you could say it again and give me more details perhaps I could make some sense out of it all.' She was craving her usual morning stimulus but sipped on her flat white instead. The caffeine would have to do. She needed to maintain her composure.

'You think I'm crazy.'

'I think you're self-destructive but that's not in question here is it? What is in question is why you thought it would be a good idea to call me in the middle of the night and leave me some garbled message about nightmares, ghosts and murder.' She could feel her anger building in her head and she immediately squashed it. She had been taught how to control her emotions, to keep all but the most valuable elements of her volatility in check, and she wasn't going to let this buffoon get the better of her.

'You would have read it in my report from the Richards case. I assume you *have* read it?'

She nodded. 'Of course.'

'I knew things about those murders that no one else knew, things that I couldn't possibly know without having some sort of … premonition.' He visibly shuddered as the words left his mouth.

'Give me a break, Raven. This isn't an episode of the twilight zone.' She wiped foam from her upper lip, being careful not to smudge her expertly applied lipstick. 'This is real life, the real world, not some fantasy, and from what I can gather, you're alleging that you have some sort of backdoor entrance into a case that we have been investigating, away from the public gaze, for the last six weeks. Who is your source?'

She was calm, calculated and emotionless. It was how she had earned her nickname – she knew it – but she didn't give a shit. If being ice cold got the job done then by god she was willing to live with the ridicule and backroom gossip.

'There is no source. I don't need one.' He leaned forward and lowered his voice. 'I know that murders have been committed on that beach, I've seen where they occurred, I've been there in my dreams, and I'm telling you, what you have on your hands here is a serial killer with…' He paused to look around him. The coffee shop was near empty. 'With a taste for human flesh.'

She laughed. 'Oh come on, Raven. You've got to be kidding.'

'I'm not joking. It's been keeping me awake at night. While the dreams are a little symbolic in nature, I've learned how to read them. I learned from the last time. The mistakes

178

I made. I'm willing to bet everything I own – which, granted, isn't a lot thanks to you – that what you have on your hands here is a vicious, cannibalistic serial killer. It sounds crazy, I know, but I've been thinking about it a lot, at night mostly, and it all adds up.' He downed the dregs of his coffee and peered over the rim of his mug at Deveraux who was raising her right eyebrow churlishly. 'I'm also willing to bet that somewhere near that beach there's a cookhouse full of dead bodies.'

'There is no evidence of any of that.'

'But you can confirm that there have been killings?'

She shuffled uncomfortably in her seat. 'As a suspended member of my team I ought not to be sharing details of an ongoing case, but …' she smiled coldly, 'as you are still officially part of the law enforcement profession.' She caressed the rim of her coffee cup with her forefinger. 'Yes, we believe there have been several murders. One confirmed and four suspected but it is becoming more and more likely that they too are deceased.'

Raven bashed a hand on the table and grinned. 'I knew it. And I bet you've found a severed limb too.'

Deveraux's mouth fell open and she quickly shut it. They had fought vehemently to keep that out of the press, arguing that it would compromise their ongoing investigation. They had even managed to convince the children and their parents that what they had seen was no more than the remains of a dead sea creature that had been washed up on the beach.

'I'm sure I can even describe your suspected victims. A couple of young lovers out for a late night stroll, both of them no more than very early twenties, a middle-aged gentleman who was a midnight swimmer and wearing nothing but a pair

179

of swim shorts and a cap, an elderly homeless lady looking for scraps of food for her and her dog and an overweight fella in a trilby and a bright coloured polo shirt who had downed a significant amount of alcohol.' He folded his arms and nodded.

She took a second to compose herself. Everything he said sounded plausible based on the limited information they had. 'I must insist, ex Detective Inspector, that you declare your source immediately. This is a matter of breaching police protocol and I will not stand for it.'

Raven was getting increasingly frustrated with the Chief Super's ambivalence and it showed. 'Look, Christy. I know you don't like me and, frankly I'm not too fond of you either, but I'm telling you – I see these things. I don't know how or why and, for the love of god I wish I didn't, but I do and there you have it. I needed to get it off my chest and now I have and you can do with it what you will. Or not. It's your choice now.'

Deveraux looked at him, amused, and waved a hand dismissively. He fidgeted under her gaze. After a moment he grabbed his jacket and went to stand.

'Wait.' She couldn't hold it off any longer. She had the urge. Her hand was in her trouser pocket and casually pressing the tip of her long index finger onto the sharp point of the hairpin that she kept hidden in there for just this type of occasion. She could feel the piercing pain as the metal entered her flesh and shuddered as the blood trickled down her knuckle. 'You need to share with us what you know, but only to a select few.' She bit down on her lower lip. Her little moment of self-flagellation couldn't hide the dissatisfaction she felt at the direction their little encounter was taking. She hated bringing him back into the fold in any way but she knew it would be foolish to be completely dismissive. She needed to stay close to him. He had a source and she intended to find out who it was. 'I'll put you in touch with the DI I have on this case. Randall Kipruto.'

'I know him.'

'I want you to take him through what you know in detail and keep him up to speed with any new...' she grimaced, 'developments.'

'Okay.'

'I want to know it as soon as you do but I want it kept between us.'

'Sure.'

'I'm serious. If any of this gets out you can kiss any chance of a reprieve goodbye.'

There it was. The precious word he had clearly been looking for. *Reprieve*. 'Got it.' He stood and looked down at her with scarcely hidden impatience as she casually finished the last of her coffee. 'Is that it?'

She swallowed and raised the little finger of her left hand. 'One more little thing. The Butler woman.'

He dropped his jacket and there was a soft clunk as his hip flask struck the back of the chair. 'What?'

'I know that you've been meeting with her.'

His face flushed red and he clenched his fist. 'Have you been spying on me?'

She winked at him. 'I too have my sources.'

He placed both hands on the table and glared at her. 'I do not appreciate being tailed. You have no right!'

She spoke calmly and meticulously. 'I do if I think it's linked to my case. I have every right in the world.'

'Wha…?'

'Tell me,' she peered up at him, placed her free hand on the table and smiled knowingly. 'Have you ever heard of an organisation known as The Legion?'

'The what? No I…' He was confused and backfooted and she was enjoying it.

'Please,' she beckoned to him, 'take a seat and we can share.'

Chapter 29:
Lisa Leaves a Message

Lisa couldn't stop thinking about it. The man with the grey hair, the kind face and the beard. The card with Raven's surname on it. And that phrase.

Here's *our* little boy.

Raven had tried to disregard it, but she knew the truth. It had affected him deeply, and that was only natural.

'I've got to get on, Lis. I'm working a case and I've got to meet Wesley to give him a debrief. Don't want to be late … again. I'll call you. Soon. I promise.'

And just like that, he'd left.

Lonnie, of course, was no help at all. 'The guy's a screw up, Lisa. He always has been, always will be. He'll let you down every day from now until forever until you learn to cut him loose. You've just got to hope and pray that he,' he pointed down at Harry who was still playing with his toy cars, 'doesn't have the gene.'

'What the hell does that mean?' Lisa stood and confronted him full on, her face at the height of Lonnie's bulging pectoral muscles.

'You know what I'm talking about.' Lonnie hooked a

lead onto the clasp of his dog's collar, the French bulldog panting and huffing around his ankles. 'Like father like son and all that? I'm just saying, these things have a habit of coming home to roost.'

'Fuck you, Lonnie! What the hell do you know?' She was seething. 'Why don't you just go out and prance around with that French fancy of yours. It seems to me that you love that dog more than you love either of us anyway!'

'Now come on, Lisa …' He dropped the lead and stepped towards her, arms outstretched. 'I was only kidding. You know I'm only joking around.'

Lisa lunged forward and swung her right arm wildly, connecting the open palm of her hand with the side of Lonnie's face with a loud *thwack*. Harry looked up from playfully crashing a truck and a Formula One car together and giggled.

'What the fu-?' Lonnie's cheek turned a bright pink with the outline of her hand.

'Don't rush back you pumped up …' she was hissing and spitting her words out like an enraged tabby, 'ponced up, steroid riddled prick!' She glanced down at Harry who was still giggling and she fought to control her language. Her temper was always there, always at the surface and ready to bubble over without a second's hesitation, but at that moment she didn't care. She wouldn't allow anyone to say a bad word about her child. Or his father. No, only she could curse Raven. He was *her* cross to bear and she didn't need anyone, especially not this oversized excuse for a bicep, wading in and causing her even more problems. 'Get out and don't come back until you've grown up!'

'Okay, okay. Peace, okay.' He grabbed his keys. 'I'll see

you in an hour or so when you've,' he smiled sheepishly, 'calmed down a little.'

She cursed under her breath as the front door opened and closed and then turned to her son. She knew she had overreacted, but she had things on her mind and a deep-seated anxiety affecting her every waking thought. She didn't even know why she was with Lonnie. Sure, while she wasn't working he kept a roof over their heads, but she didn't love him. She was kidding herself if she thought she would grow to do so. He wasn't her type and never would be. He was slow-witted at best, all testosterone and no IQ and although he was kind to them she knew that he was in love with little more than his dog and his own reflection. Raven, for all his faults, all his mistakes, had held her heart on a short string since the day they first met and she had been fighting night and day since their breakup to take a pair of scissors and sever the emotional ties. She just couldn't bring herself to do it.

She sighed and reached down to her only child who was smiling up at her, his little face full of joy and wonder..

'Come on, Harry. It's bath time.'

****

'Hello, this is Lisa Clancy. We met the other day at the park? I will be eternally grateful to you for what you did. I wanted to thank you in person so … well, I called. It would be great to meet up for a coffee. I'll bring little Harry. I'm sure he will be so pleased to see you again. If you could return my call when you pick this up that would be great. Thank you … again.'

She ended the call and looked at herself in the mirror. She didn't have a plan, not a shred of strategy or tactic, but she knew that something important had gone on between them and she was dead set on finding out what.

Raven had always told her that his father was dead, and yet here was someone claiming to be Sam Raven. Luke might want to escape his past with all the panache of a charging rhino but if her son had a grandfather they deserved to know about it..

She went on about her business around the flat but she couldn't focus. It was at the front of her mind and everything else was in a cloud. Who was this guy, the stranger that had returned their son, *our* little boy? What was Raven keeping from her? She always knew when he had something to hide, lord knows she knew all about his secrecy and lies, but this was different. This was something … personal. Why was he so coy about it? It just kept nagging away at her, irritating her like a red and itchy rash. She sat out on their shallow balcony in the bright sunshine and casually smoked a cigarette – she had started smoking again after she and Raven had separated – and all the time she thought about nothing other than: 'Raven's Interiors, for the county's best quality home furnishings.'

She leapt up with a start when her cell phone rang. She crushed out her butt, fumbled with the keypad and hit answer.

'Hi, Lisa. It's Sam.'

She composed herself. 'Oh, hi. Thanks … thanks for calling me back. It's lovely to hear from you again.'

There was a pause at the other end of the line.

'Did you speak with him?'

'With Rave- … with Luke?'

'Yes. Did you speak with him? What did he say when you told him about me? Did you give him my card?

Lisa took a breath. 'I … I did. Yes. He was … he was interested.'

'Interested?' She could hear the uncertainty in his voice.

'Yes. He was … well frankly he was taken aback.'

'I'm sure. It would have been a shock for him.'

'I wanted to thank you again for the other day. I don't know what I would have done if …'

'Forget about it, it was nothing and I was glad to help. It was wonderful to meet little Harry, he certainly is a beautiful little boy, but …' another pause. 'About Luke?'

Lisa glanced inside the apartment at Harry who was asleep on the sofa. 'Look, Sam. Are you … well, Luke told me his father was dead so you can't be …'

'I want to meet with him.' His tone was firm yet cautious.

'I don't know that he'll agree to that.'

'Then you need to help me set it up. It's in his interest. It's in *all* of your interests.'

'How would I even do that?'

'Offer to meet him for a drink. Don't bring Harry. Just you and Luke. There's a place that has booths out back that are quieter. More private. We can chat.'

'He'll never forgive me if …'

'Please, Lisa.' There was a desperation in his voice. 'This is important.'

'I don't understa-'

'Your lives could be in danger, I'm not certain yet, but I can't take the risk. I can't let anything happen to the three of you.'

Lisa leaned forward in her chair. 'What do you mean our lives are in danger?'

'I can't say any more over the phone. Tomorrow night. Eight o'clock at Dean's Bistro. Just the two of you. Don't be late.'

There was a silence on the line and for a moment she thought he had gotten spooked and hung up on her. Then, 'I'm not dead, Lisa. I've been away for a while, much longer than I'd anticipated, but now I'm back and I intend to put things right between … between me and my son.'

Chapter 30:
D4V SMDS

Chelsea Butler had said something to him that made him think. It didn't seem like much at the time but it had snuck its way into his subconscious and gradually eaten away at his neurons while he was looking the other way, distracted by the incident with his son and dead father. But slowly and subtly it had risen to the surface like a pop song, playing on repeat in his brain like some kind of euro-trash house music and he had been pondering it ever since.

I know exactly who that man was standing on the street corner ... and so do you.

Except he didn't. He couldn't. It was impossible. There was only one person he knew with those facial features, with that build, that gait and that slick attire and he had come up clean. Clean as a whistle. Cleaner than a surgically sanitised workstation in a Dettol factory.

Doctor Robert Charon.

Tony Richards' estranged father had been checked out after everything that had gone on with his son, especially after they had found Richards' mother and brother dead at the family home, but he had a cast iron alibi. At least three respectable members of the community had vouched for him and all three of those had in turn been checked for conflicts of interest. No, that double murder had been all Richards' doing, there was no question. And Robert Charon was a well-respected mentor and therapist who had more than a little influence with the county council and other assorted businessmen, women and dignitaries from around the country. Why would he waste his time standing on a street corner spying on his son's ex-girlfriend? Why would he be involved in her disappearance? What would he gain from it? It made no sense.

That didn't mean of course that he wasn't going to check it out. He wouldn't be much of an investigator, private or otherwise, if he didn't follow up on a lead, no matter how unlikely it seemed.

Furthermore, the news that Deveraux had shared with him had piqued his interest somewhat. The Legion: an elite club for the wealthy and powerful, where privileged individuals in positions of power could share thoughts and ideals and agree where and when to exert their shared influence. What they were working on he wasn't yet sure, but he planned to find out. All of which meant that before his meeting with Kipruto later that afternoon he and Wesley had some surveillance to carry out.

The Charon estate was sprawling. It didn't look like much from the front: a large, detached property with Victorian architecture and a long, open driveway behind wrought iron gates, but Raven knew from satellite images that at the rear of the property were tens of acres of sheltered space for Charon's wealthy clients to shield themselves away from prying eyes.

'How do you want to play it, boss?' Wesley was in the passenger seat munching on a Peperami.

'We just sit and wait.' Raven pulled up his collar and settled down into his seat. He planned to take a nap while Wesley kept his eyes peeled. He hadn't been sleeping well since the nightmares had kicked in again. And, after all, what was the point of having a deputy in training if he didn't let him take the reins once in a while?

'Wait for what?'

'What do you mean?'

Wesley bit into his spicy sausage and the red and oily grease ran down his pointed, bum-fluff riddled chin. Raven groaned in disgust. 'I mean, what can we expect? If the guy even comes out at all, isn't he just going to take a drive or a walk or something? What does that tell us?'

Raven shook his head. 'Well, we won't know until it happens, will we? That's why it's called a stake out. We stake out the place until something interesting happens.'

'And what if it doesn't?' Wesley rubbed his tired eyes with his oily finger.

Raven smiled and waited for the inevitable. 'Well, if it doesn't then it doesn't. Our time will have been wasted and we'll have to come back another time when hopefully something *more* interesting will indeed … happen. Those are the breaks. You just roll with them – you'll learn in time.'

'Well it seems like a bloody stupid … aagh. *Aagh shit! My eye! That burns! Luke, it stings like hell!*'

Raven fought to control his laughter, tears rolling down his cheeks as he watched his young apprentice writhe about in the car. 'What did you think would happen you idiot? You got the extra hot sausage with chillies in it!' He grabbed his sides which were aching from his fit of laughter. 'If I was you, I'd wash your hands before you take a piss.'

'Jesus, they should put a warning sign or a label or something on these things. My eye's watering like a leaky tap.' The white around Wesley's iris was bloodshot and the lid of his eye was pink and swollen.

'Bloody idiot.' Raven chuckled. 'I can always count on you to cheer me up.'

His partner huffed sulkily. 'I'm glad my misfortune amuses you.'

Raven slurped on the remains of his drink and threw the empty cup onto the back seat.

'Do you even think this guy has anything to do with the Butler girl's disappearance?'

Raven shook his head and sighed. 'Nope.'

'Then why are we here?'

'Because Chelsea Butler does and she's paying us.'

Wesley's mouth fell open. 'And what? We just got to do what she says even though we know it's a complete waste of time? That seems bloody ridiculous. What's the point of being a private investigator if all we do is follow instructions? Shouldn't we be ... investigating leads or something?'

Raven turned in his seat. 'Look, you and I both know this is a dead end. I got that. But we've drawn a blank on this case and despite my pleading with Chelsea to stand us down she seems intent on seeing this thing through with us on the payroll.' Raven raised an eyebrow. 'We can either walk away with no pay cheque and run the risk of souring our already flaky reputation or do what she says and hope that something good comes of it. And, let's face it,' Raven held up the printout of the CCTV image next to a publicity shot of Robert Charon, the doctor's black hair and trimmed goatee framing a ruggedly handsome face, 'you have to admit, the picture does bear an uncanny resemblance to him.'

Wesley turned his head to one side and shrugged. 'Yeah, I guess so.'

'Well then. There you have it. We sit, we wait.' He slowly closed his weary eyes. 'And when you see something you be sure to let me know.'

****

This dream was different. He was in a cold, dank room with stone walls. It smelled musty and old. He shivered and wrapped his arms around himself to keep his body temperature from plummeting.

There were three other occupants in there with him. They were shrouded in what appeared to be dark brown dress robes with red fringe. Raven peered through the gloom but, try as he might, he couldn't make out any discriminating features on the three, odd looking strangers. Just three vaguely human shapes that were conversing animatedly.

The door to the room opened and in walked another robed individual followed by a young woman. The woman was blindfolded and had her hands chained in front of her with iron manacles. On her head was a bronze crown with a bright green jewel in its centre. She was crying, Raven could sense the fear running through her veins like poison.

Sacrificium est purus.
Sacrificum est purus.
Sacrificium est purus.

193

The words seemed to emanate from the stone cavern itself like Raven was existing within a living, breathing, organic speaker system. It sunk into his skin and flesh and into his brain like radiation and he shook his head in an attempt to spill it out of his ears like warm water.

The girl was led to a low, stone platform where she was bound and stripped. Raven turned his head away to shield his eyes from her naked body. He felt ashamed.

She was sobbing now, her whole body trembling with fear and wretched anticipation. He tried to cross the room and grab her in his arms, to turn and carry her up the dark stairway and away from that godawful place. At that moment he would have given anything to have been able to do that.

Another shape dressed in black robes approached her from the rear of the room and ran a hand down her exposed abdomen. She shook violently at his touch.

Tu es benedictus et virtutum.

The one in the black robes took a dagger from a sheath at its side and drew it towards the young lady's face. Raven tried to scream but his throat was dry and the sound hoarse and thin.

With a sharp slashing motion the knife cut a two inch wound into the lower right hand side of the woman's throat and she cried out in pain. The shape in black held a hand under the running stream of blood, coating its fingers in the warm and sticky flow and wiped it across her forehead and cheeks. It then bent and licked the blood from its red and dripping palm like it was drinking a handful of cool and refreshing water.

Tu es benedictus et virtutum.

The one in black raised a hand in some sort of signal,

dismissing the woman. Three of the others unshackled her, covered her in her robe and led her back to the staircase. She slumped into their arms as if all her energy had been sapped by fear and they had to pick her up. Raven felt relief wash over him in waves as he watched her exit the room.

He looked over at the being in black robes and felt an immediate hatred. He could sense in that figure an evil and malevolence that he recognised. He wanted to rush over, grab the dagger and plunge it deep into the creature's throat where he was sure the blood would be black and burning and the flesh would be peeling from the bone. Images of Daisy and his former partner, Damian Barber, flashed before his eyes and he started to cry.

The creature heard, or rather smelled his tears and started to turn. It raised two twisted and blackened hands to its hood and started to lower it. From within its dark shroud there was a scream like nothing that Raven had ever heard before. Red and black eyes glared at him from its fiery depths and he saw its scaly and horned skull, its long tail with a sharp tip, its swirling mass of hate and ravenous, furious hunger.

He started to cry out but the creature opened its wide and blistered mouth. Raven saw its sharp, crooked teeth and its black, oily tongue and he held his hands to his ears as the beast screamed.

RAVEN!

****

'*Raven*, we've got movement!'

Wes was leaning over his semi-comatose comrade and shaking him violently. Raven opened his eyes, his mouth agape in horror, his pupils dilated and milky and his muscles

195

taught and agitated.

'It's Charon.' Wesley pointed out through the windscreen and towards the house.

Raven shook his head, mumbled something incoherent and rubbed his eyes. He was tired of having every moment of precious slumber terrorised by images of death and brutality. He just needed to rest.

'What …?' he coughed to clear his hoarse throat, 'what's up?'

'He's got company.'

Raven pulled himself up in his seat, gripped his still trembling hands on the steering wheel and focused intensely on the long driveway leading up to the house. There was a brilliant white Range Rover rounding the turning circle by the entrance and Charon's parking attendant was standing and waiting for the vehicle to slow to a halt.

Raven knew that car.

'This could give us an indication of who Robert Charon hangs out with, boss. Maybe give us an idea of the nature of the bloke, what he gets up to in his spare time.'

Raven waved him away and rubbed the arm of his jacket on the windscreen to clear the condensation, no doubt caused by his loud snoring and his partner's heavy breathing.

'Shut up a minute and let me think.'

'Bound to be some ponce from the council or some jumped up local entrepreneur or something.' Wesley was now snacking on a packet of cheeselets. 'Probably popping round for a glass of Chablis and a cigar, don't you know.' Wesley was attempting his best Downton Abbey accent and failing miserably.

'It can't be.' Raven was shaking his head. He re-read the

number plate.

D4V SMDS.

'Why would he be here? I don't get it.' Raven was frantically scrolling through his notepad. 'He never declared a conflict of interest when we were investigating the …'

'Oh yes, Doctor Charon. I would love to come and play polo in your garden. What's that you say? Would I like to have a swim in your Olympic sized pool? Well of course, but I haven't bought my swimsuit. Naked you say? Well, why the devil not?'

'This can't be right … it *can't* be.'

The Range Rover stopped outside of the house and Charon's valet approached. At the same time Robert Charon himself appeared in the open doorway, resplendent in a black polo top, black trousers and black leather boots. He stepped towards the pavement. He was smiling broadly, his whitened and perfectly straight teeth gleaming and with his arms outstretched in what was clearly a warm and familiar welcome.

Raven watched in disbelief as his old Chief Inspector and dear friend and confidante, Dave Simmons, exited the vehicle, handed over his keys to the valet and hugged his host like he was embracing a member of his own family.

Chapter 31:
Delilah

Delilah was becoming a nuisance. More than a nuisance, actually. Delilah was an obstacle.

Molly didn't mind her at first. She was reasonably polite, she didn't leave a mess in the bathroom and she didn't interfere in Molly's business – ultimately three things that got her a trio of large, bold and double underlined ticks in Molly's copy book.

Even when they shared classes, she was fairly benign and background material at best. Molly herself wasn't great at concentrating in lessons but she was intelligent and cunning, a combination that she had found immensely useful throughout her formative years, and she managed to pick up things quite quickly even when she had spent the whole double lesson imagining dissecting a dead fox or preparing one of her deceased treasures for eternal captivity in a jar of pungent formaldehyde.

All that changed when Teddy noticed *her*.

It wasn't sudden and it certainly wasn't deliberate but gradually, over a number of days and weeks when they were using the shared bathroom or coming back from the dorm cooking area after lashing together a tasty dinner of chilli, beans on toast or curried pot noodle, she spotted Teddy … *looking*.

Delilah was an attractive girl. Quite tall and thin, fair skinned, long red hair and cute freckles speckling her nose, cheeks and forehead. She was from a wealthy family and she spoke with the perfectly clipped consonants of someone who had been dealt a pretty good hand in life. She was also big in the boob department and Molly knew that Teddy liked that. He liked what Molly had which was ample but Delilah was an upgrade and then some.

She pulled him up on it one evening after dinner.

'You like her, don't you?'

Teddy looked up from the TV. 'Like who?'

'Delilah.' Molly couldn't meet his gaze and so continued to anxiously thumb through her magazine.

'I … I don't know what you mean. What?'

'I saw you. I've seen you a few times now. Looking at her.'

Teddy reached over, grabbed the remote and turned the TV off. 'No, Molly!' He grabbed her arm. 'No way!'

She brushed her hair from her face, straightened her top and looked intently into his dark eyes. 'Don't lie to me, Teddy.' She shrugged. 'It's okay if you do, it's not as if we're married or anything. I would just appreciate the truth, that's all. Just a little … honesty.' She pushed his hand away. 'I think I deserve that.'

Teddy sighed and smiled. 'Of course you do, Moll. Of course. But, I promise you, I don't know what you saw or what you think it meant. If I was looking at her it was absent-mindedly and with no other intention, certainly not

199

attraction. I care for you … deeply.' He put his hand on hers and squeezed. She didn't pull away. 'You know that.'

There was a moment's silence.

'She's pretty though, right?'

Teddy paused to consider his response. 'I guess?'

'What do you like about her?'

Colour started to build in his cheeks and arms. 'I … don't know what you mean.'

'Well, you *guess* that she's pretty. Why is that? Just tell me.'

He folded his arms and looked out the window. 'I think you're trying to trap me into saying something and I'm not going to fall for it.'

Molly jumped up from the bed and opened the window. 'You can only fall into a trap if there's something there to be trapped for.' She took a long, perfectly rolled joint from her dressing table drawer – the distribution of marijuana around the campus was rife and she had become a casual user along with at least half of the other residents – lit it and inhaled deeply. After a moment she blew a long, billowing plume of pungent smoke out of the open, second floor window. 'Otherwise you have nothing to be afraid of.' She handed him the joint and smiled knowingly.

Teddy inhaled and laid back on the bed. 'I don't know, Moll. She's attractive I guess, but nothing like you. You're,' he shrugged, 'more interesting'. He passed back the joint.

'Interesting, interesting. Wow, there's a compliment.' She took another drag, held it in her lungs for another few seconds and exhaled. 'You want interesting, go fuck Miss Mctierney. She has an IQ of 140.' She huffed and turned from him.

'Oh, Molly. *Come on.* Delilah is attractive in a conventional way but you're ...'

'*I'm what*?' She turned and shot him a look of defiance. '*Unconventional?*'

'Yes! That's exactly what you are.' He leapt up from the bed and put his arms around her. 'You're not like any other girl. You're special.' He kissed her neck and then her lips. 'You're individual and I love that about you.' He looked deep into her eyes, his soft hand on her cheeks. 'I love you.'

Those three words hit home. She hadn't heard them in ... well, ever.

'Don't you dare fucking hurt me.'

He smiled and kissed her cheek. 'Never.'

****

Delilah had to go. There was no way around it. Teddy, despite his protestations, was infatuated and Delilah, in stark contrast to her feigned innocence and alleged virginity, had started to respond. As much as Molly didn't want to upset her time there at Elderflower Heights – she had fashioned a life there that she enjoyed, with no consequences and certainly no repercussions from her father – there was no fucking way that ginger bitch was going to come between her and her man.

There were two ways she could go about it. Plan A was that she would discredit Delilah in some way, plant something on her or in her room that would later be discovered by someone of authority, confirming Delilah to be a woman of compromised moral fibre and ultimately lead to her expulsion from the highly respectable and extremely expensive boarding school.

Molly chose plan B.

'We've got to sort her out, Teddy.'

Teddy was climbing a hazelnut tree and peering into Molly's squirrel trap. 'Do what?'

'Delilah.' Molly was lying on the grass and yawning. She had *so* moved on from squirrels but Teddy was still obsessed with them. He seemed to love chewing on bar-b-q squirrel legs dipped in mustard and mayonnaise.

Teddy looked down from the thick branch he was straddling. He was wearing nothing but a pair of shorts and Adidas trainers. His chest was broad and muscular and his arms were thick and strong – none of which went unnoticed by Molly. 'What do you mean sort her out?'

Molly lay in a star shape and looked up at the blue sky. 'She needs to be taught a lesson.'

Teddy jumped down from the tree and shook his head. 'Nothing in that one. We'll have to take a look on the other side of the hill.' He sat down next to her and lay back on the bark and mulch that covered the small area of patchy grass. 'What do you mean lesson? Like a prank?'

Molly smiled. 'Sort of.'

'Like, humiliate her in public?' Teddy was smiling at the thought.

'Mmm … worse.'

'Worse than humiliation?'

'You're gonna have to go with me on this one.' She sat up and rested her weight on her elbows. 'No backing down.' She leaned over and licked his cheek. 'You promise?'

Teddy put an arm round her shoulders and kissed her hard on the lips. 'I promise.'

****

Delilah liked sambuca. She was a sucker for it, which was odd because otherwise she rarely drank.

There was a party in the grounds to let off steam before the end of year exams, which ultimately signalled the second year students completing their A-levels. The school itself served as both a sixth form college and a university specialising in both sciences and arts and the students rarely attended for less than five years. Teddy, Molly and Delilah were in their second.

There was a buffet, balloons and bunting, bales of hay to sit and throw around and a loud and heavily illuminated disco. And, of course, there was booze – all of it contraband, naturally.

Teddy was dancing with Delilah and plying her with drink, as per Molly's plan.

'Where's Molly tonight, Ted?' Delilah was throwing her loose, flaming red hair to the side while sipping on her shot. She'd had three of them already on top of three bottles of Corona and lime.

'Oh, she couldn't make it, Deli. She was feeling unwell. Something about seafood upsetting her stomach.' Teddy was dressed in smart denim trousers, a tight white shirt and a straight black tie. He'd had a few beers but was restraining himself from having any more. He was under strict instructions. 'We can party without her though, right?'

She staggered to her left and he steadied her. 'I...I don't think she likes me.'

Teddy feigned ignorance. 'Sure she does.' He eyed her

appreciatively. 'What's not to like?'

Delilah downed her shot and winced. 'Do…do you like me Teddy?'

Teddy swallowed and glanced over at Molly who was watching from afar. She was not smiling. Just peering at them, unblinking over the flame and smoke of the barbeque like a fiery goddess.

'Of course I do.'

As the evening went on, and the alcohol flowed, Delilah's dance moves became more haphazard and flamboyant and Teddy had to feign drunkenness in order to socially justify some of the shapes he was throwing. The dance area in front of the disco, which itself was manned by a wild eyed Pete Tong wannabe, was a square area of lawn that had a portable faux wooden dancefloor assembled upon it. It was packed with around a hundred or so students of all ages, many of which were intoxicated beyond what would be considered sensible. Teddy was counting as Delilah downed four more sambucas and moved onto tequila.

'I'm having such a lushly time with you Teddy.' She was slurring and mixing her consonants.

'Yeah, me too, Delilah. It's been great.'

'I'm shorry Molly couldn't be here.' She threw her arms around his shoulders. 'But I'm shecretly glad she isn't.' She leaned in to kiss him and belched. Teddy caught the whiff of aniseed and bile. He tilted his head to one side, avoided her chemically toxic mouth and hugged her.

A thought occurred to him and he frowned. 'Cindy Parsons told me that you thought I was…weird. Is that true?'

Delilah ran her hand through his dark hair and chuckled. 'That wash then Ted…Teddy.' He heard her stifle a belch.

'That wash before.'

Teddy grinned, vindicated. 'You wanna go somewhere quiet, Deli?' He glanced at his watch. It was a little past midnight, the time that Molly had targeted.

Delilah leaned back, staggered, held out her arms for balance and then smiled. 'If you're sure.'

Teddy nodded and winked but he could feel his heart beating like a sledgehammer in his chest. 'I've never been more sure of anything in my life.'

He grabbed her hand firmly in his and quietly and discreetly pulled her towards the forest.

****

Molly was in the clearing, she had moved to that spot around twenty minutes earlier, but she could still see the dancefloor, bathed in swathes of LED fluorescent lighting and dry ice. She watched through the trees as her man grabbed a hold of the bitch's hand and pulled her down the hill towards their planned meeting spot. The fury had been building within her all evening as she watched the red headed vixen try all of the tricks in her devious little book to woo Teddy. It was a fucking joke. Really. Molly had thought that she would be okay using Teddy as the bait but she really wasn't. At least twice that evening she had to hold back tears. It was embarrassing and she had chastised herself for being such a little baby. Gretchen wouldn't have stood for it.

She pawed at her scar absentmindedly. It was too much. She was furious. She considered their plan and decided it needed … amending.

She could hear Teddy's laughter and Delilah's giggles

and she swore under her breath. Was he fucking enjoying this?

As they emerged through the foliage and out into the open, Delilah staggered, turned and threw her arms around Teddy, planting her lips on his mouth and kissing him passionately. Molly could hear … slurping. Teddy looked over her shoulder at Molly and raised his eyebrows. Molly brushed her hair from her face and loudly cleared her throat.

Delilah spun round, almost tripped over a root and spotted Molly standing by the old, dilapidated well.

'Molly!' She grabbed the limb of a tree to steady herself. 'Shit, Molly. I didn't …' She looked up at Teddy. 'I swear … I didn't mean to …' She belched again.

'It's okay, Delilah. Honestly.' Molly smiled and opened the top button of her shirt, revealing the soft crease of her cleavage. 'We're into it.'

Delilah frowned and looked at Teddy again who had stepped towards Molly.

'That's why I brought you here.' He put an arm around Molly. 'It's what you wanted.' He kissed Molly on the lips. 'Isn't it?'

Delilah looked at them furtively and then back through the trees at the party which was still raging. 'Maybe I should get ba …'

Molly stepped towards her and held out a joint. 'Try this. It'll help.'

Delilah looked at the burning spliff as if it were the strangest thing she had ever seen in her life.

'Come on. It's just marijuana. It's not like you haven't done it before … is it?' Molly pushed it towards her again and Delilah took it tentatively.

'I guess …'

She placed it between her lips, inhaled and then coughed repeatedly, doubling over and holding her abdomen as if she was going to spew the contents of her alcohol filled stomach all over the clearing.

Molly and Teddy laughed as Delilah regained her composure. Her eyes were red and bloodshot. 'It makes you woozy doesn't it?'

'It sure does.' Molly ran a hand through Delilah's red hair and fought the urge to rip the follicles right out of her scalp. 'Try it again.'

Delilah had another drag and this time managed to maintain her composure. She blew out the smoke and started to giggle at nothing.

'Now,' Molly took the joint from Delilah and crushed it out, 'about that thing.'

'What thing?'

'You know …' Molly delicately ran a finger down Delilah's bare arm.

'Oh, I … I don't know, Molly.' She looked at Teddy with his bulging torso and dark, brown eyes and Molly saw her eyes darken with desire. Then she looked down at Molly with her dark curls, imploring stare, scarred cheek and short, but well-formed stature and wondered. 'It's … weird.'

'Not to us it's not. It's the most natural thing in the world.' Molly leaned in and kissed her gently on the lips. She reached up and put her arm around Delilah's shoulders as they embraced, then unzipped the back of her dress, running a hand down her spine as it slowly fluttered to the floor leaving Delilah standing there in nothing but her underwear. Her black, six inch heels were still somewhere at the side of

207

the dancefloor – she had removed them earlier that evening after she had almost stacked it while coming back from the toilet.

Teddy walked over, kissed Delilah at the base of her neck, ran a hand through her hair and unclasped the back of her bra. At the same time Molly stooped down, kissed her stomach and gently slipped her knickers over her waist and buttocks and down her long, pale legs. Delilah sighed with anticipation and closed her eyes.

'Look at you, Delilah,' Molly was chuckling, 'all dressed up with no place to go.' She was holding Delilah's pale blue dress and black underwear in her hands. Teddy was standing next to her looking more than a little ashamed.

Delilah peered at them blearily and then down at her bare skin. She crossed her arms over herself. 'What? What's going on? Teddy?'

'Sorry. It's …' Teddy shrugged.

Molly glared up at him. 'Don't apologise!' She pointed at Delilah. 'She's had this coming.'

Delilah was confused, cold and embarrassed. 'What did I do?'

Molly huffed. '*You know*. You've been after Teddy since the day that we got together and you haven't been shy about it either.'

'I didn't do anything?'

Molly's blood was boiling. 'Well that's very interesting, Delilah. Very interesting indeed. If you didn't do anything then why the hell are you in this clearing, with my man,' she held out her clothes, 'butt naked?'

'You tricked me.' The tears were now starting to flow down Delilah's cheeks.

'We only played on emotions that were already there.' She held Delilah's clothes over the well. 'You tricked yourself.'

'Don't do that Molly, please!' She was sobbing now. 'I'm sorry. For whatever I've done, I'm truly sorry.'

Teddy shuffled his feet uncomfortably next to Molly.

'I don't think that's good enough. You've embarrassed me in front of my boyfriend, you've secretly tried to seduce him from right under my nose, you've pretended to be my friend and now you expect me just to forgive you because you're cold and humiliated.' She shook her head. 'Not gonna happen.'

'Molly, come on.' Teddy put a hand on her shoulder. 'She's had enough.'

The rage burned in Molly's gut and she snapped at him. 'Fuck off, Teddy! I'm dealing with this!' She pushed his hand away. 'What you're going to do now, Delilah my darling, is walk back up that hill, through that crowd of people and back to your dorm, naked as the day you were born and showing the whole world what a dirty little man grabbing whore you really are.'

Molly glanced at the clothes in her hand, grinned and then let go.

'*No!*' Delilah raced across the clearing towards Molly and clawed at her arm. Her mouth fell open as she watched her dress flutter to the bottom of the well. She placed her hands on the sides of the low wall, gripped hard and gritted her teeth. The mortar crumbled in her fingertips.

'You fucking bitch!' She turned, roared with anger and clawed at Molly's eyes, one long nail catching the mottled flesh of Molly's scar and tearing a chunk of skin from it.

209

Molly screamed in pain.

'Get off me!' Molly kicked out and struck Delilah in the shin with her boot. Delilah grunted but she continued her naked assault, grabbing at Molly's curls and pulling hard.

'You think I'm a pushover but I'm not! That prick Rupert Ackhurst found that out when he tried to force himself inside of me and all he got was a dinner fork in his testicle!' Delilah was sobering up fast. 'You've messed with the wrong bitch!'

Molly's confidence evaporated. She looked up at Teddy who was frozen on the spot as if catatonic and she knew she had to defend herself. They rolled on the ground, Molly in her jeans, shirt and denim jacket, Delilah naked and vengeful, and Molly knew she was beaten for size and strength. She looked around her at the ground as Delilah mounted her and slapped at her face and chest, clawing at her neck and arms. She grabbed at the earth and grass but knew that it wasn't going to help her.

'You're a weirdo, Molly! You always have been! The whole school thinks so too, it's not just me.'

Molly looked up at her, confused and terrified in equal measure, and she could feel the tears building again.

'You don't belong here, around normal human beings, around people like Teddy!' Delilah had her pinned to the ground with her knees and slapped her hard across the cheek. 'And I'm going to make sure that you never show you're disfigured face around here ... ever ... AGAIN!'

Molly looked back over her shoulder and saw a small, fist-sized rock, just out of reach. She looked up at Teddy and pleaded, mouthing to him: *'You promised'*. He looked back at her but the fear and shame was etched in every line of his disillusioned face. He looked at the rock, realised what

Molly was about to do, shook his head with a dreadful knowing and then kicked it reluctantly towards her.

Molly grabbed it, hollered a bloodthirsty scream, swung her arm in a wide arc and connected the rock hard with Delilah's forehead.

Delilah stopped her onslaught instantly and looked down at her as if puzzled. She stood up gingerly, lifted a hand to her cracked and battered skull and gazed in horror at the blood and gore on her fingers and palm. Blood ran from the laceration in rivulets, trickling down her furrowed brow, into her eyes, down the long bridge of her nose and into her open mouth. She spat it out.

Molly stood, brushed herself down and laughed at her. 'I hope that fucking hurts you … you *slut*!'

Delilah smiled through the torrent of blood, red goo on her teeth and lips, and held her arms outstretched. 'I don't think we're finished here yet, are we?'

Molly looked back at Teddy who was shaking his head. 'No Molly. That's enough.'

She could feel her pulse beating in her temple; murderous rage coursed through her veins, the smell of human fear in her nostrils and the taste of death on her tongue. She wasn't done yet.

Molly launched herself forward with all the strength that her small frame would allow and shoved the startled Delilah hard in her naked chest. Delilah uttered a loud guttural cry, stumbled backwards, tripped on the uneven ground, hit the low, stone wall and tumbled into the open mouth of the well. Her head hit the rough limestone on the opposite side with a loud crunch – the surprise still evident in her eyes as she looked imploringly back at Molly – and her body folded in two as gravity took a hold of her and sucked her downwards into the well's cold, dark embrace.

Molly stopped, leaned over and peered into the darkness of the well. There was nothing. No sign of Delilah. No sound, no fear, no anger. Just peace.

She took in a large gulp of air and glanced over at Teddy. He was on his knees, his face a mash of revulsion and regret.

She laughed.

Chapter 32:
The Newborn

Raven's mate Jonjo came through and the ducting turned up a day early. We spent all that weekend in an empty warehouse out by the docks building a mock-up of the Greenbaum's air conditioning system and, even if I say so myself, we did a pretty good job. It wasn't quite as big, we just didn't have the head room to emulate the descent from the rooftop to the basement, but we managed to fit in all the difficult to navigate sections for young Wesley to squeeze himself through.

All of us were there, with the exception of Raven who was allegedly working a case. Most probably a case of scotch, I remember thinking at the time. Me, Del, Ronny and Wes stood back and looked up at our construction, bolted on the side of a scaffolding tower like an upmarket rubbish chute, and smiled in satisfaction. We were all nursing hot drinks and chowing on scones that Dynamite Del had brought along. His wife really is an excellent baker.

'Good job, well done, lads!' Ronny was as buoyant as ever. 'A bit of hard work and sweat and look what we've achieved. John D. Rockefeller himself would've been proud.' I took a large mouthful of scone filled with strawberry jam and clotted cream and grinned, the sticky, sweet jam trickling down my chin and onto my Kings of Leon T shirt. 'Now all we've got to do is push little old Wesley here in one end and,' he chuckled, 'hope to god he pops out of the other.'

Wesley smiled. 'Not a problem. I've done a lot of pot holing in my time, my cousin used to take me as a kid to a site in Somerset, and I've gotten through far smaller tunnels than that.'

Ronny turned and slapped him on the back, almost dislodging the coffee cup from his hand. 'Excellent! Sounds great. But as I always say, a job well rehearsed is a job well done. Del!' Del was perched on a can of spent bitumen and wiping the cream from his twirly moustache and tiny goatee. He looked up. 'Get the lube!'

Ronny had decided, as a precaution, that the safest way to get Wesley from point A to point B without any risk of blockage and therefore a failed operation, was to grease him up with petroleum jelly. Dynamite Del, being the collector of all exotic, highly flammable and dangerously explosive chemicals that he was, had managed to get hold of a gallon drum of the stuff.

Wesley stripped down to a pair of tight swim shorts and a vest and we set to work on smothering him in the slippery and highly pungent grease, ensuring that every inch of his vertically challenged frame was completely covered, allowing Wesley himself to wipe jelly over the parts that gentlemen like ourselves would be too polite to touch. Ronny, not being bashful in the slightest, cupped a hold of Wesley's nuts and hollered, 'yep, they're good and doused!'

I'll never forget the sight of seeing Wesley standing at the top of that scaffolding tower in just his shorts and vest and wearing a pair of swim goggles to prevent the grease from running into his eyes. He looked like the world's worst ski jumper.

'You ready?' Ronny was standing at the bottom of the makeshift flume and waving.

Wesley cupped two hands to his mouth and called down in a mock RAF pilot's accent. 'Chops away, chaps! Don't worry yourselves, I'll be back on terra firma in a jiffy!' And with that he vanished into the open mouth of the steel tubing.

It's an odd feeling, seeing someone disappear into a rat run like that. Anti-climactic. We all just stood there in silence, hoping and praying that the poor bloke wasn't going to get jammed in one of the right angle sections and go into some sort of panic attack, potentially folding himself into a position where oxygen couldn't get to his lungs and dying of asphyxiation before we could cut him loose. Del, for his part, was standing armed with an angle grinder and a ladder like some sort of slightly deranged fireman.

There was a lot of clanging and knocking and a couple of times I wondered whether Wes was smashing his hands on the side of a section of ducting to signal that he needed rescuing. Ronny, calm as ever, just stood with his hands on his hips, glaring at the end of the chute like an expectant father.

It felt like an age. With each passing minute, I could feel my heart pounding louder and faster. What if the scaffolding wasn't secured well enough and the weight of the ducting, along with the movement of Wesley himself, toppled it over like a collapsed leaning tower of Pisa? What if we hadn't joined the sections adequately and the lower half just came away, leaving Wesley's legs dangling out of the open mouth of the remaining half like the exposed limbs of a man-sized funnel spider? There were so many things that could go wrong and only one thing that could go right.

And shortly thereafter it did.

With a slurp and a clang and a little shout of triumph the diminutive form of little Wesley Pollock slid out of the steel tubing like a newborn.

'And that's how it's done.'

Ron grabbed him by his arm, hauled him to his feet – which took some doing given he was as slippery as a kipper – and the four of us hugged and jumped up and down as if we had just won the world cup.

I can honestly say that was the happiest moment I had – that I'm sure we all had – during the whole, long gestation of that caper. The joy of a successful trial run, the relief of there being no injuries or any other disaster for that matter, the happy camaraderie that the four of us shared at our collective achievement. It seemed to make it all … worthwhile.

From that point onwards things started to take a turn for the worse.

Chapter 33:
Terry

Randall was at a loss. The whole episode at Applewood House had left him bewildered and once again at a dead end. He had been sure they were onto something. The science pointed them squarely at that location and at that individual but, unless Miss Hanscombe had an accomplice who carried her along the beach in some sort of makeshift, adult bearing papoose, there was just no way that she could be linked with any of the disappearances. No judge in the land would accept a single hair bearing the DNA of a cripple as evidence that the same cripple could have possibly killed or maimed multiple victims. And, furthermore, Doctor Weir's decision to leave it until the last minute to reveal Lorna's disability, along with the smug look on her face as they left the facility with their tails between their legs, made his blood boil.

All of which left him with the question of how that hair had got there, and who on earth had been in contact with both Lorna Hanscombe and their victim, Simon Farrington, a.k.a. swim shorts man? It was something to follow up on at least, even if it wasn't the slam dunk he had been hoping for.

Which led him to his next appointment. Luke Raven.

Deveraux had called him and suggested he meet up with his beleaguered predecessor – something about dreams or premonitions and Raven being convinced that he had information that could be important to his case. Deveraux thought it was all a ruse to get back into her good books and Randall had to agree. It wasn't that he didn't believe in the supernatural – his mother would often have friends over to read their tarot cards or talk about their future as derived by their star signs, and he himself had seen the ghost of what he was sure was his deceased grandfather when he was quite young – but linking nightmares to murder victims and purported evidence was quite the stretch. It beat accusing a women with no legs of murder, hands down.

He parked his car in Marine Parade and descended the shallow steps to the boardwalk. To his right was the fairground, the arcades and various amusements, cafeterias, gift shops and bars, all bustling with holiday makers purchasing tokens to spend on the rides – the big wheel, rollercoaster, log flume, ghost train and the like – or spending their loose change on two penny machines, one armed bandits or buying long sticks holding large swathes of pink sugar candy floss. The air was filled with the scent of pop-corn, sizzling onions and cockles smothered in vinegar. Even though it was only two thirty in the afternoon Randall spotted at least a dozen young men and women already sozzled, sun burnt and ready to call it a day. The beach, he mused, and more importantly the hot weather, turned ordinary, normally semi-civilised human beings into something close to the Neanderthals that they had evolved from. He unfastened the top button of his shirt, loosened his tie and stepped onto the sand.

Raven was halfway between the boardwalk and the sea and perched on the edge of a deckchair, arguing with an attendant.

Randall approached Raven who winked at him impishly as the attendant walked off, huffing angrily.

'If he thinks he's getting a fiver from me for this sad excuse for a deck chair, he's got another thing coming,' Raven muttered.

Randall stopped and caught his breath. 'What did you say to get him to leave?'

'I told him I was with the inland-revenue and we were investigating beach trader fraud on the Hampshire coastline. I told him you were my boss.'

Randall sighed. 'Shit, you can't go round impersonating government officials.'

Raven stood. 'Well, firstly, you are a government official and secondly, I'm still currently part of the local constabulary.' He eyed Randall cautiously. 'Well, for the time being at least. So,' he shrugged, 'at worst what I told him was a little white lie.'

Randall sighed and removed his jacket. He could feel sweat patches forming under his arms and a slick sheen coating the dark, bare skin of his forehead. 'Whatever. I really don't have the energy to argue.'

'Good. Me neither. Did Deveraux fill you in?'

'Yeah, she told me about some sort of dream or foresight or something.' Randall glanced at the holiday makers surrounding them and decided to lower his voice to a respectably discreet level. 'Sounds a bit odd to me.'

'Well, say what you like, I've had these premonitions before and ignored them.' Raven shoved his hands deep in his pockets as if being scolded. 'I won't be making that same mistake again.'

Randall withdrew his notepad and a pen from the pocket of his discarded jacket. 'Okay, well, tell me about them.'

'I think I can do better than that.' Raven waved at the deckchair attendant who was still seething and glaring at him with the look of a man who's convinced he's been conned. 'I can show you.' He gestured to Randall. 'Follow me.'

Raven headed east along the shoreline, away from the crowds and the congestion surrounding the shops and bars. Randall watched him for a few moments unmoving before deciding that his best option was to go after him.

They trudged with heavy feet past the low dunes to the end of the board walk – at this point Raven removed his shoes and socks – strolled underneath the yellow flag that signalled the end of the family section of the beach and exited out onto the long, open stretch that allowed dog-walkers and their many varieties of canine. Eventually they came to the point where the seafront road climbed away from the town and up into the emerging cliffs, elevating higher and higher until it was some hundred or so feet above them. The dunes to their left became huge, rolling hills of golden sand speckled with bracken and couch grass, the dry earth riddled with large splits and cracks. The route downwards was scarred with a maze of rustic footpaths that had been etched into the land by beach goers that had abandoned their cars in the free spaces along the elevated tarmac.

'Where are you taking me?' Randall was tired and he had the distinct feeling that this was a waste of his time.

'You'll see.'

'All I can see is a beach – a beach that we've been to a

thousand times before and had officers crawling over for evidence. This isn't anything new.'

'We're not there yet.' Raven continued to head east with Randall four or five steps in his wake.

'What are you trying to achieve with this little charade of yours?' Randall wiped the salty sweat from his eyes. He was hot and sticky, he had sand in his shoes and he was more than a little annoyed. 'I mean, what is it with you? You want your old job back? You want *my* job?'

Raven raised his eyebrows. 'You think that's what this is about? *Your job?* You know how degraded I felt even picking the phone up to Deveraux about this? Do you have the faintest idea of how humiliating it is to suggest that you have some kind of clairvoyant – if that's what this is – ability?' He shook his head. 'Even hearing myself say the words makes me feel ashamed.'

Randall snorted. 'Oh come on, Raven, you and I both know this is some bullshit scheme that you've dreamt up to get back in the Chief's good books.' He laughed. 'You've got someone on the inside ... Ruby, Wodge? Don't tell me it's Crusher? Someone loyal to you that's feeding you the inside track on this case?'

Raven sighed. 'Look, Randall. I like you. I do. I couldn't have picked a better replacement for ... well, for me. You're organised, you're thorough and, above all, you're sharp.' Raven smiled. 'And sharp people like you don't throw away leads, no matter how obscure or how bizarre the source.' He tilted his head. 'I'm guessing so far you've come up short of a home run on this one.'

Randall looked out at the rolling tide and nodded reluctantly. 'It seems that every sniff we get at what's going on here, the path ultimately leads to a cul-de-sac.'

Raven smiled empathetically. 'Then do yourself a favour and follow this old drunk has-been along this beach and see what's at the end of the rainbow.' He placed a hand on Randall's shoulder. 'You just might get a nice surprise.'

Randall pushed away his hand. 'Why do I feel you know more than you're letting on?'

Raven laughed. 'Let's see shall we.'

They trudged through the dry sand and bracken for more than half a mile more, the cliffs rising higher on their left and the tide rolling in to their right. The sun was high in the sky, just starting to dip to the west, and their company on the beach started to drop to no more than the odd jogger, enthusiastic dog walker and a couple of opportunistic metal detectorists. The dunes themselves ranged from the small – six to seven feet in height – to the downright enormous.

After twenty minutes or so Raven stopped dead in his tracks.

'This is it.'

He looked up towards the top of the cliff, some two hundred and fifty feet above them, and pointed out a tree. It was completely barren as if it had been struck by lightning and scorched until the leaves had burned, the bark had turned to ash and the sap had run dry.

'That's where it sits.'

Randall followed the direction of Raven's arm. 'Where what sits?'

Raven looked back at him as if it was obvious. 'The Hawk.' He turned back to the tree. 'A Harris Hawk, I think. I looked it up.'

The DI took a mental note to check back with the bar staff

at the Swan and find out when Raven last made an appearance there.

Raven gestured to the shoreline. 'The kid stands there.'

'The kid?'

'Yes, the little boy. No more than seven or eight. Devious little shit.'

Randall gasped. 'A little boy? And you didn't think to mention this sooner?' He shook his head in disbelief. 'Could he be in danger?'

Raven didn't hear him. He was climbing the dunes in his bare feet and grabbing onto the grass and bracken for purchase. Randall hastily bent down and untied his laces, tossing his shoes to one side as he haphazardly followed him.

'Raven, I need some more details about this kid. He's not on our list of disappearances and I'll need to follow up on …'

Raven stood at the top of the small rise and looked down at an area just in front of him. 'This is where I sank.'

Randall was slipping and sliding on the sand like a novice ice skater, almost lying face down on the incline to pull himself up to Raven's vantage point. He spat sand from his mouth and pulled thorny bracken from his shirt.

'Where you what?'

Raven pointed towards the spot near his feet. There was a sink hole in the dune. The dry shrubs either side of the hole had been pulled up by the roots and were lying scattered on the ground around the odd-shaped depression.

'This is where I climbed out.'

Randall shook his head. 'In your dream?'

Raven nodded.

'But how can …?'

223

Raven shrugged his shoulders. 'I don't know.'

Randall laughed. 'Are you having me on?'

Raven ignored the question and turned suddenly, climbing hastily up the next incline. Randall swore under his breath. 'You've got to be kidding me.'

'If I'm right, you won't regret this.' Raven was scrambling fast up the dune, kicking sand and grass out from behind him which slid down the slope towards the pursuing DI.

'I sure hope not. This is getting weird in the extreme.'

Raven reached the top of the next dune, went over the ridge and out of sight and then hollered. 'I fucking knew it!'

Randall quickened his pace. He still didn't believe a word of what Raven was insinuating but he was so far into the ruse he was desperate to see how it ended.

After a moment he reached the top of the hill and spotted Raven in a shallow dip around thirty feet to the south. Raven was staring at an old footpath sign that pointed along the shore and then towards the cliff where a series of concrete steps had long since perished under the constant battering of the inrushing and unyielding ocean. There was something large hanging from the sign.

'What's that?'

Raven looked back and beckoned him. 'Come and take a look.' He grimaced. 'But you might want to hold your nose.'

Randall slid down the side of the dune, righted himself and then strolled casually across the sand to Raven who was turning his own nose up.

Hanging from the twisted and rust riddled sign was a medium sized, long since deceased animal. Its fur had been split down its stern and its innards had been removed, the remaining pocket of flesh riddled with black goo and maggots. The maggots had crawled out of the cavity and were now feeding on the dead beast's eyes and tongue, its rotting carcass deteriorating fast under the glare of the hot sun and the feasting insects. The air was thick with the scent of rotting meat and the incessant buzzing of flies nursing their feeding young. The smell reminded Randall of the time his parents' freezer had packed up and the chicken and pork chops inside had started to fester. He would never forget the scent that had hit him like a hard slap across the face when he opened the faltering appliance door. It had made him want to instantly throw up. He turned and placed a hand to his mouth. It wasn't just the odour. He just didn't know what to believe. If it was a hoax it was an elaborate one to say the least.

'I told you, Randall. I told you! This is exactly what happened in my dream …'

Raven's voice and the constant buzzing faded into the background as the young DI considered what had just happened. He thought of Felix the Indestructible with his limited teeth and his half chewed whelk and, despite what he thought of Luke Raven's bullshit story, he was willing to lay a very large wager that what they were looking at was the decaying corpse of the recently missing Mystic Mags' unfortunate mutt, Terry.

225

Chapter 34:
The Curator

Christy Deveraux sat on her balcony, overlooking the top of the high cliffs and the sea below, and sipped on her large glass of Malbec. She enjoyed the sweet, nutty aroma and the smooth taste of the delicate red wine. She had had a long day and she just needed to take the edge off. Luke Raven was getting closer to the truth and she needed to stay two steps ahead of him. The discovery on the seafront was just the beginning. Their little adventure was starting to get more than a little exciting and she planned to direct the route ahead in a way that a conductor might direct an orchestra, every note in tune, every beat in glorious syncopated rhythm.

There was a light breeze that felt good as it cooled the skin on her angular but not unattractive face and ruffled her platinum hair. She had removed her jacket when she entered her apartment and was now reclining in navy blue trousers, light blue blouse and bare feet. She had made her play with Raven; he had taken the bait all too easily and now she needed to wait and see where he went with it. The important part was that she was manoeuvring him, not the other way around.

Her cell phone rang on the coffee table beside her. She checked the number and smiled.

'Hi.'

'Was this you?'

Christy nodded. 'Yes it was.'

The man at the end of the phone sighed. 'I hope you know what you're doing.'

'It was the smart move to make.'

'You've brought him closer to us.'

She casually played with the sharp object in her pocket. 'It's better this way. I can keep him close but at a distance.' She could feel the anticipation coursing through her veins. 'This way he remains … malleable.'

The man at the end of the phone chuckled. 'I know you enjoy the thrill of the game, but be careful. This is not a gamble you can afford to lose.'

She felt the cool breeze on her arms and neck and yet beads of sweat were forming on her upper lip. 'I never lose. You know that.'

There was a grunt. 'Don't underestimate him. We've been here before and it hasn't ended well.'

Christy withdrew the hairpin from her pocket and held it up to her eyes. 'I won't.' She ran its tip along the inside of her forearm. 'You have me on the job now. I'm not like the last buffoon you had in this position, and … well, you know what I mean.'

'Arrogance is a weakness. Just get the job done without….a mess.'

She rolled back the sleeve of her blouse and traced the tip of the hairpin along the inside of her elbow. She smiled as she stroked a finger across the scar tissue there, remembering the many moments she had enjoyed drawing deep, burning sensations from the empty vessel of her body. 'You can count on it.' She necked the last of her wine and wiped a trickle of red from the corner of her mouth.

'Christy.'

'Yes.'

'There's been another ... development.'

She let out a long breath and leaned back in her chair, running a hand through her hair and closing her eyes as she felt the wine coursing through her veins and her stress levels dissipating. 'A development?'

'Yes. The Curator.'

Christy frowned, puzzled and leaned forward. The Curator? That rank hadn't existed for five years or more. 'I don't know what you mean.'

'He's returned.'

Christy shook her head. 'That can't be. Are you ... are you sure?' The last Curator had been cast out for his calculated treachery many years ago and had then been ... taken care of. She stroked the tip of her chin as she remembered the details.

'He has been seen.'

'Your source must be mistaken.'

'There's no mistake. We have been following him.'

Christy smiled. This was a development she could get behind. 'You want him ... resolved?'

'We want him alive.'

She slipped the tip of her hairpin under the layer of skin on the inside of her upper arm and felt the sweet pain emanate along her bicep, across her shoulder and up the side of her long neck. Her eyelids fluttered. 'Give me the details

228

and I'll make it happen.'

'Christy … together they will be a problem.'

She shook her head. 'Together is exactly where we want them.' She grinned and drew the pin across a two inch length of skin, slicing the top layer in two and drawing a thin trail of warm, pulsating blood that ran down her arm and into the pool of her elbow. She stifled a groan of taboo pleasure as little shards of electricity danced at her nerve endings and rippled in the taught muscles of her arms and abdomen. She felt an exaltation and exhilaration like no other. 'Two birds.' She smiled. 'One stone.'

Chapter 35:
Forever

Teddy had been different since that night. He was agitated, furtive, cold and constantly checking his phone. Molly didn't know what to say to him. It wasn't as if she had meant to kill Delilah but, she had to admit, the way it had panned out was satisfying.

There had been police of course. Lots of them. And it hadn't taken them long to find Delilah's twisted and broken body at the bottom of the well, her skull caved in, her spine severed and her bones shattered. Molly wondered how she smelled when they had found her. She had been there for three days after all. Festering. She often imagined the scent, particularly at night while Teddy lay on the opposite side of the bed, awake but pretending to be asleep as if any kind of physical contact between them would be considered vulgar.

They had been questioned too, especially Teddy who had been seen dancing with her all night. He was their main suspect for a few weeks after the discovery but, clearly, there was not a shred of evidence linking him to what eventually had to be considered a tragic, drunken and drug induced accident. Not that her parents saw it that way and who could blame them. Their little princess had been taken from them in a way that was completely out of keeping with her character, but what could they do? Molly learned a lot from the whole experience. She had even made notes.

Once the whole media circus had calmed down Molly turned her attention to fixing her relationship and she only had one, brilliant idea in mind.

'I'm going away for a couple of days, Teddy. Will you be okay here on your own?'

Teddy was sitting at the desk and pretending to study. 'Huh?'

'Away ... for a couple of days.' Molly had gained her driving license in the spring and her father had even sent her a car as a congratulatory gift – a little white 1.2 litre Vauxhall Corsa. She hated the colour but the car itself was perfect. 'Are you going to be able to survive without me?'

Teddy turned and faced her. 'You want me to come with you?'

Molly shook her head and smiled. 'No. I won't be long. Just a ... family thing.'

Teddy shrugged and returned to his books. His face was still ashen, bags were visible under his dark eyes and she knew he wasn't sleeping. She felt sorry for him but she also couldn't understand why he was taking it so hard. The bitch was dead. So what? At least she was out of their hair forever. 'Okay. Drive carefully and keep an eye out. There are some maniacs on the roads.'

She chuckled. The irony wasn't lost on her.

The trip actually took almost three days. The journey was a lot further than she had expected and the traffic was horrendous, but she quite liked the time away. It gave her time to think. Think about her life, her schooling, Teddy, her father and Gretchen, her dogs, the shooting accident that had left her scarred forever and about … her mother. It was as if all those things that she had buried deep down in the furthest recesses of her mind came to the surface in one jumbled heap of forgotten trinkets and the time away helped her to separate and itemise them. It gave her the space to tidy her thoughts and organise her emotions. It was satisfying.

And the whole thing went entirely according to plan. Without a single hitch. She couldn't wait to tell Teddy the good news. Only, when she got back to her room – dragging her small case up the stairs, bursting through the door and tumbling onto her bed, exhausted – he wasn't there. And neither were his things.

'What the fuck?'

She jumped up and ran to the bathroom. She rifled through the cabinet that was attached to the wall to the left of the basin and was relieved to see Teddy's purple toothbrush, deodorant and acne pills in his usual spot on the top shelf.

She crossed the hallway and banged on his door loudly.

'Teddy, you in there?'

She banged again, impatiently.

'Teddy! It's me, Molly. I'm home!' She could hear the desperation in her own voice and it upset her. She was angry but also afraid.

After a moment the handle turned and the door opened a crack. She saw Teddy's eye and the left hand side of his face.

'Molly, it's late. I'm sleeping.'

She shoved the door open hard, knocking him backwards towards his small desk.

'So what? Didn't you miss me?'

'Of course. I …' Teddy was standing there in just his boxer shorts, his body pale from lack of time outdoors and his shoulders slumped, his arms hanging limply.

'Where are your things? Why did you move them out of my room?' Molly was agitated and she could feel her blood rushing to the surface of her skin.

Teddy sat on the edge of his bed and put his face in his hands.

'Molly, we have to talk. I … I can't do this anymore.'

Molly shook her head. 'What do you mean you can't -'

'We killed her. *You* killed her.' He dug his fingers into his cheeks. He looked grey, exhausted.

Molly kicked the door shut with her heel and sat down on his stool facing him. 'So what?'

His mouth dropped. 'What do you mean so what? It's murder for god's sake!'

She urged him to keep his voice down. 'You're upset. I get it. Me too. I didn't mean for it to happen and neither did you, but it did so there's that.' She went to hold his hand in hers but he withdrew it from her. She bit down on her lip. 'We need to move on.'

'I can't. I've tried, *really hard*, but I just can't.' He ran a hand through his dark hair. 'I'm not sleeping, I'm not eating. I just can't get her face out of my head, the shock in her eyes.' He shook his head. 'And the fear.'

'You know she was going to kill me, don't you?'

'Prime suspect. That's what they called me. Prime bloody suspect!' He plunged his face into his hands again. 'I could have ended up in prison for life!'

She moved to the bed and sat next to him. 'But you didn't,

233

Teddy. You *didn't*.' She grabbed both of his hands within hers. Her fingers looked tiny next to his. 'We got away with it.' She smiled. 'We got away with murder.'

He looked at her. 'But Molly, I …'

'Do you love me, Teddy?'

He stopped and took a deep breath. 'Yes.' He couldn't meet her gaze but whispered a soft, 'I do.'

'And I love you. We were meant to be together. Me with a father that hit me.' She ran a finger down her scar to embellish the lie. 'And you with your abusive …' she raised her head and peered up into his eyes, '*mother*.'

He jumped as if startled. 'What do you mean …?'

Molly stood up. 'Oh come on. It was obvious. From the moment you told me I knew it wasn't your dad that hit you.' She paced the room. 'The way that you jolt every time we have a play fight, the way that you do everything I ask without arguing or remonstrating.' She picked up his wallet and opened it. 'And this photo of your family with your mother's face faded and smeared as if someone has tried to erase it.'

'You've got me all figured out haven't you, *Molly*.' He hissed her name through gritted teeth.

'I looked it up. I found police records of phone calls from your house. Calls from your father requesting assistance because he was being attacked by your mother. No arrests of course, these things weren't taken as seriously back then, a man being attacked by his wife. How could that be assault? Surely the man could defend himself?'

Teddy played with his hair and started to make a low humming noise.

'But they didn't know, did they? How bad she could get.

234

How vicious, how *nasty*.' She started to pace. 'How downright *evil* that woman could be. And all because of … what? Disappointment? Regret? She hated your father and because of that she also hated you.'

He nodded and his humming grew louder, now rising and falling like the swelling tide.

'*You*, because you look so much like him don't you.' She picked up his wallet again and withdrew the bent and tattered photograph, holding it up to the light as she pointed at it. 'A spitting image I would say, the two of you. Two peas in a pod.' She shook her head and chuckled. 'I bet she couldn't *stand* to look at the two of you together, a double shot reminder of how shitty her life was. In fact, I bet the only one in that house that didn't feel the effects of her violent rage was your brother, Thomas.' Teddy shuddered at his name. 'Because he doesn't look like you at all. Or your father. He barely even looks like your mother. Blonde hair, slight build, pale skin, tall lanky frame.' She showed Teddy the picture but he looked away. 'He wasn't even your father's, was he? A product of your mother's infidelity and a trophy for her. A precious monument of how she could punish you both for being who you are. But it's okay, Teddy.' She sat down on the stool in front of him and grabbed his hands. 'It's okay.' She nodded. 'I took care of it.'

He looked up, tears still running down his cheeks. 'You what?'

She smiled a warm, knowing smile and nodded again. 'I took care of it. For you.'

'Took care of what?' His sobbing had abated and his breathing had slowed.

'Of her.'

'Of her … how?

She reached into her rucksack and pulled out a long red jewellery box. She carefully handed it to him. 'You'll see.'

'I … what is this?'

She grinned. 'Open it. It's for you. For everything you've ever been through at the hands of that awful woman.'

He wiped the back of his hand across his running nose, gripped the lid between his finger and thumb and pulled it upwards. There nestled in blue tissue paper was a finger, topped with a long, pink fingernail and adorned with two gold rings, one with a green emerald at its centre. The tissue at the knuckle was dark red with dried, flaking blood.

Teddy dropped it like it was scalding hot and pushed himself back across his bed to the wall by the window.

'What the fuck!'

'Don't worry. She didn't suffer. I gave her that much respect, not that she deserved it.'

'You … you killed her?'

Molly was smiling but the edges of her mouth faltered with sudden uncertainty. 'For *you*.'

He pointed at her. 'Don't say that. You keep saying that!' He pulled his knees up to his chest. 'Don't fucking say that!'

Molly reached out to him but he recoiled. 'But she hurt you! She deserved this!'

'Murder! Murder is not a rational way to deal with … issues!'

'Don't you get it?' She held her arms out. 'Now you can be free from all of it. All of the fear and anxiety and worry for your father.' She pointed at the severed finger which had spilled from the box and was now lying on the bed like a discarded cigarette. 'She can't hurt either of you anymore.'

236

She was crying now and she didn't know why. 'It's over!'

Teddy was looking down at the bed and shaking his head. He paused, nodded and spoke in a low whisper. 'It sure is.'

She smiled and wiped tears from her cheeks. 'That's right. It's finished.'

A whisper again. 'Forever.'

She nodded vigorously. 'Forever.' She loved him so much. She wanted to hold him in her arms and comfort him, lie on the bed and lay in a tender embrace until the sun came out and a new day bathed them both in its promise of glorious possibilities. 'Like our love, Teddy. It *will* last forever.'

Teddy stood and opened the window. 'Not in this world, Molly.'

With that he stepped over the ledge and dropped out of sight. Molly heard the thud and crunch as he hit the concrete three storeys below.

She screamed.

Chapter 36:
Buried Revelations

'Is it him? Is it who we thought?'

'I can't confirm that right now, Chelsea. Let's just say the information is ... well it's promising.'

He could hear a sigh of exasperation down the line. 'This is all taking way too long, Luke. Jane could be ... I don't even want to even think what might be happening to her right now.'

'I understand but this moves us further forward at least. As I said, my resources are limited and if you choose to go to the police instead I won't ...'

'And as I told you: *fuck* the police.' She rarely swore and when she did it served to truly emphasise her agitation. 'I don't trust them. I don't believe what they say and I won't allow the most important person in my life to be placed in their incompetent hands.' He could hear her stifle a tear.

'Well ... we're doing our best.' He too was deeply concerned about Jane. It had been way too long with no contact from anyone. No ransom demand, no gruesome note in the post, no phone call. Nothing. 'Wesley and I are following up every possible avenue of investigation. If she can be found she will be. I can tell you that for sure. I just can't …' he grimaced, 'I can't promise a happy outcome. Not yet. Not until we know more.'

She grunted. 'Just do the job I'm paying you to do. And fast.'

The call ended and Raven stood on the corner of Hutchinson Street with a silent cell phone attached to his ear. He shook his head, put the phone in his pocket and again wondered what the hell he was doing.

Lisa had called that morning. She'd sounded upbeat and full of energy. He hadn't heard her speak to him like that since … well, since before. He'd shaken himself out of his slumber – his sleep had been fitful at best, his dreams riddled with the carcasses of dead dogs, human remains and faceless women in rusty shackles – and had sat at the table of his kitchenette, eating a giant bowl of Cheerios, drinking strong, home-made coffee and wondering what in god's name had just happened.

She had asked him out on a date. Just the two of them. Alone.

Of course, as a detective, trained to analyse every fact, every conversation and every scenario, he figured that something was amiss. There was a detail he wasn't seeing. Why would his ex, with all the anger and frustration between them, with the shadow of her current boyfriend looming over them like some disfigured incredible hulk, and with the added complication of their young son and the five hundred or so pounds of child support he still owed them, suddenly decide that all of that was in the past and that they both deserved a second chance?

It just didn't add up, not by a long shot, but he found

himself going along with it anyway. Out of intrigue certainly, but with more than a hint of hope too. A hope of reconciliation. He would pay anything, *do anything*, for that.

The sky was a beautiful crimson and blue, the sun just starting to disappear to the west, and the air was just beginning to cool. The humidity had been high all day and Raven had been careful to apply an extra layer of anti-perspirant under his arms. The last thing he wanted was to be sitting in a hot restaurant trying his best to woo back the only female who he had ever come remotely close to saying that terrifying word 'love' to, with giant sweat patches tarnishing his dark, checked shirt.

He rounded the corner of Admiral's Hill and saw Lisa standing outside of the restaurant. Her red hair looked terrific in the early evening light and her body looked stunning in a figure hugging black dress that ended just above the knee.

'Hi.'

'Hi Luke.' She looked a little nervous.

'You been here long?'

'No. I just came out for a cigarette. I'm still trying to give them up. *Again*.' They both laughed. 'I've let them know we're here.' She eyed him up and down. 'You look … smart.' She smiled.

He brushed a hand down his shirt. 'Oh, you know. I thought I'd make the effort.'

'Thanks for coming.' She put a hand on his arm and a warmth spread through his body like hot butter. It felt good.

'I wouldn't miss it for the world. You know that.'

There was a moment of beautiful, unspoken communication between them. 'Shall we go in? I'm starting to get cold.' She shuffled on the spot, her black heels tapping on the concrete.

'Why the hell not.' He smiled, held out his arm and she took it. They walked into the restaurant as if they were an old married couple out on an anniversary dinner. He liked that. He could get with that program, no problem.

Dean's Bistro was a small place built into the shell of an old, long since abandoned church. Consequently it was deep and narrow and the ceilings were incredibly high. It gave the place a cavernous feel with a reverb that bounced off every block of stone and ornate architrave. Raven liked it. He thought it was different from all the other run of the mill restaurants that dotted themselves along every main road, side street and alleyway. It seemed nowadays that if you owned a building in a coastal town, just stick a café or artisan coffee shop in it and Bob's your uncle.

The waitress, a pretty black girl who said her name was Sheena, showed them to their table at the back of the half-full room.

Sheena placed their cutlery on the table and straightened their napkins. 'Special occasion?'

Raven waited for Lisa to answer. 'Oh, we're not together like that. We're just friends.'

He felt his heart sink.

'Oh, well how nice.' Sheena stood back and looked at them both. 'Well, if you don't mind me saying, you would make a beautiful couple.'

Raven felt himself blush and he glanced at Lisa who was smiling coyly. 'Well, you never know.' He chuckled. 'By the end of the night we could be engaged.'

Sheena laughed. 'That would make my evening. Now,' she withdrew a notepad and pen from her apron, 'can I get you some drinks?' She turned to Lisa. 'For the lady?'

'I'll take a red wine please. Large.' Lisa turned to Raven and he could feel the heat of her gaze.

'Sure, and for the gentleman?'

Raven looked at the bar and could see the full range of optics – whiskey, rum, brandy, gin and vodka – and knew he could take his pick. 'I'll just have a diet coke,' he glanced furtively at Lisa who was pretending not to notice. 'With ice.'

'Sure thing.' Sheena handed them two, large leather bound menus. 'When I come back with the drinks, I'll take your order.' She placed her pad back in her apron. 'I can recommend the duck with braised artichoke and dauphinoise potatoes. It's absolutely gorgeous. Or, if you want something spicy,' she leaned over and turned the page of Lisa's menu, 'the seafood marinara with tomatoes, garlic and chilli has a real kick.'

Raven looked up and smiled. 'That's great. Thanks. We'll be sure to bear that in mind.'

The waitress smiled warmly and left them to make their choice.

As soon as she left, Lisa leaned over the table and placed her hand on Raven's. Again his heart skipped a beat.

'I've got a confession to make.'

Raven sighed. 'I guessed as much.'

'You did?'

'Well, I knew there was more to this than meets the eye.' He peered over the table at her. 'There always is.'

Lisa sat up. 'And what's that supposed to mean?'

'You tell me.' Raven could feel the mood of the evening turning and they were only ten minutes in. It didn't surprise him. It was the way they were with each other. 'You're the one with the confession.'

Lisa crossed her arms and he could see the bright orange flames burning behind her eyes. 'Well if you're going to be like that.'

Raven smiled. 'I'm only kidding.'

'No, if you don't want to know you don't want to know.' She looked over his shoulder at the door. 'I couldn't care less one way or the other.'

Raven swore under his breath. She could be stubborn at the best of times. 'I didn't mean to offend you. I'm sorry.'

She glared back at him and then raised a hand to someone or something behind Raven in greeting. She turned back to him. 'Just try to act like a normal, rational human being won't you.'

Sheena returned with the drinks and began to set another place at the table next to Lisa. Raven looked up at the smiling waitress, puzzled.

'Someone's here, Luke. Someone you know.' Lisa leaned over and grabbed his hands in hers. 'Be nice.'

Raven's eyes narrowed. 'Why do I get the feeling I'm being ambushed.'

Lisa sipped her wine, looked over Raven's shoulders and nodded. 'Hello again.'

'Hello Lisa.' Raven turned to look at the source of the familiar voice. 'Hello Luke.'

Raven could feel bile rise in his throat and a burning sensation behind his eyes. He spoke through gritted teeth: '*Dad*.'

****

The meal was muted. Lisa tried her best to engender a happy, friendly discussion but no amount of fake cheeriness could mask the truth: that Sam had faked his own death and abandoned his son and wife. It wasn't just something that evaporated over a pan roasted duck and a glass of merlot. Or, in Raven's case, a glass of coke.

'So where you been?' Raven spat out the words as if they were stuck in his throat like shards of glass, 'why the secrecy, the lies. Why not come directly to me?'

'I needed to get away.' Sam Raven was in his early sixties – grey hair, grey beard and lines round his eyes that betrayed a troubled past.

'From what?' Raven was pushing the bloody remnants of his sirloin around his plate. He suddenly had no appetite. 'From me? From Mum? What did she do to deserve that?'

'I didn't mean to hurt her. Or you.'

Raven didn't lift his gaze from the table. 'Then why did you do it?'

'There were people.' Sam glanced around nervously at the busy restaurant. 'Bad people. People that wanted me to do things that I didn't want to do.'

Raven grunted. 'And because of that you ran.' He shook his head. 'Ran away from the family that had stood beside you through everything. All the shit that you had put us through.' He pointed his fork at his father. 'You screwed around behind her back, despite her devotion to you, and you were never there for me.'

'I know.'

'Everyone at school thought I was from a single parent family because you were never around.'

'I know.'

'Jesus, you didn't even come with us on family holidays!' Raven dug his fork into a remaining slab of meat. 'And then you left her.'

Sam shuffled uncomfortably in his seat. 'What can I say, Luke? I was … wooed by delusions of grandeur. I believed everything I was being told, all the guidance they gave me on how to be successful, I fell for it hook line and sinker.' He looked across at Lisa who was eyeing him sympathetically. 'I wanted to do what was right for my family but I ended up doing everything for me and me alone. If I could turn back the hands of time I would do it in an instant.'

Raven looked up at the bar and wished he could telekinetically pour himself a double bourbon. 'So why are you back?'

'Things have … changed.'

'You can say that again.'

Raven looked up at Lisa who stared back at him, urging him on. 'Your father told me that we could be in danger, Luke. That's why I arranged this meeting.'

Raven laughed. 'That's horse shit! That's what he does,' He glared at his father. 'He makes up some bullshit story and then expects you to play along with his little, self-serving game.' He finished his coke and felt a deep sense of empty dissatisfaction. 'My mother fell for the same trick all the time. She never learned.'

'That's not fair, son.'

Raven slammed his hand on the table so loud that the family sitting behind Lisa and his father looked up in unison. 'Fair? *Fair*? Are you kidding me?' He clenched his fist. 'I buried you!' He could feel tears welling in his eyes and his voice became a hoarse whisper. 'I fucking *buried* you.'

There was a long silence.

'I regret it. I've regretted it every day since and I'll regret it every day until the moment I leave this topsy-turvy world.' Sam reached across the table towards his son but Luke pulled away. 'But I won't let anything happen to you or my grandson. I'll do whatever it takes to make things right.'

'Lisa, I know you were hoping we could play happy families here but this was a very bad idea.' Raven stood and threw two fifty pound notes on the table. 'That should do it.' He turned to his father. 'Look, I think it's great you're alive. I really do. But you have to make things right with Mum before you even think about making things right with me.' He shuffled along the booth and out into the narrow walkway between the tables. 'It will take a lot of time and a lot of effort though. You might not think it's worth it.'

'Luke!' Sam grabbed his son's arm. Luke tried to shake it off but his father's grip was resolute. 'Sit down. I'm not kidding!'

Lisa went to stand.

'And you too Lisa. Sit!' Sam looked from Luke to Lisa and back again. 'Please!'

Raven's mouth opened and he went to speak. His father raised a hand.

'It's about an organisation known in private circles as The Legion. It's about a very dangerous man called the Cardinal.' Sam's eyes dropped to the table. 'And it's about a league of very powerful people that will do whatever it takes, including taking your son, to protect the sanctity of their precious establishment.'

Lisa looked across the table at Raven for re-assurance. Tears gleamed in the corners of her eyes.

'And if you think the police, or any other person of authority is going to protect you, then think again.'

Raven didn't know what to do or say. He was backfooted.

'This goes to the very core of what you believe. Of everything you've tried to protect, Luke. Of everyone you've ever worked for. Of every friend you thought you had.'

Raven looked up at the bartender. He was a young guy of maybe twenty-two, short black hair, an earring in his left ear. He was pouring a double shot of vodka and a slug of orange juice with ice. Raven could have crossed the fifteen feet or so between them in an instant, grabbed the glass and knocked it back like it was nothing. But he chose not to. He chose sanity and restraint. Not like the estranged pensioner sitting not two feet from him. The man who had acted like a child when the only child he had ever conceived had needed him - had needed his father's support, his father's advice, his father's love.

'This is all bullshit. Come on, Lis. We're getting out of here. Why don't you go back to whatever hole you crawled out of and continue doing whatever the hell it is that you've been doing for the last five years.'

Lisa stood up and grabbed his arm. She was visibly shaken. Together they exited the restaurant, leaving Sam Raven to nurse the remains of his meal and the last of his scotch on the rocks.

Across the restaurant a dark stranger eyed the older man with interest. He grabbed his mobile phone from the inside of his jacket and hit speed dial. They were going to want to know about this. A little more grey in his hair, a few more lines on his face and a new beard, but he could never forget the man that had vouched for him at his inaugural presentation to the Masters. He would have staked his reputation on it. It was the Curator alright.

Chapter 37:
Forbidden Needs

Molly returned home for her father's birthday. It was a big one – fifty – and in any case she couldn't concentrate on her schoolwork. She couldn't concentrate on anything at all, actually. Sure, she'd drafted a note from Teddy admitting that he had killed the poor, tragic Delilah and that he couldn't bear to look at himself in the mirror anymore and despite her grief, which was deep, unyielding and painful, she was proud of her handiwork. It turned out she could forge a pretty good letter when she put her mind to it, a talent that she thought could be valuable in the future.

Daddy's parties were always fun. She could fade into the background like plain wallpaper and watch all the other guests mingle and gently erupt in intellectual orgasms with their posh frocks, glittering jewellery, big cigars and over-inflated egos. It was like play time at the asylum.

And she wanted to see Gretchen again. Before she passed.

Her father was pleased to see her. 'Molly, my dear. You're home. How have you been? How was the journey?'

Molly looked around at the big house and she smiled. She'd had some happy times here. The place brought her a sense of comfort and peace that she hadn't experienced since leaving for Elderflower.

'Hello Father. I …' she looked up at the towering presence of her dad and she could feel her scar begin to throb and the right hand side of her face start to stiffen and ache. 'I've missed this place.'

'And I'm sure it's missed you too, my love. Did you bring your party dress? It's going to be quite the occasion.'

Her father glanced to his left at the group of young workers who were decorating the reception area and great hall respectively. Flowers streamed down the grand sweeping stairway, bright red and white bunches of roses and chrysanthemums, and large, ornamental lanterns in the guise of forest trees with brilliant white streamers tied around their many branches, giving them the illusion of being smothered in snow and ice, stood in a perfectly symmetrical pattern either side of them. Tables were erected and enclosed in crisp, white linen. There were more flowers scattered sporadically and there were dozens of crystal glasses placed meticulously in orderly rows of eight for the champagne reception. The floor had been polished and waxed and a large red carpet had been rolled out neatly from the foot of the first floor staircase to the bottom of the concrete steps that led down to the large driveway at the front of the house. White and red balloons were tied with ribbon and placed every ten feet or so and at the back of the great hall there was a small stage area where Molly suspected a jazz band might entertain the guests later that evening.

'I did. It's in my bag. Is … is Gretchen here?'

Molly's father was distracted. 'Toby … Toby! For god's sake, Toby will you listen?' A young man by the water fountain looked up, alarmed. 'The cake stand? Did you collect it from the larder?' Toby looked at Molly's father, perplexed. 'For the love of … Molly, dear. Would you mind? I'll see you later at the party. Don't be late now.'

And with that her father departed, leaving her standing there in the middle of the reception hall like a spare part.

She picked up her rucksack and trudged to the top of the stairs, taking care not to bash into the decorations that severely narrowed her passage. She reached the summit and looked down at the organised chaos below. She thought of Teddy and how we would have loved to see this – the extravagance, the expense and the vulgar display of wealth. He would have laughed until the tears flowed, his nose ran and his sides hurt, and she would have laughed with him. She didn't feel like laughing now.

She glanced to her right and Molly's Place beckoned her. She would go there shortly but she had someone else to visit first.

Gretchen's room was off the corridor that ran along the north wall, past Molly's Place and at the far end of the long hallway. It was the smallest room on the first floor but Molly liked it nonetheless. It was the room where Gretchen would show Molly some of her things. There were pictures of Gretchen's family in Bavaria – which Molly now knew was a region of southern Germany but in her younger years believed to be a magical land of princesses, dragons and castles – trinkets and jewels that Gretchen kept in a small, white wooden box and, best of all, a large, wooden clock in the shape of a Bavarian cottage, complete with a farmer and his wife who came out of their house on the hour when the clock chimed. Molly dearly wanted to hear that clock chime

251

once more.

She approached Gretchen's door, which was just ajar, and paused. She hadn't seen her childhood nanny since she had left for Elderflower Heights, and even then, there had appeared to be something amiss between them. They had been so close – Gretchen had been like a mother to her – but Molly knew that she had changed since puberty and Gretchen seemed to resent that. Or fear it.

Molly reached out her hand and pushed. The door swung open slowly revealing a cluttered dressing table, a thin, dusty wardrobe, a large hanging mirror that reflected Molly's own anxious image and a small, cream and white single bed. Within the thin and fraying bedsheets was the still and delicate frame of an old, frail woman in a white nightgown. She looked a little like Gretchen but faded like an old photograph. Molly's father had warned her that she was ill but she hadn't expected her to be quite so … translucent.

Gretchen opened her eyes as Molly entered.

'Molly my dear. How wonderful.' She cleared her throat which was dry and hoarse. 'Please. Come in.'

Molly stepped towards the bed.

'Take a seat, dear, I won't bite.' Gretchen pointed toward the cushioned stool that was perched to her right.

'Gretchen, I …' Molly found herself lost for words.

'It's okay.' Gretchen cleared her throat again and reached for a glass of water on the dresser by her side. 'I'm old, that's all, old and so tired. Pretty soon I will be on my way to the next life and that will be that.' Molly gasped. 'That's okay, Molly. I'm looking forward to seeing my Christian once more.' She pointed to a picture on the wall. It was a photograph that Molly had seen many times before. A much younger Gretchen with long blond hair in tightly wound plaits and a strong, handsome looking man with short, brown hair and a thick moustache. He was holding an axe in large, bullish hands and he had the look of a man that wanted to get on with things. They were standing in a forest with a log cabin in the distance to their left. There was a large, black dog between them – Molly thought it to be a Rottweiler – and a rolling brook or stream running through the forest to their right.

'Gretchen, I'm sure you will get well soon and be back in our kitchen making apple strudel or one of your wonderful roast pork and dumpling dinners.' Molly held Gretchen's hand in hers and she could feel every bone and wasted muscle under her wafer thin skin.

'I don't think so. My heart is not as strong as it once was. One more kick from this old ticker of mine and I will be done for.'

Molly could feel the tears starting to swell again. 'Gretchen, don't say that.'

'It's okay my love. It's okay.' The old lady smiled and Molly once again saw the Gretchen that she knew – full of life, vigour and a determination like no one Molly had ever met since. 'It is my time and I am reconciled to it. No need to feel upset or sad.'

Molly wiped a tear from her cheek. 'But … your family.'

'All gone I'm afraid. Well … the ones that matter anyway. No,' Gretchen looked around her, 'I gave my life to this place. To you and your father. And it's fitting that it's here that I will breathe my last breath.' Her face hardened. 'No matter what I have seen here, or what I have fought so hard to forget.'

Molly eyed her curiously. 'What are you -?'

'Molly, you know as well as I that there are things that go on here that are not for the likes of us to meddle with. Some of the things that your father and his associates entertain themselves with, well …' Gretchen placed both of her frail hands on Molly's and sighed. 'Stay away from it. It is unnatural and ungodly and I pray that my looking the other way doesn't condemn me to an afterlife in the *Teufel's* own company.'

Molly remembered her father crouching over the lady who was shackled to the bed. She heard the crack of the stick as it struck flesh and the grunt from the woman as the pain tore through her body. She felt her heart start to gather pace and sweat start to form on her forehead and upper lip. Her scar burned and pulsed and her hands trembled under Gretchen's loose grip.

'I don't know what you mean.'

'Oh, don't be so *foolish,* girl!' Gretchen had once again become the strong and firm handed nanny of her youth. 'Open your eyes and see what has gone on here! It has been the one true shame of my life that I allowed it to continue while every inch of me was screaming to say something, *anything*!'

Molly looked at the wooden clock on the wall and silently begged for the farmer and his wife to come out and rescue her.

'And don't think I didn't see what you became as you grew, Molly.' Gretchen lifted a thin and trembling finger and pointed in Molly's direction. 'I saw you. The *real* you.'

Molly's mouth fell open. 'You have always seen the real me. *Always*.'

'Your little hoard of dead animals stashed in your room. The awful torture you put those poor creatures through before disembowelling and dismembering them.' Spittle formed on Gretchen's lips and chin and Molly resisted the urge to wipe it away. 'I saw the grim fascination grow in your eyes and in your mind and it terrified me. Your urges, your *impulses*, became more morbid and spiteful day by day.'

Gretchen reached for her water but Molly moved the glass out of reach. The old witch was starting to annoy her. 'You've obviously been spending too many lonely nights drinking your schnapps. It's affected your mind.'

Gretchen looked at Molly with alarm, and then her expression hardened. 'I thought that the blood of your mother was strong enough in you to expel your father's influence. But I can see that I was wrong.'

Molly once again looked at the clock. It was five minutes to the hour and she so wanted to hear the melodic chimes once more. 'My mother abandoned me.'

'Your mother was taken from you!' Gretchen tried to sit up but did not have the strength. '*They* took her from you! Once your father had grown tired of her and after she had given him what he wanted - a child - he tossed her aside like a broken toy. She found out about it, of course, about his sick obsessions. And when she threatened to expose him to the world, it was the last straw. He set his thugs on her like a pack of vicious dogs. She didn't stand a chance!'

'No!' Molly reached over and grabbed Gretchen by the shoulders and shook her. 'Liar! Liar! *Liar!*'

Gretchen flailed on the bed like a delicate rag doll, her head lolling from side to side and her bones creaking and

255

groaning under the force of the young woman's furious rage. 'Let me go, you … you *hexxe*!' Gretchen tried to reach for Molly's throat but the young woman was far too strong. 'Molly, *let me go*!'

Molly could feel the intensity of her anger building in her chest and arms, her muscles taught and her body slick in a cool, salty sweat. She released one of Gretchen's shoulders, swung her arm and connected the back of her right hand on her nanny's thin and haggard cheek. There was a crunch as Gretchen's cheekbone shattered and she screamed in shock and pain.

'If it was so *awful* here, if my father was so terrible, *why did you stay*?'

Blood trickled from the corner of the sobbing, elderly lady's mouth. There was a gurgling sound as she attempted to speak. 'Because I was afraid.' She coughed and spittle and blood sprayed across the white linen of her pillow. 'Of you both.'

Molly reached over, grabbed Gretchen's handkerchief from the bedside table and screwed it up into a tight ball. She sighed wearily as she leaned over the bed. 'Perhaps, my dearest Gretchen, you were right to be.'

As the Bavarian clock began to chime to the beautiful music of the German Alps, and the farmer and his wife came out of their kitchen to see what the day had brought to them, Molly opened Gretchen's mouth with strong, urgent fingers and pushed the handkerchief deep into the dazed and bleeding nanny's throat. There was a struggle but not a strong one and after a moment she was still and Molly was sobbing. She felt the life essence drain from the body in her grasp and the warmth seep from the old lady's flesh.

Molly removed the handkerchief from Gretchen's mouth and raised it to her own eyes, gently wiping away the tears. She held it to her nose and breathed in the decades old scent of the kind and tender woman that had raised her. She bent down, wiped Gretchen's white hair away from her face and kissed her sunken, lifeless cheeks.

'Goodnight Gretchen.'

****

Molly prepared herself for her father's party by taking a hot bath. She could feel her shoulder muscles starting to stiffen from the fight with Gretchen and she thought that the warm water would help soothe her. It didn't.

She had left her dress hanging on the wardrobe door in her room and when she returned from the bathroom she looked at it like it was an alien presence to her. It was long and purple, with short sleeves and a plunging neckline. She hadn't even tried it on. She'd ordered it online without thinking about it and had simply thrown it in her rucksack while still in its packaging. Now that she saw it for the first time, she thought it was hideous.

She let her hair dry naturally which was the way she liked it. It couldn't be tamed by any hairdryer, hair straighteners or hair care products and so she let it be what it was. It was like her. Wild, free and unleashed.

She opened the door of her wardrobe and rummaged in there for something that would be suitable for her father's party but not make her look like an over-dressed fool. She stopped as she saw the empty jars where she had kept her little treasures and she stooped to breathe in the scent of formaldehyde.

Ultimately, she settled on a blue, sleeveless top and a pair of tight, black trousers with ankle length boots. The dress, she concluded, was doomed for the furnace.

She glanced around Molly's Place and smiled. Her small bed, adorned with black cotton sheets, looked beautiful to her. Her low sofa with its light green, cushions where she would spend evenings reading, watching TV or planning her treasure hunts. The dog baskets where Bert and Ernie would sleep. The family pictures of her with Gretchen, with her father and his friends and one, small picture of the woman she only remembered in her dreams. Her mother. Her mother with her beautiful, ebony curls and topaz blue eyes. Her mother whom she hadn't seen since she was a four-year-old toddler.

She reached out, stroked a finger along the silver picture frame and then tipped it face down on her dresser.

She left her room, walked along the hallway towards the stairs and looked over the handrail at the party below. The reception hall was already more than half full and she could see tens of other guests starting to fill out the great hall. The jazz band was already in full swing and she could hear the faint strains of *Fly Me to the Moon*. The guests were all dressed in ballgowns and dinner suits and Molly looked down at her smart, casual attire and frowned. It would have to do.

Her father was at the doorway greeting yet more prestigious guests alongside his best friend and confidante, Bobby, a man who had spent many evenings at their house, often occupying one of the spare rooms. It always impressed Molly how casually charming her father could be without coming across as pompous or grandiose. Bobby on the other hand could be stern and authoritative and had scolded the younger Molly on more than one occasion. She generally avoided him as a result. She also recognised Mayor Chester Wood in the doorway, another who had been at their house many times in the past four or five years, both before he became Mayor and since he had taken up office. She raised a hand to him and he spotted her and raised a hand in return. A lady stood by her father's side, her hand casually resting on his shoulder in what appeared to be a gesture of warm, familiarity. She was tall and slim and had shoulder length, platinum hair. Molly hadn't seen her before but she was instantly taken with her. A lady that appeared to have strength, presence and sexuality in a room full of testosterone and male dominance. She liked her for her father. He needed someone like her.

She heard footsteps behind her and turned. A man with salt and pepper hair and a moustache loomed over her.

'Hello Molly.'

Her face cracked into a broad smile and she opened her arms to hug him. She buried her face into his chest.

'Sam, I haven't seen you in such a long time. I'm so happy you're here!'

He laughed and hugged her back, his long limbs enveloping her diminutive frame. 'The feeling's mutual.' He broke their embrace, placed his hands on her shoulders and looked down at her. 'You've grown into quite the young lady. It looks like the time away has been good for you.'

She sneered. 'It's been interesting, let's put it that way. But it's good to be home.'

'You don't seem too enamoured with … Elderflower

Heights, isn't it?'

She nodded. 'It's okay.' Her smile faltered. 'It's just that I've had a few ups and downs recently.'

The tall, middle aged man spotted her consternation and peered at her earnestly. 'You gonna ride them out?'

She glanced over her shoulder at the crowd below. 'We'll see.' Her eyes narrowed. 'I haven't made up my mind yet.'

Her father was beckoning Sam to join them. He raised a hand in acknowledgement. 'Well, look,' he placed a hand on Molly's arm. 'If you want a change, I happen to know that our new, dim witted Mayor is good friends with the Chief Inspector at the Westhampton Police Department and they're just about to start this year's recruitment drive. He put my son forward a few years ago when he was working his way through local council and I'm sure if I had a word with him he would do the same for you.' He smiled warmly at her. 'After what you've been through, something like that would be good for you.'

She thought it over. 'I … I don't know. Father wouldn't like me leaving without at least attempting a degree.'

His brow furrowed. 'Your father has a lot on at the moment and … well, his daughter taking up an honourable profession like that would look rather good for him, I think.'

She had to admit, she liked the idea. The possibilities it opened up for her … little extravagances excited her. 'I'll certainly think about it. Thanks.'

'No problem. Just say the word.' He grinned. 'Look, I need to get down to your father. I think he's going to burst a blood vessel if I don't hurry so I'll bid you farewell for now and see you at the party.'

She laughed. 'You're right, I think he's heads going to

explode.' She looked down at her dad who was approaching the foot of the stairs, his expression barely hiding his increasing level of agitation. 'You'd better move it Sam or he's going to come up here and carry you away.' She smiled. 'I'll see you later.'

Sam Raven raised a hand in farewell and descended the stairs two at a time. He and her father immediately entered into a deep and serious conversation. She watched them walk across the reception hall and disappear into the amassed throng of guests. Sam had always been so kind to her and yet her father was so demanding of him, always speaking down to him as if Sam owed her father a debt of eternal servitude. She wondered about Sam's family, about the toll it must take on them, him being at her father's beck and call every minute of every day.

Talk of becoming a police officer tweaked her barely suppressed desires and she decided to take a detour. There was an enclosed staircase at the end of the south wall hallway and she took it. It led to the kitchen at the back of the house, a room that still smelled of Gretchen's home cooking and cheap perfume. The scent made her stop in her tracks. She thought of events earlier that day and she became saddened. She caught a reflection of herself in the large, polished-steel American refrigerator, her dark curls shrouding her small, pretty face, her bare arms hanging loose by her sides. She looked like a little girl lost, not the cold blooded murderer that she knew she had become.

She wondered when that had all changed but she couldn't remember. She was just aware of being in her current state, not who she once was. She was both confused and thrilled in equal measure. Whatever had happened to her was meant to

261

be. She was sure of that.

There was a locked door to the east of the kitchen. She knew where her father hid the key, in the nook under the microwave, and she grabbed it. It was heavy, black anodised metal and it felt cool in her hand. She had used this key many times before without her father's knowledge, and she intended on using it again.

She approached the door, which was set into the wall in a dark corner of the kitchen, inserted the key and turned. The deadbolt slid from the catch with a satisfying clunk. She pushed and the door opened inwards. The air from the stairway beyond was cold and smelled of damp and many forbidden memories. There was a light switch to her right but she didn't use it. She liked the darkness.

She descended the stairway, running her hand along the cold, smooth wall, and felt the excitement build behind her eyes. This was father's secret place. The place where he did secret things. She reached the concrete floor below and turned to her right.

The room was large, with a further room through a door at the back wall. The room she stood in had a low, white panelled ceiling, smooth stud walling which covered the soundproof foam that she knew was sandwiched behind it and the red brick beyond, and rows and rows of shelving which housed many dusty and fragile volumes of books that her father had studied and researched. She had read some of them but in the main they bored her. Early versions of most of the world's religious fables – the Christian Old Testament, the Buddhist Tripitaka, the Hebrew Tanakh, the Hindu Bhagavad Gita, the Muslim Quran and the Zoroastrian Avesta – to list but a few. Her father knew these texts inside out and recounted tales from them over dinner or during conversation. It was as if the history of the world's religions was an addiction for him.

There were also books that listed the many member of her father's secret society, the elite club that he had put together meticulously over the past two decades. It was a collection of people with power, money and influence. Molly also knew that it was a group of people with shared needs that had to be satisfied in unconventional, left-of-centre ways.

The Legion.

It was the right hand wall that fascinated Molly. It was where her father, the unorthodox philanthropist that he was, kept his artefacts. Instruments of torture. Items that could inflict terrible pain. Historical relics that proved beyond doubt that mankind harboured an unyielding need to inflict pain upon itself. There were leather whips, pliers for removing fingernails, metallic hoods with pins on the inside, wooden stocks, an iron instep borer, a black thumbscrew, a rack for stretching the human body, a scavenger's daughter for compressing it. There was even a large, dark metallic iron maiden with its door open like a gaping jaw revealing the sharp teeth inside. Molly loved touching these objects and feeling the excitement build as the pain and suffering that had been absorbed into the iron and steel seeped through her fingertips and into her nerve endings. Her lips would quiver and her eyelids would flutter as she imagined the blood that had been spilt by the very objects in her small, fragile hands.

Her father had created this basement area not long after Molly had spied him striking the lady held captive in his bedroom. She had often wondered whether he had realised she had seen him and it was for that reason he had moved to a more discrete location. He never mentioned it to her but he had modified his behaviour with her somewhat, being far more cautious and subtle with his language and tone. She had secretly hoped that he'd always known that they both shared an unspoken secret. She had watched him build his basement room through a crack in the kitchen door and had spied him carrying down his books and his artefacts. Every time he returned from a 'business' trip she wondered what other item he had procured for his secret laboratory underneath the house. The more she watched the more curious she became until one day she built up enough courage to take the key, unlock the door and enter the world beyond. It had changed her.

But it was the small room behind the closed door in the rear wall that Molly was most excited about. This was where her father brought his guests. He wasn't fussy. Men and women, both young and old, had been brought down here to the basement and through that door. It was where he fed his fetish, where he was able to mete out the very acts that satisfied his deepest, forbidden needs. She knew it was wrong but she didn't judge him. She too had her own forbidden needs.

She turned the cold handle and pushed. Beyond was a small room with enough space for a double, four poster bed. The walls were painted a deep, charcoal grey and the floor was dark linoleum. There was one single, dim lightbulb set in the ceiling overhead. The room was cast in long shadows and there was a scent of sweat and fear. A muffled sound emanated from the bed.

There, with his hands and feet tied to the tall, walnut posts in each corner of the thick bed frame was a young man. He had dark hair, dark eyes, thick chest and biceps and was naked except for a pair of boxer shorts and white socks. His torso was emblazoned with long red welts that criss-crossed each other like a maze of busy roads, small rivulets of blood running from the jagged wounds and pooling on the bedsheets. His mouth was gagged and Molly could see the sweat running from his forehead and into his eyes. She didn't know this man but it didn't matter. All she could see was Teddy.

She bent down and smelled him. He tried to yell but the gag prevented it. He could only manage a low, muffled growl. She licked the sweat from his legs and arms and shuddered. He tasted of Teddy. She wanted to taste him some more. She turned and left the room.

Behind her she could hear the man attempt a scream but it washed over her like a cold mist. She could just hear Teddy laughing with her. She wanted to be with Teddy. She needed him. It was perhaps the strongest desire she had ever felt in her short, eventful life.

She reached up to the shelf on the wall to her left and found what she was looking for. She turned the surgical scalpel in her hand and saliva formed in her mouth as she ran a finger along its razor sharp edge. A trickle of blood escaped from the point where the blade had sliced her. She licked the red liquid from the wound, its salty warmth settling on her teeth and tongue and ran the bloodied fingertip down the length of her throbbing scar. She turned back to the doorway of the bedroom and smiled.

Act 3:
Generations

They'll hing ye ap an cut yer throat
An they'll pick yer carcass clean
An they'll yase yer banes tae quiet the weans
In the cave o Sawney Bean

The Ballad of Sawney Bean by Lionel McClelland

Chapter 38:
Slam Dunk

The August bank holiday in Westhampton was always a busy and well-orchestrated event and this year was going to be no exception. There was to be a carnival during the afternoon – a long procession that would commence with dancers and acrobats dressed as characters from movies and west end shows, jugglers and clowns mingling amongst the gathered crowd and entertaining the excited children while collecting loose change for next year's event from their parents. Large floats would be made to look like pirate ships, moon rockets, submarines, battle-tanks and the like, all sponsored by the local businesses and inhabited by their enthusiastic staff, and the finale at the end of the long procession would be a float hosting the town's beauty queen and her princesses, all waving their hands and smiling until their jaws ached, their wrists were limp and their lips were dry and sore.

Along the beach-front during the day there would be steel drum bands playing alternative versions of pop music hits, stalls selling a multitude of gifts and artistic creations from local artisans, street food merchants offering aromatic jerk chicken from the Caribbean, Pad Thai from Thailand, steak sandwiches from Argentina and other greasy and tasty delicacies from around the globe, mime artists sprayed silver and gold and standing perfectly still like statues from ancient Greece, only to terrify the young children by moving and re-positioning when they came too close. Plus more fairground rides erected in the closed off car park that sat just north of the seafront, the noise from the dodgems, carousel, helter skelter, ghost train and the waltzer booming from large speakers while their exuberant occupants screamed and whooped.

The day was the big cash cow event for the town's local businesses and they made the most of it every year. Their success or otherwise during that single twenty-four hours of pure and unabated capitalism, would determine whether their season had been very good or particularly disastrous. Their year hinged upon it. Some businesses would prosper and go on to cement a place in the town's history as a store that could be depended upon to ride out any economic tidal wave, and others would crash and burn, like a ship bearing gold and cinnamon that came a little too close to the rocks at Bishop's Crag during an almighty storm.

The town council, however, was ambitious and each year tried to out-do the last. They had held fireworks shows from the pier, with tens of thousands of pounds of local taxpayers' money exploding in shards of colour over the Solent while loud music played over the PA system. They had shown movies from a thirty foot screen that was erected on the beach with hundreds of beach goers huddling together to watch the latest re-imagined superhero movie. They had held a sports event where amateur athletes entered into a competition to see who could navigate the gladiator style assault course, culminating in a sprint up a large, moving travellator. That particular event had to be finished early as a couple of the more inebriated and locally notorious contestants engaged in a fist fight over who had completed the course in the fastest time. They had even held a sailing event where people were encouraged to build vessels created to look like odd creatures or objects and navigate them along the shore towards the small port of Fisherman's Catch that resided at the end of a long spit of sand and shingle at the mouth of the estuary. Again, that event ended in disaster when a rickety boat that was built to look like a world war one bi-plane had capsized and almost drowned a father and his two young children.

This year they had played it safe. They had erected a large stage at the western end of the long, golden beach and there was going to be a pop and rock concert. It was sponsored by the local radio station, WHFM, and they had obtained acts from the eighties and nineties, some of which were well known, others less so.

And to the delight of the townsfolk the weather forecast for the bank holiday weekend was hot, sunny and without the hint of a breeze. The Monday, in particular, was going to be particularly good. Thirty degrees in the shade.

'I don't like it, Ron. Too many people.' Ronny Valentine and I were sitting on a bench, overlooking the gathering throngs of deckchairs and parasols. I was never one for the heat, as you know, and the thought of rummaging around in a locked vault and making our escape through a hot and humid cave tunnel filled me with nausea and dread.

'You're fucking kidding me. That store's going to be

271

rammed all weekend with people bursting with excitement and ready and willing to part with their hard earned cash.' Ronny was animated and as excited as a young kid at a shopping mall Santa's Grotto. 'The Greenbaum vault will be bursting at the seams with cash.'

I shook my head. 'There's going to be thousands of people on the streets. Thousands of potential witnesses.'

Ronny huffed dismissively. 'They'll all be down at the front watching some prat in spandex singing Walking on bloody Sunshine. No,' he pointed at me and winked, 'don't you worry about witnesses William, my boy. We'll be in and out of that vault before the Greenbaums can say Buster Edwards.'

I wasn't convinced. 'I hope you're right. I could do without a long stint in Dartmoor.'

He patted me on the back and I almost dropped my ice cream. 'You're so negative. Don't think about the inside of a prison cell.' He rubbed his hands together. 'Think about all the beautiful cash you're going to be able to spend on that lovely wife of yours.'

I smiled. It wasn't that I hadn't thought about it. I absolutely had. I'd even dreamed about how we could treat ourselves. Maybe a holiday in Mauritius or a cruise around the Caribbean. You know I love rum, and the thought of sipping a Cuba Libre while sitting on a sun lounger in the shade by the pool, reclining in nothing but my swim trunks and a pair of flip flops while listening to Bob Marley made me very happy.

'With our little mate Wesley primed and ready to go we've got a plan that can't fail.' He chuckled and took a large bite out of his choc ice. The chocolate fractured like a tiny earthquake, much of the ice cold and brittle confectionary dropping onto the floor where it immediately began to melt into a brown, sticky puddle on the hot paving slab. He didn't seem to notice or care. 'Yep, it's a slam dunk of an operation if ever there was one.'

I liked Ronny. I still like him. He had been good to me and he had been good to my dad and that meant a lot. As far as I was concerned Ronny was like family, even if he did scare the living shit out of me. But, even with all of that in mind, even with the thought of Ronny looking at me with eyes that screamed betrayal and vengeance, there was no way I was going to risk everything I had worked so hard to build.

Because the thing was: I knew something that Ronny didn't know. Something really important and something that the person who had told me, a person who I probably owed my life to, had made me swear to secrecy.

Luke Raven, the guy that had taken down the Pale Faced Killer and most probably prevented us from being next on his list of victims, was planning to shop the whole thing to Chief Superintendent Deveraux in return for his badge.

Chapter 39:
Captive

Raven had had enough of the nonsense. He'd had enough of being left on the scrap heap by the people in charge of the only job he had ever cared for. People who had demonstrated time and time again that they didn't have the slightest clue what they were doing. He'd had enough of being abandoned by his father and then being expected to welcome him back with open arms. He'd had enough of not being able to sleep or to get the brutal images of torture and bloodshed out of his every waking thought. He'd had enough of the Jane Butler case. And he'd had enough talk of this so-called secret society known as The Legion. It sounded like bullshit to him and he intended to prove it.

'So, tell me again what the plan is?' Wesley was by his side and sipping on a can of energy drink.

Raven nodded. 'We're breaking in.'

'Just like that?' Wesley was nonplussed.

Raven nodded again. 'Just like that'

'Okay then,' he pursed his lips. 'Sounds fine and dandy.' He shook his head, confused and exasperated. 'Why not?'

Raven withdrew a small pen like object from his pocket

and switched it on. A powerful, red beam instantly leapt from the end and projected a small red spot on a saloon car three streets down from them. It was a little after midnight and the streets were deserted aside from the odd passing car and a scavenging fox or two.

'Right, young Wesley, when I say *now*, we're going to casually cross the street, I'm going to boost you over the wall while keeping this laser spot located squarely in the centre of that CCTV camera,' Raven pointed to a rotating, white cylindrical camera that was positioned on top of a silver, metallic pole located behind the high, stone wall in front of them. 'Then you're going to reach down, grab my hand and pull me over with you. Got it?'

'No probs, boss.'

'And then we're going to see what all the fuss is about.'

Wesley nodded. 'Indeed we are.'

Raven breathed in a huge gulp of air and re-positioned the laser. The red spot immediately appeared in the centre of the camera lens. 'Now.'

Within a few seconds they'd crossed the wide street, Raven had helped Wesley up with one hand while continuing to point the red spot at the watching eye of the CCTV camera and then Wesley had leaned over, reached down and hauled Raven up and over with him. Raven knew that a security guard would be down to check on the camera within a couple of minutes but by that time they would have moved across the wide expanse of lawn ahead of them and hid in the shadows cast by the large stately manor owned by none other than Doctor Robert Charon.

He glanced at Wesley who was visibly excited. 'Let's go.'

They were both decked out in dark clothes, Wesley in his black combat trousers and black, long sleeved T shirt with a black baseball cap on his head and Raven in black jeans, black sweatshirt and a black beanie with a charcoal grey rucksack on his back. They moved across the lawn in unison, rounding the large, ornate water fountain, stepping down onto a wide patio area, through a row of hedges that served as a maze of paths that ultimately led out onto the golf course, and then past the large, round koi carp pond and into the dark recess of the round turret that guarded the eastern wing of the building.

They watched in silence as a golf buggy rolled across the grass, through the trees and towards the wall that they had just vaulted.

'He'll be there for a while figuring out what's up with the camera. The laser's probably left a sunspot in the middle of the sensor which will render the thing useless.' Raven pointed to the rear of the property. 'Let's head that way.'

They kept low and close to the wall of the large building, ducking once or twice to stay beneath the large, dark windows that overlooked the grounds. As they rounded the corner at the south wall Raven spotted a light burning bright in a ground floor window. He held up a hand to his partner to signal him to halt.

'Keep watch here. I'm going to take a look.'

Wesley shrugged. 'What if the security guy comes round with the buggy?'

'Give me a howl.' He smiled. 'Like a wolf.'

Raven ducked down, keeping to the dark shadows that stretched out across the grass like black, languid ghosts and approached the bright glow of the window. The rear of the property was overlooked by tall pines and low hedges and it contained none of the ornate features that decorated the side that proudly faced the street. Raven placed a hand on the low windowsill and peered into the room beyond.

Seated at a large walnut desk was Robert Charon. He was sipping on a cognac and conversing with his visitors. Raven recognised one of them. He'd seen him at a police gala event a year or so prior. He couldn't recall his name but he knew he was a senior ranking official in the town council. He didn't recognise the other gentleman with them but he appeared to be the one in charge. He was also tall, broad and with a face that looked like it had been carved out of granite. A strong jaw, deep-set eyes, dark, neatly combed hair, a nose that looked like it had been broken at some point in the distant past and a gaze that was steadfast and firm. Raven immediately knew that it was the guy his father had spoken of. *The Cardinal*. He had a presence about him that was unnerving. It was his eyes. They were … cold.

The Cardinal was angry, Raven knew that much. He was pointing at the still seated doctor and spitting something angrily at the back-footed council official.

Charon held his hands up in defeat and stood. He rounded his desk, placed down his cognac and attempted to appease his large, angry colleague with the crooked nose. The Cardinal turned to him abruptly, pointed his thick finger at the approaching doctor and mouthed his words clearly enough for Raven to be able to lip read. '*No! I want you to sort it immediately, Robert. Not him. You. In person!*'

With that the Cardinal turned and exited the room. Raven watched as Charon turned to his colleague who was clearly shaken. They both entered into an animated conversation

277

which Raven could not interpret and shortly after they too left the room. Within an instant the small study was plunged into darkness.

Raven turned back to Wesley who was crouched in the far corner. He was waving his arms. Raven shuffled along the wall.

'What's up?'

Wesley pointed at the front of the house. 'I think a light just came on out front. Could be security.'

'I think it's more likely the guy I just saw leaving. He looked important.'

Wesley eyed him curiously. 'Charon?'

Raven shook his head. 'No. Someone even more important than the good doctor.' He considered what he had just witnessed. 'If my father's right, it's someone with a lot of power and with the desire and means to use it.'

Wesley looked confused. 'Then aren't we in the wrong place? I mean, if this guy that you just saw is the boss, shouldn't we be tailing him rather than skulking around in the shadows here?'

Raven thought about his next move. 'I don't know. I've got a hunch. This is the place, right here. I don't know if it's just my nightmares playing tricks on me or whether it's my instincts subconsciously drawing all the pieces together. But something inside of me says that if we're going to find Jane Butler,' he gazed across the acres of tended grass, putting greens and shallow, sandy bunkers, 'we're going to find her here.'

Wesley shivered. 'You want to keep looking tonight?'

Raven shook his head. 'No.' He watched as the golf buggy approached them, clearly doing a reccy of the grounds after finding their camera deliberately tampered with. 'I think we've outstayed our welcome.' He pulled his beanie down over his ears. 'We'll come back some other time.'

With that the pair moved speedily west along the rear wall, hunched over like poorly trained paratroopers. They rounded the opposite end of the building and headed out of sight.

****

Some five hundred metres east of them, past the silky smooth green of the eighteenth hole, over the calm waters of the fishing lake and through the gently swaying pines of the surrounding woodland stood a small stone building. The building was known by the residents as The Church. A building that held a sacred testament for each of the members of The Legion.

From deep within its inconspicuous embrace there emanated a lonely and desperate mewl. It echoed through its wooden door and along its cool, damp staircase, through its musty and cavernous interior and along a further, smaller staircase. The building seemed to revel in the cries of cold and vapid desolation. Another wooden door guarded the entrance to three, stone cells. Two of the cells were empty, their inhabitants had been removed some weeks ago by the very people that had imprisoned them there in the first place, but in the furthest cell, hunched in a corner and tethered to the wall by a damp, frayed rope, was a young lady. She was draped in a dirty, beige smock and the dust and dirt from the grimy floor and walls was smeared on her hands, feet and within the coarse lines of her haggard face. She had a two inch wound on the base of her neck that had clearly bled profusely, the dried blood caking her neck, shoulder and chest, but her eyes remained fierce and her lips pursed in a grim and resolute determination. Her hair was long and straggly and tied back in a loose ponytail. She may have been beaten, she may have been slashed and whipped like a stray dog and she may have been mentally ravaged by her nameless captors, but she wasn't broken. She was going to escape. Jane Butler had never been as certain of anything in her life.

Chapter 40:
Balthazar

Molly spent many hours considering Sam Raven's recommendation. For countless afternoons she skulked in her room, mulling over whether she should commence a career with the police force. Yes it was an organisation that up to this point she had roundly despised and fiercely avoided, but at least it meant she wouldn't have to spend another three years at Elderflower Heights. She'd grown tired of having to avoid the idle stares of teachers and students who had heard the many and varied rumours of how Delilah Yardley had come to meet her fate and how Molly had driven the poor, desperate Teddy Palmer to suicide by her depressing emo tendencies and her violently possessive nature. The more she considered it, the more she decided that her time as a student was done. She needed to get out, and fast.

Finally, after much consternation and half a bottle of red wine she made the call.

'Sam, it's me. Molly.'

'Hi Molly. Is there something you need help with?'

She instantly sensed a nervous undertone. Her father had

obviously spoken of the nefarious events that had taken place in the basement during the big celebration.

'Well, actually yes there is.' She took a breath. 'It's about what you said. About your son. Luke isn't it?' He was maybe ten or so years older than Molly but she remembered his face.

'Yes. Yes, Molly it is.' There was a pause. 'What about him?'

'You told me that Mayor Wood had found an opening for him with the police training academy. And you,' she hoped he remembered. 'You suggested that he might be able to do the same for me.'

There was a silence at the other end of the line and she could feel her heart beating in her chest. Had she blown it by not being able to control her inner most desires? Surely her father couldn't punish her for…spending some quality time with the stranger in the basement. After all, what was he going to do with him?

Her mouth filled with saliva at the memory of the coppery tasting fillet of flesh that she had carved from the stranger's taught thigh. She suppressed a satisfied sigh.

'Are you sure about that?'

She swallowed and wiped her moist lips with the back of her hand. 'Totally.'

'It's what you want?'

'Yes.' Her tone hardened. 'It most certainly is.'

Silence again and then a shuffling of papers. 'You'll need to control yourself. You know that, right?'

Molly glared at the phone. 'I'm in control. Completely and utterly.'

She could hear Sam's shallow breathing, the thoughts churning through his head. He hadn't been in her father's good books of late but she knew that he would bend to her will. 'Okay, I'll make the call.'

Less than three months later she was in her car and on her way to the Hampshire police headquarters and ready to embark on a Police Constable Degree Apprenticeship. It was exactly what she was looking for. She could learn her trade doing the job rather than spending thousands of hours behind a desk, listening to dull, monotonous lectures. Her skills were more ... practical in nature. She was free from the stifling bureaucracy of Elderflower and, more importantly, free from the watchful eyes of her father and his cronies.

She took an apartment less than half a mile from police HQ, something her father subbed her for, and revelled in owning her own living room, bedroom, kitchenette and a bathroom that she could spend as long as she wanted in. It was a freedom she had never felt before and one that she relished with every ounce of her being. In three years she knew that she would be a fully qualified police officer with every chance of progressing quickly through the force, what with her father's powerful connections, and she could barely imagine the things she could get up to without fear of recourse with a badge in her hand and the protection of the Staker brand in her back pocket.

But it was in her third year, while attending to a call with two other fully qualified constables, that the course of her life took a tangent that she could never have anticipated. And that change came in the name of Balthazar Bean.

'Car five, car five. We need you to attend to an altercation in Halfacre Avenue. Over.'

PC Paul Barker reached over and grabbed the radio. He winked at his partner, PC Natasha Green, and spoke into the intercom. 'This is car five. We are about three minutes from the location. Over.'

'Reports of four young male individuals causing damage to public property, using offensive language and threatening to assault residents. Over.'

PC Green raised her eyebrows. Another night dealing with the drunk and disorderly. She made no secret of the fact she hated this part of the job. Lowlife scum intent on causing mayhem and chaos without any perception of the consequences of their actions.

PC Barker spoke again. 'Got it. Attending to the scene now, over and out.' He pushed a switch on the dashboard and all of a sudden the darkness of the night turned blue and red and a piercing wale of a siren drowned out the angry roar of the rapidly accelerating, souped-up Ford Fiesta.

Molly sat in the backseat, her eyes wide and her heart racing. This was her first call out and she was loving every second of it. She inwardly hoped that the violence would be fierce, blood would be spilled and they would be confronted by an angry and baying mob.

'No need to worry, Ms. Staker.' PC Green had turned in her seat and was attempting to calm their young apprentice. 'This is just a routine call out. Probably just a bunch of herberts out of their heads on skunk and alcohol and egging each other on.' She smiled warmly and Molly smiled back. She found the PC attractive but in an unconventional way. 'Just follow our lead but stay away from any trouble. PC Barker and I will handle it. You're just here to observe.'

Molly nodded enthusiastically. 'Of course, no problem. And,' she leaned forward in her seat, 'don't worry. I'm not anxious at all. Just thrilled to get to see the two of you in action.'

PC Barker laughed. 'Well, you won't be disappointed. PC Green and I are a crack squad who can deal with any concoction of knuckleheads, dipshits and crackeroos. These little bastards won't know what's hit them when PC Green here tears them a new one.'

Natasha Green groaned. 'Don't listen to him, Molly. He's just as bad as they are.'

They rounded the corner at the base of the hill and swung the car into the narrow street. Up ahead, to their right and on a patch of land between two semi-detached houses were a group of young lads. One was wearing a traffic cone as a makeshift hat, one was lying on the floor and puffing on what looked like a crack pipe and two others were confronting an older gentleman who was wearing red, checked pyjamas and carpet slippers. A grey-haired lady was standing in the open doorway behind him with a telephone to her ear. The taller of the two lads swung an aimless punch and narrowly missed the older man's chin.

PC Green smiled at Molly who was watching the scene with an obvious, morbid fascination. 'Here we go then.'

Molly nodded as the two PCs opened their car doors and adjusted their hats. Molly followed them.

PC Barker hollered. 'Police, stay where you are!'

The two boys with their fists raised took one look at the approaching officers, glanced at each other, nodded sheepishly and ran for the alleyway between the two properties. Traffic cone head looked out from under his makeshift hat, tried to run but tripped over crack pipe boy, who simply giggled inanely as the traffic cone went tumbling onto the wet grass along with its single occupant. PC Green and PC Barker took off after the hastily departing offenders, leaving Molly alone with the two prone lads and the middle aged man in his PJs.

'Well, I hope you're going to arrest these two, Officer.'

Molly was looking down at crack pipe boy. His eyes were spinning in his head and a long line of snot ran down his cheek and onto the grass.

'Oh,' she looked up at the older man and smiled, 'I'm not a police officer. Not yet anyway.'

The older man frowned at her. 'Then why the heck are you dressed like one?'

'I'm an apprentice. I'm in training.'

Traffic cone boy sat up on the grass. 'Like a Jedi?'

Molly laughed. 'Yeah, kinda like a Jedi.'

Pyjama man grumbled something inaudible. 'This is no laughing matter, young lady. These young ruffians were attempting to assault me.'

Molly withdrew her notebook from her pocket. 'What, these two?' She pointed at the two lads on the lawn. 'These two right here?'

The man sighed. 'Well, no. Not these two. The other two.'

The lady in the doorway shrugged her shoulders as if questioning what was going on.

'So … not these two?'

'No, I just said that. But they were loud and raucous.' He folded his arms. 'They were disturbing the peace.'

Molly raised an eyebrow. 'These two or the other two?'

Pyjama man shook his head. 'Well, I'm not sure. I didn't see them. I came outside to ask them to quieten down, when the other two,' he pointed at the alleyway, 'not these two,' he pointed at the two prone boys, 'tried to assault me.'

'Okay, got it.'

The man in the pyjamas took a step towards Molly. 'Look, this is a nice, quiet neighbourhood. We don't get any trouble around here, not usually anyway. I want these louts arrested.'

Molly placed her pen back in the pocket of her jacket and turned to face the increasingly agitated resident. 'Well, if they've committed a crime we can do that, sir. Not a problem. And I'm sure PC Green and PC Barker will apprehend the two gentlemen who attempted to assault you and they will be dealt with appropriately.' She nodded. 'As for these two, I'm almost convinced this young man will be charged with possession.' She pointed to crack pipe boy. 'But I'm not sure this other one has broken the law.' She chuckled. 'Aside, that is, from stealing a traffic cone and acting like a buffoon.' Traffic cone boy looked at her and shrugged his shoulders as if to say 'hey!'

Pyjama man growled in frustration. 'Well, sometimes I wonder what I pay my taxes for when I have to deal with this ineptitude.' He threw out his arms in agitation and trudged over to the grey-haired lady in the doorway.

Molly shrugged and walked over to the young man who was now removing the traffic cone from his head and brushing himself down. 'What's your name?'

He held out his hand to her and she took it. He hoisted himself up, winked and smiled. 'Balthazar.'

'Balthazar?' Molly laughed.

'Don't laugh. It's a real name.' The boy was short and skinny and roughly the same age as Molly.

'It's an odd name.'

287

Balthazar gave a mock look of indignation. 'Well, it's a name nonetheless and it's the one my mother gave me. Balthazar Bean. Ancestor of the notorious and once roundly feared Sawney Bean.'

Molly shrugged. 'Never heard of him.' She peered over at the alleyway as the two PCs returned, both of their fugitives handcuffed and sheepishly walking in front of them like convicts on a chain gang. Pyjama man smiled smugly.

'You've never heard of Sawney Bean? The great Sawney Bean? Well I'll never.'

'Why? Should I have?'

'Sawney Bean my dear was the first serial cannibal ever convicted on these great shores.'

Molly's jaw dropped and her pulse quickened. She switched her gaze abruptly to Balthazar, her eyes wide. 'Did you say *cannibal*?'

Chapter 41:
Sins of the Father

Lisa had had enough of Lonnie. It was getting to a point now where the mere sight of his face – all suntan, designer stubble and cheeky smirk – made her blood pressure rise like boiling water in an Icelandic geyser. She knew she had to get away from him once and for all but with Sam Raven's stark and terrifying warning still ringing in her ears she just couldn't set her mind to the important task of breaking it off. There was only so much drama she could stomach in her life.

But when Lonnie smacked her backside as she bent down to pick up Sly's dog bowl from the kitchen floor, the bulldog's slobber and left over chow mashed into the linoleum like baby food, she snapped.

'*Don't ever do that again*!' Her ears were ringing with rage.

'What?' Lonnie was leaning against the fridge freezer and grinning like a Cheshire cat on laughing gas. 'You used to like it.'

'Let me get one thing straight.' She took two steps towards him and pointed a sharp, dark purple fingernail into his chest. 'Not only did I never like it – and, by the way, I suspect that not one self-respecting woman has ever enjoyed the feel of your stinging palm on her rear end – but when you do it, it makes me so sick and angry that it's all I can do not to punch your dimly lit lights out.' She was speaking calmly and with some precision but even so her skin was prickling with heat and her vision was swimming in a cloudy crimson ocean.

'Okay, okay. I get it.' Lonnie was backing away. 'It was just a joke, that's all. Jeez, I didn't realise you were so touchy.'

Lisa desperately fought to keep her temper in check. She knew it would do neither of them any good. She took a breath.

'I'm going out.'

She scooped up Harry and started strapping him into his pushchair.

'Where you going?' Lonnie had lost interest in their debate and was now thumbing through a glossy fitness mag. 'It's warm out there. You might wanna, you know, cream him up and stuff.'

She growled. 'We'll be fine. I've got everything I need in my rucksack.'

'Okay. Very high UV.' He rolled his eyes. 'That's all I'm saying.'

She mumbled under her breath. 'Oh piss off.'

Lisa and Harry took the elevator down to the ground floor and briskly strolled out into the morning sunshine. The little square across the way from their flat was ideal for a lazy morning mooch and she intended to stay out for a good couple of hours. She couldn't bear the thought of returning to the apartment and spending more time with the half a brain cell she had once thought a catch.

She mulled over the dinner with Luke and Sam. She just couldn't get it out of her head. Despite Luke telling her it was all a complete fantasy and to ignore every terrifying word of it she just knew that there was more to Sam Raven's story then a desperate attempt to reconcile with his long lost son. It just didn't feel right to her.

To be fair, Sam's talk of this organisation, The Legion, and their leader the Cardinal sounded pretty ludicrous but what if it was real? If they really did pose a threat to her son then she had to take it seriously. She shuddered at the thought.

Harry gurgled and shook her out of her daydream. They had crossed the square and were now continuing down the alleyway connecting the two main streets. It was long, maybe half a mile, and was enclosed by the rear wall of a line of garages on one side and tall garden fences on the other. The pathway was rough and riddled with stones, the suspension of the buggy more than man enough to handle the off road action, but the day was so nice that Lisa had decided to stretch out their walk to the larger park across the other side of town. Why not, she thought. It wasn't as if she had anything to rush home to.

She bent down and kissed her son. He smiled and gurgled at her.

'What you saying, little man? You talking to mumma?'

Harry nodded his head and laughed. He pointed at his mum. 'Maaaaa.'

'That's right, Harry. Your ma. I'm your ma.' She laughed and ran a hand through his floppy blond hair. 'Although I prefer Mumma. It's what I used to call my mum, you know.'

His speech had been slow, something she blamed on her and Luke's breakup which must have had a negative effect on their tiny son, but more recently it had started to pick up.

'Tall Maaaa.' Harry was pointing and laughing.

'No, Harry. Mumma's not tall. Daddy, yes, but Mumma, no.' She was five foot two at a push and even that was a stretch, so to speak.

She heard a crunch of gravel behind her and turned. There was a blur of movement, a hard shove on her back and neck and Lisa found herself tumbling to the ground, her knee connecting with sharp gravel and her face and arms crashing into the nettles and thorns that lined both sides of the path. Her forehead scraped against brick and mortar and she screamed out in pain and shock.

She rolled onto her side and looked up. A dark figure stepped over her and stooped towards the stationary buggy. Her attacker's gloved hands reached down and unclipped the restraints. She could vaguely make out Harry's arms and tiny fingers reaching up towards the new stranger in excited anticipation, could hear his voice cooing and calling.

Within a second Harry was being lifted towards the stranger's chest, tucked under his arm like a miniature and delicate roll of carpet and carried hastily away towards Park Avenue.

'No!' Despite her injuries Lisa leapt to her feet, took in a huge gulp of air and set off after her attacker. 'That's my boy, you piece of shit!' She was quick for her size and the person she was pursuing wasn't as sprightly on their feet as perhaps they ought to be given the task at hand. Harry was crying, his legs poking out from beneath the crook of his kidnapper's elbow, his little head shaking from side to side as his tiny body shook vigorously. Lisa pushed the thought of the pain her son might be experiencing firmly to the back of her mind. The single thought she focused on, like a laser beam targeting a would-be assassin, was getting her boy back.

She was within six or seven feet now, the black hoody of the fleeing kidnapper almost within arm's reach. The end of the alleyway was some hundred feet or so in front of them and Lisa knew with an impossible certainty that if the kidnapper reached the main road there would be a car waiting for him to jump into. She couldn't – *wouldn't* – let that happen.

She could feel her heart pounding in her chest, the blood running down her forehead and into her eye and the graze on her shin stinging like buggery but her jaw was set firm and she was putting the many months of pounding the treadmill in a desperate attempt to banish the thoughts of her poisonous and dead end of a relationship to good use.

With fifty or sixty feet to go before the path ran out Lisa threw herself at her attacker but gasped for a moment in mid-air when she thought she had mistimed her jump and was about to come crashing to the ground in a futile and painful heap. The relief was immense as she felt her fingers grasp the bottom of a sweatshirt and she gripped it with all of her might, pulling sharply with arms that were seemingly powered by nuclear fission.

The kidnapper uttered a loud '*eeurgh*', wheeled around as if surprised, dropped Harry like an oddly shaped and rather hot potato, and fell backwards into the nettles.

Lisa frantically crawled on her hands and knees towards her shaken son who by now was screaming for his mumma.

He was on his back, a small cut on his cheek where he had landed roughly on the loose stones and dirt, waving his arms while trying to catch his breath mid holler. Lisa scooped him up and clutched him into her chest. She was sobbing but a furious rage burned in her belly.

She looked over at the fallen attacker and growled under her breath. The stranger stood up and dusted himself off and she could see a face under the hood of the sweatshirt. A face with dark eyes, tanned skin and dark goatee beard. He was tall and broad and she knew that there was an evil within the dark shroud – an evil that she did not want to confront. She pushed back with her feet like she was kicking away a rampaging hound but the man loomed over her like an ominous and devilish presence. She stifled a scream.

'The boy is mine, Lisa. Give him to me.'

'How do you know my name?'

'Let's just say we have a shared … acquaintance.' The man wiped blood from his lower lip with the back of his hand, raising it to his eyes to peruse is it with interest as the warm liquid trickled down the side of his thumb and onto his wrist.

'He is my son and I won't let you take him.' Her voice didn't sound nearly as convincing as she had hoped.

'This isn't open for discussion.'

Lisa continued to kick out her legs and pushed herself and her son towards the garage wall behind her. There was no escape. She looked up and down the desolate alleyway, desperately searching for someone, *anyone*, to help her.

'*Please*,' she could hear her sobs from a world away.

'There are important and powerful people that would like to spend time with your child, Lisa. Neither you nor I can stand in their way.' She could see a look of steely resolution in his eyes. But, perhaps, fear also. 'It would not end well.'

Lisa shook her head. 'I don't know what you mean.'

'You knew my son.'

Lisa looked up at him in disbelief. She had no idea who the man in front of her was but she knew in her heart that there was poison in his veins and a hatred for her and her boy. Panic rippled through her body. 'I … I don't know you.'

He spat out his words as if every consonant was bitter. '*He* took him from me, just as I was beginning to know him again. Wrenched him from his father's love like a disused object. Like he was worthless.' He grunted and pointed at Lisa with a long, steady finger. She could see the outlines of large rings under his black gloves. 'Actions have consequences. Debts are owed.' He held out his hands. 'The children must pay for the sins of their fathers.'

Lisa looked down at Harry, tears streaming down her cheeks. 'He's just a child!'

The man stepped towards her and reached out for her son. Harry was still sobbing breathlessly into his mother's shoulder. 'It's time.'

Suddenly there was a loud CRACK and the man jerked to one side. A red splatter of blood sprayed in a thick jet onto the green slats of the garden fence behind him. The man looked up in shock and there was another CRACK, this time the blood spurted from his lower torso and onto the ground, turning the gravel beneath him a dark shade of crimson. The man staggered back, held his hand out for balance and left a smear of blood from his long fingers on the fence post and garden gate.

He glared at Lisa, mouthing something soundlessly as he

stooped down and wrapped his bloodied fingers around her son. Harry's screams resonated down the long, enclosed alleyway like a long and looping siren of fear and confusion as he yanked him from his mother's desperate grasp.

'*Noooooooooooo!*'

The stranger turned and fled as another bullet struck a concrete fence post behind him, the cement flying off in splintered chunks. A man rushed past her from her left but Lisa barely noticed. Her son. Her *son*! She staggered to her feet, held onto the garage wall for balance and shuffled along the path as fast as her trembling legs would carry her. She could see the cars rushing down Park Avenue, the onlookers standing with their hands to their faces in shock and confusion and she heard another shot as a car door slammed. There was a screeching of tyres, the beeping of car horns, expletives tossed out as if they were futile and powerless. She knew.

Within a few hollow moments a man walked slowly towards her from the mayhem that had been left behind him. Blue jeans, dark boots, a red plaid shirt and holding a smoking pistol. He was bleeding from a shoulder wound.

'I'm sorry, Lisa.'

Sam Raven held her in his strong arms as Lisa Clancy sobbed as if her life-force had just been torn from her still beating heart.

Chapter 42:
The Divinity

'She's becoming a problem.' Christy Deveraux was standing in the dark and musty study of the large, ornate house, a thin ray of morning sunlight penetrating the semi-closed blinds and illuminating the right side of her face. Her silver hair glistened as the warm rays caressed her skin.

'It's a phase and it will pass.' The man was reclining in a leather study chair and idly playing with the nib of a fountain pen.

'It's not passing and I cannot contain it forever. Kipruto is getting closer and, despite my initial belief that keeping Raven close at hand would be a wise and risk-free strategy, I'm starting to worry that the two of them together might … unravel things.' She picked a loose hair from her ash grey jacket.

'Then stall them.'

Christy sighed. 'That's what I've been doing, sending my DI on pointless errands to keep watch on that self-destructive degenerate like a highly paid babysitter.' She glanced at the thick books on the wall, dusty tomes of heroic episodes from their glorious past. She loved sitting and rifling through them when she had spare time, revelling in the tales of wanton heroism and necessary pain and bloodshed. If only the world knew what had to be done to keep order. So many naïve humans, so few of their kind to maintain a semblance of what most people considered to be normality. 'There's only so much I can do to keep this … under wraps. She's,' she paused for effect, 'out of control.'

The man laughed affectionately. 'She's always been a wild one, that's for sure. I couldn't tame her when she was younger and I'm pretty certain I'd have even less success now.' He tapped the pen on the mahogany desktop.

'If it gets back that she's one of our rank then questions will be asked. My position will be reviewed.'

He shook his head. 'That's within our control.'

'The commissioner, yes. But not Fitzwilliam.' Clarence Fitzwilliam was the Member of Parliament for the New Forest East district and was famously incorruptible. The man was a devout Christian and a vehement idealist. 'He's already got his eye on me and would not hesitate to force me out of the chair.'

The man nodded slowly. 'I'll see what I can do.'

Christy let out a long sigh. 'Thank you, Bernie.'

Bernie Staker stood and came around the right side of the desk. He placed a large hand on Christy's shoulder and she shuddered. She immediately recalled Father Regan, the pastor at the care home she had grown up in after her parents had abandoned her. The vice like grip of his calloused and nicotine stained fingers, the foul stench of his putrid breath in her nostrils, the taste of him on her mouth and face. Bernie wasn't like him – she knew that much – but the memory remained just the same.

'Do you have the Curator?'

'We have eyes on him.'

'And the boy?'

She smiled. 'There was a situation.' She grimaced as she recalled the bloody wounds that Robert Charon had sustained. Sam Raven would pay for his insubordination. The pain would be long and slow. She eagerly looked forward to that day. 'But we have him.'

'The society thinks well of you, Christy.'

'I am grateful.'

'You will be rewarded.'

She felt in her pocket for her hair pin and pushed the sharp point into the tip of her index finger. Father Regan's hateful and eczema ridden face immediately vanished from her thoughts. She gasped. 'I need no reward, my lord.'

He bent and kissed her on each cheek, his smoky scent entrancing her like opium. She gazed up at him, the sharp beam of light from the window illuminating his dark brown and grey hair like a roaring fire. She spoke as if whispering to her lover. 'I mean your daughter no disrespect.'

'That is wise.' He turned and faced the window. 'One day she will lead The Legion into its next glorious phase.' He glanced at her over his shoulder as she pushed the hair pin into the soft flesh between her thumb and forefinger. The hot pain shot up her forearm and into her elbow. She sighed.

'We will rule the earth as our ancestors foresaw.' They spoke in unison as Bernie Staker pulled the blinds and the blazing sun erupted into the gloom of the study, banishing the darkness to the deepest recesses of the room and ravishing their bodies like a warm and sensual ocean.

'And all those that question our birth right will burn

within the fires of our furious wrath. *He* will bless us with his unyielding compassion and forgiveness.'

Christy's voice crackled with emotion as she felt the centuries of pain and suffering enveloping her body like a soft and familiar blanket. A tear ran from the corner of her eye and she sobbed silently.

'Praise be the one true divinity!'

Chapter 43:
Spring Tide

'I had a strange dream last night. Maybe not as surreal and as detailed as Raven's but a strange one nonetheless.'

DI Randall Kipruto was standing with his hands on his hips and looking up at the summit of Bishop's Crag.

'Okay, boss.' Ruby Cropper was smiling and nodding her head enthusiastically but she had no idea what her DI was going on about. She was starting to think that all detectives, or at least the ones she had worked with, could do with spending some quality time at Applewood House.

'I mean, my mother always said there was something in it, you know? The power of the subconscious and all that.'

'Yeah, got it.' Ruby fought to dampen down her sarcastic tone. Her mum was always having a go at her about it and she had become a dab hand at hiding it when necessary.

'I mean, Raven knew. He really did!' Randall pointed at the dunes. 'He knew that the dead dog was going to be tied up on that footpath sign and he knew that there would be a sink hole in the sand dune. I mean,' Randall looked down at her, his eyes bright and beaming and his smile thick and broad, 'how would he know that?'

The young constable shrugged. 'Maybe he'd been out here before and saw it. Used it to gain your trust, trick you into believing he really could see things?' She didn't like speaking ill of her friend, but he had really lost the plot after the whole Richards thing and needed professional help - and not from the undead or whatever it was that her boss was insinuating.

Randall shook his head. 'No. No way. He'd dreamt it alright, or saw it in some vision of his.' He looked along the shoreline. 'I'm beginning to buy what he's been telling us, for better or worse, and the more I think about it the more I'm starting to believe that the answers are all right here.'

'We've been scouring this beach for weeks and every piece of evidence we've found has led us absolutely nowhere.' She frowned.

'You're wrong. It's led us here.'

'Which is right back where we started.'

'And that's my point, Rube'. That's my *point*.' He shoved a finger in her direction.

Ruby glanced at her watch. It was six pm already and she'd been on shift since seven am that morning. She was tired and ready for a microwave curry and a film night with her boyfriend.

'Ruby. They're here.'

She was getting frustrated. 'Who?'

'The bodies.'

Her mouth fell open. She looked up and down the beach and held out her hands. 'Where?'

'There's a cave.'

'There's lots of caves. It's a cliff.' Her sarcasm was starting to get the better of her. 'On the coast.'

'But not like this one. I dreamed it,' he nodded again. 'And then I googled it. Annie's Cove. You heard of it?'

'Yeah, of course I've heard of it. I was born here remember?' Ruby unfastened the top button of her shirt. The air was thick and humid and she'd been outside in the heat for most of the day. 'It's a bay about a mile and a half from here. Out towards Fisherman's Catch. It's very popular with paragliders and windsurfers.'

Randall clapped his hands together. 'Correct. And do you know what's peculiar about Annie's Cove?'

The young constable's mind had already moved onto her chicken passanda and a bottle of Corona but she humoured the animated and newly crazed man in front of her. 'What's that?'

He clapped his hands together again and the loud crack almost made her jump out of her skin. 'Spring tides!'

Ruby laughed loudly. She was beginning to like this version of Randall Kipruto. He was funny. 'Spring what?'

'It's okay. I'd never heard of them either. It's when the tide is at its lowest point. They only occur twice a month, normally when there's a full moon and a new moon. At those two moments the sun, the earth and the moon are all in a straight line,' he held out his forearm and ran two fingers along it, 'and the power on either side of the earth from those two titanic entities stretches the sea to its furthest point. Like elastic.' He shrugged. 'It's all very interesting.'

Ruby laughed again. 'Clearly.'

'There's a smugglers' cave down there at Annie's cove. One that's been there for centuries, but it doesn't exist on any of the modern online maps.' He scratched an itch beneath his goatee. 'I had to look really hard for it and even then the location's not precise.'

'Okay'. She really had no idea where he was going with this.

'The cave's called Barbary's Hole.'

Ruby almost choked on her own saliva. 'Barbara's Hole?'

Randall laughed. 'Barbary pirates used to terrorise European sailors off the coast of Africa way back in the seventeenth century.' He waved a hand at her dismissively. 'Barbary's hole … *pirate's cave.*'

'Oh, got it.'

'It's right at the base of the cliff's edge, somewhere down there on the western face of the cove and too deep to be seen from the shoreline.'

'Right …'

'And do you know the only time you can gain access to this cave?'

Ruby put the pieces together and her mouth fell open in a moment of profound realisation. 'At spring tide?'

'At spring tide. And do you know when the next spring tide is at Annie's Cove?'

'August bank holiday Monday?'

Randall grinned. 'Bank holiday Monday. Tomorrow.'

They both looked at each other and smiled.

Ruby withdrew her notebook from her jacket pocket. 'We're going to need to brief the Chief.'

'Scratch that, Ruby.' He winked. 'We're gonna need a boat.'

Chapter 44:
The Custard Express

The darkness of her room comforted her. She could hide in the darkness. She could be still in the darkness. She could reveal her real self without others seeing, especially that overt sexual predator, Cecil. He had attempted to get his hand under her nightgown on several occasions, his indelicate wandering hand clawing at her thighs like a hungry crab. On just one occasion she had let him get the faintest essence of a feel, just long enough to distract him from his day job. Just long enough to get what she wanted.

Lorna, you see, was no longer living under the cloud of the mental illness that had tortured her mind and body for almost two decades. Lorna was back.

Doctor Weir was smart. If she suspected something, if she got even an inkling that one of her patients was trying to pull the wool over her eyes, she would not rest until she uncovered the truth. And uncovering the truth usually meant some form of torture – either mental or physical. Doctor Weir wasn't fussy and Lorna had come to suspect that she got a real kick out of it.

Cecil, however, was as blunt as a claw hammer and as

slow as a sloth on Valium. While he pulled and tugged at her in the darkness, his breath quickening as he got whatever pleasure he could from her dismembered form, she had slipped his key card from the chain that hung around his waist and pushed it beneath her pillow. It had been days ago and for the first two or three of those days Lorna was sure that Cecil was going to come crashing through the door of her room, spittle running from his mouth in long gloopy strands and his cheeks as red as fire, screaming at her to return what belonged to him or threatening to crack her good and hard with his stick. Or the good doctor with her Taser turned up to full volume, her gown unbuttoned and a maniacal grin spread wide on her voluptuously red lips. But no one had come. And minute by minute, hour by hour Lorna lay still and waited patiently in the darkness for her moment. For the time when she could finally return home.

That moment had come.

She slid down the length of her bed, constantly watching the internal window of her room for late night passers-by. There were none. She had hidden a knife from Cecil's dinner trolley under her mattress and she casually worked her fingers between the bed frame and the plasticised material of her duvet, clasping her fingers around the blade and sliding it towards her. She knew she would need its steely protection. There would be blood spilled tonight and she did not intend for it to be hers.

Lorna quietly dropped onto the wheelchair at the end of her bed, swung what remained of her legs into a sitting position and released the brakes. Almost instantly the chair started rolling forwards. She listened for a squeaky wheel – the very thought of which had kept her awake at night, its existence threatening the success or otherwise of her well laid out plan – but fortunately she heard none.

She swung the chair away from the bed and towards the door, Cecil's key card hanging around her neck.

She pulled the card downwards, the spool of string attached to the little plastic wheel in the centre of the lanyard giving her plenty of slack to slide the key card against the door lock. The first time it didn't work, the red light on the lock flashed as if to say *'beware, beware, there's a patient escaping from her room. Send armed guards immediately'*, but on her second attempt, while Lorna frantically attempted to calm her pounding heart and throbbing temples, the green light flashed and she was relieved to hear the powerful door magnets release.

She pulled the door inwards and a rush of air entered the room. It was cool and refreshing and she paused for a moment to let the slight breeze caress her skin and what was left of her hair. She wasn't the elegant beauty she once was, *he* had robbed her of that a long time ago, but the delicate touch of the summer night air on her face made her feel like a millionaire. She was young again.

She looked left and right along the corridor and saw no one. She was alone in the darkness. She looked upwards and saw the red blinking light of the CCTV camera. She didn't have long before they came but she wouldn't need much time to do what she was planning to do.

She turned the chair hard to her right and spun the large wheels as fast as she could. She had strength in her arms – she had been lifting her water-filled jug above her head repeatedly for about a month and her triceps and forearms were as toned as they ever had been – and using her muscles

307

for something positive felt good.

She passed old man Benjamin's room and raised a hand in salute. The old guy was sitting on his windowsill and picking his nose as she passed by. She wished she could have bottled the look on his face when he saw her. The mixture of excitement and surprise was priceless.

She couldn't remember exactly when her old self had returned - after being in Applewood for so long every week seemed to merge into the next. Little by little and day by day her conscious thought came back, as did her long term memory. She remembered things, remembered people, but, more importantly, she remembered herself. Who she was and why she had come to be in this situation. She was not ashamed but she was sad. Saddened by what she had lost and the opportunities she had missed. The loved ones she had left behind.

She had almost revealed herself to the two police officers, especially the young lady with the dark hair. She had a kind and compassionate face, the kind of face Lorna thought she could trust. But she knew she couldn't risk it. There was no telling what Doctor Weir would have done if Lorna had sprung it on her like that, in front of other people, especially people with authority. She would be embarrassed in public and that would not do. Lorna would have been made to pay.

She passed Emily Feeley's room and looked in. The young lady had murdered three men with nothing but a spoon and yet she appeared as sane as the next person. That was, of course, until you offered her dinner and then she would attempt to gouge your eyes out with her fingers. Her brother had raped her as a child while she was eating the spaghetti and meatballs her mother had set out for her while she was out prostituting herself to keep her children in clothing and with a roof over their head. Emily, who had been no more than five years old at the time, had been traumatised beyond compare. The three men she had killed had all been suitors of one fashion or another and didn't deserve what had happened to them but Lorna felt a sadness for her just the same.

Lorna heard a noise from behind her and turned to see Cecil lurching through the doorway to the corridor that attached A wing to B wing. He looked furious and liable to do her some serious damage if he caught up with her.

'Oi, you! What the hell do you think you're doing?'

He was maybe thirty metres behind her and carried a stoop that impaired his mobility, but she was acutely aware that he had two fully able legs and her wheelchair skills were in need of some significant practice. She turned away from him abruptly and focused on the dimly lit corridor ahead. The room that she sought was around the next bend and behind another set of double doors that would require key card access. She knew that she needed to gain some distance between her and her pursuer if she was going to have enough time to do what she had planned.

Her hands were burning from thrashing away at the thin rubber and aluminium of the wheels of her chair and her arms were throbbing and aching with the intense and strenuous exercise. Years of being motionless on a steel cot had affected her in ways that she could have never imagined and she knew that she was going to need some urgent physiotherapy if she was ever going to regain a semblance of her prior self.

The corner up ahead was getting closer but she could hear

309

Cecil's heavy breathing and his boots shuffling along the corridor like she was being pursued by a wounded geriatric. He was screaming abuse at her but she knew the gap between them was growing and she allowed herself a laugh. She was approaching the bend at some speed and once she reached it, she would round it in a sweeping arc, pull on her key card, swipe with her right hand and push through the double doors with ease.

Just then there was a clunk and a terrible grinding sound and her wheelchair listed violently to one side. There was a moment of awful realisation when she saw the right hand wheel spin away from her as the bolt that held it in place sheared in half like a torn piece of old linen. Lorna yelled in shock and held up her hands for protection as the chair spun out of control, hitting the ground hard on its side and spilling Lorna out like apples from a barrel. She screamed as she slid along the hard tiled floor and crashed against the wall at some speed. Fortunately her hand prevented her head from smashing into the metal skirting but she cried out as she felt her little finger dislocate at the middle knuckle.

She looked up and saw Cecil shuffling towards her. She reached for the key card around her neck and gasped in despair as she realised it had come dislodged in the crash and now lay helplessly on the other side of the corridor. She looked to her right and saw the double doors, only some four metres away, but they may as well have been on the other side of the planet. She knew that there was no way that she would be able to crawl to regain the key card and then drag herself to the doors before Cecil would be on her like a hungry jackal.

Still, she had to try.

She held up her hand, hollered in pain as she pulled at the little finger of her right hand and clicked it loosely back into place, and then set on the task of pulling herself along the floor to regain her lanyard. The picture on Cecil's key card leered at her while the real Cecil bore down on her like a lunatic set loose in the asylum. So many ironies, she thought, so little time.

The tile was smooth and her skin was slick and she moved across the floor with some ease. Cecil was approaching fast but she felt sure that she would make it to the discarded lanyard before he did. She reached out her pained right hand and clasped her finger around the key card just as Cecil rounded the corner and swung a boot in her direction.

'No you don't you bitch cripple!'

His foot connected with her hand and she felt her finger pop out of its socket once more. She screamed again but this time more in rage and frustration than in pain. The pain was secondary.

'Get off me you filthy creep!' She grabbed at his ankle and pulled with all her might and he span sideways, tripping over the stricken wheelchair and uttering a loud grunt as his back connected with the hard floor.

'You deceitful little slag!' He rolled onto his front angrily but she could see the hint of fear and a weakening confidence behind his eyes. 'I knew there was nothing wrong with you. All these years living off the good nature of Doctor Weir and all along you were just playing dead. Like a little kid, just pretending to be asleep.'

Lorna grabbed the lanyard and looped it over her neck. 'Believe what you want, you old pervert.' She pulled herself along the floor towards the door lock. She knew that one

311

swipe of the key card around her neck and she would be away from this fool.

Cecil got gingerly to his knees. He grinned and she could see his five or six remaining teeth, all black and yellow, spittle hanging from his lip and sweat pouring down his forehead and cheeks. The poor guy had probably had a year's worth of exercise all in one evening. 'Pervert, me? I bet you got your kicks, didn't you? He laughed. 'I bet you looked forward to old Cecil visiting you every day. I bet you even dreamed of me when I wasn't there, you with your two stumps for legs and a brain full of mush and sludge. Let's face it, what else are you going to get in here? A feel up from old Benny Moon?' He hooted with laughter and tears rolled down his cheeks. 'I don't think so. Not with that finger permanently stuck up his hooter!' He doubled over with that, spit spraying all over the floor as his terrible cackle reverberated down the long hallway.

Lorna took advantage of the distraction and gained a few extra feet. She was out of breath and her body ached as she approached the doorway but she made it nevertheless. She leaned back against the wall, took a large intake of oxygen and pulled on the lanyard. The string didn't unspool as it had before and there wasn't enough slack in the cord to reach the lock. She almost sobbed with desperation until she realised that all she had to do was pull the lanyard from around her neck. Before she could reach up and slide the key card across the receiver Cecil was upon her.

'No you don't, you bitch!'

He grabbed her arm and yanked the lanyard from her hand, his left forearm smashing into her jaw with some force. Her head hit the wall behind her and her vision swam like

312

ripples on a lake.

'Cecil, no!' She gathered herself and desperately pushed herself away from him, but he was stronger than he looked and intent on exacting some revenge.

'You think you can embarrass me in front of the lovely Doctor Janet by stealing my things? You think you can get away with that? *Do you?*' He slapped her with an open palm on her right cheek and she collapsed in a heap on the floor. He saw the opportunity and climbed on top of her, reaching down to unzip his trousers as his heavy breathing intensified. 'I'll show you what happens to little slapper cripples who try to get the better of my good nature!' She looked up at him as he pinned her down with his hands, drool spilling from his lips and sweat pouring from his face and arms. 'There'll be no fumbling in the dark this time Loony Lorna. Tonight you'll be getting the real deal!'

He released one hand to reach down and pull at his trouser leg and that was one mistake too many for the hapless Cecil. Lorna took the opportunity to withdraw the knife from her nightgown and plunge it into his eye socket, all the way down to the handle. She grimaced as she heard the gristly pop of his eyeball and felt the dark red goo run down her arm in a thick stream, some of it spilling onto her face and into her mouth.

Cecil froze as if struck by a stun ray and then started to shake and judder like he was sitting on a vibrating platform. His mouth fell open and his tongue lolled to one side and he started to hop and twist. He looked down at Lorna, the knife protruding from his eyeball like a grotesque handle and mouthed the word 'daddy'. With that, he fell to one side and crashed onto the tiled floor like a discarded toy.

Lorna sat up slowly, wiped the gore from her face and spat its salty and sticky remnants from her mouth. She reached out and grimly pulled the lanyard from the now still Cecil's loose grip. She cried out in desperate exaltation as she swiped it on the key card receiver and heard the magnets disengage.

She lifted Cecil's legs out of the way, pushed through the double doors and closed them behind her. She was almost there.

The entranceway to her left opened up onto the laundry room and the waste disposal chute. Lorna had one thing on her mind. Down that chute was a skip. Once she was out of that skip, probably covered in decaying food and human faeces, there was a short drag towards the banks of the River Solace – a steady stream that rolled down from the hills, through the town and out to sea. She knew from looking out of her bedroom window countless times that tied up on the side of that river was an old yellow rowboat that Cecil used on occasion to bring in supplies from town. From her bedside chair, idly gazing out of her window and watching the rolling stream as it swam merrily away from Applewood and towards the ocean, dreaming of the day that she too would be free from the marshmallow prison that she was trapped within, Lorna had nicknamed the weather beaten, brightly coloured vessel the Custard Express. Cecil couldn't drive – he'd had his licence taken away for multiple drink driving offences some years ago – and so Doctor Weir humoured her cheap and loyal lackey by buying him his own boat and allowing him to use it to collect supplies from the local cash and carry. She clearly hadn't been picky on the colour.

It was the Custard Express – complete with its two bright

yellow oars – that Lorna planned to use to make her escape.

And to find the one person she loved more than life itself.

Her Molly.

Chapter 45:
Rag Doll

The boy was alone. He was sitting in the shallow sea water and sobbing, his eyes red with tears, his cheeks moist with salty rivulets and his body shuddering with long whooping wails.

Raven was sitting next to him in the water but he couldn't feel the cold tide lapping around his legs and buttocks.

'What's wrong, little man?' Despite the crimes the young guy had committed with his murderous raptor, Raven couldn't help but feel sorry for him. He looked lost, like someone who had committed a heinous act and was now way out of his depth.

The boy looked up as if startled. He reached a hand out to Raven and prodded him as if checking that he was real.

'What makes you so sad?'

The boy wiped the back of his hand across the underside of his nose. He spoke in the alto pitch of a young man not yet into puberty. 'Doesn't love me.'

'Who doesn't love you?'

The boy shook his head and looked down at the water. He continued to sob.

'Look, little guy, I can't help if you don't confide in me.' Raven attempted to give him a gentle, compassionate pat on the back but was dismayed to learn that he couldn't move his arms.

The little boy thrashed a hand in the water angrily and the flying droplets rained over Raven. He expected the shock of cold water on his face and body but felt none.

There was the faint sound of cawing overhead. Raven looked up and saw the distant outline of a circling bird. The boy looked up and pointed skyward.

'Don't love me.'

'What?' Raven shook his head. 'The bird?'

'My hawk.' The boy began to sob uncontrollably again.

Raven looked to the west and saw the bright lights of the fairground and the amassed crowd at the bank holiday concert. Thousands of people were flocked around a flashing and smoky stage, flags and inflatable characters were being vigorously waved, arms and hands jutting towards the sky like spears and kids and adults alike dancing and gyrating to the soundless and hypnotic symphony.

He glanced up at the barren and blackened tree at the top of Bishop's Crag and saw a huge bald eagle perched on its sturdiest branch. Lightning erupted behind it like a bolt from the gods and thunder rumbled from within the black and billowing clouds. The eagle was gazing up at the hawk, transfixed.

'Can't you do anything, mister?' The boy was pulling at Raven's shirt sleeve imploringly.

'I ... I don't know.'

'Please ... *please*. He's confused her.' The little boy pointed at the eagle and shook his fist angrily.

317

'I don't understand. What are you trying to say?' Raven looked to his right, out towards Annie's Cove. Fisherman's Catch was beyond, the light from the shallow water warning beacon spinning slowly and peacefully in the darkness. Lightning flashed like a strobe and the jolt of intense brightness burned into his vision like a sunspot. Try as he might, he couldn't piece it all together.

'My hawk. My bird!' The boy now had both hands on Raven's shirt and he was trying to drag him into the water. 'She's mine, don't you see? Not his!' He turned to face the clifftop, pointing a short finger at the eagle and spitting as he hollered. 'She's *mine*!'

Raven watched as the eagle looked up at the circling raptor and nodded. There was a loud screech, followed by a pregnant pause. Raven glanced back at the eagle who now turned, opened its huge, graceful wings and took off north towards the beckoning storm. It had achieved what it had set out to do.

Behind him he heard a whoosh, a tearing sound like a fork through pulled pork and then a terrifying and bloodcurdling scream. He felt the small fingers that were gripping his shirt violently wrenched from him and he turned to see the boy's stupefied expression. The hawk's talons had pierced the skin in the boy's fleshy sides and blood now poured from underneath the kid's vest top and dripped into the ocean, turning the tide crimson and slick. The raptor span its head towards Raven and he was sure he saw a wink from one of its black, emotionless eyes.

'No, don't! Leave him!' Raven tried to grab the thrashing bird by the neck but his arms were numb and motionless.

With a flap of its dark, sleek wings the hawk was

airborne, the boy dangling from her talons like a large, flaccid rag doll.

Raven followed the raptor's flight as it carried the young boy out to sea and within a few moments they were enveloped by the darkness. An overwhelming sorrow that he couldn't explain hit him. He was ashamed that he couldn't save him, that he couldn't do more for him. Self-loathing consumed him.

He was vaguely aware of the water rising and his legs sinking into the soft sand underneath the ebbing tide. Within a few moments he was waste deep, his hands trapped in the rocks and silt, and the water was level with the underside of his chin. He looked back towards the crowd of people for help but the lights were all out, the stage was bare and the dancefloor was empty. He looked towards Annie's Cove and saw the vague and disappearing outlines of DI Randall Kipruto and PC Ruby Cropper heading into the distance. He tried to call out but knew it was fruitless. The scorched tree above Bishop's Crag leered down at him like an all-knowing Oracle, its sharp fingers pointing at him as if accusatory, its blackened bark blistered like burnt skin, its jarring silhouette lit up by shards of lightning from way up in the ether. Water began to fill his mouth and he felt it run down his throat and into his lungs. He knew he was about to die and felt nothing. Nothing but love for his son and a burning regret that he would never see him grow old.

****

Raven opened his eyes and was surprised to see the white and mottled brown ceiling of his flat. He gulped down

319

oxygen and sat up on his elbows. He was sure he had been dead but clearly what they said about never dying in your dreams wasn't true. He had died alright. Died right there in the ocean while he sobbed about some kid he didn't even know. He didn't understand it, but he knew it was important.

He looked on the floor for his phone and had a vague recollection of dropping it on the pavement outside and then treading on it on his way home from the Golden Swan. The screen was cracked and the LCD behind it was discoloured and unreadable. He swore under his breath. He knew today was important and a phone would have been invaluable to him but once again he was going to have to improvise.

He was due to meet Valentine at two pm and that only gave him an hour to get his shit together. He had a million and one things to do in less than half a day, not least of which rob Greenbaums jewellery store.

Chapter 46:
Black Agnes

Molly watched it happen. Saw the whole thing unfold before her eyes like some sort of neo-classic Greek tragedy. The Pale Faced Killer. What a name. What a rush. The murder, the bloodshed, the deceit, the media frenzy. The corridor whispers of what they had seen – a demon rising from the fiery pit, the tip of its tail razor sharp, its scales black and oily, its eyes crimson and evil. She was more than morbidly curious. She was jealous. She was *insanely* jealous of the Richards boy and what he had achieved. Shit, he had even killed the Mayor in front of the Chief Inspector! Sure, her father was displeased with the loss of an important ally, but still! The audacity of Anthony Richards. The cunning, the guile, the ingenuity!

From the moment she attended the first media event at her father's friend, Chief Dave Simmons', behest she knew that she was born to make her mark. Her time in the police force had been benign at best up until that point – four years of walking the beat, making meaningless reports and attending dull and pointless meetings. She felt like she was treading water, watching paint dry, cooling her heels – all the clichés – until the moment she stood in front of the parents of Tracey Webb and breathed in all of their grief, their tears and their black and tortured despair. She licked it up like honey. It aroused her.

But even then she didn't know what to do with it. Her fascination was interesting – it kept her awake at night, imagining what she might do in that situation, with blood on her hands and the police on her tail – but it had no meaning. Sure, she'd killed people before, but they were deeds of passion, acted in the moment like a muscle reflex. Spontaneous. What she craved was the calculation of it all. The planning. The structure.

Bal changed all of that. He gave her purpose. He was her muse.

'A thousand people, can you believe that! He and his clan killed and feasted on over one thousand people in just twenty-five years!' Balthazar lay back on the sofa and swigged on an energy drink.

'And you say there were over forty of them?'

Balthazar nodded. 'Yep, forty or so.' He leaned forward. 'But the beauty of it was that they were all family, so there was never any question of loyalty or having a snitch in the camp.' He grinned. 'They were all in it together.'

Molly laughed. 'And remind me of his wife's name again?'

Balthazar set down his drink and held out his hands, shaking them theatrically for effect. 'Black Agnes Douglas.' He winked. 'She was a witch.'

Molly chuckled, crushed out the butt of her joint in a saucer and closed the apartment window. She liked the thought of her. Black Agnes. She was probably a strong woman, not afraid to do what was required, to lead her family to death if that was what it took. She leered at Balthazar. 'And this Sawney Bane …'

'Bean.'

'Sorry, yes. He got away with it for a quarter of a decade?'

Balthazar nodded enthusiastically. 'I guess my ancestor was a cunning old fox like me. He even had the King of Scotland, James VI, after him and yet time and time again he managed to give him the slip.'

Molly poured herself a glass of wine and smiled. 'It's amazing. I can't believe I'd never heard of them before.' She swigged her glass of merlot and wiped a drop of the red liquid from her lips. 'And you say they kept the meat fresh by pickling it?'

'And hanging it from the roof and covering it with salt, like beef.'

Molly shivered; her eyes glazed over as if in a daydream. 'They were like predators. Like hunters.'

Balthazar shrugged. 'I guess.'

'Carnivores, descending on their prey like glorious and terrifying beasts.'

Balthazar picked at a callous on his hand. 'I suppose so.'

'And your parents told you all of this?'

'My stepdad, yep. He told me all about it.' He grabbed his can and gulped down the fizzy, sharp liquid. 'He's from Glasgow and he knew my old man before he died. Told me all about my dad's ancestors, what they did, what happened to them and how Sawney's daughter got away when Sawney, Agnes and the other children were arrested by King James and his soldiers. They were taken back to the village of

Girvan, up there in Ayrshire. Sawney and his family were executed like dogs; the men's genitals, hands and feet cut off and thrown into the fire while they were left to slowly bleed to death. And Black Agnes and the girls were all burnt at the stake like witches. But my great, great, great, great, great …' he trailed off, counting the greats on his fingers, his face wrinkled in confusion. With a shrug he continued, 'Grandmother managed to escape and set up home. She befriended a local man, Connor Barclay, who she later married and had children with.'

Molly was idly gazing out of the window, watching the distant sea roll into shore like a watery comfort blanket. She'd phased out Balthazar's slightly irritating voice moments ago. She was still thinking about the salted limbs hanging from the roof. She could practically see the blood draining onto the floor, could smell the coppery scent of the red and sticky liquid, could feel the tepid warmth of the taut skin, the density of the severed muscle tissue. She could taste the earthy sweetness of the flesh. She wiped saliva from the corner of her mouth and wrestled her conscious self back to the moment.

'Where did you say they hid the bodies?'

Balthazar stood up. He was wearing a baggy Animal surfer T shirt and a pair of loose fitting, shin length shorts. He wasn't attractive, Molly knew that. He was certainly no Teddy, could *never* replace Teddy in her heart, but he had his uses. Like a cheap tool. 'That was the beauty of it, Molly. It was ingenious.'

Molly finished her wine, set down her glass and shrugged.

Balthazar put his thin, wiry hands on her shoulders and

kissed her gently on the lips. He tasted of apple and sugar and smelt of cheap body spray and sweat. Molly kissed him back, fantasising about grabbing her wine glass, smashing it on the edge of the worktop and shoving the sharp fragments deep into his carotid artery. She resisted.

Balthazar lifted his head, gazed at her affectionately – his breath pouring over her like toxic fumes – and placed a sweaty hand on her cheek. 'Have you heard of Bennane Head? It's a small rock outcropping at the northern end of Ballantree Bay in Scotland.'

Molly shrugged. 'Should I have?'

'Yes, you should have.' He raised his eyebrows dramatically. 'Because it is the essence of what happens next.'

Molly felt her pulse start to quicken and her face flush a pale crimson. 'What happens next?'

'Molly, isn't it obvious? Isn't it smacking you in the head like a cold kipper?' He slapped the palm of his hand hard on his own forehead and the percussive sound was quite audible. 'All we need is our own Bennane Head, our own little hidey-hole away from prying eyes and sanctimonious do-gooders and we can make our own piece of history. Our own Bean clan.'

Molly laughed but she was intrigued. 'But we don't have a hidey-hole, Bal.' She felt the anticipation coursing through her bloodstream like high octane heroin. 'And we are at least five hundred miles away from the coast of Scotland,' she chuckled. 'And I don't want to live up there in the bloody cold.'

Balthazar smiled and winked mischievously. 'We won't need to do that.' He pulled his phone from his pocket and

325

opened Google maps. He scrolled up with his finger to the south coast and pinched the screen to enlarge it. 'We have everything we need, right here.'

Molly looked down at the blue hue of the screen and smiled. She was looking at a red triangle on the map highlighting a familiar place to the east of Westhampton, not five miles from where they were sitting.

Annie's Cove.

Chapter 47:
Frankenstein's Monster

She'd done it! She'd really done it! It had taken all her patience, her willpower and what little strength she had left in her thin and fragile arms, but Jane Butler had done it.

She had read once that if you moved an ancient boundary stone you encroached on the fields of the fatherless. It was some useless, nameless proverb that had stuck in her mind for no other reason than it seemed nonsensical to her. Except right now, sitting in her stone cell and with her hands and feet freed from the shackles that had ensnared her for what seemed like months, she knew exactly what it meant. The boundary stones had been moved alright and the bastards that had put her in that hell hole of a prison were about to get encroached and encroached hard.

It was just a little thing, a piece of loose flint that was jammed into some decades old mortar that she had managed to work loose over the course of a number of days. She had cut into the tips of her fingers from gradually rocking the exposed piece of stone back and forth, and each time the flint moved just a little further, the dry and brittle sand and cement crumbling from within the stone block sandwich that it nestled within. When the sharp green and grey rock fragment came away in her hands she had almost whooped with joy. It was a small victory but by no means a hollow one.

After taking a moment for self-congratulation, one which felt good despite the many weeks of desolation that had almost crushed what was left of her normally stoic optimism, she went to work on her shackles. They were old, the bolts that held them to the wall were rusty and malleable and she felt sure that with some muscle they were bound to give way.

Day after day she dug her little flint tool into the crevice between the iron bolt and the brickwork. She had considered trying to shear her ropes with the flint but they looked and felt strong and sturdy and seemed like the much more difficult of her two escape options.

She was sweaty and dirty and was sure she smelled as filthy as a discarded piece of wet carpet left out in the sun for weeks on end. The stone kept slipping from her grip and on more than one occasion went flying across the floor of her cell, very nearly out of range of her desperately reaching grasp. The more she scraped the more the dust flew and little pieces of flint split away from the main body of her makeshift chisel, but her resolve was undeterred.

The danger was imminent and very real. Twice a day a male visitor would slide her some mashed vegetable and potato or some tepid soup with a jug of warm water and she would have to tuck the flint under her bottom or between her legs. She had no real measure of time – there were no windows in her cell – so day and night was not a concept that mattered to her. She relied solely on her thankfully impeccable hearing and her sensitive nerve endings picking up on small vibrations in the ground to warn her of

328

impending visitation. She had almost been caught out once but she swiftly turned on the tears and her suspicious waiter span on his heels and scarpered.

There were two bolts - just two of them - one restraining the rope around her wrists and the other the slightly tatty rope around her ankles. Two little fastenings that kept her tethered to the wall like a wild animal. She found the whole thing degrading and disgusting and completely self-deprecating. But, of course, the mistake had been all hers.

She knew who had done this to her. She'd sat there in her kitchen with Tony staring at the computer screen and watching a video of Doctor Robert Charon not long after Tony had originally learned the name of his long lost father. He had been there at the funeral, sitting at the back of the crematorium in the late afternoon shadows and regularly checking his phone, which Jane had thought absurd given they were saying a final farewell to the body of his mentally tortured son.

She had seen him that day, standing on the corner looking at her when she went in to the store, and her instinct told her something was off but her internal calculator didn't put two and two together until it was way too late. She had left the store, bottle of mineral water in hand and a sunny disposition on her face, jogged not more than half a mile along Cockleshell Way and then suddenly in a moment of tragic epiphany had realised the identity of her lone watcher. Within a millisecond, there was a hand on her mouth, an arm around her waist and she was being shoved into the back of a transit van.

She had been tied up, beaten up, cut like a slab of cold meat and left for dead in that damp and gloomy sweat box and was left pondering what she had done to deserve it all. She had loved the guy, for god's sake. She had loved Tony Richards with all of her being for more years than she cared to remember and, even with everything that happened, she still cared for him. She hadn't put the gun in his mouth, had she? And she certainly hadn't pulled the trigger. No – that had been the result of a deep and ugly psychosis, more than likely brought on by his sense of violent abandonment from his estranged and ill minded parents.

And the more she pondered the more she scraped, and the more she scraped the more the bolts worked their way loose. She would hear herself use all the best swear words as she threw all of her anger and resentment into her work and she would feel the beautiful and very real aching in her fingers, her forearms and her biceps as she sliced the flint back and forth, back and forth.

When the bolt holding the rope around her feet to the wall came free, she shrieked with delight. The iron rod clattered to the floor like a pebble from heaven, the clanging of metal on stone singing a resounding and clanging symphony of glorious exultation. Her own vocals just added to the orchestral arrangement. She knew that with that single battle won the war was almost over.

Within moments she had turned back to the task at hand and had set to work on the remaining fixing. She did this with a renewed vigour and a shot of acidic energy that could only emanate from such a resounding and potentially life-saving success. Her arms and hands moved like an electric bandsaw, the flint slicing between metal and stone like an angle grinder in the hands of an experienced stone mason. The blur of her hands and limbs was entrancing and hypnotic and the sweat that formed on her arms, in her hair and on her back and face only served to oil the cogs of her whirring, high performance engine.

Just as she felt the bolt start to move within its fixing hole she heard the door at the top of the stairs open and close. She held her breath and listened and, sure enough, she could hear the gradual descent of feet on cold, stone steps. Her heart raced in her chest and the sweat turned icy on her skin. She grit her teeth and continued to grind the flint into the mortar and with the sound of every downward step she gave a little grunt of effort. She was damned if she was going to be defeated. Not after everything.

She heard the slow creak of the heavy hinges as the big wooden door at the bottom of the stairway swung open. A soft gasp escaped from her mouth and she felt her lips and cheeks trembling like rye grass in the afternoon breeze. She knew she had but a minute or so before her lunchtime delivery arrived and her whole escape plan would be exposed.

She doubled her efforts and crashed the flint repeatedly into the small crack between iron and stone, putting the noise she was making out of her mind and focussing solely on driving her blunt blade into the crevice that was starting to open little by little.

Footsteps down the hallway, the sound of a man whistling an old Rolling Stones song. She used the melody to inspire her work. She was steadfast and determined.

She had maybe twenty seconds to finish the job and she felt the beads of desperation start to form in her eyes. She was so close, *so close*. She'd given it her best shot but what did she expect? Little Jane Butler and her tiny piece of stone.

It was a stupid plan, *stupid*! It was doomed to failure from the start, she was too blind and too exhausted to see it for what it really was. Just a crazy, ridiculous thing that had no basis of reality. She was going to die there in that dark and dingy cell and her body would rot and her bones would crumble into ash and dust. All that would remain of her would be a memory and perhaps a ghostly visage that would appear to errant visitors from time to time. The ghost of Jane. She could be a part of folklore.

She heard the key enter the lock, the latch begin to turn and a man utter: 'What the?'

With one last monumental effort Jane threw the flint to the floor, put both hands around the thick rope and pulled. With a heave and a defiant scream she felt the bolt shear in half and she swung her makeshift sling with all her might, whirling round at her captor with her teeth gritted together in a deathly grin, her eyes narrowed like a warrior goddess and her arm muscles taut and sinewy like those of a crazed beast. The remaining half of the bolt struck the surprised visitor in the soft temple tissue in the side of his head, the sharply sheared iron penetrating the skin, tissue and the blood vessels beyond. The man whom she had seen before, a middle aged gentleman with brown hair, clean shaven face and dressed in a smart shirt, beige slacks and keenly polished shoes, stopped in his tracks as if he had been slapped in the face. He dropped the plate of gloopy food and glass of dirty water, the items shattering on the floor and spraying their contents across the bare concrete and onto Jane's legs and smock, and his arms started shuddering like he had received a sharp jolt of electricity.

Then Jane saw the blood. It ran from the underside of the

332

bolt which was now protruding from the side of the young guy's head, giving him the almost comical appearance of Frankenstein's monster in smart casual attire. It ran down his face and neck, into the collar of his shirt and then spread across his body and arm like a red and salty tie dye. He tipped to one side, took a knee and then fell to the floor in a heap.

Jane knelt, wiped the hair from his eyes, kissed his forehead tenderly and pulled the bolt from his skull like King Arthur's Excalibur from the rock.

She stood, opened her arms, lifted her face to the heavens and screamed.

Chapter 48:
Grease Monkey

The Greenbaum place was right in the centre of the high street, near the large Natwest and across the street from the constantly overcrowded Primark. It couldn't have been more conspicuous if it was covered in a banner that said: 'Open for Burglaries', but their bed was made.

'The access to the roof top is just around back.' Ronny Valentine was pointing down the alleyway between the jewellers and the card shop. 'We'll need to boost each other over the wall, I've got some bolt cutters for the metal gate on the other side, and then there's an aluminium staircase that leads you to the top of WH Smiths.'

Raven already had half a hip flask of single malt in his belly but even he spotted the problem.

'Hang on – Smith's isn't attached to the jewellers. It's a detached building.' He pointed at the alleyways either side of the property. Greenbaums had once been the home of a wealthy landowner in town, before Westhampton had become the huge conurbation that it now was, and consequently stood out as being the only freestanding building along that stretch of the High Street. He reluctantly asked his next question although he was sure he knew the answer. 'How the hell are we going to get on to the rooftop of the jewellers from way over there?'

Ronny looked at all of them in turn; Del, Billy, Raven and Wesley, and nodded. 'That's right, boys. We're all gonna bounce like kangaroos today.'

Wesley clapped his hands together and laughed. 'Awesome!'

Billy West groaned. 'I don't know about that, Ron.'

Dynamite Del huffed and twiddled with his moustache. 'With my knees?'

Raven growled. 'That's an eight foot jump. Eight foot! I don't know if all of us can make that.' He pointed at the diminutive but stocky Derek Luscombe, a large bulging rucksack slung over his shoulder. 'He's carrying bangers for god's sake.'

'We can make it. No problem. Del,' he patted the visibly unsure demolitions expert on the shoulder, 'is as fit as a fiddle and as springy as a March hare, aren't you, Del?'

Dynamite Del sighed, 'I guess.'

'And Billy, I've seen you on a rugby pitch and watched you leap for the try line like a young Jonah Lomu.'

Billy blushed. 'I don't know about that.' He chuckled, but the flattery had worked. 'More like a much older Joe Marler.'

'Who cares? I know you can make that jump!'

'Look, Ron.' Raven grabbed him by the arm. 'The only guy that needs to get on that roof is the one guy that's going down that pipe.' He turned and faced Wesley. 'And that's young Wesley here.' Wesley clicked his heels together and saluted. 'Why risk the whole operation for a boy's own version of Commando with a bunch of over the hill misfits like us? Wesley can get up on that roof, make the leap across to Greenbaums, slide down that chute and let us all in the vault.' Raven huffed. 'Rather than risking our lives, and the loot, we can just walk in off the street like any regular punter.'

Ronny pondered this. He plunged his hands into his salmon coloured trouser pockets and smiled. 'When you're right, you're right, Raven.'

Raven let out an audible sigh of relief and nodded.

'Except there's one little thing you're missing.' Ronny was looking at Wesley and waving his hand. 'Someone's got to lubricate little Wesley here and carry his clothes back down.'

Raven knew what was coming next.

'And as you're the fittest of the lot of us, Raven, what with you being an ex-copper and all,' Ronny said the last part with more than a hint of cruel sarcasm. 'Well, I guess you get to carry the lube up there for our little grease monkey.'

Chapter 49:
Valium

Lisa was exhausted. She'd been in Accident and Emergency with Sam all night; the gunshot wound he'd received at the hands of Charon and his cronies smashed into his collar bone breaking the bone and cartilage. The doctor had cleaned his wound and inserted several stitches but luckily the bullet had made its way all the way through the older Raven's body. Lisa thought it was now probably lodged in someone's fence panel, ready to be discovered at a later date when some genial homeowner gave the garden fence its annual lick of wood preserver. And, despite her terrified protestations, Sam had convinced her not to call the police.

'You'll just make things worse.' Sam attempted to sound commanding. 'These people have friends in high places and anything you say to the authorities will make its way back to them.'

'But I don't understand, they have my son! Your grandson! What am I supposed to do?' She was sitting on a plastic chair by the side of the hospital bed with her head in her hands and tears streaming down her face and neck. 'I can't just sit here and do nothing. He could be anywhere.'

'I know where they'll take him.' Sam winced with every word as if clout nails were being driven into his shoulder. 'I know exactly what they're planning.'

'Well then for god's sake fill me in, because at the moment I feel like I'm dying inside.' She went to grab Sam's arm but gripped the edge of the bed instead. 'I need to do something, I need to do something *now*!'

'I know it's hard, but just give me an hour.' He took two of the painkillers the doctor had given him and sipped water from a plastic cup and winced like even swallowing the codeine hurt like a bitch. 'Once they've discharged me, I'll take you to him. I promise.'

Sam's skin was ashen, which wasn't surprising to Lisa given the amount of blood he'd lost, and his eyes were bloodshot and jaded. She was concerned for him – he wasn't a young man. She had known him for less than a few weeks and yet he had shown her and Harry more love and tenderness than most of her previous male companions put together. Nevertheless, she silently cursed Sam Raven and his bastard son.

Luke had been uncontactable all evening, despite her calling his cell phone umpteen times and leaving him countless messages; the first message a mess of tears and desperate shrieks, her sentences barely intelligible, the last an expletive-laden rant about how Luke had never been there for her, how he was a no good alcoholic has-been and that he didn't deserve a son as beautiful as their little boy. Sam had listened to all of this and had stared quietly at the floor as if being chastised himself.

'I'm sure he'll be in touch soon enough.'

'Yeah, right. You don't know your son very well, do

you?' Lisa reached into her pocket for her cigarettes. 'He's not the reliable type.'

'I haven't set him a good example.'

Lisa huffed. 'Luke's pretty good at this disappearing act. If he gets that from you then I'm afraid you'll get no thanks from me.'

'I'm sorry.'

'No need to apologise. He's a grown man and can make his own decisions.' She felt for the engraved lighter in the rear pocket of her jeans. 'I've known Luke long enough to know that when he wants something, he'll come find me. But until then I'm on my own.' She flicked the lighter and idly watched the yellow and orange flame as it slowly burned under the bright hospital lights. 'Which is just fine and dandy by me.'

'We'll find Harry.'

'Oh, *I* plan to.' She wiped a tear from her cheek and a strand of bright red hair from her eyes. 'I need a cigarette.' She stood. 'I'll be back in a few minutes.'

'Don't do anything silly, Lisa.' Sam tried to sit up but winced with pain.

'Besides smoking?' Lisa smiled and touched his leg tenderly with a hand that bore a tattoo of an oriental red dragon, its body snaking in a sweeping curve from her wrist to the end of her forefinger. 'Don't worry, I'm not planning on getting myself into any dangerous situations. Harry needs me.'

She left through the swing doors and headed for the exit. She had a million things racing through her brain and she needed to get out of there. Her son needed her and she was damned if she was going to sit by and wait for a knight in shining armour to do her dirty work for her. She was more than able to sort out her own mess.

She raced through the automated slide doors at the front of A&E and pulled her phone from her pocket. She knew exactly who she was going to call. The one person who Luke Raven would never have wanted her to contact.

She lit a cigarette, inhaled and felt the nicotine hit her lungs. She knew she should quit, but right know she needed to calm her racing heart and soothe her erratic and unpredictable emotions.

She found the number she was looking for and hit dial.

'Hello? Yes. This is Lisa Clancy. I need to talk to Chief Superintendent Christy Deveraux.'

Chapter 50:
Grandpappy

Doctor Janet Weir stood with her hands on her hips, her cheeks puffed out in exasperation and her red lips pursed together in grim knowing. She'd lost one. She knew it had to happen at some point but if she had to guess who would make an unauthorised exit from her hospital under the nose of her well trained, if slightly abnormal staff she would have never picked Loony Lorna. Not in a million years. Not in a trillion. And poor old Cecil. What had he done to deserve such a gruesome fate?

She watched as the ambulance staff zipped up Cecil's hunched body in a black, oversized bag and groaned. The old boy had been a pervert, she knew that, but he was loyal. That kind of unquestioning obedience was going to be hard to replace. Especially on his salary.

She turned to the attending detective – a rather large, smartly dressed black woman with a long, dark weave that tumbled over the shoulders of her light blue suit jacket – and hissed. 'She won't have gotten far. This one is severely physically disabled and mentally challenged. I doubt if she's even half a mile away by now.'

Allison Bailey, affectionately known as Crusher by her pals in the force due to her commanding presence and booming voice, watched the gurney carrying the deceased orderly getting loaded into the back of the ambulance and pursed her large lips. 'Well, disabled or not, your Miss Hanscombe sure made short work of Mister Barker over there,' she looked back at the rear doors of the hospital, 'and seemed to have no trouble in getting around your security system Doctor ...' She paused.

'Weir.'

'Yes, sorry. Doctor Weir.'

The doctor took a step towards the young detective and clasped her large, meticulously manicured hands together. 'With Cecil's key card she could have opened a great many of the secure doors inside our facility, but there was no way she could have exited A-wing without a master card.' She grasped the card that hung around her neck on a red and white lanyard. 'The likes of which are only provided to me, as the supervisor of this facility, and my boss.'

Bailey took the card in her hand and held it up to her face to peruse the image of the doctor, her face beaming and yet somehow slightly sinister, the word MASTER emblazoned underneath in large red letters. 'And yet here we are. One employee deceased and one patient on the run.' She grimaced. 'So to speak.' The detective walked around the side of the building towards the loading bay. 'Do you have any idea how Miss Hanscombe might have made her getaway?'

Janet made no attempt to hide her impatience. 'I would say that was very much your department.'

'I'm just looking for anything that might help our

investigation here. Anything at all.'

Janet walked slowly towards the loading bay and groaned at the litter strewn across the yard. So untidy. She had told the boys on the dock to ensure that they kept the place clean. That was the Applewood way. Spotless. Shiny. Immaculate. Her brow furrowed and she drew her lips together in a thin, crimson line. She followed the line of refuse sacks, cereal boxes, milk cartons and empty tins towards the neatly planted petunias that ran along the edge of the riverbank and then down towards the murky waters of the stream. Something was missing but she couldn't place it.

'Did Miss Hanscombe have any visitors at all? Any family member that could have aided her in her escape?' Bailey appeared agitated.

Janet couldn't hear the detective. She was thinking. The unusual mess on the forecourt. The crushed petunias. Something wasn't where it should be.

'Doctor. Anything you provide me now will only help in the investigation. We have a very small window in which our chances of success are high. Beyond the first twenty-four hours our percentage starts to evaporate very quickly.'

The River Solace was rolling quite quickly and the perpetual hiss of the water was drowning out even the loud, thickly Caribbean infused boom of the detective. Something was usually there, on the riverbank, occupying a small space at the bottom of the path. Something odd. Something out of place with the clean lines of Applewood. Something that she had acceded to on the incessant pleading of her quirky but wilful employee.

The detective hollered. *'Doctor!'* Janet turned. 'Doctor Weir, I need your statement and I need it now! If you refuse,

I will have to assume that your plan is to frustrate this investigation for reasons I do not …'

'That bloody luminous yellow contraption.' Janet suddenly said, triumphantly.

Bailey frowned, confused. 'The what?'

'Cecil's boat.'

Bailey shook her head. 'I don't understa …'

'Loonie Lorna's not as loonie as we thought.'

****

The boat had rocked quite aggressively from side to side on her journey down the usually gentle flow of the River Solace but Lorna kept herself huddled under the tarpaulin. It had been difficult enough hauling herself into the battered old vessel without spilling out the other side into the freezing and no doubt filthy water and she had no plan to make any sort of sudden movement until she had made it to her ultimate destination.

She felt bad about Cecil. She had never killed anyone before and she certainly hadn't anticipated how things had unfolded, but the old boy had it coming. If it hadn't have been her it would have been someone else, she was certain of that. In the end everyone had to pay for their sins. Lord knows, she had.

Of course, she knew that news of what had happened at Applewood would be out very quickly and she was under no illusions. She wasn't exactly difficult to spot. She hadn't been out of the hospital for almost twenty years and because of that she had no emergency number she could call or any inkling of what new-fangled modes of transport she could hope to utilise. And her lack of two limbs was going to make things difficult.

But, still, she had a plan. It wasn't an ideal plan, wasn't even an okay plan, but it was a plan nonetheless and one that she felt sure would work. He owed her after all. If he was even still alive, that was.

So when she made it into the boat, after flying down that rubbish chute like a kid on a log flume and into the rusty old skip full of shit and muck and all sorts of germ infested waste, she set her mind to the task at hand. She would hide under the tarpaulin until she made it as far as the tributary that diverted a narrow stream away from the River Solace towards the old water mill. Then she would grab the two yellow oars, emerge from her olive green shroud like a phoenix from the ashes and steer her little escape vessel down that little stream. It would take her past the Priory with its large nave to the north and sweeping chapel to the east, under the low stone bridge that served as a pedestrian crossing from the old town to the new town, and towards the quay.

It hadn't been easy. Just as the river pushed her almost as far as the mouth of the stream, a rowboat with a couple of guys with fishing rods passed to her left and she had to wait patiently for them to be out of eye contact before she made her move. That made sure her timing was off and by the time she had propped what remained of her legs against the struts across the boat the stream had almost passed her by. She nearly cried out in desperation but bit her tongue. Plunging the heads of both oars into the river, almost losing one clumsily in the strong current, she yanked with all of her strength and managed to spin the head of the boat towards her right. She hissed a '*yes!*' but then realised that the current had grabbed the back end of the boat and had whipped her tail around to almost face back the way she had come.

Lorna hadn't spent the last few months readying herself for this moment only to fall at the last hurdle. She set her jaw, bit her lip and yanked on the oars with all her fragile might. The boat juddered and groaned and the waves of the river splashed over the bow and into the cavity that housed her tiny form but she didn't care. The water was cold and it soaked her pyjama bottoms so that they were wet through but that was fine. She could change her clothes later on. This was her one and only chance of escape. The stern of the boat spun so that it was now side on to the current and it listed to her left and groaned like it was about to spill its delicate contents into the murky depths. She yanked again and the bow surged forward into the reeds that separated the river from the stream and with one almighty pull on the oars – one that screamed of revenge and restitution – the Custard Express emerged through the thicket like a long and severely jaundiced baby from the womb. As it righted itself on the gentle flow of the stream, calmness resumed and Lorna exhaled a long, slow breath.

Things hadn't changed much, she was relieved to learn. The Priory still stood where it had always stood, a large bunting at the front declaring a cake sale and choir recital for the bank holiday, the bridge still straddled the water, luckily almost entirely vacant aside from an old lady pushing a shopping trolley across its tarmac spine and, as luck would have it, the water mill was still turning.

She steered the boat alongside the low, paved walkway and looped the rope across the iron bulkhead. With that she spun herself rearwards towards the path and sat her bottom on the cold paving. She looked along the path and spied a young couple headed towards her. They were arm in arm and looking cheerily at the ducks as they waddled along the low stream and she knew she only had moments to get herself out of their eye-line.

Placing her hands firmly on the paving slabs, she swung her bottom half to her left, spinning around so that she faced the walkway that led away from the stream and towards the mill house. With that she leaned forwards, placed her hands again at a forty-five degree angle forward from her shoulders and swung her lower half so that her residual limbs landed alongside her hands. She repeated this motion several times until she had almost made it to the thick wooden entranceway of the mill house. The door was partly opened and, whether it was occupied or not, she intended to get inside before the lovebirds spotted her. She congratulated herself on what had been an almost herculean effort on her part.

And then it hit her like a hard slap in the face and she almost burst into tears.

The boat. She couldn't leave the boat there. It would lead that bitch Doctor Weir straight to her. She felt the despair return – a long, dark hallway of melancholy that had been her home for such a long time. Darkness started to creep in at the corners of her vision and her face felt numb and soft. She wrestled with the creature in that hallway, the one that would seek to ensnare her with its hot, sharp whip – a molten iron strap that would loop around her neck like a venomous snake. In her mind she turned and saw the doorway back to reality, kicked the creature in what she guessed would be its nether regions and fled.

She had too much to do.

And a daughter to rescue.

She glanced along the path and could see the young couple. They hadn't seen her – not yet – but they would. She had no more than a second to react.

She spun and faced the stream, looked down the short slope to where the Custard Express gently rocked on the steady but stable current, and pulled herself forward. She could hear her own heavy panting; her heart was beating hard in her chest and the muscles in her arms and shoulders throbbed in protest. She reached the bulkhead and grabbed the rope which she had only loosely tied. She heard a noise to her right and turned to see two cyclists hurtling towards her from around the bend and knew it had to be now.

She threw the rope into the yellow boat and pushed it away with all her strength. Initially the vessel caught in some reeds and didn't move. She pushed again, hard, and the stern released itself and she watched through salty tears as the yellow beast rolled away from her.

She looked left and saw the young couple, turned right and saw the approaching cyclists and span swiftly on her hands as if her very life depended on it. She pounded up the path, back towards the mill house with its door semi-open and beckoning her in like a terrible but inevitable tomb. She could hear the lilting voice of the young girl behind her, could also hear the monotone and low retort from the young man and could feel the spinning wheels of the speeding cyclists reverberating through the ground and resonating through her fingertips and up her arms and across her shoulders. She pushed them out of her mind just like she brushed the hot, salty sweat from her eyes and hammered towards the mill house like a rabbit bolting towards the safety of its warren. She felt alone, vulnerable and terribly afraid.

She screamed with elation as she pushed through the heavy door and into the dark, musty entranceway.

'Who the *hell* are you and why are you in my mill house?'

Lorna leaned against the cold, stone wall and heaved in huge, lung filling breaths. Her hair was slick to her forehead, her hands were sore and bleeding and her clothes were wet and clinging to her body like tissue paper. She peered across the gloomy room through sweat and tears and spied the old man with a long grey beard, sitting in a battered and torn armchair and smoking a pipe. The sweet and acrid scent drew her a back to a time when she was much younger and her life still held so many possibilities.

'Grandpappy. It's me. Your Lorna.'

Chapter 51:
The Hound

They had to be patient. The entranceway to their hidey hole was only exposed twice a month and only for a couple of days at a time.

Molly couldn't wait. She still yearned for the stranger in her father's basement. It hadn't been a long encounter – her father had unfortunately caught her in the act while the man howled in agony and the blood was still wet on her lips – but it had been life changing. She had let herself go, had allowed her deepest, darkest wants and desires to rise to the surface and control her in a way that was both despicable and deeply erotic, and once that door was opened there was absolutely no closing it.

'Tonight, Moll. We'll do it tonight.' Balthazar was jumped up on energy drinks and sweets and was bouncing around her apartment like a cat on a hot tin roof.

'And you're sure the tides are right?'

'Of course I'm sure.'

Molly sipped on her coffee and shook her head. He was impulsive and a little annoying but, despite appearances, he was surprisingly sharp.

'Well then,' he grinned, 'tonight it is.'

Molly allowed herself a moment of anticipation. 'Midnight.'

Balthazar reached into the refrigerator and grabbed himself another drink. 'Come again?'

Molly felt her scar pulse and sweet saliva fill the inside of her mouth. 'It has to be midnight.'

Balthazar gulped down a huge mouthful of the green and sickly-sweet fizzy liquid and burped. Molly turned up her nose but giggled like a little schoolgirl just the same. 'Then midnight it is.'

****

They watched from the tree as the revellers filled the seafront bars and clubs. They waited silently while the sun set to the west and the beach lights erupted in luminous eruptions of radiant colours. They listened to the house and techno music leaping from the fairground speakers like ear worms of repetitive beats and synthesised and incessant melodies. They fucked under the stars. Not because Molly wanted to, but because she needed something to occupy her mind and help kill the time.

And then the moment arrived. The hands of the clock aligned at twelve and, as if by magic, they came.

The girl was first, running through the sand in her bare feet and yelping and squealing like a crazed banshee. The boy pursued her but he was slow and ponderous and had little hope of catching his prey. Molly watched still and silent from her perch while Balthazar descended the steep slope of the sand and clay bank.

She was the hawk. Balthazar was her hound.

At first, she thought the boy was going to kill the girl, and while that would have completely ruined her plan, it might have been interesting to watch. Someone else murdering for fun. Like a snuff movie.

But then she realised it was a game of chase. Kiss-chase maybe, and the girl was simply acting that way to draw him in. Like she had her own prey. She was fishing for him, like the other vacuous girls had at Elderflower. Like Delilah.

Molly watched as the young lady fell backwards into the sand and waved her arms and legs up and down, creating the illusion of an angel spreading its wings. The boy ran up to her and slumped to the sand in a heap. They started making out and Molly decided that enough was enough. She moved down the steep path silently and swiftly and came up behind Balthazar who was crouched behind the nearest dune.

'Are we doing this or what?'

Balthazar looked up at her and she instantly saw the fear and uncertainty behind his eyes. 'Of … of course .' She felt disdain and anger. 'I was just waiting for the right moment.'

Molly felt the blade in the sheath by her side. 'That moment is now.'

He stayed prone on the floor and looked at her like a lost puppy begging for its first meal. 'Oh … right now? I thought we were …'

'Oh for heaven's sake!'

Molly leaped over the dune and strode towards the young lovers. Balthazar stayed back, dumbstruck and more than a little embarrassed.

She approached the couple and watched them for a moment. They looked pathetic, writhing down there in the sand and fumbling at each other's clothes like desperate, love-struck teenagers. They disgusted her.

The male sensed her presence and turned to face her. She immediately noticed the fear behind his stubborn glare and it aroused her. Her scar throbbed and pulsated as she withdrew the knife from the sheaf and dragged it across his throat. As the blade tore through flesh and sinew she once more heard the retort of the rifle, felt her cheekbone shatter. The blood poured from him just as the blood had spurted from the wound in the deer's throat.

The girl screamed and started running. Molly smiled and looked back at Balthazar. If the idiot didn't step up now she would have to find a way to dispose of the hapless fool.

Fortunately for him, after a moment of uncertainty and a clumsy fall down the steep incline of the dune, he rose to his feet and gave chase. He had made his living out of being a shifty little bastard so he was light on his feet and he immediately gained ground. Okay, the girl was sprightly – she'd give her that – but Balthazar soon caught up with her.

A hard shove, pushing her to her left and into the water, was all it took. Molly watched with morbid curiosity as he pounced on her and held her head under, his arms shaking like jelly and the tears flowing from his cheeks, the snot dripping from his upper lip.

Once it was done, he sat back in the water, hanging his head. Molly felt that familiar disdain again. He looked terrified, ashamed. She, on the other hand, felt exhilarated. Alive.

'Well come on then,' she said, approaching him. She had to contain her frustration. She was hungry. 'We need our boat.'

Chapter 52:
Buggy

The sunshine caressed her face and it was the sweetest, most delicate thing she had ever felt in her life. She paused for a blessed moment in its embrace. She let her body absorb it like a sponge might absorb moisture. She felt an almost holy elation.

And then the hatred returned.

Jane looked around her at the meticulously trimmed lawn. She had absolutely no idea where she was, just that she had emerged from a small stone building that looked out of place from the clipped and bright green grass, neat hedgerows and equi-spaced fir trees that surrounded her.

She still had ropes around her wrists and ankles but they were long enough that she could walk. She just had to carry the heavy bolts that she had pulled from the stone walls. It was an inconvenience but one she could live with. She was free after all, and just a few moments ago that was something that she could only dream of.

She glared across the long rolling landscape towards the large house in the distance. That was her destination. He would be there. She could sense him.

She decided to make her way across what looked like an eighteen-hole golf course, bordered by a large fishing lake, keeping to the shadows of the shrubs and trees. She knew it would make her journey that much longer but she looked an absolute fright and she couldn't rely on strangers taking pity on her. She had no idea what company she was in.

That was, of course, until she spied a familiar face on the fourteenth hole.

She would never forget those present at the moment the man she had once loved blew his brains out. That was a picture that was emblazoned on her memory like a tattoo. It was eternal.

This was one such individual. A man in his late fifties/early sixties with a healthy paunch, grey and thinning hair and a hearty laugh. The Chief Detective on the case of the Pale Faced killer. Dave Simmons.

She thought for a moment whether she should go to him for help. He and DI Raven had saved her life after all. But distrust held her back. He was, when all was said and done, on the grounds of what she could only assume was an estate owned by the sinister Doctor Charon. Could she really believe that the Chief knew nothing of what this man was capable of? Of what he had done? She couldn't take the chance. No, she was alone and she was going to have to make her peace with it.

She peered past the Chief, who was standing chatting to another gentleman who was getting ready to take an eight iron swing at his ball, and spied a lonely golf buggy. That would do the trick.

She rounded the edge of the fairway, keeping behind the low hedges, and inched towards the static vehicle. She convinced herself that if she moved quickly, while the two men were eyeing up their shots, she could get into the buggy, get it started and accelerate away without either of them realising it was gone. By the time they discovered their loss she would have made it to the house and would be free to wreak her vengeance. She was dead set on it.

The buggy was maybe ten metres beyond the edge of the fairway and she knew that she would have to be both sprightly and silent. She gripped the bolts in both hands, making sure they didn't rattle or clunk as she ran, and counted down from five.

Five

She swallowed her saliva and took in a deep, heaving breath.

Four

She put her left foot in front of her right foot and semi-crouched in a sprinter's starting position.

Three

She looked up and saw Simmons' golf partner take a hard swing at his ball.

Two

She looked across at the house and imagined Charon sitting inside, smoking a cigar and drinking a large cognac.

One

She ran. She crossed the first four metres in record time and felt the elation build in her throat and face as she could almost feel the grip of the steering wheel and the rush of the acceleration as she pulled away. A smile spread across her face like sunshine and her fingertips started to tingle with excitement.

Then her foot caught in the rope between her ankle and

arms and she tumbled forward, spilling the bolts from her hand, one smashing into the buggy with a loud clatter and clang, and span head over heels, her head finally coming to rest violently against a motionless tyre. She looked up, shook the stars from her eyes and gasped at the rotund silhouette that blocked the sunshine from above her.

'Jane! Jane Butler! Is that you?'

Chapter 53:
The Jump

The jump was more like nine feet and looked way too far to Raven. Despite what Ronny had said, he wasn't fit at all and had not been keeping in any kind of shape since being on suspension. In fact, he hadn't kept in any real shape since his twenties, and that seemed like eons ago.

'What d'ya reckon, boss?'

'I reckon we're bloody idiots, Wes. Bloody idiots. Look mate,' Raven turned to face his partner, 'I haven't said it yet, but I'm really sorry for getting you into all this. You really didn't have to say yes, you know.'

Wesley laughed. 'Are you kidding? It's the most exciting thing I've done since setting off fireworks in the school playground during the Guy Fawkes assembly.'

Raven chuckled. 'Well I know there's a thrill to it, I've felt it too, but it's doomed to failure, you know that, right?'

Wesley turned to him and shook his head. 'What do you mean?'

Raven put a hand on his shoulder. 'Well, let's just say that Ronny Valentine isn't the kind of villain who can stay out of the Klink for long. It's like he hatches these lunatic plans just to get himself a free ticket back into her majesty's custody.'

'No, that's not right. I've gone through the plan back to front and I think we've got a real chance.' Wesley's face was starting to turn an odd shade of mauve.

'A chance of what? A chance to walk away with a few hundred grand each and a wanted sign hanging over our heads like the sword of Damocles?'

'I don't know what this sword is or who Damian Cleese is, but I do know that I could use the money.' Wesley was gazing across at Greenbaums from their side of the gaping void. 'Like *a lot*. I'm grateful for the job you've given me, Raven, I really am, but on the odd occasion when you have a job to do I'm only kept half busy and the hourly rate isn't that spectacular.'

Raven nodded. He was right. Raven's PI business hadn't exactly been buzzing. Just the one live case and that wasn't really getting anywhere. He had been distracted – a lot. Distracted by Lisa and Harry, distracted by the return of his once deceased father, distracted by his god awful dreams, by trying to get back his old job and by this bloody ludicrous attempt to become a big time jewellery thief. Chelsea Butler deserved better. *Jane* deserved better.

'Look, Wes. I've got something. Something's going to happen.' He chose his words carefully. 'To us. When we get inside.'

Wesley bent down and tightened his boot laces. 'What do you mean?'

'Well, let's just say that I have a get out of jail free card and I plan to use it.'

'A what?'

'You could be in on it too. I *plan* to get you in on it. It's

359

just Ronny that they're interested in. And god knows that perp deserves it. I've been chasing the old boy around town and locking his arse up for as long as I can remember.'

Wesley looked perplexed. 'What are you saying?'

Raven paused. 'Look, let's just do the jump and try not to kill ourselves.'

'No, no, come on. You started it.' Wesley pointed at him. 'You're up to something. You're bloody up to something. Typical Luke frickin' Raven.'

Raven smiled. 'All I'm saying is when we get in that vault and things start to go downhill – which they will – just follow my lead.' Raven slung the rucksack over his back. 'Follow my lead and everything will be just fine.'

'You've got a bloody screw loose, you really have.' He eyed Raven up and down and shook his head. 'Anyway, whatever. Let's do this.'

He bent down, blew out his cheeks and pumped his long, streaky legs like his life depended on it. He hit the tarmac five feet out like a long jumper, jammed the hi-top of his right foot into the kerb at the edge of the building and leapt into the air, his feet out in front of him, his arms wind-milling like rotor blades and his mouth open in a gnarly expression of both fear and exultation. Raven watched him fly across the open space as if in slow motion and he crossed his fingers and toes. He had no desire to scoop young Wesley up from the pavement some forty feet below them.

Wesley cleared the gap by some way and hit the flat top of the Greenbaum building at pace, his legs splayed out, his back skidding across asphalt and his fingers gripping for purchase. He crashed into the building's elevated rooftop doorway and crumpled into a heap.

360

'Wes? Wes!' Raven called across the gap between the two buildings in a loud whisper, being careful not to be overhead by the multitude of pedestrians below. 'You okay?'

Wesley's thumb came up in a gesture of painful triumph and then a hoarse, 'Piece of piss.'

Raven afforded himself a laugh. The kid really did crack him up. He was the closest thing to a real friend since he had his old partner, Damian Barber, and he was damned if he was going to let tragedy beset young Wesley the same way it did poor Damo. No way.

'I'm coming over.' He smiled. 'Now you can see how the pros do it.'

Raven backed up to the rear of the building the same way that Wesley had done, but gave himself a few extra yards. He wasn't as young as the kid, certainly not as skinny and in no way as agile. But he had the edge on experience and guile and nicking a longer run up was at least going to give him half a chance to make the leap. He gulped and thought of Harry. There was no way he was going to let his end be defined by a failed jump from the rooftop of WH bloody Smiths.

'Do it for your kid, Raven.' Wesley called across the rooftop as he dabbed at a large graze on his forearm. 'You're gonna need all the strength you can get later on.'

Raven looked up. 'What do you mean by that?'

Wesley smiled. 'You know, for little Harry?'

Raven's face hardened. 'Why will I need my strength for Harry?'

Wesley's face shifted and he placed a hand on his mouth. 'Oh, nothing.' He coughed. 'It was just a turn of phrase.'

Raven pulled the straps of the rucksack tight. 'Well

fucking phrase it better in future.' He shook his head. 'That's not something to joke about.'

Raven gripped his hands together in tight fists, pulled in three or four large gulps of air and grunted. With a huge effort his legs started pumping and his arms started chugging like the pistons of a steam engine. He felt his face turn hot and red and the sweat form on his back and torso as he leered at the onrushing cliff edge of the newsagents. He imagined himself falling, felt the sickening crunch of his skull connecting with the pavement, heard the screams of the terrified onlookers, the blood as it jettisoned from his body like the strawberry jam of a burst donut … but then his boot connected with kerb and he uttered a loud '*EURGH*!' as he stretched every muscle and sinew of his body across that deep and voluminous cavity. He saw his arms reach out, his fingers claw at the air, his legs pin-wheeling like a cartoon character, saw the hordes of shoppers below blissfully unaware of the peril just a short distance above their unknowing heads. The rucksack felt like a lead weight on his shoulders and he realised, way too late, that he should have thrown it across the gap before attempting the jump. He was sure it would be his fatal undoing.

But with a thud and a crash his right foot connected with the rooftop while his left leg hit the side of the building with a loud thwack and he span head over heels four times across the coarse gravel that was buried into the thick black bitumen. He came to a rest on his back, his forehead grazed, his left leg battered and sore and his spine bent across the arc of the back-pack as if he were an upturned beetle.

Wesley was looking down at him like a concerned son. Raven coughed out bile and forced a grin.

'And that's the way it's done, kiddo.'

Chapter 54:
Quay Executive

Lisa crushed out her cigarette with the toe of her boot, ran a hand through her tousled and brightly dyed red hair and raised her hand to the intercom. Number thirty-five.

'Deveraux.'

'Chief Inspector, it's Lisa. Lisa Clancy.'

'Come on up.'

Lisa heard the latch disengage and she pushed inwards.

Deveraux's apartment building was plush to say the least. White clean walls, large white leather sofas in the entrance hallway, bold, illuminated blue letters hanging on the rear wall declaring the building as the Quay Executive.

Lisa strode across the bright, marble tiled floor and pressed the arrow pointing upwards on the elevator control panel. She heard the soft ding of the lift descending to the ground floor and the velvety voice of the female automated announcer declaring that the doors were indeed opening. Lisa idly fiddled with the piercing in her left ear, a silver cross that Raven had bought her as a birthday present, and entered the shiny, brushed steel encased enclave. She looked down at her black, skinny Rancid T-shirt and scuffed black-denim jeans and wished she'd dressed better for the occasion. She pressed the button for floor three.

She felt desperately afraid. She couldn't wrestle her thoughts away from the image of Harry in awful pain, those evil men standing over him and beating him savagely, his screams of terror piercing the night sky like the cries of a lone wolf, his tears streaming down his soft cheeks like molten fear. She jammed her teeth together and her eyes narrowed. She wasn't going to let her emotions set her path. She had a plan and she was going to stick to it – whatever the consequences.

She gripped the colourful red, pink and green tattoo of water lilies on her left arm. She was no shrinking violet, not a girl that was prone to tears. She had fought her way through life like a furious ball of violent energy and if those bastards thought they'd bested her they had better think again. She was coming for them at high speed and with dangerous intentions. No one fucked with her son.

The automated announcer informing her that she had reached floor three and that the doors were once again opening jolted her back to reality.

Deveraux was at the end of the hallway, her platinum hair set firmly in place, her dark blue suit neatly pressed, her make-up subtle but perfectly applied.

'Lisa, hi. It's good to see you.' She smiled a thin, expertly judged smile.

Lisa had often thought Raven was just blinded by what had happened to him – honestly, how tough could this woman really be? – but now that she was standing in front of her, face to face and with all of her senses picking up every vibe and every beat, she knew that Raven was right. She was a woman not to play games with. Lisa knew she was going to have to be on top of her game.

'Chief Super …'

'Christy, please.'

'Christy, yes. Thank you. Thanks for seeing me.'

Lisa followed Deveraux to the right and through the cream and soft, padded doorway marked 35.

The room was enormous, much bigger than Lisa had expected. When she heard that Christy Deveraux lived in a flat by the sea front, she had envisioned one of those concrete prefab places, buildings marked by years of petrol fumes and muck and shit from the streets below, their balconies full of clothes hanging from long lines, pots full of under-watered plants, cigarette butts overflowing from ash trays that rested on plastic patio furniture and graffiti on the walls of hallways that were strewn with litter and sewage (she knew it was a cheap and easy stereotype but it helped to settle her nerves). This room, however, was gorgeous. Cream sofas, a coffee table that smacked of artistic integrity, a large painting of naked lovers on the rear wall, a semi-circular bar that housed Chivaz Regal, thirty-year-old, single malt scotch, and Beluga Noble Russian vodka. A large set of French doors were to her left and they opened onto a sweeping balcony containing cushioned, rattan sofas, three large sun loungers and two stainless steel, free standing patio heaters. Lisa gulped.

'Would you like a drink?'

'It's a little early.'

'Nonsense. It's a bank holiday after all, and lunch is way behind us.' Deveraux smiled warmly. 'I would say that ticks enough boxes to justify at least a small tipple.'

Lisa stepped further into the room. 'Just a small vodka, if that's OK.' And before Deveraux could ask: 'Neat, no ice.'

Deveraux nodded knowingly. She walked over to the bar in a manner that was both graceful and determined, grabbed a tumbler, pulled the bottle of vodka from the refrigerator and poured Lisa a shot that was way more than a tipple. 'This is about your son?'

Lisa caught a sob in the back of her throat and forced it away. 'Yes, my Harry.'

'Some men took him?' Deveraux's back was to Lisa but she could sense her considering every word very carefully.

'Late yesterday, yes.'

'And you were alone?'

'I was with a friend.'

'A friend?'

Lisa paused. 'Yes, a male companion.'

Deveraux turned and eyed Lisa with suspicion. 'And how is this ... companion?'

'A little wounded but he'll pull through.'

Deveraux turned to the bar again and reached for the brandy. 'And where is he now?'

'Harry?'

'Your companion.'

'He's safe.'

Deveraux paused and Lisa was sure she saw her shoulder's tense through the soft material of her jacket. 'And you called me directly why?'

Lisa considered her next sentence very carefully. 'Because my son's father, Luke Raven, believes your office to be compromised.'

Deveraux turned and paced across the room towards her,

her hands holding two tumblers, one of which contained Lisa's ice cold vodka. God, she needed that drink more than oxygen. 'Well, with respect,' Deveraux gave her the tumbler and Lisa necked the vodka almost instantly, 'he would say that wouldn't he?'

Lisa nodded. 'Perhaps, but I know Luke well enough to see through any acrimony.' She handed back her glass. 'And this isn't sour grapes.'

Deveraux sipped her brandy and held out her hand. 'Won't you take a seat?'

'I'm fine standing, thanks.'

Deveraux shrugged. She took another sip from her brandy. 'Another drink?'

Lisa nodded. 'I saw the men, you know?' She took a moment. 'Well, one of them at least.'

Deveraux smiled. 'That's good.' She turned and walked back to the bar. 'That will help with any ... enquiries we might make.'

'I could pick him out from a crowd without any trouble at all.'

Deveraux's shoulders tensed again and Lisa was sure she heard a sigh of regret. 'That's ... good.'

'The man was wounded quite badly by my companion. Not mortally, at least I don't think so.'

Deveraux didn't react.

'He had a very distinctive face. Tanned, dark hair, goatee beard, dark eyes ...'

Deveraux turned sharply. 'What do you want from me, Lisa?'

'I want you to get my son back.'

Deveraux finished her brandy and poured herself another.

'And how do you expect me to do that?'

Lisa strode across the space between them and took her vodka. 'I think you know how, *Christy*. I think you know *exactly how*.' Lisa necked her drink once more. 'And I swear to god, if you don't take me to my son this instant, I will be reporting all of this to Clarence Fitzwilliam faster than you can say *I offer my resignation*.'

Deveraux paused and Lisa could hear the gears in the senior police officer's sharply tuned brain whirring. Her eyelids fluttered for just a split second and that was all Lisa needed to be sure that she had hit her mark. Deveraux ran a hand through her platinum hair, sipped her drink slowly and turned and walked to the French doors. 'Strong words indeed.'

'You'd better believe it.' Lisa could feel her arms shaking and her heart pounding in her chest, but she was resolute.

'You know what you're getting yourself into, I assume.'

Lisa nodded. 'I have a pretty good idea.'

'And the danger that lies there.'

'Bring it on.'

'It's not for the fainthearted. I should know that more than anybody.'

'Being fainthearted's not my thing.'

'Yes, Raven told me as much.'

Lisa grunted. 'I bet he did.'

There was a muted silence between them, the only sound the low hum of the refrigerator and the dull call of the gulls overhead.

Deveraux turned, her face and jaw set hard and her eyes steely and cold.

'I'll make a call.'

Chapter 55:
The Sea Lion

PC Ruby Cropper watched dutifully from the quayside as Detective Inspector Randall Kipruto smiled excitedly from the deck of the twenty foot motorboat. The sky was a beautifully rich blue and the sun was hot and fearsome and, despite her fear of the water and general trepidation at what they might find in Barbary's Hole – that was, of course, if they found the alleged smuggler's cave at all – she also had a sense of anticipation at cracking her first big case. Working with Randall certainly beat desk duty by some considerable margin, even if her boyfriend, and mum for that matter, preferred her home at a more predictable hour.

The ship's captain, a sun-dried older gentleman with a thick, dark beard and a blue and green tattoo of a fifties showgirl on the side of his neck, swung the red and white vessel into the dock as Randall hollered across at her.

'Ships ahoy, Rube! Let's go find our underground mortuary!'

The DI was wearing a police issue, navy blue polo top with loose black slacks and black leather, ankle length boots. As usual his tight curls were neatly trimmed, as was his short goatee and sideburns, and his dark glasses and dark attire rounded off the look perfectly. Ruby thought him to be a handsome and respectful boss and housed a growing affection for him. She grabbed his hand which was warm to the touch and allowed herself to be pulled on-board.

'The sea's calm today so there's no need to worry. Captain Gary here said that the conditions are perfect for a little aqua exploration.' Randall was as excitable as Ruby had ever seen him.

'Very true, Detective Inspective. Very true indeed. Welcome aboard. It's a pleasure to meet you.' The ship's pilot turned to face her and Ruby was surprised to see that their captain's left eye was glass, the centre of the white marble emblazoned with a black anchor. 'Captain Gary's my name and I'll be hosting your little expedition today. If I might ask that you both wear the standard issue life vests over there, we'll be doubly sure of your safety if by chance the unpredictable maidens of the sea decide to surprise us with a little push and shove.'

Ruby glanced at Randall a little uneasily but he smiled and patted her on the shoulder reassuringly. 'No need to worry. Just a safety measure, isn't that right, Captain.'

Captain Gary lit a loosely rolled cigarette, smiled and winked at them both with his good eye. 'Aye, if you say so.' He turned, fired the boat back into life and pulled away from the Quay.

Randall turned to Ruby. 'So, I read up on it some more. While much of this part of the coastline is clay and sand – basically from Poole all the way through to Calshot on the other side of the New Forest – and is constantly being hammered at by the sea, causing much of the coastal erosion and slumping you can see at places like Barton on Sea and Highcliffe, Annie's Cove is different.' The boat juddered to the right and Randall instinctively grabbed the hull. Ruby in turn grabbed his shoulder to steady herself. She blushed a little at this but the DI was too deep in his own conversation to notice. 'Annie's Cove is peculiar in that it is hewed out of a large slug of limestone that stretches as far inland as Beaulieu. It's in that slug, somewhere on the western side of the bay, that our little entranceway resides. Some suggest that the cave is actually a mouth to a maze of zig zag tunnels, many of which head along the coast towards Westhampton itself.'

Ruby was focusing on the horizon to prevent her inevitable nausea from rising to the surface. 'And how do we know we'll be in the right place? How do we even know that our killer has been using this cave to dispose of the bodies?'

'We don't. There's no suggestion at all that this is a killer's retreat, which is why it's just you and me and the captain on this fishing trip.' He sighed. 'I didn't dare report it to Deveraux – she would have laughed me out of the station – but I have a hunch, a real pang of knowing that I can't put my finger on, and one thing I've learned in my short time on the force is to follow a hunch.' He gazed out across the Solent towards the Isle of Wight and shook his head. 'And, that thing with Raven – it got in my head, you know? How did he know what he knew? That wasn't a stunt, I genuinely believe that. He had a sincerity and a belief that I hadn't expected from him. That guy has cracked a case like this before, using whatever hocus pocus premonitions he has and, knowing that, understanding it the way that I do, how can I ignore what he told me?'

Ruby thought of her old boss, how unreliable and reckless he could be. How violently outspoken. But he was a good copper and a good bloke deep down and she couldn't help but agree with Randall. They would be foolish to just leave his intel to rot away in some case file somewhere. They had to at least give it a try. What else did they have?

'I'm with you, boss. Whatever this is, I'm willing to go along with it, if only out of morbid curiosity.'

Randall smiled. 'And that may be all we get out of today. A sating of our own personal wonderment, but,' he took her shoulders in his large hands, 'at least the time won't have been wasted.'

They skirted the shoreline about half a mile out to sea and watched as the beachfront passed into the distance and the section of the vast and spellbinding New Forest that kissed the ocean came into view. Swathes of tall, green pine trees butted up against the coastline, interjected by thick tufts of green and brown heathland and the odd detached property with their private docks, sheltered gardens and shallow beaches. Further in the distance they could see the spit of Fisherman's Catch, jutting out into the Solent like a bony, accusatory finger, pointing at the Isle of Wight as if chastising it. Boats launched from within the spit's thin solitude by the dozen – fishing vessels, pleasure cruisers and ferries carrying tens of passengers across to the beckoning seaside town of Yarmouth. The day was beautiful and the hordes were enjoying their long weekend with their families, friends and loved ones by doing something that made them happy. Ruby thought of her boyfriend, Dan, and how he would have loved for them to be on one of those boats and heading out to some seaside location, spending their day eating fish and chips, drinking cold lager and swimming in the beautifully blue ocean. That wasn't the life that she had chosen and she wasn't sure that he had the stomach for the one that she had.

'Annie's Cove coming up on the left!' Captain Gary, puffing fiercely on his cigarette, his beard billowing in the wind like a thick, woollen scarf, pointed ahead.

Sure enough, the yellow and tangerine sandy shoreline that they had followed from Westhampton Quay turned to a grey and black lump of sharp, angular rock that hung out in the ocean like a thick and gnarly limb.

'We'll have to be a little careful around this area. The rocks beneath are vicious and unpredictable and a slice from one of those suckers will cleave us in two like a lump of soft cheese.'

Ruby once again found herself swallowing her saliva and holding on to the boat to right herself. She didn't have sea faring legs and talk of being split in two like a lump of cheese was doing her anxiety no favours at all.

'Where's the cave, Captain?' Randall was leaning over the cockpit like a naval officer.

'Well, if I was a betting man – and I am! – I would put my money on somewhere between those two outcroppings just as the bay starts to widen.'

Randall looked across at the Cove, its yellow, sandy centre covered in sun worshippers, jet skiers and swimmers, the beachfront stalls selling ice creams, cold drinks and various assortments of snacks and meals. Either side of that centre were ever growing rocky outcroppings that climbed into large, overhanging cliffs that gave Annie's Cove its rich reputation for being the hidden jewel in Hampshire's coastline crown.

'Well if that's where you're putting your money Captain,' Randall had to holler above the roar of the boat's motor and the constant hiss and whoosh of the ocean. 'Then I'm willing to go all in!'

With that the boat lurched forward towards the rocks.

The tide had been gradually receding since two p.m. that afternoon and was about an hour from its lowest point. Randall was hopeful that by now they would at least see the beginning of a hollow in the cliff face.

Ruby was sitting in one of the blood red plastic benches that ran along the side of the boat and trying to hold her intestines together. For a supposedly calm day she thought the waves to be the largest and most aggressive she had ever had the misfortune of witnessing.

Captain Gary steered the ship with great care as they moved through the deeper parts of the water. Ruby looked down and could see rocks jutting up from the sandy seabed, their black and sharp edges almost beckoning them towards their watery and bloody graves. She felt her lunch, a tuna and cheese melt, rise in her throat and she reached for a bottle of water.

Randall was oblivious. 'Is that a cave there? To our right?'

Captain Gary shook his head. 'Not much more than a crack in the rock.' He looked up and smiled. 'We'll know it when we see it. If this was truly used by pirates and smugglers then mother nature should lead us straight to it.'

The boat lurched and Ruby was caught off guard, vomiting up her lunch all over the bench she was sitting on.

The captain laughed. 'Don't worry, my dear. We've had

376

worse.'

'I'm so, so sorry.' Ruby's face was a milky pale and yet her cheeks were flushed scarlet. She retched again.

'Get it out, girl! She won't do you any favours sitting in your stomach like a fiery blossom!' The captain swung the boat to the right, narrowly avoiding a rock that seemed to leap from the ocean like a gnarly, barnacle encrusted, fist.

The boat rounded the edge of the Cove, just in eyeshot of the throng of beach revellers and the captain swung to his right to steady the ship against the retreating tide. Randall lost his balance, tripped and fell onto the bench next to Ruby. He groaned as he felt warm vomit soak into the seat of his slacks. Ruby turned to him and her mouth fell open. 'I'm so sorry Randall. I really am.' Ruby was chugging on a bottle of water but she couldn't keep in the belly laugh.

Randall turned to her as if offended and then his lips parted and he started to laugh along. 'I have puke on my arse, Ruby!'

Ruby held her stomach as she doubled over, tears streaming down her face. 'Don't, *don't*!' She grabbed him by the hand. 'I'm going to be sick again if you keep on!'

'Puke … on … my … *arse*!' Randall was laughing hard and his cheeks hurt from the giggles as he wrestled a handkerchief from his pocket to wipe the brown goo from his trousers. 'I can't believe it!'

Ruby turned to him, her own face screwed up in a tight ball of laughter, and their faces paused a few inches from each other. There was a moment, she felt it. She could sense the desperate but forbidden longing in both of them. It was screaming to be set free like a surprising but urgent desire, but then it was gone.

'That'll be her, Detective!' Randall turned from Ruby, the spell instantly broken, and looked up at the captain who roared back at him. 'If that's not Barbary's Hole then I'm not Captain Gary Sealion, the finest boatsman this side of Weymouth!'

Randall and Ruby leapt up and peered across at the rocky crag.

There, at the base of the cliff and still partially covered by the receding green foamy water was a black, crooked hole, maybe six or seven feet in diameter and peering out at them from the rock face like an all knowing eye. It was large enough to fit a human through. Maybe a human carrying a sizable cargo. A *human* sized cargo.

'Take her in, Captain. We're going fishing.'

Chapter 56:
Little Orchid

Lorna stared at the old man. One eye was filled with a creamy, thick cataract, the other was grey and weary. His pipe smelled of her childhood; happy memories of sitting on a swing in the park while her Grandpappy and Nonna took turns in pushing her, all the while both reminding her that she needed to do her writing and arithmetic when she got home. Those were the last really good times that she could remember. That and giving birth to her little girl.

'You been gone a long time, Lornie.'

'Too long, Grandpappy.'

'And not a call.' Her grandfather stoked his long wooden pipe with a metal spoon and heaved in a big lungful of Prince Albert.

'I ... I've not been myself.' Lorna was seated on the room's only other armchair. It was tucked into a dark corner of the living room, a single thin beam of light coming through a small lead paned window that was almost entirely covered in ivy from the street outside.

'You can say that again. Your Nonna always said that since you met that ... man ... that *fiend* ... that you were lost to us.' He huffed and looked away.

'You didn't look for me?'

He shook his head. 'You were long gone by then.' He sighed, a weary breath that sounded so much like exhaustion and longing. 'Long gone.'

'But my baby?'

'You think we didn't care?' He stood up and walked over to her. 'You think we didn't want you and our great grand-daughter here with us, where you belonged? You think your Nonna didn't lay awake every night sobbing until the tears ran dry and the sadness washed away like spoilt milk?'

Lorna looked up, tears running down her cheeks and her eyes wide and pleading. 'I made … bad choices. Choices that I couldn't change. That I couldn't get out of.'

Her grandfather stooped down and rested a hand on her arm. He was crying too. 'You were swayed by the fancy life. The dinners, the dances, the weekends away with people that had money and influence. He turned you onto something that you enjoyed a little too much.' He pointed at her. 'And look what he did to you.' He was sobbing now, his chest heaving with long, wailing cries. 'Look what that bastard did to your legs. *Look what he did*!'

She reached for him and wrapped her arms around his swollen stomach. He was old and unwell but she could feel a strength in him. The strength of ten men, fifty even. He had been her rock and she had abandoned him. Him and her Nonna.

'What happened to her?'

He waited until the sobbing abated and walked back to his chair where he tapped out tobacco from his pipe. 'The cancer got her. Nine years ago. First it hit her stomach, then it spread to her spine.' He looked towards the door as if he half expected her to walk back in. She could see the deep remorse behind his cataract. She knew he missed her like he would miss his own heart. 'She fought it like the strong old battle axe that she was, but eventually even she had to concede it had her beat. She called for you before she passed. Called for you and the littl'un.'

Lorna placed a hand to her mouth and gasped. She felt more tears welling in the corners of her eyes. 'I miss her.'

Her grandfather shook his head ruefully. 'You and me both.' He gripped the edge of the chair. 'You and me both.'

'I want to get her back.'

'Nonna?'

Lorna smiled. 'My baby.' She leaned forward in her chair. 'My daughter.'

'She's lost to you. And look at you.' He pointed to where her legs would be and she pulled her shirt down over her stumps as if ashamed. 'What match are you for him?'

Lorna's face hardened. 'I got out of that hospital, didn't I?' She slammed her hand on the arm of the chair. 'I beat that black hole of a depression, didn't I?' She raised her voice angrily. 'I bloody well got here *on my own,* didn't I?'

Her grandfather held up his hand in surrender. 'Okay, enough! I get it. But where would you even start?' He stood up and filled a tin kettle from a tap that squawked as the water poured. 'You don't even know her anymore.'

'She is, and always will be, my little orchid. My beautiful little rare flower with a face that could light up the darkest of rooms and a laugh that could melt the coldest of hearts.' Lorna held her hand to her cheek. 'Nothing in this world – not him, not that bitch at the hospital, not the police – could ever change that.'

Her grandfather sighed. 'She was always your little special one.'

'So special.'

He poured hot water into two coffee stained mugs, paused for a moment, considering, and eventually nodded. 'What do you need?'

'I need a chair.' She pointed at her Nonna's old wheelchair, folded in the corner like a rusty old bicycle. 'And I need a driver.'

Chapter 57:
The Gift

Molly was addicted.

After those first two it was all she could think about. She would lie awake at night running the memory of the kills through her mind over and over on repeat like a cheap slasher movie. Their faces, so afraid. The sound of the blade as it tore through skin, muscle and bone. The blood. So much blood. The weight of the bodies as they hauled them into the boat.

Balthazar was less enthused but he played along. She knew that he was doing what she asked of him because he liked her, perhaps even loved her. She also knew that she needed him. There was no way she could move that amount of weight that far without another pair of hands. As strong as she was, she wasn't superhuman.

The swimming guy was a little more difficult. He fought back. He had gotten his hands around her throat and he'd even managed to thwart Bal's pitiful attempt at a chokehold while he kept one hand around her windpipe. The knife had penetrated his sternum with a satisfying crunch however, thereby ending his valiant struggle. She had been flustered, afraid even, but only for a moment.

The homeless lady was a piece of cake, as was her yapping dog which she hung up in the sunshine to dry out like an old raisin.

The fat guy was pretty simple, if a little gross, and much more difficult to move. The guy must have been twenty-five stone and change.

Body after body piled up and no one came to call. She kept her ear to the ground at the station, listening out for tittle tattle on what that young DI had gathered in terms of evidence, but despite a few whisperings about DNA being found (which she didn't believe because she had been so careful) and the discovery of the dog (which she had left there anyway because why not?) there was nothing. It was as if she was free to do as she pleased – just like Sawney Bean, way back when DNA hadn't even been thought of and there wasn't yet any such thing as the internet or the Police National Database. It made her even bolder and with every satisfactory kill her fantasy of being an invincible and notoriously mythical being blossomed.

She was lounging on her bed, casually smoking a joint – Bal was out doing something or other of little significance – when her phone rang. It was her father.

He knew what she was up to of course. They all knew. The whole Legion. They'd been keeping tabs on her since she was out of nappies. They knew all about Delilah and Teddy's mother. Hell, they probably even knew about Gretchen although nobody ever dared to mention it. But what were they going to do? That lot and the stuff they got up to. It made Molly's little killing spree look like a day out at Disneyland.

'What do you need, Dad?'

'Now, now. Don't be like that.'

Molly grunted. 'I'm busy. Hurry up.'

'Are you still doing … your thing?'

Molly looked at her hands and scolded herself. She needed to be more careful. She was lying there in her police uniform after all with the dried blood of a murder victim under her fingernails. That was wrong on so many levels.

'I don't know what you mean.'

She heard a sigh. 'Listen, while I disapprove of what you're up to, we think it may have its uses.'

Molly stared out at the crowds of people gathering around the hastily constructed beach stage. She hated the August bank holiday. It was so commercial. So plastic.

'I don't do requests.'

'Not even for your father?'

Molly felt the scar on her face itch and throb. She held a warm palm to her cheek to help soothe the irritation. She closed her eyes and heard the kick of the rifle, the crack of the stick on the faceless lady's back. She thought of her blanket that was now tucked away in the corner of her wardrobe. The image of the cow with the suckling calves, the young, bright eyed girl with the blonde pigtails and the milk churns. She smiled. 'Come on, then. Spill.'

There was a pause on the line. 'I have a young lady here with me that our friend Robert has been allowing to sleep over at his for some considerable time.'

Molly's pulse quickened. 'And?'

'She would very much like to meet you.'

Molly felt sweat form on her brow and anticipation build in her veins. 'And why would that be?'

She heard her dad grunt impatiently. 'Molly, she's a gift.'
She gasped. 'A gift?'
Her father sighed. 'To do with as you please.'

Chapter 58:
Little Bird

'I've dealt with it.'

Robert Charon lay in his bed, his face ashen and his arm attached to a drip filled with saline, another with morphine.

'How?'

'Don't worry about it. I'm getting done what you should have done months ago.' Bernie Staker stood by the window, his large shoulders filling the space occupied by the window frame, and groaned. 'You used to be better than this.'

'I was saving her. For later.'

Bernie walked towards him, his hands clasped together in an almost prayer like state. 'Robert, Robert. When are you going to learn from your mistakes? Look what happened to your son.'

Robert Charon grimaced as he tried to right himself in his bed. 'That was the Curator's boy. Luke.' He coughed. 'Him and that imbecile Simmons.'

Bernie chuckled. 'What was that? Imbecile?' His mouth dropped in mock surprise. 'The same imbecile who just returned your escaped prisoner to you, saving your ass from a humiliating and costly brush with the law. *Again*?'

Charon grunted. 'He didn't know what he was doing. He thought he was rescuing her.' His face hardened. 'He believed she was delirious, the buffoon. He'll wilfully accept anything we tell him as long as we look after that boyfriend of his and his hair-brained business schemes. It's amazing what a hundred grand of debt will buy you.' He frowned. 'But sooner or later he'll put two and two together.'

'And that will be dealt with.' Bernie placed a hand on the bag of saline. 'Later, when all of our other loose ends have been tidied away.'

Charon frowned. 'The boy?'

Bernie waved a hand dismissively. 'The boy, yes. And the Curator.'

'He knows too much.'

Bernie smiled. 'Which is why we have his grandson.'

Charon looked down at his bandaged wounds. 'He almost killed me.'

'You were careless.'

'And the girl?'

Bernie placed a hand to his chin. 'Yes, that's a delicate situation.'

'We could summon … *him*.'

Bernie slammed his hand on the table. 'And look where that got you last time! We serve *him*, we are here to do *his* bidding, not the other way around!' He growled. '*He* is not a weapon to use like some cheap handgun.' He turned away. 'You acted foolishly and you're now paying the price, lying in a bed convalescing. Robert, you were only moments from passing to the other side just a few short hours ago!'

Charon nodded and there was a moment of silent acknowledgement. 'What next?'

Bernie's phone rang and he pulled it out of his jacket pocket.

'Hello?' He listened. 'She does?' He nodded and smiled. 'Yes, that's good.' A pause. 'Okay. Bring her to the house.' He growled. 'No, the boathouse … yes. That's right.' He eyed Robert over the rim of his glasses. 'We need to make a deposit on the way.' He ended the call and brushed a hand through his neatly trimmed hair.

Charon shifted himself uncomfortably in his bed. 'What was all that about?'

'That was Christy.' He laughed. 'As reliable as ever.'

Charon leaned forward. 'And?'

Bernie picked up a pen from the bedside table and pressed his finger forcefully on the nib. 'It seems like our little bird is coming to us after all.'

Chapter 59:
Any Change?

We waited for what seemed like an age before we saw them both appear at the top of the building. Wesley went first, leaping across the alleyway like some sort of double jointed tabby, and then came Raven who was far more agricultural. We all groaned as we saw his left leg hit the edge of the building with some considerable force but, despite being about as graceful as a donkey with four left feet, he made it across.

Ronny chuckled. 'Lucky boy.' He turned to us. 'He was about two inches from being fish paste there.' I got the impression that he wouldn't have been too disappointed if that had been the final outcome.

It took about another ten minutes before we saw Raven make his leap back, this time the rucksack going first, Raven following a few moments later; a more a cautious attempt that didn't get anywhere near as close to being fatal.

Once he was back on the ground, grumbling about the knock on his chin and large, red graze on his elbow, we all gave him a hearty slap on the back.

'Well done, Luke my boy, a fine endeavour indeed.'

Ronny had a broad smile on his lips and a glint in his eye.

I turned to Raven. 'How was Wes when he entered the air con duct?'

'Smiling, as usual, and about as slippery as a wet bar of soap. But otherwise fine.' Raven was glaring at me with a grim knowing. I tried my best not to give the game away but my heart was pounding hard in my chest and the hairs on my arms were standing on end. I was starting to feel bad for Ron. The guilt was eating away at me. I wanted to be anywhere else but there, on that High Street on that day.

'Right, it's time for us to pay the Greenbaums a visit.'

Ronny went first, then Dynamite Del with his sensitive package slung over his shoulder like any regular rucksack – although this one of course could go flash, bang, wallop at any moment – then me, then Raven. The street was packed with holiday goers and shoppers and we were well hidden among the masses although we were all well aware that it would only take one person with a suspicious, nosy nature for the whole thing to unravel like a tightly wound spring.

We entered the open foyer of the jewellers, the large glass windows on either side displaying silver and gold wedding rings, necklaces, bracelets, watches and various ornaments and trinkets.

'William my boy, you're up.'

There was a CCTV camera in the foyer but Ronny's mole Lulu had let us into the shop's little secret. The black box that pointed out to the High Street day and night with a red blinking light and a single, green coated lens was a dummy. Mister Greenbaum, it seemed, was one tight son of a bitch.

I strode forward with my tool-bag under my arm. The access panel was an old one – an SRS DC60 with mechanical buttons rather than the more modern touch screen version – and overriding it was a doddle. I hadn't done it live before but any goon with access to the internet could learn how to do it. It hadn't taken me half an hour to master the technique at home with a couple of locks I'd bought from Amazon.

The trickier task was shutting down the alarm system which was hooked to the door mechanism. As soon as I overrode the door lock, de-activating the magnets that latched the door to the frame, I knew that I had twenty seconds to either input the alarm code or access the alarm panel, remove the fuse from the system and instantly disconnect the leads to the internal battery. Failure to do both simultaneously would mean game over for our whole operation.

I put on the latex gloves that Raven had provided us with and routed a wire around the keypad mechanism for the lock. Ronny was looming over me like a school headmaster while Del and Raven kept watch. With the other end of the wire in my hand I prepared to connect the stripped end to the corresponding terminal. Once done I knew that I needed to move swiftly.

'You ready, Ron?'

'Ready as I'll ever be.'

My mouth was as dry as concrete but I gulped anyway, wiped sweat from my brow and pushed the wire against the metallic connection point. There was a loud click and the door swung outwards. I heard Ronny utter a whispered *'come on'* behind me but I was already moving.

I knew from Lulu's plans that the alarm panel was situated behind the counter and underneath the till. I pressed go on my digital stopwatch, scooted round the display case, my tool bag slung over my shoulder like a shopping basket, and dived underneath. I heard Ronny, Raven and Del come in behind me and close the door.

At first, I couldn't see the panel. My eyes were still adjusting to the gloom and I could barely see my hand in front of my face. I moved my hands around under the counter, frantically searching for something that felt like the plastic box that I was looking for and, in my haste, dropped my screwdriver which I then also couldn't see.

'Fuck, fuck, *fuck*!'

Del called from above. 'You okay under there, Billy?' I could hear the tremulous nervousness in his usually assured tone and instantly felt sorry for the old boy.

'Fine,' I reassured him. 'Just … working my magic.'

By this time my eyes had adjusted and I had my screwdriver in my hand and was removing the last of the screws holding the burglar alarm panel's cover in place. With that removed I had access to the wiring underneath.

The fuse was set just above the digital display and the battery was the other side. I glanced at my watch which was telling me in bold black numbers that I had but eight seconds left before the whole place erupted in a cacophony of sound.

'Come on! This is taking way too long!'

I ignored Ronny and placed the thumb and forefinger of my left hand on the fuse while gripping the two battery terminals in my right hand.

'Cross your fingers, guys. The moment of truth.'

I pulled and the battery terminals came away but the fuse didn't budge. I swore loudly.

'Oh shit!'

I grabbed my screwdriver just as the first whoop sounded,

levered the flat edge under the base of the fuse and gave it a hard push. With a crack and a snapping of plastic the fuse leapt from its socket like a glass eye and rolled across the hard floor like a marble. I breathed out, counted to three and raised my head above the counter.

Raven was glaring out the shop window.

'Did anyone notice?' My face was flushed red and covered in a sheen of sweat.

Raven walked to the other end of the shop and looked out of the other window. 'I don't think so.' There was a moment of muted silence as we all half expected the old bill to come crashing through the door. Ironic really, given what Raven was planning.

Ronny leaned over the counter. 'I think we'll give you a B minus for that little exercise.' He patted me on the head. 'Must try harder.'

'Sounds like my school report.' I packed the tools back into my bag and stood. Dynamite Del's face was ashen and his hands were shaking. 'You gonna be alright, Del?'

He nodded. 'Jesus. You had me there.' He wiped a handkerchief on his bald brow. 'I thought that was game over for sure.'

'Nonsense.' Ronny was pointing to the door that led out to the back of the shop, which in turn provided access to the basement. 'Just a little hiccup is all. Nothing to worry about. Now – William? Will you do the honours?'

I walked through the door, past Ronny, and pointed to the CCTV unit that Lulu had informed us was there. It was an old VHS recorder, in keeping with Mr Greenbaum's tight-wad nature, and I disconnected the cameras and removed the tape. I waved it at Ronny. 'You might want to look after that?'

Ronny smiled. 'I do love a good home movie.'

'Boys? We have a problem.' It was Raven. He was facing us with his back to the front door and a look of bemusement on his face. Behind him, from the other side of the shop door, an elderly lady was waving her hand and pointing at the display case to her right. 'It seems like we have an eager shopper.'

There was an audible groan from Del who was looking increasingly under the weather.

'Well don't just stand there.' Ronny was gesticulating wildly. 'Get rid of her.'

Raven sighed and turned to the front door and I heard him holler, 'We're closed!'

The old lady, her hair dyed an odd shade of pink and her lipstick smeared on thick in a matching pink gloss, shouted back. 'It's about the bracelet I bought!'

'Okay, that's very nice, but we're closed!'

'I just need to talk to Mr Greenbaum!'

'Lady, I just said we're CLOSED!'

The lady wasn't giving up. 'But Mr Greenbaum said if it didn't fit I should just bring it straight back to the shop for an exchange!'

Raven was waving his arms. 'Mr Greenbaum's not here and we're … oh this is ridiculous.'

Raven opened the door and stuck his head through the gap. I could see the lady was quite animated and Raven was shaking his head as if empathising. Their speech was inaudible but I could see that the woman was giving Raven what for and he was taking it on the chin like the true sport that he was.

Ronny was getting anxious. 'What the hell is he up to?'

I chuckled. 'She's determined. I think he's playing along.'

Ronny grunted. 'What the hell for?'

'I guess he's humouring her.'

The old lady removed a silver bracelet from her right hand and handed it to Raven. Raven eyed it curiously and shook his head. The old lady removed a phone from her pocket and scrolled through her contacts and Raven waved his hands animatedly. He looked to his left side and nodded, pushed the door closed, rounded the rear of the display case that was just behind the shop window and pointed at a fabric square containing a dozen or so bracelets. The lady nodded eagerly. Raven leaned over, withdrew a bracelet, replaced the fabric square and returned to the door. He handed it to the old lady who placed it onto her right wrist. She held her arm to her face, closed one eye, broke into a smile and almost whooped with joy. She leaned forward and planted a big kiss right on Raven's open lips and patted him on the cheek. With that she turned and left.

Raven closed the door and shook his head wearily. 'Some people.'

Ronny strode up to him with intent and slapped him hard on the shoulder. 'Well played my friend, well played!'

Del stood behind Ronny and was giggling like a schoolchild. 'I ... I don't like your lipstick much Raven.'

Ronny, who was chuckling under his breath and nodding, pulled out a polka dot handkerchief from his pocket and wiped the pink goo off Raven's lips. 'I don't think this is your colour.'

I coughed and spoke up. 'I ... I've overridden the

basement lock.' I'd continued with the task at hand while Raven had worked his magic. 'Shall we … take a peek?'

'A sound idea!' Ronny came barrelling down the hallway. 'A sound plan by a hell of an electrician!' He gripped me in his large hands. 'Let's see what's behind door number three!'

Raven and Del joined us in the small hallway as Ronny pulled the basement door open.

Behind it stood a thin, greasy looking creature with a flushed face and wearing nothing but a pair of yellow gloves, a blue vest and a pair of bright green speedos. Wesley Pollock beamed back at us like a child that had just been given the keys to the sweet shop. In his right hand he held a tight bundle of fifty pound notes.

'Has anyone got any change?'

Chapter 60:
Follow that Car

Grandpappy pushed her along the path in her nonna's old wheelchair to the side of his car. Lorna was amazed that the battered old thing was still mobile.

'Your old house? That's where we're headed?' Her grandpappy was only just able to shuffle along the path in his open toed sandals and Lorna felt helpless being cared for by her fragile, elderly custodian.

'That's where she'll be. I'm sure of it.'

Grandpappy hoisted her into the car's passenger seat with a loud groan and more than a few creaks of his ageing bones. 'Well, I hope you're right.'

'You and me both.'

The old car started with a squeal and a holler and petrol fumes leapt from the exhaust in a thick cloud of billowing smoke. 'Don't worry.' He smiled and placed a hand on her arm. 'She hasn't let me down yet.'

Lorna smiled tenderly and kissed him on the cheek. 'Thank you.'

He smiled back. 'For what?'

'For being ... you.'

They pulled away from the Millhouse, turned left and were soon making their way through the old town with its terraced cottages and cobbled streets, and then headed out to the thin and winding, farmland-bordered Westhampton country lanes.

A few minutes later a black Audi A4 pulled up in the Millhouse's open driveway, followed by a squad car with blue flashing lights. Detective Allison Webber emerged from the car in front, closely followed by a large lady in a white uniform with bright red lipstick and red nails to boot. Doctor Janet Weir looked down at the stream, a bright yellow oar floating idly in the murky green liquid, and up at the Millhouse's ivy strewn façade. She smiled.

'Loonie Lorna's been here alright, Detective.' Her brow furrowed. 'Now,' she clasped her thick fingers together, 'where to next?'

****

Lorna felt a sharp pain in what remained of her legs as they pulled up outside of the estate. She immediately recalled the hot steel of the surgeon's knife as it cut flesh, the jagged edge of the saw as it severed bone, the mind numbing agony that ripped through her nerve endings. She shuddered and groaned and thick tears rolled down her cheeks.

'Are you okay, Lornie?' Her grandpappy was peering across at her from the tatty driver's seat.

She nodded. 'Yes. I'm fine.' She gripped the passenger door's arm rest. 'It's just ... been a long time.'

He smiled ruefully. 'Too long.'

She wiped the tears from her face and looked across at

the large iron gates opening up to a limestone driveway that she knew would curve through rolling meadows on its way to the large, Victorian mansion with red brick and black trim. The house that she once called home. She recalled her dressing room in the east wing that was nestled at the apex of the large circular, imposing turret. It was a beautiful space full of dresses worth many hundreds of pounds, jewellery that wouldn't look out of place in a palace and shoes that could adorn the feet of the wealthiest women in the world.

She cursed herself for becoming the victim of the terrible vanity and self-infatuation that had coursed through her mind and body at that time. She no longer knew that person. The mother who had spent little to no time with her one and only child. The woman who was rarely seen without a glass of Chardonnay in her one hand, an ornate cigarette holder in the other and some man by her side. She didn't deserve her little girl.

Her grandpappy touched her hand. 'What next, my love?'

Lorna looked at the gates. 'I … I don't know.'

They stared in silence at the property across the street from them and waited. Waited for inspiration.

Lorna could feel that despair again, the one that she knew would always be just around the corner, waiting to grab her in both its spindly, wiry hands and drag her towards the bottomless and vacuous pit that she had once used as her shelter, her safe place. She envisioned sunlight and flowers and the face of her baby daughter and little by little the darkness was pushed back to the cobwebbed corners of her imagination.

As the sun started to cut across the sky to the west and the shadows started to elongate and mis-form on the ground below there was a sound of locks unlatching and metal moving on stone. The gates swung inwards and Lorna watched as a large, navy blue Lexus pulled out of the driveway and swung to its left.

'I never thought I would ever say this, Grandpappy, and certainly not to you,' she pushed her semi-shaved, red and black unwashed hair out of her eyes and smiled, 'but ... follow that car!'

Chapter 61:
The Mannequin

Captain Gary Sealion pulled the boat up to the shoreline and beckoned Randall and Ruby to jump out.

'You're best taking your leave here,' he said to them both as he helped Ruby out. 'I'll swing around the bay a few times while you do whatever it is you're here to do and come back for you in thirty minutes or so.'

Randall shook his head. 'You might want to make it an hour. We have quite a lot to do.'

'Well you won't want to leave it much longer than that.' The Captain held an arm out to the ocean. 'She'll be coming back in before you know it and you don't want to be trapped inside that cave overnight.' He growled. 'It could drive a man insane, spending the night in those cold, dark and ghost ridden tunnels.'

Ruby smiled uncertainly but felt her pulse quicken.

Randall nodded. 'Then an hour to the minute it is then.' He shook Captain Gary's hand. 'Thanks for getting us out here in one piece, Captain.'

The Captain sneered. 'Thank me when you're out of that cave and back on dry land, Detective.'

With that he gestured towards the shore and Randall and Ruby stepped into the shallow water. Ruby immediately felt the cold of the Solent enshroud her walking boots and socks and she grimaced. 'That's icy.'

Randall held out his hand and she took it. 'Try not to fall in. You'll catch your death of pneumonia.'

They sloshed through the water towards the cave and watched as the red and white motorboat turned and headed out to sea.

'You ready, Rube?'

She looked up at him and pursed her lips. 'Well, if I'm going to find my first corpse since becoming a fully-fledged police officer, why not find it here,' she pointed at the gaping black and ominous hole that loomed in front of them, 'in an underwater cave with nothing but a flashlight and the fear of being left inside to drown and float around with half a dozen or so dead bodies like a waxy and terrifying mannequin.'

Randall chuckled. 'My thoughts exactly.'

Chapter 62:
The Boathouse

Lisa looked out of the car window as the coastline approached. She had no idea where the suspiciously calm and placid Chief Superintendent was taking her but she could see it was certainly going to be somewhere near the water.

She had tried Luke's phone again while she had waited for Deveraux to bring her silver Audi TT Coupé around the side of the apartment building, but to no avail. She cursed him but she knew there was little point. His vanishing acts were just another annoying trait that had led to their relationship's ultimate demise. While she had hoped of a reconciliation, something she knew that he wanted too, she was all too aware that if he couldn't be there for her and their son then there really was no future for them.

That was, of course, if she made it out of this alive.

'He'd better be there, Christy.'

'He will be.'

'Or you'd better believe that I will bring your whole world crashing down around your ears.' Lisa wished her voice sounded more convincing. Her plan was thin and sketchy at best.

'Oh,' Deveraux turned to face her, 'I have no doubt of that.' She pulled the car onto a shingle covered driveway and turned a corner to pull up beside a single storey, large wooden lodge. 'No doubt at all.'

Lisa was surprised to see that there were no other cars at the property. 'Well, where is he?'

Deveraux opened the driver's side door. 'Don't worry.' She hooked out a leg and turned back to Lisa. 'They're on their way.'

Lisa exited the vehicle and brushed a hand through her hair. The forest was to her left and the Solent to her right. She could see the Isle of Wight across the thin patch of sea, and when she turned behind her, she could see, in the distance, the large wheel of the busy fairground and the illuminated stage of the Bank Holiday beachfront celebrations.

'Nice place.'

'Our host is a man of great wealth.'

Lisa sneered. 'Forgive me for not admiring him.'

Christy beckoned her towards the front door of the lodge. 'Oh, trust me, my dear. There is a great deal to admire.' She smiled. 'He does a huge amount for this unforgiving community.'

Lisa laughed sarcastically. 'Like stealing children from their parents?'

Deveraux turned to face her. 'You crossed him.'

Lisa's mouth fell open. 'I did no such thing.'

'You associated with an old enemy.'

Lisa exhaled loudly. 'Sam Raven? *Sam Raven*? Is that who you mean?'

Deveraux's face was unmoving. 'The Curator betrayed us

badly, in ways that you could never imagine.'

Lisa took a step towards the statuesque woman. 'Fuck you! Fuck the lot of you and your little … club. Because that's what it is isn't it?' She was fighting the anger that was building in her veins and behind her widening eyes. 'Some self-important rich playboy club that holds all sorts of misguided, bullshit delusions of grandeur!' She kicked at the shingle under her feet. 'And what are you? Their muse? Their moll?' Deveraux's expression betrayed nothing. 'What drew you to a gang of wealthy, perverse middle aged white men with a tactic of bullying others into doing what they want and using their children as bait if they didn't?'

'You have no idea …'

'I have every idea!' Lisa held out her hands. 'As a mother, with a little boy who was snatched away from her trembling arms while she cowered on the floor in fear, I think I have every idea of what your *Legion* is all about!'

There was a muted silence, save but for the hiss of the ocean and the faint sound of live pop music as it drifted in their direction on the gentle breeze from the busy sea front celebrations.

Deveraux's face hardened and she turned to unlock the door. 'You'll have your son soon enough. You just need to play along.'

Lisa looked behind her, took a deep breath and stepped gingerly into the boathouse.

Chapter 63:
Daddy's Girl

They'd drugged the girl which was good. Molly thought that without Balthazar, who was still MIA, she would have struggled with a live and animated adult woman. After all, she had to get her to the tunnel entrance, navigate along its winding and crooked maze of tributaries and intersections and eventually emerge into her secret and sheltered place.

She pulled up at the cliff top in her Vauxhall Corsa and unfolded her fabric and plastic trolley onto the grass and dirt. She knew it was strong enough, they'd used it for another of their victims who was at least two or three stone heavier than the blond woman in the boot of her hatchback, and while she knew that pushing it over the rock strewn pathway of the network of cave tunnels would be tricky, she was sure that she was more than capable of the task.

She clicked a button on her key fob and the boot opened. Inside lay the prone, sleeping and muck covered form of the very beautiful – despite her condition – Jane Butler.

'Well, I don't know what you did to piss him off, Jane,' Molly pulled her by the legs towards the empty trolley. 'But my dad and his friends certainly want you out of the picture.'

Molly grunted as Jane's body slumped into the rectangular basket. Her mouth watered. 'And I am in no mood to deny daddy dearest.'

She closed the boot of her car and pulled the trolley towards a dense, coppice of shrubs that covered the entranceway to their tunnel. Not many people knew the hole was there, least of all her father, and she and Bal had been using it as the backdoor exit from their dark and damp mortuary since the third murder. This was the first time she would use it as an entranceway and she was keen to see whether it was as effective as the watery doorway they had been using to this point.

She turned to face the girl in her basket and groaned. 'So pretty, Jane. So slim and radiant.' She stroked a hand across her warm, unmoving cheek. 'I will take my time with you, slow and patient as if we are secret lovers.'

She pulled the trolley into the darkness as the scar on her face burned with an intense heat and the hole in her heart echoed with the emptiness of an open plain. She recalled Gretchen's bloodied and terrified face as she pushed the handkerchief into her dry and ashen mouth, the old lady's body convulsing and flailing as the life force evaporated from her sick and sallow body. 'I'm only here to make Daddy happy after all.' Her voice echoed off the damp and ancient limestone walls like the voice of a distant ghost. 'I'm Daddy's little girl.'

Chapter 64:
Bang Bangs

Raven checked his watch. It was ten to seven which meant they had ten minutes before all hell would break loose.

Billy, Wesley and Ronny were loading great armfuls of cash and jewellery into the canvas sacks that they had brought with them while Dynamite Del was outside the vault in the narrow entranceway, shoving thick sticks of nitro glycerine onto carefully placed holes that he had drilled around the concrete and brick tunnel entrance with his battery powered hammer drill.

'Well, this is a lot more than even old Lulu had predicted. A *lot* more.' Ronny was grinning from ear to ear. 'We're gonna struggle to carry all of it at this rate.' He was spitting as he enunciated his words, the intense excitement rippling through his huge frame. 'I reckon there could be up to half a mil each here.'

Wesley cackled. 'Yeah, we're gonna be loaded, Ron. Loaded!'

Billy looked up at Raven, his face a light shade of pink and sweat pouring from his thick brow. Raven nodded casually.

'Luke, would you go and see how Del's getting on with the bang bangs?' Ronny chuckled. 'There's only one way out of this place with this much loot, and that's through that concreted up escape hatch.'

'Yeah, no problem.' Raven turned to the vault's exit but then paused and turned back. He just couldn't help himself. It had been building. 'Ron?'

Billy looked up with a start and shook his head violently. Raven ignored him.

'What's up? Come on, hurry it along.' Ronny had his head buried in his canvas sack and was re-arranging the loot to make more room.

'Remember that time, when you almost got me sacked for suggesting I'd misappropriated some of the stolen goods that you'd half inched from the local cash and carry?'

Ronny's head appeared from his loot bag and he laughed. 'Oh yeah!' He pointed at Raven. 'You're not still sore about that are you?'

'No, no. Not at all.' Billy uttered a low groan. 'But … do you also remember the time when you slept with that girl I was seeing?'

Ronny sighed. 'I do. I really do. Daisy was her name and a right feisty bird if ever there was one.'

Wesley uttered an intentionally comical *'phwoargh!'*

Ronny continued, 'Raven obviously couldn't satisfy her in the sack so Granddad Ron had to step in. I never heard her grumble once after that.'

Raven bit his tongue as he remembered how he had cradled the dying Daisy Reynold's body in his arms after she was brutally stabbed by the Pale Faced killer. How he had felt her fragile final breath as it spilled from her soft lips.

'Ha ha. That's right, yes.' Raven looked out at Del who had his thumb up and a trigger switch in his right hand. 'And you remember the time, Ron, when you tried to get my dad thrown in the slammer for fraudulent accounting, even though he was laundering money for you and your deviant little business enterprises?'

Ronny stood up, his face flushed red. 'Now, you know that's bullshit!' He threw down his sack and took a step towards him. 'He ripped me off to the tune of fifty grand, that lowlife scumbag!' Ronny grabbed Raven by the shirt collar and pushed him backwards. 'Your old man was as shifty as they come and sly with it!' He leaned forward and exhaled cigar infused breath into Raven's stubbornly resistant face. 'I should be taking the debt out of your end.' He growled. 'I for one don't miss him.'

'Get your fucking hands off me, Ron, or this could get very ugly, very quickly.'

Ronny continued to breathe heavily and grunt like an ox in a bull-fight. He was flustered, Raven knew it, which was exactly where he wanted him.

'Del,' Ronny pointed at the animated explosives expert. After the consternation of earlier on, when Del looked like he was on the verge of a nervous breakdown, he now appeared excited and eager to get on with it. 'Blow that fucking hole and let's get the hell out of this hot tub before one of us gets killed.'

Raven smiled at Billy as they all took their places behind the concrete and steel wall of the vault. He checked his watch and it was one minute to. His hackles were up, his body tense and energised with the eager and yet nervous anticipation of imminent action.

Del rounded the corner with his hand on the trigger switch, and Ronny placed his own hand over the top. They both counted down in unison.

'Three, two, one …'

Their fingers depressed simultaneously and there was an explosion loud enough to rattle their brains and scramble their senses. Dust, smoke and brick dust filled the vault like a dense and suffocating fog. Raven heard a *'bloody hell!'* and *'Jesus, Del!'* and a couple of whoops from Ronny and then, as if timed to perfection, the door leading to the ground floor staircase came crashing in.

'Police – don't move! Everybody on the ground, now!'

Raven could barely see a thing, the concrete and cement dust clouding his vision and filling his lungs. He brushed some of it out of the air like a vapid apparition and saw Billy crouched next to him. He nodded.

He looked around at the brick and muck strewn floor of the vault and saw Ronny laying down face first with an anxiously flustered Del next to him. Ronny was glaring at Raven with a look that screamed hatred and betrayal. Raven scoured the vault for signs of Wes but he couldn't locate him. He glanced through the opening into the vault's entrance hall and saw three men with handguns. No ballistics vests, no masks, no identification. The men were middle aged and all looked like they'd just walked out of the trading floor of the London stock exchange. He immediately sensed danger.

'Billy.' He whispered.

Billy nodded.

'We're getting the fuck out of here.'

Billy looked up at him, confused. 'But …'

'We've been double crossed by that bitch Deveraux.'

412

Raven shook his head. 'I should have seen this coming a mile off, but maybe I'm getting slow and a little too trusting of others in my old age.' He cursed himself for his naivety.

Billy was dumbfounded. 'So those aren't cops?'

'They're as much a bunch of cops as you're the chief of police, Billy.' Raven pulled Billy up by his thick arm. 'Now let's hustle.'

Raven used the confusion caused by the explosion to slip out of the vault door. He looked back and saw Ronny lying prone on the floor, murderous venom pouring from his eyes. 'You're fucked, Raven! When I get out of this, I'll be coming for you. You'd better count on that!'

Raven smiled back and blew him a kiss. 'I'd be disappointed if you didn't, Ron my old love.' He turned and almost walked into a tall, blonde haired man wearing a beige sweatshirt and blue jeans.

'Where the hell do you think you're going, Raven?' The man raised his pistol at the two of them and beckoned them to the low couch that lined the back of the room. Behind him were two other men who were deliberately blocking the escape route that led up the staircase to the ground floor.

Raven glanced over his shoulder at the still smouldering tunnel entrance. He winked at Billy once more who cottoned on immediately and nodded cautiously.

'I don't think so fella,' he retorted. 'Here's one for the old chaps.' He raised his knee as hard as he could into the man's testicles. A loud '*oof!*' emanated from the blonde haired man's lips and he crumpled to the floor in a heap. Raven grabbed the gun out of the man's trembling hand and pulled Billy towards the tunnel, just as the two men behind him hollered in disapproval.

He heard crushed testicle man shout, 'Get after them you prats!' as he and Billy dived into the black unknown of the newly re-opened Westhampton underground tunnel network and hastily plunged themselves into the damp darkness of its murky abyss.

Chapter 65:
Pirate Hunting

Lorna watched from afar as the Lexus drew up alongside the little white Corsa. She gasped as two men pulled what appeared to be a dead body from the rear of their vehicle and shoved it into the boot of the little hatchback. Then her ex-husband pulled his hulking frame from the rear seat of the Lexus and walked over to the smaller car. A beautiful young girl stepped out into the open and stood next to her father.

Lorna gasped. She felt as if all of her dreams, all of her moments of grim but desperate optimism, had erupted into reality before her very eyes.

'Molly.' Her low whisper was cracked and hoarse.

Molly stood there in her blue jeans, black short sleeved top, pale blue trainers and hair that tumbled over her shoulders in ebony, untamed ringlets. Lorna had never seen anyone more beautiful in her whole life. Her heart skipped in her chest. She wanted to reach out to her and hold her in her bosom like the baby that she once was. Oh, how she wished she could take all of those forgotten years back and start everything over. Things would be so different.

Her grandfather sighed. 'She looks like your nonna. She

really does. Back when I first met her.' He groaned. 'But it looks like she's gotten herself into a whole world of trouble.'

'But it's my Molly, Grandpappy.' She reached for him. 'It's *our* little girl!' She was grinning.

Her grandfather shook his head. 'She's had almost twenty years of her father's influence, my dear.'

'I refuse to believe it.' Lorna was shaking.

'Then tell me what we're seeing here.'

Lorna watched as Bernie and Molly held a short, emotionless discussion. Bernie appeared to be giving Molly some sort of direction and Molly appeared to be rebutting with her own instructions.

'I don't know. I can't piece it together.'

Her grandfather turned to her. 'Well, I'll tell you, then.' He pointed at the two cars. 'Your ex-husband, the man that did …' he pointed at her legs, '*this* to you, is clearly up to more of the same, although this time he's followed through on his murderous intentions. Something I am sure he had meant to do to you, if you hadn't had the good sense to get away from him. And he's gotten your daughter, my great grand-daughter, all mixed up in some despicable plan to dispose of the body! Like he hasn't got the wherewithal to do that himself! Does that sound plausible to you?'

'Nothing sounds plausible to me at the moment.'

'Well then open your bloody eyes!' He was spitting as he hollered. 'Look at what's right in front of your face!'

Lorna sobbed. 'I can't!'

Her grandfather placed his hand on her shoulder. 'You must.' He hugged her. 'Lorna, sweetheart, the apple doesn't fall far from the tree, especially when the only loving influences in Molly's life were taken away from her!'

There was a moment of solemn silence, Lorna staring down at the floor and her grandfather looking on.

'I failed her.'

A tear rolled down her grandfather's cheek. 'No, Lornie.' He kissed her. 'He failed you both.'

Lorna sobbed into her elderly patriarch's shoulder and he allowed himself a tear or two. Emotion poured from her battered body in great waves of sadness. She felt the many years of detachment come flooding back to her like a bitter and sallow memory, one that she had hoped had been vanquished to the dusty corners of her brain.

The tears soon subsided. She looked up just in time to see Molly and Bernie getting back into their respective cars. After a moment, the Lexus rolled around the smaller car and raced off into the distance. She felt a hatred boil in her stomach with the acidity of neat alcohol. She slammed her hand on the dashboard. 'I can change her, *goddammit*! I can bring her back!'

Her grandfather held her hand tightly. 'That's a hell of a gamble. Is it one that you're willing to bet your life on?'

Lorna nodded slowly. 'What else am I going to do?'

Her grandfather groaned and looked west at the slowly setting sun. He pursed his lips sombrely and shook his head in grim acceptance.

'Then where are we headed?'

'The only place I want to be.' She pointed as the little white car pulled away. 'Wherever my daughter is going.'

****

Grandpappy stayed a good distance from the car in front,

417

which was wise as they were the only other vehicle on the road.

'We seem to be heading out towards the coast.' Grandpappy had his eyes glued firmly to the bumper in front and both hands on the wheel.

'It seems that way.' Lorna was glaring over the dashboard at the white car ahead. She couldn't believe that her little baby knew how to drive, let alone how to get rid of a corpse. 'If Westhampton is that way,' she pointed, 'over there to our right, then what lies this way?'

Granpappy shrugged. 'Could be Fisherman's Catch, could be the cliff top at Bishop's Crag.'

Lorna gasped. 'Do you think she's going to launch the body off the cliff?'

'Maybe. People have done stupider things.'

'We have to stop her.'

Lorna's grandfather nodded. 'Well that part, my girl, I'll leave up to you. I'll just steer you to within earshot.'

Lorna nodded. She felt sure, as sure as she had ever been of anything in her life, that she could get through to her daughter. Her little orchid. Her baby.

Molly's car swung to the right and headed down a roughly gravelled dirt track. Grandpappy almost overshot the turning but hit the brakes hard, narrowly avoiding being rear ended by a Range Rover that was hurtling past them at some considerable speed.

'*Stupid prick!*' Lorna heard a male voice holler as the Range Rover tore off into the distance.

Grandpappy turned to her. 'Well that was a little too close for comfort.'

He turned the stiff and frayed steering wheel to his left

418

and swung the car onto the rough and bumpy track. Molly's Corsa was already some four hundred yards or so further along the path and turning right onto a new, even less well marked trail. Grandpappy followed on behind at a slow and deliberate pace.

'Don't lose her!'

'Do you want her to see us?'

'No, but I don't want her doing anything stupid either.'

'I think that ship has already sailed.' Grandpappy gripped his hands tight on the wheel which was shaking violently, the Granada's old and tired suspension struggling to cope with the many divots and stony lumps. 'It's difficult to come back from murder, no matter what the circumstances.'

Lorna wheeled on him. 'Don't say that. We don't know she's murdered anyone.'

Lorna could see the sea on the horizon and the approaching precipice of the clifftops in the distance. Molly's car suddenly swung hard to the right and parked diagonally next to a raised copse of bushes. She watched as the diminutive form of her daughter leapt from the driver's side door like a circus clown and skipped to the back of the car.

'She seems merry.' Her grandfather had his spectacles on and was watching with grim curiosity.

Lorna just observed in silent contemplation.

Molly unloaded a collapsible trolley and pulled the body from the rear of the car, dropping it into the vacant basket.

'What's she doing?' Lorna was astonished.

'Wait. I know what that is.'

'What do you mean?'

He pointed. 'That cluster of brambles. There, to the right

419

of the car? When we were kids, a long time ago, way before I met your nonna, we'd go down there.' He chuckled. 'Old Alfie Taylor would play Blackbeard and Tommy Sharples and I would play the British naval officers. We'd run around those tunnels as if they were our own little rat-run. A little adventure playground that only we knew existed and that no one, not even our parents, could ever be allowed to find out about.'

'Tunnels? What tunnels?'

He turned to face her. 'The tunnels. Over there. Deep and winding tunnels, tunnels that would make your senses spin. Damp and dark like the inside of a sewer but sweeter smelling and as pretty as a postcard.' He nodded. 'They lead down to Barbary's Hole.'

Lorna recalled something from her schooldays. 'Barbary's Hole? Isn't that a legend or myth or something about pirates and smugglers that used to bring illegal alcohol and contraband into the town?'

He nodded.

'But wasn't that just an old wives' tale?'

'That was what we all thought. Until we found that tunnel.' He was pointing in the direction that her daughter was headed. 'Which as far as I know is the only open culvert to the underground tunnel network that winds beneath these cliffs and underneath the town. They go on for miles, you know, tens of miles even.'

Lorna watched with a growing unease as her daughter pushed the trolley containing the corpse – a young woman – through the thicket, the brambles closing in behind them like a thick and impenetrable stage curtain. Within an instant they had vanished.

'Well, we need to follow her. Right now! Before we lose her!'

Her grandpappy turned to her and grabbed her firmly by the shoulders. 'Lorna, my dear. I may look young and sprightly, but I'm an eighty nine year old man with crumbling hips, a cataract that gets worse by the day and curvature of the spine that makes me stoop over like a bloody ape.' He suddenly looked very old to her. Perhaps she had been too preoccupied in her own endeavour to notice. 'And even if I could, even if there was an outside chance that I would have the strength and agility to do it, I'm not convinced your nonna's old wheelchair would make it all the way down that tunnel without coming apart in my hands and spilling you onto the rocks and muck.'

Lorna felt tears welling in her eyes once more. 'But … *Molly*.'

They both stared at each other for what seemed like an eternity, neither wanting to admit that their disabilities were going to ultimately cause them to fail in rescuing their beloved kin. The shadow of her grandfather fell on Lorna's tired and distraught face and she felt like the darkness was sucking her whole world out from within her body and gobbling it up like it was a hearty and satisfying meal.

Suddenly her grandfather's eye twitched and he checked his watch.

'Wait a minute.' He raised his wrist to his good eye. 'Six thirty. That's good.'

Lorna raised her eyebrows. 'What's good?'

He re-fired the Granada's old engine. 'Pat Feeley's boat hire shop doesn't close until eight and this time of year the Spring tide lasts until around seven thirty.' He swung the car around. 'It's been a long time, but I still think I've got it in me.'

'Got what in you?'

'Sailing, my girl!' He winked with his good eye. 'Lorna, we're going pirate hunting!'

Chapter 66:
Arrival

Lisa stood in front of the large bay window and watched the boats sail by on the smooth waters of the Solent. Deveraux was reclining on the sofa behind her, sipping a Malbec. She had removed her jacket, exposing a peach-coloured shirt and a silver and diamond encrusted pendant in the shape of a dagger. Lisa wanted to rip the necklace from her body and drive the dagger into the devious woman's eye.

'Where are they?'

'They won't be much longer, I'm sure.' Deveraux pointed to the large, oak bar that ran across the back of the property. 'You sure you won't join me in a drink?'

'I have nothing to celebrate.' Lisa turned back to the window. 'I came here for my son, and I intend to take him safely back home with me.'

Deveraux sighed but there was a hint of sarcasm in her tone. 'Does your anger come naturally or do you have to work at it?'

Lisa was unmoving. 'Naturally. It's served me well so far.'

'Couldn't keep you two together though, could it?'

Lisa wheeled around. 'What do you mean?'

Deveraux chuckled cruelly. 'You and Luke?' She leaned forward, cradling the half full wine glass between two fingers. 'The father of your child? How long was it? Six months? Seven?'

'Fourteen months and it's none of your business.' She leaned against the internal wall separating the front porch of the boathouse from the living area.

'And where is he now in your hour of need?'

Lisa shrugged. 'I have no idea, and neither do I care.'

'I would have thought he should be standing where you are, Lisa, rather than leaving you to deal with this whole sorry mess on your own.'

'I'm more than capable of looking after me and my son!' She took a breath to collect herself, quietly considering her riposte. 'Single, aren't you, Christy? Live on your own in that great big apartment of yours?'

Deveraux smiled but Lisa could see that the sharp barb had stung. 'I like it that way.'

'I bet you do. I bet this lot,' she held out her arms at the vastness of the property, 'I bet they get their wicked way with you whenever and *however* they want.'

Deveraux sipped from her wine glass and swallowed slowly. She breathed out. 'It's not like that.'

Lisa huffed under her breath in audible disbelief. 'From what Sam tells me, these cretins wouldn't think twice before stripping you naked and flagellating you like a piece of cheap, raw meat.'

Deveraux's eyes flitted anxiously. 'I've known these men since I was a teenager. They've been good to me. Helped me to rise to this position of power within the police force. You think it's easy being a woman in my profession, having the responsibilities that I have, rubbernecking with middle aged white men at endless dinners, negotiating with grey-haired bosses with sticks so far up their arses that they couldn't bend to an idea if their lives depended on it?'

Lisa held up her hands. 'I'm sure.'

'You think that apartment pays for itself? You think these clothes buy themselves? You think that fucking car just fell off the back of a lorry and landed in my lap like some cheap perfume?' Deveraux stood up and walked towards Lisa, bearing down on her angrily. 'I came from nothing! Nothing! Fiddled with by a pervert of a priest at an orphanage, thrown onto the streets for fighting with the nuns and spitting at the other cruel and spiteful kids, left to sleep in shop doorways with nothing but a cardboard box and a paper cup full of loose change for comfort!' Lisa could smell the wine on Christy's breath and the bitterness oozing from her. Deveraux whispered her last sentence with a desperation and defiance that couldn't be masked. 'Do you think that if I didn't do what I did,' her eyes were steely and determined, 'the *way* that I do it, that I would be able to lead the *life that I lead*?'

Lisa looked up at Christy, unthreatened by her imposing frame and caustic tone, and responded calmly. 'Well, I hope it's worth it. Because from where I'm standing, you look very much like a bruised and fragile woman who needs to get away from the poison that has been intoxicating her for far too long.'

There was a moment of silence save for their shallow breathing. Their arguments were spent.

With a crash and a whoosh of escaping intensity the front

425

door opened.

Lisa turned and watched the arrival of a large and statuesque gentleman. He was pushing a wheelchair carrying the bandaged and pale form of the tall man that had snatched her sobbing son from her arms. Lisa growled under her breath.

The man pushing the wheelchair held out his huge hand. Lisa did not respond.

'Lisa, isn't it?' The large man smiled but Lisa could see the evil intent behind his eyes. 'Bernie Staker's the name and it's a pleasure to meet you.' He pointed at the man in the wheelchair. 'I believe you've met Robert. Or, at least, you shared a moment of passion in a quiet alleyway.' He laughed. 'I hope you like my little boathouse and that everything is to your ... taste.'

Lisa grunted. 'I don't care who you are, or who this prick is in the wheelchair.' Robert Charon leered up at her and she snarled back viciously. She stepped towards Staker and shoved her finger hard into his barrel of a chest. 'All I want to know is,' she leaned forward and spat out her words like sharp spears of hate, 'where's my *fucking* son!'

Chapter 67:
Smugglers' Morgue

There was a wide stream that ran through the base of the cave and Randall and Ruby had to climb up the side of the rocky face to make it to the much drier elevated walkway. The rock was hard and jagged and Ruby lost her footing more than once, bashing her legs and elbows on the sharp limestone outcroppings.

'Shit!'

Randall leaned towards her. 'Do you want a hand?'

'Thanks. No.' She smiled but she was breathing hard. This was more physical exertion than she'd had in at least a year back at the station. 'I can do it.'

The light couldn't penetrate more than twenty or so feet in. As Ruby hauled herself up to the base of the rocky path, she peered into the darkness uncertainly.

'Don't worry, Rube.' All of a sudden, Randall's smiling face was illuminated in a bluish hue. 'I brought torches.'

The relief in the young PC was palpable. She eagerly grabbed the small, circular LED light from his hand and looped the black, elastic straps around her forehead. Together they both looked like a pair of science fiction cyclops and she chuckled at the image.

'Be careful with your footing here, Rube. The rocks are uneven and slippery.'

She smiled. 'I'll be okay.' Almost instantly the foot holding her slight frame slid to her right and she wheeled her arms frantically. Randall grabbed her elbow in his firm but tender grip and steadied her.

'You alright?'

She nodded but she could feel her face blushing a fiery crimson in the darkness. 'I … I will be putting a call into the council about this footpath when we get back.'

Randall laughed cheerily.

They proceeded ahead in silence, the sound of the ocean echoing through the vast open chasm of the cave around them and the daylight disappearing from their rear view mirror. The place was much larger than Ruby had imagined, the top some ten or fifteen feet above them and the rear wall way out of reach of their headlamps. On their side of the running stream the path was around six feet wide, and on the other there was a narrow walkway of around two feet. Ruby could imagine smugglers bringing their longboats into the cave along that stream and stashing their barrels and crates at the back for the shoremen to haul inland along the tunnels that Randall had informed her criss-crossed underneath the town like a railway network. It was fascinating to her, but also terrifying. She dreaded what they might find.

'Up ahead, Ruby. Do you see that?' Randall was pointing diagonally to her left at what appeared to be the remains of a campfire. It was on a platform that was some three or four feet above them. Ruby climbed upwards and peered at the smouldering embers of tree branches and kindling and a tripod of metal skewers holding a tin kettle above what would have been roaring flames.

'Someone's been here.'

Randall nodded sombrely. 'Doesn't mean it's our guy, but it's something alright.'

Ruby pulled herself up onto the platform and Randall followed. She looked around at a large, flat slab of stone with sleeping bags off to her left and a black, open space to her right. Almost instantly the smell hit her. It was like strong pickle, salt and rotting meat. She held a hand to her mouth.

'Ugh! What is that?'

Randall stood next to her and pulled two small, white handkerchiefs from his pocket. 'I had a feeling we would need these.' He handed her one. 'I've sprayed them with room deodorizer. Don't worry, it's not used. Hold it to your face and it will take the edge off the smell.'

She held it up to her nose and almost immediately she felt better. 'What the hell is that?'

'I have a suspicion.' His face took on a grim seriousness. 'Let's find out.'

They crossed the flat, rocky area in large strides, Ruby two steps behind and peering all around her for signs of life, friendly or otherwise. Randall was bold in his strides, like a hunter who has caught the noxious scent of his prey. Ruby knew with a morbid certainty that they weren't leaving the cave empty handed, at whatever cost.

Up ahead she spied something. 'What's that?'

Randall turned to face her. 'Where? What?' He was energised, excited.

'Over there, by that large boulder.'

Randall turned and peered into the darkness. He stepped

429

cautiously in the general direction that Ruby was pointing. She watched him disappear into the gloom and held her breath. The darkness of the cave enveloped her and the low hiss of the ocean whispered in her ear like the gentle, melodic voice of a harpy.

'Leave here now, leave here now, leave here now.'

She gulped and looked around her. Black shapes swirled around her head like dancing fairies; dark, looping circles of death lassoed her arms and legs so that she couldn't move; an ebony snare of invisible tether gripped her throat so that she couldn't speak or even breathe. She wrestled with the silent, invisible demons with all her strength, her eyes wide and panicked, her hands clenching and unclenching like she was being electrified by her own terror. She wanted to run, to leap from the rocks and into the shallow stream below, swim with all her might and leave the black and damp mouth of Barbary's Hole to the ghosts of the long forgotten. She wasn't meant to be there.

'Don't come over here, Rube.'

'What is it?' Ruby fought to calm her trembling voice.

'Well, if I had to guess I would say we've found the body of Simon Farrington. Well, most of it.'

Ruby gasped. 'Oh god.'

'Oh god indeed.'

Randall returned to Ruby and she thought that she had never been so glad to see someone in all her life.

'It's a mess,' he said, running a weary hand over his face. 'Arms, legs, head – all cut off. Vital organs and intestines carefully removed.'

She grabbed his hand. 'Are you okay?'

He looked at her and then at her hand in his. He smiled

and peered down at her warmly. 'I'm fine.' He touched her cheek. 'Are you?'

She felt the warmth of his fingertips on her skin and she shuddered. Her emotions were in such a raw and fragile state that she knew the electricity pulsing through her nerve endings was abnormal. But still, it mattered to her. She thought of Dan, at home alone and watching some shit on the TV or playing on his beloved Xbox. And she thought of their situation, her and DI Kipruto, holed up in that cold and sodden smugglers' morgue with nothing but dead bodies and each other for company. For protection. She wanted to hold him, to feel his chest against her body, to feel the comfort in his strong arms. It couldn't be fake, could it? She wanted it, didn't she?

'Let's push on.' Randall broke the tension between them. Or did she imagine that too? 'There's more here, I'm sure of it.'

They turned to go back in the direction that they had previously been headed, Ruby reluctantly so, when a yellow glow emerged from up ahead, followed by a clatter of wheels on stone and a sweet melody being hummed by a lilting female voice. Ruby walked forward, her fear swiftly abating and her mouth falling open in a look of utter bewilderment.

'Staker?' The girl up ahead stopped dead in her tracks. 'PC Molly Staker. Is that you?'

Chapter 68:
Keep Left

We ran down that tunnel like a couple of field mice and all I kept thinking was, 'What if we get lost down here?'

I could hear Ronny behind us giving the fake coppers a good seeing to and I half expected him to race down the rocky tube after us to finish the job. I didn't dare imagine what he would do to Raven and me if we were caught alone with him in a small, restricted space.

'So I guess we keep going until we come to the other end of this thing?' I sounded as unsure of myself as I felt.

Raven was impassive. I had my phone held out in front with the torch switched on but I only had fifteen percent battery left and I was dreading the moment the lights went out.

'I don't think it's as simple as that, but here's hoping.'

I gulped. I knew you were going to be worried sick and I hated the thought of you finding me down there, cold and dead like a frozen slab of festering meat.

We came to a fork in the tunnels and I looked at Raven. 'Which way?'

Raven shrugged. 'Beats me.' He turned to me. 'Flip of a

coin?'

'Flip of a coin? Flip of a *coin*? Surely you've got something better than that?'

Raven stopped to consider it. He took a metallic hip flask from his pocket and held it out to me. 'You want some?'

I gasped. 'What the …' I hesitated. 'What is it?'

'Scotch, single malt.' He glugged from it like he was drinking from a bottle of Evian.

I shook my head, took the flask from his grip and swallowed a large mouthful. The whiskey hit my insides like an inferno and I relished the peaty taste as it coated my mouth and throat. I felt the tenseness in my muscles and in my face start to relax a little. With that came an epiphany. 'I've got it!'

Raven shook his head. 'Got what?'

'I read it somewhere, about mazes and that kind of thing.'

'Mazes?'

'Yeah, like this. You know, puzzles?'

Raven took his flask back. 'Billy, this isn't some stupid game. This is our lives.' He took another hit, swallowed and wiped his mouth with the back of his hand. 'We get lost down here and its game over for the both of us.'

I grabbed the flask back and swigged a little more myself. 'Keep left!' I smiled.

'Keep left? What the hell are you …?'

'I read it in one of Sal's puzzle magazines. You know the ones with anagrams, word searches, crosswords, that kind of thing?'

'Yes, but …'

'It was in the hints and tips section. At the back.' I grinned because it was the first place I'd go to when cogitating over

433

one of those bloody things. 'The cheat sheet. It's what you do when cracking a maze.' I pointed to the branch on my side of the tunnel. 'Keep left!'

We raced down the left hand branch until we came to the next intersection, and then we went left again. I was sure, as sure as I'd ever been of anything in my life, that we were going the right way.

The noise behind us had disappeared entirely and all I could hear was the drip, drip of filtered water through limestone, and our heavy footfalls on the rocky path. We took another left turn down a tunnel that was much narrower and with a slightly lower ceiling. We both had to stoop while we were running and were now shoulder to shoulder. I was panting furiously.

'I might have to take a breather, Raven.'

Raven was breathing heavily himself. 'I'd rather just push on, if we can. We've got no idea how that fist fight back there turned out, but I'm backing the three guys with guns.' As if to emphasise the point a loud crack, like a pistol going off in a tin can, resonated down the tunnel like the sound of our impending demise.

I nodded eagerly. 'Let's keep going.'

We kept on moving down that rapidly narrowing track, my claustrophobia gnawing at my every thought like a hungry rat on a piece of mouldy, blue cheese. My breathing became shallow and my vision started to become a little out of focus. The blue haze of my torch started to dim.

'My battery's going to die, Raven.'

'Then let's keep moving for as long as we have light. The faster we go the further we'll get.'

'I … I don't know how long it will last. Maybe another

434

minute?' I was becoming panicked. I started to lag behind him, just a couple of steps at first, but then three steps, four. Raven was pushing hard and I just couldn't keep up. I know you'll say that you've told me countless times that I should lose some weight and work on my fitness. If I had I wouldn't have gotten myself into that … mess. But I've always been big, my old man was big, so I've always been fighting a losing battle, really.

'Raven … I …'

'Come on, keep going. I can feel cool air coming from somewhere!' He was shouting back at me but I could barely hear him. My mind was all fuzzy and the oxygen level to my brain was depleting. I think, looking back, that I'd started to have a panic attack.

'Cool air? Where …'

'Another left hand turn! Just one more!' He was now fading into a low echo. 'I think you were right. Go left! Genius!'

My left foot trod wearily on my right foot and I found myself tumbling onto wet stone and sludge. My phone slipped out of my weakening hand and went crashing onto the rock, the already fading torch light now blinking out completely. I was in utter darkness. I called out tamely.

'Raven?'

There was nothing. No voice, no footsteps, no breathing except my own frantic panting, my lungs expelling hot and sticky air.

'Raven?'

I listened again, hoping against hope that Raven would appear in front of me with a fully powered torch, a glass of brown ale, a cheeseburger and a smile declaring victory. I could almost taste it.

All of a sudden, a light appeared before me, a thick white light with a thin shadow beyond.

'Is that you, Raven?'

A face loomed down over me like a harvest moon. Blonde, spiky hair, spotty face and crooked teeth.

'Wesley?'

'One and the same, my friend.' He crouched down.

'How did you get away? We looked for you but …'

He placed a finger to his lips. 'Never mind that,' he whispered. 'What I want to know is, why are you down here in my little space?'

'Your little space? What are you talking about? Raven and I …'

He grinned. 'Yeah, yeah. I'll get to him. But first,' he took out a long line of black cord from his rucksack. I thought it looked a lot like the backpack that Del had been carrying. 'Let's get you prepped.'

I had pushed myself to a sitting position but I was still severely disorientated. The only focal point I had was Wes' face and the white beam of bright light from the large torch that lay on the ground, facing us. 'Prepped for what?'

'You mean for who.'

I was confused and started to get annoyed. 'What the hell are you talking about?' Wesley tried to tie the cord around my wrists but I pushed him away. 'Fuck off, Wesley! What are you doing?'

'Just sit still, will you.' He grabbed my hands again and I kicked out at him.

'So help me god, I'm going to beat the living crap out of you if you try that again!'

He reached into his bag and pulled out something long and shiny.

'Suit yourself.'

Too late I saw him raise his arm and swing what looked like a socket wrench at my head. I heard a loud thud from far away, felt warm liquid run down my cheek and chin and then everything went dark.

Chapter 69:
Ghosts

'Billy, Billy!' Raven was in complete darkness with nothing but his fingertips on wet stone helping him to head in any sort of straight line.

He had somehow gotten too far ahead of Billy. His internal warning indicator was screaming at him to get the hell out of there as quickly as he could, and he hadn't realised that Billy had dropped back so far. It was only when the fading torch light had been completely extinguished that he realised he was completely on his own.

From someway behind him he heard Billy shouting, firstly for him and then someone or something else. It was shortly followed by a thud and then silence. He'd turned to go back to him but had become disorientated, the last fork he had taken had scrambled his senses in the black. He no longer knew if he was on the same tributary or whether he was now on the right hand side of the fork and descending deeper and deeper into the cave network.

'Billy! You there?'

He tripped on a raised outcropping in front of him and almost fell face first into a hard slug of limestone. His hand scrambled for a grip on the smooth and wet tunnel wall while his other hand took most of the ground impact. He grunted loudly.

He sat, one knee on the ground and one raised in front of him with his elbow balanced upon it and caught his breath. They must have run a mile or more into the rabbit's warren and he still felt no closer to finding the exit. A cool breeze caressed his cheek and he reminded himself that he'd felt that just moments before. He knew it must be coming from an opening somewhere close. He regained his composure and pushed on.

He hadn't spoken to Lisa in almost two days and he wanted to take things forward with her. They were reconnecting, he could feel it, and he felt a strong, burning desire to see where it could take them. He'd learned from his mistakes. He wanted to be with his son, more than life itself, and not just as a part time father. No, as a real dad, someone that would be there when the kid needed him, when his partner needed him. Not like his old man. The guy was never there, not for him, not for his mum. He was too interested in hob-knobbing with his wealthy pals, running errands for complete strangers who paid well and got him invites to swanky dinners and dances and fraternising with the many beautiful women that hung around the rich boys' club. That wasn't what a father did. And now he thought he could just waltz back into Raven's life, after both he and his mother had gone through the trauma of burying him, *mourning* for him? No way. Raven was no soft touch. He wanted something, something he didn't deserve and he wasn't going to get it from him, from Lisa or from his boy. Raven would make sure of that.

But then, there had been good times. A long time ago. His

439

dad would take him fishing and they would sit for hours on the lake and pray that the big one would finally take the bait. Or he would read to him at night when he was in bed – one of the good books, not the kiddies' ones. *The Hobbit* was a favourite, or *Lord of the Flies*. His dad would scrunch up his body and act out the parts, do the voices. The young Luke would giggle or shriek in fear and his mother would come in and chastise them and yell at his father for scaring the kid. He had loved his dad, once. Before everything went to hell.

The tunnel wall that Raven was tracing with his right hand suddenly disappeared and he found himself in an opening. There was still no light at all and the absence of a wall immediately made Raven feel exposed, with nothing to prevent attackers coming at him from all sides. Whatever had gotten to Billy was now out there with an open shot at him. Raven knew it was either Ronny, the three armed attackers or … something else.

He heard a voice from somewhere buried deep into his psyche. A growl and a breath. Red eyes, pointed tale, blackened tongue. Something that swam through a swirling dark mass, its claws reaching for him, it's teeth dripping with the blood of the undead. He shuddered.

He opened up his arms to feel for something, anything, but all he found was a wide, open space, with a cool breeze on his fingertips and in his face.

He was at the exit, he was sure of it. All of a sudden he could feel Lisa's lips on his, his son's arms around his shoulders, the musty scent of Lisa's perfume. He was getting out of there!

He stepped forward purposefully towards the direction of the breeze but his right foot failed to find solid ground. He was falling face first into the dark abyss, his arms and legs flailing as his hands clawed desperately for something to prevent him from plummeting to his death. He saw his father at the restaurant, leering over his dinner plate with sordid tales of murderers and philanderers, Lisa screaming at him for abandoning her once more, his son alone in an empty room with a single light bulb and calling for his dadda to come get him. He'd let them all down, every one of them.

His head connected with something hard and cold and he felt his senses swiftly depart. His eyes rolled back in his head and he slumped into the blackness.

And then the ghosts came.

Chapter 70:
Shots Fired

'Harry, baby. I missed you so much my sweet, sweet boy!'
Lisa was hugging her son to her chest, sobbing and laughing
in equal measure.

'Mumma, Mumma.' Harry had his little arm around her
shoulders and was kissing her on the cheek again and again.
The feel of his warm skin on hers flooded her body with a
relief so palpable that she could taste it, like the sweetest of
honey or a fine wine that never corked.

'I'll never let you go again, Harry. *Never*!' She looked up
from her son at the two men: one propped against the bar and
smugly sipping an expensive brandy, the other in his
wheelchair and glaring at her with malicious intent.
Deveraux stood by the window, no longer with a glass of
wine in her hand, and was looking at Bernie cautiously as if
expecting instruction.

'It warms my heart, it really does.' Bernie was smiling
like a man watching an entertaining show. 'What do you say
Robert, does it warm your heart?'

'Deeply.' Robert Charon's face was unmoving, his dark
eyes penetrating Lisa's own gaze like a black and boiling oil.

'What do you say, Christy?'

'I don't … I don't know.' She nodded. 'Lovely … I guess.'

Lisa looked behind her at the door.

'We're going to leave.' She stepped backwards, gingerly. 'Now.'

Bernie set down his glass. 'Well,' he smiled, 'that's certainly one way to go.'

Lisa looked to her left, at Deveraux who was still standing in front of the window, and then down at Charon who was still silently seething. She glanced up at Bernie Staker, the man she knew to be the Cardinal.

'That's the way I'd like to play it.' She hugged Harry to her bosom. 'And that's the way it will end, with nothing else said.' She stepped backwards once more. 'No repercussions.'

Bernie stepped towards her. 'And that is very gracious of you,' he nodded at Deveraux. 'Don't you think, Christy?'

'I do.' She looked uncomfortable.

Bernie continued. 'Very gracious indeed. Especially after what the good doctor here,' he pointed at Robert, 'did to you and your beautiful young son. Harry Raven is it?'

Lisa nodded anxiously.

'Because some mothers, single mothers like yourself, they use their own surname, don't they? When naming their kids.' He smiled but not with his eyes. 'Yours is Clancy, isn't it?'

She nodded again and took another step back.

'But he's not a Clancy, your boy?' He pointed at her son. 'He's a Raven, like his dad.' He grinned and his white and even teeth were visible through his open lips. 'Luke.'

443

Lisa could feel her heart pounding hard in her chest and her blood racing through her veins. She felt like an artery could burst at any moment.

'The one that killed *his* son?' Bernie waved a hand at Charon.

Lisa corrected him. 'Anthony Richards killed himself.'

Charon leapt up. 'Because Luke Raven hounded him! Because he created a groundswell of hatred towards him, backed him into a corner and dared him to bite, like a *dog*!' He was half standing and spitting out his words with hatred and bile. 'He was trapped and had nowhere to go. Because … of … *Luke Raven*!'

'He was a murderer!'

'He was a saviour!'

Bernie waved a hand at his compatriot. 'Potato, Pot-ah-to.' His smile faded as he turned to Lisa. 'And then there's the other Raven we all know and love of course. We called him the Curator, but that was a long time ago and now frankly I don't give a shit.' He rubbed a huge hand on his smooth chin. 'Sam Raven is his name. Raven. Like old Lukey. Like Harry.'

Lisa swallowed the saliva that was pooling in her mouth and felt her lower lip begin to tremble.

'All fucking bastards as far as The Legion is concerned!' He walked forwards, looming over Lisa and her son like an ominous and terrible beast. A dark shadow descended upon her. 'And all must be sacrificed in *His* name.'

The lights in the room flickered and Lisa could have sworn she felt the earth shudder, just a little. She looked around her for a friend but she had none. Not even Deveraux, who was now skulking behind an upright lamp. Lisa

444

suspected that deep down she wanted to help, but she didn't have the nerve. She was going to have to act alone. She felt the blood rise to her cheeks and the anger burn behind her eyes.

'Get away from my son!' Lisa spat in Bernie Staker's face, a long gloopy string of mucus that hit him squarely in the left eye and ran down his cheek. He pulled back a hand and struck her hard in the chin and she slammed back into the door, barely keeping a hold of Harry. She slowly slid to the floor.

As she looked up at the much larger man, his mouth open in a snarl and his eyes glaring at her like tiny infernos, she heard the back door cave in, heard a loud retort of a gun being fired and saw the ceiling above her shatter into dust and plaster.

'Step away from her, Cardinal.' Bernie wheeled around. 'This is between you and me.'

Lisa looked back and saw a wounded but mobile Sam Raven, his legs shoulder width apart and his hand gripping his Glock as if ready to cast Bernie Staker back into the ether. His expression was hard, determined. He nodded at Lisa. She called to him.

'Sam!'

'Aah, and here he is! Right on cue!' Bernie turned to face him. 'The recently reincarnated body of Sam Raven, our one time *Curator*.' Bernie was chuckling. 'The guy that relieved us of a considerable amount of investment and who tried to dissolve our organisation by spilling his foul lies and conjecture to his friends in the government.'

'Let them go, Bernie.' Sam's eyes were furtive and rapidly flitting from side to side. 'This has nothing to do with them.'

'On the contrary, my good fellow.' Bernie plucked a cigar from the breast pocket of his jacket and placed it between his lips, a sudden, forced calmness returning to his previously furious expression. 'This has everything to do with them.'

'I've returned to put this to bed.' Lisa could see that Sam's shoulder wound was bothering him and she wondered how long he could hold the gun in a shooter's position. She wanted to go to him but couldn't risk her son. 'Once and for all.'

Bernie lit the end of his cigar and blew out a long plume of billowing smoke. 'And that is most admirable, ex-Curator. Most admirable indeed.' Bernie looked down at Charon who was shuffling in his chair and reaching slowly into his inside jacket pocket. 'But we are under strict instruction from the immortal. Isn't that right, Robert?'

Charon nodded.

'An eye for an eye.'

'Then take me.'

Bernie shook his head. 'Your sins are too many and too profound, my friend.' Bernie took another drag on his cigar. Lisa couldn't believe how relaxed he was. It was like he was having an after dinner chat with his chums. It was perverse. 'Your tepid little soul won't satisfy *Him*. You know that.'

Sam laughed. 'You and your 'higher being' bullshit.' He glanced at Lisa. 'I used to believe it, you know. They had me fooled too. That there was no good, no light, no morality. That the very presence of religious texts was all just a counterpoint to the real truth.'

Lisa shook her head, not understanding.

'That we are all controlled, that we're just pawns, ants in

a box if you like, for the thing that plays with us like we're its little toys. Pushes us into position and poses our arms and legs, moves us from one place to the next so that we can do *His* bidding, only to rise up and sweep us from the game board like chess pieces whenever he tires of us.' He shook his head solemnly. 'Call him what you will. The devil, Beelzebub, Angra Mainyu, Shaitan, Mara … it doesn't matter. Every religion has a name for the same thing.' He sighed. '*Evil*.'

Lisa spoke up. 'Sounds like fanatical bullshit to me.'

Bernie wheeled on her. 'Does it, Lisa? Really, *bullshit*?' He glared at her, the smoke wafting from his cigar like the fire from a dragon's breath. 'Think of it, think of all the suffering, the pain, the genocide. Man killing man, woman killing woman. And for what?' He laughed. 'Because that's just what we do? The absurdity of it all. The beautiful chaos!' He held out his arms. 'There is no good, no god. You must know that, deep in your soul. Reach down there and find the truth, it's within your reach.' Bernie turned back to Sam whose arm was now visibly shaking. 'If you let go of your fictionalised notion of good then what are you left with?'

Lisa slowly started to push herself up to a standing position.

'I'll tell you. You are left with us, The Legion. We are many and we are strong and when *He* asks us to do his bidding, we do just that.' He grinned. 'Famine, war, terror, bloodshed. These things don't just happen, Lisa.' He was speaking to her from the back of his head, his eyes still firmly transfixed upon Sam Raven. 'They happen because we make it so.'

Lisa spoke up. 'You mean to tell me that your …

447

organisation deliberately causes pain and suffering, on a widespread scale, because of your … your what? Your *god*?'

'There is no god.'

'Your higher being tells you to do it? Some demented belief that you have an other-worldly deity that you need to satisfy by sacrificing the human race for *Him*?'

The room shook once more and Lisa thought she heard a low, rumbling groan.

'We have *saved* the human race, my dear. Without the sacrifices that we have made to appease *Him* we would have all been cast into the pit of damnation a long time ago. We prevented it and we continue to prevent it every single day. Just watch the news!' He turned back to her. 'Explosion in Baghdad? That was us. A train derails in New Jersey? That was us. A contagion takes the lives of tens of thousands? Us too!'

Lisa's mouth fell open. 'Murderers!'

He shook his head. 'Heroes!'

'You bastards!'

Another low, guttural growl and the floor shook like it was about to split in two.

'*He* is here.' Bernie closed his eyes.

'This is utter crap and you know it.' The room shook again and Lisa felt a cold chill race through her veins and the hairs on her forearms stand on end. She suddenly felt a deep sorrow like nothing she had ever felt before. She fought back the tears.

'I'm getting out of here.' She looked across at Sam who was nodding to her.

He smiled solemnly. 'Tell Luke I've always loved him.'

Lisa looked at him, *really* looked at him, and saw the

compassion in his aged face. He wasn't the monster that Luke thought he was. Misguided and easily influenced, yes, but he was atoning, completing his penance. He smiled at her warmly.

'Come with me, Sam.' Even as she said it, she knew it couldn't be. The sorrow gripped her in its icy and sharp mandibles. She grabbed the cold door handle and pushed.

'You aren't going *anywhere*!' Bernie lunged for her, the cigar spilling from his lips like smouldering dynamite as his hands clawed at her back.

There was a loud crack and blood spurted from his shoulder and splashed into Lisa's face and torso.

'Run, Lisa. *Run*!'

As Charon drew his gun, Christy dived to her left, also pulling a weapon from her hidden ankle holster. Multiple shots were fired from both ends of the boat house and Lisa saw a bullet strike Sam high in the thigh. She grit her teeth, narrowed her eyes and swung the door open with all her strength and ran with her son in her arms and the wind in her hair. She ran for Westhampton beach because that was the only place she could think of to go. And she cried tears of fear and of rage with every sound of a firearm being discharged and of the shouts and hollers as bullets struck flesh. She wanted to go back for Sam, but she knew it was too late. He had been her hero but she couldn't think of that now. She thought of The Legion; the demon that they served, the low, ominous groan in the boathouse, the ice in her veins, the walls shaking, the floor rumbling, the bullet as it struck Bernie Staker's back and the blood in her eyes and on her clothes.

She had to find Luke.

Chapter 71:
Boo

'Ruby? Is that you?

'What the hell are you doing down here? How did you get in?' Ruby was slowly walking towards the bright beam of light spilling from the torch in Molly's right hand. She was holding something else too. A bag?

'Dawes sent me,' Molly paused. Her voice was ... odd. 'Something about a case he's been working on.'

'Dawes?' Ruby glanced back at Randall who was shrugging his shoulders. 'Why would Dawes be working on a case that leads him here of all places?' Ruby was trying to piece it all together. 'And why would the lazy sod send a junior PC, all on her own?'

Molly dropped the thing in her left hand and started moving to her left, Ruby's right. The flashlight beam struck odd looking objects as it moved from side to side in Molly's hand. Things hanging from the cave ceiling like misshapen limbs, shadows creating monstrous caricatures of terrifying beasts, their teeth sharp and their talons crooked and barbed.

'Oh, you know Dawes.' Molly continued moving. 'He barely gets out of bed in the morning, let alone go on a field trip.' She was semi-joking but there was no humour in her tone. 'I was glad for the extra shift.'

'But down here?' Ruby walked towards her as the shadows grew longer and Molly's face began to fade into view.

'This is my case, PC Staker, and Detective Dawes has not consulted with me on any intel that he may have uncovered.' Randall was behind Ruby and she could sense the agitation in his tone. He was about to crack the biggest case of his career and here was a fellow DI, butting in on his own good work and without the courtesy of letting him know.

'Obviously I can't comment on that, DI Kipruto.' Molly stopped. 'I just do as I'm told.'

Ruby shook her head. 'This is so odd, Molly.'

'I know, right?'

Ruby laughed. 'I mean, this is a terrifying hell hole, one that we didn't even know existed until yesterday. And yet, here we all are, working the same case and without ever knowing we were heading to the same misbegotten place.'

Molly's tone was flat and impassive. Ruby still couldn't quite see her expression, the shadows were too deep and the flashlight was between them, glowing like a moonbeam. 'That's weird alright.'

'Can you help us?'

'Of course.'

'Because, we found a body, over there.' Ruby pointed to her left. 'A hanging corpse, arms, legs and head removed.'

Randall stepped forward. 'Disembowelled.'

'Oh, really?'

Ruby nodded. 'And we think there are more. We just need more light and your torch will really help us.'

Molly lifted the torch and the beam caught her face momentarily. Ruby thought she looked pale and ashen, like a corpse. Her lips were red but her eyes were black. Ruby heard a sound like metal being pulled through cloth but the danger failed to register.

'Hello …?' There was a thin voice, followed by a hacking cough and a shuffling sound. 'Is anyone there? Please?'

Ruby turned to the sound that was coming from behind her, back towards the approximate place where she first spotted Molly holding that thing in her left hand. 'I don't know where I am and I can't move. Please …'

Ruby turned back to Molly who was now grinning maniacally in the white hue of the flashlight beam. She leaned towards Ruby as the light moved from her face to her hand holding the long and brightly gleaming knife. Ruby felt Molly's breath on her face as the lights went out.

'Boo.'

Chapter 72:
Rockfall

'Is it done?

   'I don't know?'

   'Tell us it's done? Please?'

The ghosts came to him, one by one, pleading for him to release them from their hellish purgatory. He saw each and every face, felt their terror penetrate his soul, cried tears of sorrow with them, told them that he wished that he could do more, could have *done* more. The young lovers, their lives taken before they could make any sort of connection, the swim shorts guy who had left behind a loving family, the homeless lady – what had she ever done to anyone to deserve such a horrendous and bloody fate? And they were stuck in this wet and dark place until what? Until Raven could release them? How the hell could he do that? It was as if his hands were bound by some invisible and yet immensely powerful force.

He spat out the cold and salty water which had now soaked his entire left hand side, and gradually stood. His head hurt and he felt blood trickling down his face. He didn't know how deep the wound was but it felt like a little man was sitting on his shoulders and pounding his head with a mallet. He reached around to the rear pocket of his jeans but the handgun was gone. He cursed aloud.

He turned back towards the open tunnel and saw a shadow holding a torch. It bent down, moved to its right and disappeared.

'Hello? Is anyone there, please?'

There was a giggle, like a little boy playing a humorous but cruel prank. The sound moved from Raven's left to the right, like a soundtrack in Dolby surround sound.

'Hello? Billy? Is that you?'

There was a fizz, a pop and then a detonation that shook Raven to the core. Rock and dust hit him in his side like molten bullets and the shockwave shoved him back into the water like he had been hit by a speeding car. Carbon dioxide escaped from his lungs and surged out of his mouth like the air from a burst balloon. He splashed into the water, his arms flailing, but grabbed onto the edge of the raised platform.

In the flash of the explosion he momentarily saw the space that he was in. A small cave with an opening to his right that spilled out into what looked like a larger space. Water poured in from the opening in a gushing water fall and Raven knew that he had but a few minutes to move into the larger cave before the room that he was in completely filled with sea water. The tunnel back from where he had come, and hence the only other escape route, would now be just a pile of smouldering rubble.

The cave was once again completely black, aside from a low light from the hot and molten rocks to his left. He dragged himself through the thigh high water until he reached the sound of the waterfall. The ghosts were with him

455

again, he could feel them, and he hoped with all of his failing optimism that they were there to help him. God knew he needed them. Whoever had followed them from the vault had the upper hand and was using it to great effect. He hoped Billy was okay, but he couldn't worry about that now. He needed to get out, to get to Lisa and Harry, and do what the ghosts had asked him to do. Solve the case and release them. He had promised.

'Help me … please!'

He heard a voice from the larger cave. A woman's voice. A voice he recognised.

'Jane?'

'Is anyone there?'

He heard a scuffle, shouting. He pulled himself up through the thick stream of falling water, the salty liquid stinging his eyes and filling his mouth, and dragged himself onto a large, rocky platform. A familiar smell hit him but he shook it off.

'Ruby, are you there?'

It was Randall Kipruto's voice and it sounded afraid.

There was another loud thud and the sound of Randall grunting and his body striking the floor.

'Kipruto? Randall?' Another woman's voice, young but very professional. Ruby Cropper? 'Randall, be careful she's armed!'

Raven couldn't see anything at all but he could hear every detail of the chaos that was playing out up ahead. He was confused and disorientated. Were his ears playing tricks on him? How could all these people that he knew well, characters that helped to complete the colourful story of his life, all be in this dark and ominous place with him? Was he still dreaming? Did the explosion knock him unconscious and if so, was he now drowning? He had to wake up!

There was a loud, blood curdling scream and a horrifying cackle.

'I am the Hawk and you are all my prey!' Another laugh. 'You think you can catch me but you can't. I am undefeatable! I am invisible!'

Raven could just make out a small, diminutive looking woman holding a blood soaked knife. She was pacing. He reached for something, anything to disarm her with. His hand found a fist sized rock on the floor to his right and he picked it up. He had the element of surprise and he knew that it would be his biggest ally. He had to be silent and stealthy.

Suddenly he heard a match being struck and a flame leapt from a burning torch to his left. Behind it stood someone that he knew very well. He smiled.

'Wes?' Thank god it's you,' Raven whispered. 'There's a crazed woman over there and I think she has just attacked two police officers.'

As Raven spoke, he looked behind the still and smiling form of Wesley Pollock and glanced the horror that was spread out before him. Hanging from the low cave ceiling were dismembered torsos, all limp and flaccid like boiled meat, heads removed and bloodied necks exposed, disembodied arms hanging from the wrists like joints of beef, thighs suspended in the air like they were being aged like good steak. He looked around the walls and saw heads in large glass vats. They were floating in a pale liquid, their eyes open, mouths pulled back in grimaces of fear and rage, their lips purple, the hair stuck to their faces like shrouds of death. He saw the young girl, the fat man, the old lady. He placed a hand to his mouth and groaned. He had found them. Found them all. What the hell had gone on here?

He looked across at the platform on the other side of the river of sea water that was pouring in from somewhere down a wide tunnel to his right. He knew it must be the watery way out. Randall lay on the floor, presumably knocked unconscious, and Ruby Cropper was on her knees, her hands clutching a bleeding and gaping wound in her side. She looked up at Raven, silently imploring him to help them. Behind her stood the bedraggled and waif-like form of another woman. Raven thought this to be Jane Butler. She was holding onto the cave wall to steady herself. She looked like she was half in this world, half in the next.

The young woman with the black curls and scar running down her right cheek looked up at him and laughed.

'Balthazar, you've brought me a new one!'

Who was she talking to? Raven looked around him and saw Wes, his partner, his friend, smiling and nodding at her.

Wes raised a glistening, blood-soaked socket wrench in his right hand. He smiled at Raven.

'That's right, Molly my sweet.' He winked at Raven and spoke in a knowing whisper. 'I am the hound.'

Chapter 73:
Motuh Bi!

Lisa's legs were throbbing with pain as her feet pounded through soft sand. Her lungs were burning and her face was flushed and pink. The sweat poured from her forehead and cheeks in the hot and sticky summer heat and she could feel a warm river pouring down the curvature of her spine. All of a sudden, and as if she had willed it to be so, a thick flash of lightning scorched the sky above, closely followed by a loud and deafening crack of thunder.

She heard shouting from somewhere behind her and she pushed on. Harry was hugging her like his life depended on it and he was giggling in her ear like he was enjoying the game. She smiled at the morbid hilarity of it all.

She heard the roar of an engine being fired and instantly knew what it was. She had seen it on the way into the boat house. A quad bike. A dread descended upon her, as thick and black as the rapidly billowing clouds above.

The crowds of people gathered around the brightly illuminated stage were still half a mile ahead, and Lisa knew that they may as well have been an eternity away. She would never make it in time. She couldn't outrun a motorbike, could she? She knew that despite Sam Raven's heroics, she was almost certainly doomed. She hugged Harry into her body as she continued to push her legs forward. She wasn't going to give up, no matter the odds.

She could hear the bike closing, the sound of the roaring engine rivalling the gradually building thunder and the loud boom of the concert's PA system. She knew the song well – 'I Fought the Law' by the Clash. The members of the local covers band were leaping across the stage, the singer yelling out the vocal line, his fist pumping in time with the crunching guitar and pounding drums. The crowd was lapping it up, oblivious to her terror and the imminent danger a few hundred yards away from them. She started to cry.

The bike was now almost upon her and she half expected to feel a bullet strike her back, severing her spinal cord and dropping her to the floor like some lifeless puppet. Harry yelled in her ear. 'Motuh Bi … Motuh bi …!'

'I know Harry, I know! Mummy loves you, never forget that!' She was sobbing now, thick tears rolling down her cheeks.

'Motuh Bi … *Mumma*!'

The quad bike roared past her and swung in a wide circle in front of them.

'Fuck you!' Lisa stopped dead in her tracks. 'Fuck *all of you*!'

Lightning flashed across the sky behind the bike's rider and illuminated the beach like a single and terrifying strobe light. She saw platinum hair and a sharp, angular jaw line adorned with intense but pretty eyes.

Christy Deveraux leaned over, her open hand held out while she glanced anxiously over Lisa's shoulders.

460

'Jump on! Quickly! They're coming!'

Chapter 74:
Sawney

'Ruby! Ruby!' Raven was kneeling down and looking at the long hole in the young PC's side.

'Luke? How did you get here?' Her face was white and scared.

'It's a long story. I'll tell you later.' He looked over his shoulder at Wesley. 'We need to stem the blood flow.'

Molly was dragging the flaccid form of Jane Butler towards them by the ropes that bound her hands together. She threw her to the floor next to Raven and the bleeding Ruby Cropper. Randall Kipruto was unconscious beside them. Raven grabbed her arm.

'Don't worry, Jane. We're getting out of here.'

Jane looked up at him, her eyes furtive, her mouth twitching. She looked like a beaten animal. 'Detective Raven, is that you?'

He smiled reassuringly. 'Yes.'

Jane started to sob. 'Where have you been? What's taken you so long?' Her voice was shrill and thin.

'I'm sorry. I really am.' He gripped her arm. 'But I'm here now and we're going to get you home. To your mother.'

'It was Charon, all along.' She was shaking. 'It's always been him.'

Raven nodded. He had known as much. He just hadn't acted quickly enough.

'I hope you're having a nice mother's meeting down there, because this is where it ends.' Molly strode around the prone DI Kipruto and kicked him softly in the side. He groaned.

'What's been going on here?' Raven glanced from Wesley to Molly and back again. 'Wes, is this that crazy girlfriend you're always going on about?'

Molly spat out a sarcastic laugh. 'Girlfriend, please.'

Wesley looked at her anxiously, and then down at Raven. 'Balthazar.'

Raven shook his head. 'What?'

'My name is Balthazar. Balthazar Bean, descendant of the great Sawney Bean.' Wesley puffed out his chest.

'The *cannibal*?'

Wesley nodded. 'One and the same.'

Raven rose to his knees. 'No, that's not true.' He peered up at him. 'I checked out your records before I agreed to employ you. You're Wesley Pollock, son of Sandra Pollock, a single mother that lives on the Butchers estate. You've been living off monthly benefits since you were a child because your mum's a drug abuser. I took you on because I felt sorry for you, I knew you needed the cash.'

He heard Molly grunt from behind him.

'Don't say that!' Wesley grabbed a carving knife and pointed it at Raven. 'Don't ever say that!'

Raven looked at Molly who was staring at Jane Butler like she was a slice of tenderised meat. 'I don't know what fantasy he has been filling you with but it's all fabricated by his ripe and fertile imagination.' Raven looked at her knowingly. 'The boy has ADHD and FPP.' Molly peered up at him, confused. 'Fantasy Prone Personality, or an overactive imagination.' He heard Wesley gasp. 'Not to mention an addiction to energy drinks that just fuels his hyper drive of a metabolism.' Raven nodded. 'Why do you think he's so skinny?'

'Shut up, Raven! What do you know about me?' Wesley went to Molly's side. 'You hardly ever spend any time with me. Unless you want something, of course.'

Molly pushed Wesley away.

'I knew the whole thing was made up. I'm not an idiot, Raven,' she growled defiantly, although Raven could see how backfooted she was. She'd really bought into it, hadn't she? 'I have my father's brains, that's for sure, and I can see through a lie just as easily as I can carve through human flesh.' She looked down at the knife which was caked in Ruby's blood.

Ruby grunted. 'You're sadistic. I can't believe I didn't see it sooner. You've always been weird.'

Molly laughed, but there was an uncertainty behind it. 'Define weird, Ruby. Because my definition and yours are likely to be very different.'

'I'm sure.'

Randall groaned again and tried to push himself up. Molly kicked him in the ribs and he crumpled.

'Is weird working for a police force that's run by an organisation that inflicts pain on hundreds of thousands?' Molly was pacing. 'Is weird participating in a robbery, only to snare a career criminal in the act in order to resuscitate your failing career?' Raven felt the sharp barb prick his already deflated pride. 'Is weird letting your son get snatched by the very person that imprisoned the woman that you were employed to rescue, but were too distracted by your own self-centred problems to do the job properly?'

Raven went to get up but Wesley pushed him back down. 'What are you saying? Are you talking about Harry?' He felt the blood rise to his cheeks.

Molly shrugged. 'Just the facts, Luke. No more, no less.'

'My son?'

Molly laughed. 'You'll never know, will you? You'll never know what became of Lisa, little Harry ...' Her face became serious, almost sombre. 'Or your father.'

'How do you know my father?'

Molly smiled. 'I know much more than you might think, Luke.' She pointed at Wesley. 'Like the lies that Wesley here told about his family. Do you think I really believed all of that ... crap?' She laughed cruelly as she embellished the lie. Wesley shrunk visibly. 'Sawney Bean? Give me a break? That story's not even true, it's a myth!'

'Molly?' Wesley was reaching for her but she shunned him.

'No, it was just inspiration, that's all. I was looking for the right thing to put my ... talents to. The things that my father taught me, the little infatuations that I inherited from him.'

Ruby hissed. 'Bernie Staker.' She glanced at Raven. 'That man has his fingers in almost every pie in the area.'

Jane sat up. 'Including the estate of Doctor Robert Charon.' She sobbed. 'The man that imprisoned and tortured me.'

Molly nodded grimly. 'Something like that.'

'And, what?' Raven pointed to the grim discoveries hanging from the cave ceiling. 'You were inspired to do this?'

Molly smiled. 'This and other things.'

Raven was still recoiling from what Molly had declared about his son, but he hastily put the pieces together in his own mind. 'You're the hawk from my dreams.'

Molly frowned.

Raven pointed to Wesley. 'And you're the frightened and snotty little boy.'

Wesley winced.

'Manipulated by her. Ensnared by her.' He nodded. 'You didn't want to do these things, Wes. It's not you!' He rose to his knees. 'She had you under her spell. She entranced you.'

Wesley's eyes flitted from side to side. 'No, I'm … Balthazar Bean!'

'You're little snotty Wesley Pollock.'

'No … I'm not. I'm a winner.'

Raven reached for him. 'I never said you weren't, Wes.'

'But Mum did. She called me a failure, a little hopeless failure. She said that I couldn't take care of her.'

Molly groaned. 'Oh please.'

'Then do the right thing.'

Wesley looked down at him. 'What do you mean?'

Raven held his hands out to the other three prisoners. 'Help us.'

Wesley looked down at the knife in his hand. 'Why?'

'Because you're a winner.'

'I don't know.'

Raven continued. 'I do, Wes. You make me laugh, you

466

help me get things done mate, you're the reason we get so much business. You help me win!'

'I do?'

'You do.'

Wesley looked down at Raven and smiled. 'I'm a winner?'

Raven grinned. 'Always.'

Wesley paused, his lips pursed together in a grim determination. He looked up at Molly, down at the floor as if searching for inspiration and then across at Raven. He stopped, took a breath and wiped a tear from the corner of his eye. He winked at Raven and then, in an instant, he swung the arm holding the knife around in an arc and lunged at the girl with the black curls and mottled scar on her cheek. But she was ready.

There was a crack of a handgun, an instant hit of strong smelling gunpowder and Wesley Pollock's skull shattered into tens of pieces, his skull fragments and chunks of brain exploding onto the cave walls and around the cave's occupants.

'Wes! No!' Raven stood and caught his partner as he fell. The right side of his head had disappeared. *'No!'* He turned and saw Molly Staker holding the handgun that he had taken from the blonde haired man. He cursed himself for not being more thorough in his search for it. He was so stupid. He looked down at the still body of Wesley Pollock but the life force had already evaporated from him. Another ghost in a cave that was already full of them. He shook his head with regret.

'Time to end this, guys. I've got work to do.' Molly turned and pointed the gun at the recoiling Jane Butler's face.

'Please, don't!'

Molly's finger wrapped around the trigger and she winked. 'Goodbye Jane.'

'Molly, No!'

There was a loud, hoarse female voice from the rapidly rising stream. Raven turned and saw a small rowing boat approaching.

Molly span around with the gun in her hand and pointed it at the boat's single occupant. She stopped dead, shuddering as if struck by an invisible force.

'Mother?'

Chapter 75:
Walls

Lisa climbed aboard the quad bike as the heavens opened and turned to see a 4X4 approaching. She vaguely saw the jeep's occupants – a wounded Bernie Staker and Robert Charon and two other equally menacing looking gentlemen.

Christy Deveraux turned to her. 'We need to get away from here, and fast!'

'Why are you helping me?'

'Because you were right.' She smiled at little Harry. 'Because it's been too long.' She fired the bike's engine. 'And because I've been too weak.'

Lisa gripped her side with one arm and held her son in the other. 'Thank you.'

The bike roared into action and sped down the road running parallel to the beach, behind the stage that was now being hastily vacated and through the crowds of dissipating spectators.

'Where are we headed?' Lisa had to shout to be heard above the bike's engine.

'Back to the Cardinal's house!'

'What?' Lisa instantly felt like she was being dragged to

the monster's lair.

'Don't worry. I called the Commissioner.' Christy's body tensed. 'He has a squad meeting us there.'

Lisa thought for a moment. 'Isn't he corrupt too?'

'Bernie's made mistakes, too many of them! Not least letting his daughter off the leash to kill as she pleases.' She groaned. 'I warned him about her.'

Lisa felt overwhelmed. It was like everything she knew, everything she understood to be normal, was now being tipped upside down and shaken like a dice tumbler. 'His daughter?'

'It's a long story, but let's just say the people that Bernie has influence over have run out of patience with him. He's all out of lives.'

Lisa cradled Harry like a precious and fragile cargo. 'So what happens now? What's our plan?'

'We trap him in his own home, and with a little luck,' she risked a glance back at Lisa, 'the walls will come tumbling down around him.'

Chapter 76:
The Hawk

'My Molly.'

'Mother, how …?' Molly approached the boat.

'I'm so sorry, Molly,' her mother said. She was sobbing. 'I was never there for you.'

'I thought you were dead.' Molly's voice had switched into the voice of a little, helpless girl. She put the gun on the ground and sat with her legs in the water. 'Father told me you were dead.'

'He lied to you.'

'Your legs?'

Lorna held out her hand and grabbed Molly's. 'Your father's doing. He left me for dead.'

Molly's mouth fell open. 'Father?'

'He's not the man you think he is.'

'But … where have you …'

Lorna gripped Molly's hand in both of hers and shook it vigorously. 'I've been unwell, Molly. For a long, long time.' She smiled through the tears. 'But I'm back now, and so is your great grandpappy.' She nodded her head in the direction of the exit. 'He's waiting for us in a motorboat out there, but we've got to hurry.' Lorna glanced at the rising tide. 'Pretty soon the waters will be too high.'

Molly looked over her shoulder. 'But … I'm in trouble, Mother. Bad trouble.'

Lorna nodded. 'I know, I know.' She brushed a hand gently along Molly's uneven scar. 'But whatever it is, we can take care of it. Together. You and I.'

Molly remembered the jewellery, the pretty dress, the smell of perfume, alcohol and cigarettes. She remembered Gretchen looking at her tenderly and with thinly veiled concern in her grandmotherly like stare. She felt her mother's perfectly manicured fingers on her baby skin, her red lipstick on her cheek and her departing visage as she left the room, offering nothing but a faint and listless goodbye. She stared down at the ground. 'I don't know, Mother. Father asked me to take care of some things.'

Lorna's mouth turned up in a sneer of hateful defiance. 'Your father is a bad man who has made you … made you do the things that you do, Molly.' She held her by the shoulders. 'But I can help you, my darling. I can make things right.' Lorna glanced up at the horrors that filled the cave's interior like wax models at a museum of torture. The bodies, the blood, the prisoners. It was so much worse than she imagined it could ever be. But she owed it to her daughter. She would atone for her mistakes. 'I can get you the help that you need and I swear,' she wiped tears from her cheek, 'on my life and on the lives of everyone I love, that I have *ever* loved, that I will be by your side, day and night and for every second of every hour until you are better.'

Molly shuddered as if stunned. '*Better*?'

Lorna's smile faltered. 'Yes, better.' She nodded. 'Well

472

again.'

'You think I'm ill?' Molly was frowning.

Lorna was confused. 'I think you've been misguided, Molly. I think your father has led you astray?'

'Astray?' Molly stood. 'You think I'm someone that needs to be rescued like a lost child?' She laughed. 'Is that what you think, Mother? You think you've come back, after all these years, and all of a sudden you have me figured out, like a little puzzle that you've been able to solve? You think I need your help?'

'You are my little orchid, Molly.' She was shaking. 'You are my little flower and I have neglected you. I can help you blossom once more.'

'I am the menace, mother. I am the *predator*! When I descend from the heavens people cower in my shadow. You think I'm some sort of weak-minded little girl that needs a hand to hold?'

'Molly … I …'

'I am the Hawk! I swallow my prey and I enjoy it!' She hollered. *'I am the Hawk*!'

Her voice echoed down the tunnels and out of the cave entrance. Out in the motorboat her great-grandfather caught a sense of the pain in the loud, shrieking voice and he shuddered with sick dread.

'I am eater of souls, devourer of flesh. I feed off terror and fear, I revel in watching the life-force flee from the bodies of the unwashed!' Her voice dropped to a whisper. 'I do *His* bidding!'

Lorna's mouth fell open. 'You believe your father's lies.'

'I believe in *Him*. '

'You have been turned.' Her lips turned into a sneer,

473

'*already.*'

Molly shook her head. 'I am the next generation mother.' She smiled. 'And I am all powerful.'

The walls of the cave shook and the waves in the rising stream increased in intensity. The boat listed to one side, almost spilling the distraught Lorna Hanscombe into the cold depths of the ocean.

There was a voice from behind Molly. A man's voice.

'I think we're done here. Don't you?'

Molly turned. Randall Kipruto had pulled himself to standing and was now holding the discarded handgun to her head.

Molly looked down at the flashlight in her left hand. She nodded. 'Perhaps.'

In an instant she launched it towards the burning torch, knocking it to the ground and plunging the cave back into near darkness. Randall fired the gun but she was already on the move.

****

Raven scrambled around for a battery powered torch and found one in Wesley's rear pocket. He switched it on and saw a fleeting glimpse of Molly Staker escaping through the tunnel at the rear of the cave. He turned to Ruby who was still bleeding from the wound in her side. He was pleased to see that the flow had stemmed somewhat.

'Rube, can you get Jane into the rowboat with Molly's mother?'

Ruby considered this and nodded affirmatively. 'Yes, I can.'

'Good, get into the boat with her and row the three of you out to the motorboat that this lady,' he pointed to Lorna who was still reeling from her daughter's actions, 'says is waiting out there. But be quick.' He looked at Ruby with a grim knowing. 'If she's right, you've only got minutes left until the exit is blocked.'

'Got it, boss.' Ruby realised her mistake and looked up at Randall apologetically. 'I mean ... sorry boss.'

Randall smiled. 'It's okay. Old habits die hard, I get it.'

Raven bent down to Jane. 'You're getting out of here, Jane. Once and for all. Say hi to your mother for me.' Raven smiled. 'She's a persistent woman.'

Jane smiled, but Raven could see she was exhausted and spent. 'Tell me about it.'

'Randall?'

Kipruto was holding a hand to his head. He still looked a little worse for wear but determined all the same. 'Yes, Raven?'

'Let's go catch us a hawk.'

Chapter 77:
Crossbow

The quad bike swung into the long driveway of the Staker estate and Christy gunned the engine so that they reached the front door before the 4X4 rounded the corner towards the main gates.

'Get inside. Into the study.'

'Where …' Lisa had no idea of the layout of the sprawling mansion.

'Through the open hallway, past the stairs to the left and towards the back of the building.' She reached for her handgun. 'I'll stall them.'

'But …' Lisa held her son to her body. 'They'll outgun you.'

Deveraux smiled. 'Don't worry. I don't intend to face them head on.' They could hear the roar of the approaching engine. 'Now get inside, quick!'

Lisa burst through the large wooden door and gasped at the enormity of the gaping space inside the house. The large open staircase stood before her with a huge dining room to her left and a decorated entertainment hall to her right. The building was opulent and bold and spoke of the riches afforded a man that had made his living feeding off the pain of others. She felt sick to her stomach.

She heard shouting from outside and raced through the downstairs hallway. In her panic, she couldn't remember whether Christy had said left or right. She guessed right.

She pushed through the doorway at the back of the building and found herself in a large countrified kitchen. She looked around her for a doorway that might lead to a study and saw a small wooden door tucked into the dark recesses in the corner of the kitchen, to the right of the large refrigerator. The door was standing ajar so she decided to take a chance.

'Kitchee … kitchee …'

'That's right, Harry, it's the kitchen.'

'Cookie?'

'Maybe later, my love.' Lisa was breathing heavily. She heard gunshots from outside. 'Right now we have more pressing things to deal with.' She hoped that whatever space was behind that door would keep them hidden long enough to give the armed police enough time to make it out to the Staker estate before things got even more bloody.

She ran across the kitchen, innocently unaware of the small hole in the skirting board that was obscured from her view, a hole that was now fully re-populated with a new family of small rodents. She hastily pushed through the narrow door and almost fell down the stairway beyond.

'Shit.'

She flicked a switch and the lights came on, revealing a curved staircase that led down to a basement room.

'This will have to do, my darling. Won't it?'

Harry nodded enthusiastically.

She walked down the narrow steps, pulling the door closed behind her and descended into what appeared to be a workshop. There were items resembling tools hanging from the walls and shelves full of books and artefacts.

'What do we have here, Harry? Looks like little old Bernie is a collector.'

She took a sickle in her hand and felt the smooth, wooden handle as it sat comfortably in her firm grip. Holding the weapon felt good, almost like a comfort blanket. She thought that she could defend herself at last. She felt her anger building once more.

There was a door at the back of the room and Lisa considered it a good place for Harry to hide while she waited for impending visitors.

She heard gunshots again and she hurried. She wondered whether the police were engaging in an armed shootout with Staker's gang but didn't bank on it. She needed to consider the worst case scenario and there was no way she could ever let them get to Harry. She would defend him with her life and then some. She pushed through the door just as she heard pounding footsteps overhead.

The little room at the back was small and occupied by a large four poster bed. A single light illuminated the room from above. Lisa thought it an odd place to have such a sparse and dimly decorated bedroom. She wondered with a grim knowing who would sleep down here. She sat Harry on the thick duvet and gasped as she spotted the manacles attached to each of the four bed posts. She recoiled in horror but was resolute nonetheless. She had no other hiding place for him. Harry would have to stay in that room, despite the atrocities she was sure had taken place there. She kissed him on the cheek.

'See you in a little while my darling.'

'Mumma?'

Lisa had a thought and raced out of the room and grabbed an old voodoo doll that she had spotted on the way in. Thankfully the pins were removed. It was black and brown and the face was scary as hell but she had no time to shop. She re-entered the bedroom and gave it to Harry.

'Here Harry. It's a night garden toy.'

'Ni gardy?'

'That's right. Its Upsy Daisy.'

'Yay … uppy daiz!'

'That's right.' Lisa grinned as Harry took the toy and kissed it on its grotesque and up-turned lips. 'Upsy Daisy! Now,' she bent down, 'you play here.' She groaned. 'With Upsy Daisy, and Mummy will be right back.'

'Okay Mumma …'

Lisa could hear footsteps on the first floor hastily getting closer to the kitchen, along with male animated voices. She thought she could hear the loud boom of Bernie Staker's authoritative tone and hoped his shoulder wound stung like a bastard. She wondered what had happened to Christy Deveraux, her unexpected saviour. She hoped with all her energy that she was okay.

Lisa pulled the bedroom door closed and picked up a long, nine inch blade. She held it in her left hand and the sickle in her right and stood around the corner from the base of the stairs. She heard the door above slowly creaking open and a large boot hitting the first step. She took in a silent breath and gulped. She looked down at her middle aged weaponry and wondered what chance she stood against a speeding bullet. She hoped more than anything that Christy Deveraux's cavalry turned up before she had a chance to find out.

Then she spotted the crossbow.

Chapter 78:
The Lift

Raven and Randall raced up the dark tunnel, a torch in Raven's right hand and a knife in his left, and pursued the fleeing Molly Staker.

Raven wondered what kind of life that depraved young woman had lived up to this point that had led her to commit such horrendous acts of brutal violence. Had she turned that way due to the manner in which she had been raised, or had it always been there, dormant in her psyche until she hit an age where those kind of things became real? He doubted he would ever truly understand what lurked in the minds of murderers and rapists but he hoped someday that he would know a little more. Maybe he could help them get better. Maybe.

'There's a light up ahead, Raven! Can you see?' Randall was just behind him and holding the handgun. It felt good having a partner again. Like old times.

'I see it! Let's hope she hasn't managed to get away before we get a chance to see where she's headed.'

Raven couldn't shake what Molly had said about his son and about Lisa. Was it real or did she make that up too, just like poor Wesley had become confused by his own sick lie? He knew he needed to get to them but he couldn't let the murderous harpy get away. He had promised the ghosts of her victims. He needed to get them the closure that they deserved.

'When we get to the exit, Raven, be careful.' Randall was less out of breath than Raven which was a testament to the younger copper's fitness and dedication. 'She could still be armed.'

Raven looked down at his knife but wasn't entirely sure whether he could use it on a woman, especially one as young as Molly. 'Will do, Randall. Don't worry.' He smiled. 'I've done this kind of thing before.'

They burst through the tunnel's exit and scrambled through the bracken and brambles, one clawing at Raven's cheek and tearing a chunk of skin away.

'Bloody hell!'

He heard an engine revving and the crunch of tyres on mud and stone and pushed through the shrubs to see a white Vauxhall Corsa whirling around in reverse. Molly smiled at them, her middle finger raised in an amused and satisfied defiance, as she turned the wheel and pulled away.

Raven slumped to his knees as Randall emerged from the tunnel, the gun drawn and his feet spread shoulder width apart.

Raven shook his head. 'It's too late.' He sighed. 'Unless you're a crack shot that can take out a tyre from this distance.'

Randall grunted. 'No such luck, I'm afraid.' He groaned. 'We can't let her get away. We've got to do something.'

Raven looked up from where he had slumped and

shrugged. 'Any ideas?'

There was a moment of silence as the realisation set in. They were too late.

Suddenly the sound of a large diesel engine roared over the hill from behind them, and within an instant a white van skidded to a halt. Raven looked up and smiled.

'Well, blow me!'

Billy West, dried blood caked on his cheek and chin, wound down the passenger side window and hollered at them.

'You boys need a lift?'

Chapter 79:
Jelly

'Hello Robert.'

Robert Charon had rounded the bottom of the staircase, his gun raised at arm's length, and ended up face to face with Lisa who was pointing the bolt of the bow squarely between his eyes.

'Hello Lisa.'

She feigned confidence. 'Shall we finish what we started?'

Charon was barely able to stand upright, his wounds were still fresh and Lisa could see the blood oozing through the dressings. 'I think I'm almost done.'

Lisa smiled. 'Won't your all powerful deity save you?'

Charon placed the gun on the worktop and sighed. 'That's not how *He* works, I'm afraid.'

'Then let me go. What does it matter to you?'

'I think we've come too far for that, don't you?'

Charon sighed and raised a hand to his chest wound. He pulled his fingers away and Lisa could see the blood on his hand.

'The police are on their way. Armed police.'

Charon raised an eyebrow and chuckled. 'Is that what she told you?'

Lisa hesitated. 'Yes. She told me everything.'

Charon eyed the weapon as if it were nothing but a curiosity. 'Interesting.'

'You don't have the strength. I can see that. Do yourself a favour and just step aside.'

Charon smiled. 'I don't fear death. I never have.' His eyes narrowed. 'I embrace it, drink it in like a fine wine. I find comfort in understanding that I will become one with my creator, with the destroyer of worlds. I will become all powerful, all seeing, all knowing.' He held out his arms. 'You might take away my body, you might take away this mind, this power of thought. But my soul is eternal and my revenge will be all consuming. You'll see.'

'You're a lunatic, you know that don't you?'

Charon shrugged. 'That's your perception.' He rested a hand on the gun. 'My son is waiting for me from beyond the thin veil that we call mortality.' The building shook and the lights blinked. 'I would very much like to be by his side once more.'

Lisa wrapped her finger around the crossbow's trigger. 'Then let's see what you've got.'

Charon whirled with some speed and raised the handgun towards Lisa's face, just as the steel tipped bolt left the bow's stock, the taught string hurling it along the barrel and through the air at a frightening speed. It connected with Robert Charon's left eye, shattered the socket, drilling a hole through his skull, fragmenting bone, crushing brain matter and embedding itself deep in the rear wall of the basement. Charon fell forward, his face as still and emotionless as a wooden puppet, and crashed to the ground. She exhaled.

'That one's for Sam.'

She heard more movement above and glanced at Charon's gun. After a moment of consideration she decided that she preferred the bow. It was silent, and she wanted the shadows rather than the bright lights. She listened out for Harry and she could still hear him cooing and giggling at his little toy. She opted to leave him hidden in the bedroom. She had to find out what had happened to the police. They should have been there by now.

She ascended the stairway and reached the narrow door above. She peeked through the crack and could see that the kitchen was clear. She heard more noises from the front of the house.

She crept through the kitchen as silently as her soft leather boots would allow and approached the open doorway. There was nobody in the hallway so she continued on towards the large reception area. She could hear voices.

She thought of Luke, how he had abandoned her and Harry in her hour of need. She thought of Sam, how he had sacrificed himself for her and her son. She wondered how a father and son could be a million miles apart from each other and yet share the same DNA. Why couldn't Luke be more like his dad? She could really fall for a man like that, strong and reliable, brave and unselfish. What had she done to deserve such a shitty taste in lovers? What was it about her? One thing that she knew above all else was that if she wanted something sorted, there were only two people she could count on to do it. Her and herself.

She approached the doorway, half expecting to see uniformed officers on the other side with the gang in handcuffs and a proud Deveraux being congratulated. Instead she saw a wounded Bernie Staker, blood oozing from a shoulder wound and spreading on his blue shirt and across his chest. Christy was kneeling before him, blood in her nose and on her cheeks. Bernie had her hair in his hands and was pulling her towards him and Christy looked … aroused. Lisa blinked and looked again, but there it was: a sheen of sweat across her brow and eyes ablaze with desire.

Either side of Bernie were two silent but menacing associates, one with a lazy eye that drooped towards his left cheek and the other with a side parting and thin moustache that would make an officer in the SS look positively British.

'Come out, Lisa. There's a good girl.'

Lisa glanced at the three men and then down at Christy. She desperately glared at her, silently and urgently inquiring where the hell her police rescue squad had gotten to. Christy just smiled.

'As you've made it out here alive I assume that you've finally put poor Robert out of his misery?'

Lisa nodded. 'It was me or him I'm afraid.' With a quick jerk, she indicated the crossbow in her hand.

Bernie laughed. 'Well, I can certainly empathise with that, my love. Being a hunter myself, I understand that when the shot is on,' he smiled, 'you take it.'

'I suggest you let Christy go.'

Bernie shook his head. 'Oh, I don't think so.' He pushed the pistol into Christy's platinum hair. She jumped and then groaned. 'What do you say, Christy?'

'Please don't.' Christy's eyes were alive with electricity and her skin was pulsating. 'I'm rather enjoying this, *Cardinal*.'

Lisa cocked her head to one side. 'What?'

Lightning flashed across the sky outside and the lights in the big hallway blinked momentarily.

Bernie gave a sinister smile. 'Did you really think that Christy here,' he pulled her hair again and she gasped, 'the woman that I pulled out of the gutter, would turn against me? Against *us*?'

The air left Lisa's lungs. She felt herself collapsing inwards. 'You bitch!'

Bernie tapped Christy on the shoulder. 'You can stand now, my dear. I think we've made our point.'

'Oh Bernie,' she chuckled. 'Must I?' She kissed him tenderly on the lips and glanced back at Lisa over her shoulder as if she was perusing a potential acquisition. 'Perhaps she can join us for some quiet time later on this evening?'

Bernie's face was impassive. 'Oh I doubt that very much.' He waved the gun. 'Lisa here is not really our type. Isn't that right, Lisa?' He nodded. 'You see, I had to get you back here, you and little Harry, to my humble abode. I couldn't go all thug like and kill you out in the open like that, now could I? On the beach with all of those people looking?' He glanced at Christy. 'That would just be …'

Christy smiled. 'Tacky?'

'That's it. Yes. Tacky.' He shrugged. 'Not my style at all, that.'

Lisa looked at the two henchmen either side of Staker and Deveraux and cursed herself for being so naïve. She was royally screwed and she knew it.

Bernie ran his hand through Christy's hair. 'You see, Lisa my cherub, everyone here, everyone that associates with me, has a grim story to tell. Perhaps they were raped by the vicar running the foster home, like Christy here. Or maybe they were arse fucked by their alcoholic of a daddy, like my good pal Marty over there.'

The man on Bernie's right hand side with the slick hair parting and gestapo moustache looked at the floor.

'Or left to fend for themselves on the streets like Timothy.'

The man to his left with the lazy eye nodded.

'But we give them something to focus on, something to live for.'

'You brainwash them into believing the crap that you sell! Like cheap labour! They spend their life savings in pain on the expensive membership fees that you no doubt charge for entry into this old boys' club. A club that markets death and misery. It's perverse and it's wrong and it needs to end.'

The building shook once more and Lisa thought she heard screaming.

Bernie touched a hand to his shoulder wound and grimaced. 'Your old mate got me good back there, Lisa. It seems that the dead really can wreak havoc when they put their mind to it.' He winked. 'It's a shame Robert put two bullets in his chest, but there you go. That's one less Raven to worry about.'

Lisa felt sorrow bleed into her heart like novocaine. She felt both numb and deeply sad as she mourned for her friend Sam.

'Now, just two more to go and that'll be the hat-trick.' Bernie smiled and nodded at Marty. 'One of them, of course, is in the basement where our little red-head wielding the crossbow appeared from.' He winked. 'Like the mystical

489

lady of the lake recovering her medieval weapon.'

Marty smiled and went to step forward. Lisa immediately turned the crossbow on him.

'Don't you fucking dare move!'

Marty stopped, the smile evaporating from his moustachioed lips, and looked back at his friend for direction.

Bernie laughed. 'You're out gunned my dear. Three to one. What you gonna do? Rapid load the crossbow and take us all out before we can get a shot off? Now, that is something I'd like to see!'

Lisa faltered.

Bernie laughed once more. 'I bet you wish you'd picked the handgun now, don't you?' He turned to his minion. 'Well go on then Mart!' He gestured. 'Go get the kid. We haven't got all fucking day!'

Marty stepped forward and Lisa didn't hesitate. The bolt left the bow and hit the surprised henchman high in the cheekbone, exiting from the top of his head like a silent but deadly missile. He crumpled to the floor, blood blossoming from the wound like juice from a spilt carton.

'For fuck's sake, Lisa, I'm *definitely* going to have to kill you now!'

Just as Bernie raised his gun a car pulled up outside the entrance and the driver's door slammed. Lisa looked up as a five foot nothing young woman with tumbling black curls strode into the reception area like a ball of whirling enthusiasm and energy.

Bernie turned to her and smiled. 'Molly, my darling!'

Molly walked up to Timothy, took the handgun from his startled grip, pointed it towards her father and pulled the trigger. Bernie Staker hardly had a moment to protest before the bullet penetrated his skull and turned his brains into mashed meat and jelly. He fell to the floor like a giant redwood, his head connecting with the tile with a loud crunch, his body thudding to the ground like a boxer's heavy punch bag.

Molly smiled. 'That was for mother.'

She turned to Christy Deveraux, who was still gaping in horror at the shattered face of her friend, mentor and lover, and fired. The bullet smashed into her forehead, cleaving her head in two and slicing a deep ravine in her frontal lobe. She fell to the floor as the blood poured in a thick red ravine through the silky white strands of her neatly trimmed hair. Her face came to rest opposite that of the Cardinal, the pair of them gazing at each other in a vacant but passionate death stare. Bernie Staker's left hand rested almost peacefully upon the base of the Chief Superintendent's exposed throat.

'And that was for Gretchen.'

Chapter 80:
Cannibal

Billy was racing after the Corsa that was now two hundred yards or so in front. The rain was pouring down and visibility was limited but he followed the red trail of the taillights.

'How the hell did you get out of there, Bill?'

Billy West was smiling like a kid that had just heard a dirty joke. 'Well, funny story.'

Raven glanced at Randall, who had his eyes glued on the speeding white car, and shrugged. 'Well, go on then. Spill the beans.'

'Well, I got clocked good and proper by your mate, Wesley.' Raven felt a pang of sorrow as he recalled the bullet shattering his friend's skull. 'And I blacked out. Luckily,' he crossed his chest, 'the little shit had left me for dead so when I came to and heard the explosion, I decided to take my chances and head back to the vault.'

Raven frowned. 'But, what about those hired hands with guns?'

Billy nodded. 'Yeah, I know. I was worried about that. But it turns out that Ronny had beaten the living crap out of two of them and the third must have legged it.' Billy nodded towards Raven whose mouth had dropped open. 'I get it, that means he's on the loose and will probably want his bloody revenge – if he can prove that we were in on it of course – but, either way, when I got back to the vault the money was gone, and so were Ronny and Dynamite Del.'

Raven urged him on. 'So what did you do?'

'I just walked out the front door of that place and onto the High Street like nothing had happened. After that I walked home.'

'You always were a lucky sod, Billy.'

Billy waved a hand. 'Well, you have to earn the luck you know.'

Randall turned and eyed him suspiciously. 'So what brought you to that field, out in the middle of nowhere, at that particular time? What the hell were you doing up there?'

Raven turned to him. 'Randall!'

Kipruto held up his hands. 'Not that I'm not grateful.'

Billy continued, 'Well, I got to thinking about what Ronny had said about the tunnel network under Westhampton. How the tunnels were old, medieval even, and how people had used them for smuggling back in the day. I knew that someone must have mapped it all out at some point.'

Raven shook his head. 'I thought the blueprints had been destroyed.'

Billy took a sharp right hand turn and followed the Corsa up the hill. The transit hit a deep puddle of rain water and the back end spun to the left but he expertly brought the van back under control.

Randall cautioned him. 'Lay back a bit, Billy. We don't want her to know we're tailing her.'

Billy eased his foot off the accelerator. 'There's always a record somewhere, Raven. You should know that.'

Raven nodded. He should. He'd become lazy in his old age.

'I called my old mate, Spongey, on account of him soaking up information like a sponge soaks up water. Anyway, he has a mate, Blackstuff, who's a dab hand on the dark web.'

Randall groaned.

Billy held up his hands. 'It's okay, I don't use him often. Anyway,' he turned down the pounding drum and bass a little, 'he went online and found some old website used by local criminals and various hoodlums, and it turns out they use these tunnels to hide their shit all the time. These things are all over the place, stretching from the estuary to the east, to the west towards Lymington and almost as far inland as Brockenhurst. One of the tunnels even pops out under the Golden Swan, although that was blocked up long ago too. The only open tunnel, aside from the one that you can get to from Annie's Cove of course, is the one that you guys just popped out from.' He grinned. 'So I took a gamble, jumped in my van and drove up there to see what was what.'

Raven glanced at Randall. 'Well, I for one am very happy that you did, Bill.' Raven patted him on the shoulder. 'We have a murderer to catch and without you she would have been long gone.'

Billy's mouth fell open. 'A murderer?'

Raven nodded grimly. Lightning flashed across the sky and momentarily turned the inside of the van into something resembling a butane lamp.

'I thought she was one of the gang that accosted us in the

494

jewellers!'

Raven shook his head. 'She's a cannibal.'

Billy almost swerved the car off the road. 'A cannibal! Like, she eats *humans*?'

Raven gave a sombre laugh. 'I'm pretty sure that's the definition.'

'And we're following her?'

Randall turned to face him with a look of sincere professional pride and a determination in his dark eyes. 'We're going to bring her in, yes.'

Billy exhaled. 'Jesus guys, what is this town coming to?'

The Corsa indicated right and pulled into a large driveway that led up to a huge, Victorian style mansion with tall turrets and sweeping architraves.

'That's the Staker mansion. Her dad's place.' Raven turned to Randall. 'We might need back up.'

Randall nodded. 'Let's do a reccy and see what's up.'

Lightning flashed again as Raven nodded in agreement.

Billy looked at them as he turned the van onto the driveway. 'Do I need a gun?'

Raven shrugged. 'Well, as there's only one between the three of us Bill, I would say you're out of luck.' He patted Billy on the arm. 'Just stay in the van.'

Billy sighed, relieved. 'Sounds like a good plan to me.'

They watched as Molly leapt out of the car and entered the building. Then they all jumped when they heard the gun discharge twice.

Raven turned to Randall. 'Time to move.'

Chapter 81:
Ghost Ship

Raven made it to the front door first and what he saw made him stop dead in his tracks.

There was a red head in a black T shirt and with blood on her face and a crossbow in her hands and he realised with a deep and unfathomable dread that it was Lisa. Three bodies, including Chief Superintendent Deveraux, lay prone on the floor in front of her with more blood pooling around them than Raven ever cared to see and a hapless guy with a lazy eye, his hands thrust deep into his pockets as if protecting his crown jewels, looking down dumfounded at them. Molly Staker, her right arm hanging down by her side with a pistol hanging limply in her hand, casually strutted around the dead bodies as if they were roadkill, her eyes wild and alive.

Randall crashed into his back clumsily and Raven held a finger up to his mouth. 'Let's just listen.'

Molly spoke with the authority of someone twice her age. 'Well … Timothy isn't it?'

The guy with the lazy eye nodded. 'Yes, ma'am.'

'Can I call you Tim?'

His voice cracked a little as he muttered a half-assed

response. 'Oh well …' He shrugged. 'I mean, of course, ma'am.'

'We seem to have ourselves a situation here, Tim, don't you think?' Molly was pacing from side to side, her dead father lying at her feet like a beggar hoping for a glimpse of loose change.

'I …' Tim anxiously glanced around himself. 'I don't know that I understand.'

Lisa peered over the top of Molly's sleight shoulders and spotted Raven standing next to DI Kipruto in the shadows. Her eyes widened but Raven gestured at her to hold her ground.

'Well, let me fill you in then.' Molly held the barrel of the pistol to her mouth as if she was chewing the end of a pencil. 'I've just left my mother, the one that abandoned me.' She pushed up the corner of her mouth with the gun. 'Left her back there in a cave.'

Tim nodded and Lisa beckoned Raven to enter. He held out a hand and urged patience.

'Yes, in a cave with a bunch of dead and hanging bodies. Arms, legs and heads removed of course. I mean, I'm not an amateur.' Molly laughed and the tip of her scar folded into the soft lines of her face. 'Lots of other bodies too, *cadavers* really, just waiting to be carved up and devoured.'

Raven started to move to his left and beckoned Randall to move right. They skulked in the shadows of the deep entranceway of the mansion like cat burglars, both up on the balls of their feet.

'And then I get here, Tim, without any idea of what I was planning on doing other than wanting to go back to my old room and kick back. And suddenly I thought, *what the hell*?'

Tim nodded as if acknowledging her dilemma.

Molly waved the gun at him. 'There I was, thinking she was dead.' She paused to clarify. 'My mother I mean.'

'Yes ma'am.'

'And all the while, my daddy dearest here had been keeping a very simple but really rather important truth from me.' She narrowed her eyes in deep and contemplative thought as another bolt of lightning leapt across the sky outside, thunder rumbling around them like the clang of gigantic cymbals being struck by the gods.

Tim shrugged as Raven moved to Molly's left. Lisa stood stationary with the newly re-loaded crossbow casually aimed towards Molly's bright and beaming and yet seemingly unaware, face.

'He took her, you see, took her away, beat her I suppose to a point at which her life probably didn't seem worth living.' Molly gasped as if remembering something funny. 'She even had to have her bloody legs amputated, he beat her so badly! And then he tells me, the little toddler me that is, that she had died. Just like that. And why did he do that? So that he would have free reign to mould me, shape me in his image, in a way that would prove useful to him. Made me who I am today, you might say.' She paced towards Tim, his good eye wide and anxious, his drooping eye nervously peering from under his heavy lid. 'Made me who I am! Can you believe that?' She raised her eyebrows. 'Like I needed … *making*!'

Raven glanced across the hallway at Randall who was now at a forty-five degree angle from the beleaguered bodyguard. Lisa started to inch forwards, slowly.

'I was already who I am today, way before my mother

fake abandoned me and way, *way* before my father knocked me senseless with the stock of his hunting rifle and then *apparently accidentally* let me in on his little torture session with that hopeless bimbo whose parents were members of the *club*!'

Molly was increasingly animated and Raven was becoming more and more concerned that the gun in her right hand might go off at any moment.

Lisa mouthed soundless words to him which he interpreted as '*Hayley's on the parchment.*' He mouthed back: '*What?*'

Lisa tried again, this time adding emphasis with her eyes. She nodded her head to her rear, left hand side. '*Bailey's up on Bagpus.*'

Raven watched her lips with intense interest and shrugged. '*Eh?*'

'What did he think? Those episodes in my life; the abandonment, the being left to fend for myself for days, *weeks* at a time, spying him and his buddies meting out pain and fetish based *sex torture* on young, terrified men *and* women! Did he think it would all have some kind of profound, demonizing effect on me?' She gasped, astonished. She bent down and grabbed her father's shattered face in her hands, the blood oozing between her small but determined fingers. 'Is that what you thought, Daddy? That I would become just like you?' She squeezed what remained of his fleshy cheeks, the skin splitting around the wound. 'Follow in your wondrous but hard to follow footsteps?'

Lisa tried again and this time a little sound escaped from her lips. '*Harry's in the BASEMENT!*'

Raven felt his heart sink in abject terror. Harry was there

too! His whole family, everyone he cared about, was in immediate danger. He had to do something, and soon. He moved quickly around the back of the still crouched Molly Staker and towards the fiery red head he had once called his lover. She held out her hands as if urging caution. Raven glanced up and saw Randall, the handgun drawn, making his way towards the side door to the great hall. He nodded at Raven affirmatively.

Molly raised her head towards Tim. 'I really don't care about my dad, Tim.' She wiped a tear from the corner of her eye and snorted. 'I really don't. Couldn't give a damn really, nor my mother.' She waved the gun and slammed her father's head into the floor. Blood splattered on the tile beneath him. 'Terrible parents, both of them.' Tears started to spill down her freckled cheeks and run along the pink skin of her jagged scar. She wiped them away once more dismissively. 'All I cared about was Teddy.' Molly stood and hugged herself. 'My Teddy.' She closed her eyes. 'Oh, how I loved him so. Teddy was my one.' She nodded her head. 'My one and only, my heart and soul. My breath, my air.' She was almost singing. 'My blood, my touch, my taste. My every sense. We were as one.' She kissed her arm as if kissing a lover's smooth lips. 'We were passionate, intense, raw and naked.' She started to sob once more, and her body shook with a terrible and eternal sorrow. 'I will never replace him. *Never.*'

Tim the bodyguard stayed silent, dumbfounded, keeping his eyes fixed directly on Molly.

Molly opened her eyes as Raven moved swiftly and silently behind her and Randall edged towards the newly captivated bodyguard from just out of Molly's eye-line.

'I lost him. *She killed him*!' Molly seethed as if all of the anger in her tiny frame was rising up from the heels of her boots and bleeding through her pores like hot, sulphuric lava. '*Delilah*!' Molly wheeled around and pointed the gun at Lisa. 'Like *her*!'

Lisa gripped the crossbow, startled.

Molly spat on the floor. 'Red-haired *harlot*!'

Lisa cocked her finger on the crossbow's trigger and tried to still her shaking hands. 'Move that gun away from me, before one or both of us gets hurt.'

Molly laughed, but the tears flowed from her dark eyes like rainwater from a broken gutter. 'Do you think I care? Do you think I really give a damn what happens to me?' The hand holding the gun was shaking.

Randall grabbed the distracted bodyguard around the throat and mouth and dragged him into the shadows. Tim conceded his position almost without a struggle, seemingly realising with a grim certainty that being dragged away by what he could only assume was someone with authority was much better than standing out there in the open with a volatile young lady who had confessed to being a cannibal and who also had a handgun.

Raven was in reaching distance of Molly and glanced up at Lisa who had her eyes set determinedly on the brash young woman. He didn't want to misjudge his timing and inadvertently cause an accidental squeeze of the trigger. Either Lisa would be killed or he would, and either way their son would spend the rest of his life without one or other of his parents.

'I don't know anyone called Teddy.'

Molly shook the gun at her. '*Liar*!'

Lightning flashed again and this time the building rattled as if being shaken by an invisible force. Raven looked around him and saw a darkness creeping into the corners of the room, a darkness that he had hoped that he would never have to witness again. He felt ice form in his veins and a dryness build in his throat. Randall had gagged and cuffed Tim and shoved him into the Great Hall, and when he returned he peered up at the darkness that was starting to descend upon them and glanced over at Raven, confused.

Lisa continued trying to keep Molly's attention. 'I'm not lying!'

Molly cried out as if being slapped across the face. She held a hand up to her scar and scratched at it furiously 'First my mother leaves me behind for a so-called better life. Then my father with his night-time visitors and sordid little games. Gretchen kept it all from me but I knew. And then Delilah - with Teddy. *Liars, all of you!*'

There was a roar that emanated from somewhere beneath their feet and the bodies – Bernie Staker, Christy Deveraux and Gestapo Marty – vibrated as if being shaken awake by an invisible hand.

Molly's eyes rolled up into her head and her body started to convulse. She whispered, 'Liars, liars, liars, liars ...' over and over again like a mantra. Raven reached for the gun in her hand but she turned to face him. Her voice was deep, coarse and menacing. *'Luke Raven, you have returned*!'

The room was now almost completely in the shadows, the only light emanating from a glow that had entombed Molly's small frame. Her hair stood on end like a dark and moving head dress, her skin turned a shade of jaded pink and the scar on her right cheek glowed a fiery red. Her eyes were still

502

rolled up into her skull like white and yellow marbles and her head was jittering from side to side like she was a puppet in a stop motion movie.

Randall was standing behind her, dumbstruck. Lisa moved first.

'Harry!' She turned to head back to the kitchen and make her way to the basement but the newly re-modelled Molly raised her hand.

'*Stay where you are, WHORE!*' The voice was not her own, someone or something had possessed her, but Raven sensed there was still plenty of Molly Staker in there.

'Who are you?' Raven thought he knew the answer but had to ask.

Molly laughed. '*We've met before, Luke. You know me. I came for your soul the last time I was invited back to your world, but you gave me another.*'

Raven recalled the moment his partner, Damian Barber, had been struck by the bullet. A bullet that was meant for Raven and fired from a gun which was discharged by the confused and misled Tony Richards. The man they had dubbed the Pale Faced Killer. 'You were a dream, a communal hallucination.' His mouth was drawn down in a grimace that shrieked of disgust and denial. 'You were never real!'

The ground shook again and a splinter formed in the earth, a crack that ran from the open front door and ended at the foot of the large staircase before him.

Molly Staker laughed. '*Is that what they told you, that I was a hallucination?*' Her head cocked to the side. '*I rose from the furnace, the molten and the boiled, to reach for your black and tarnished soul, exposed myself to you in my all-*

powerful, all-vanquishing glory, my body crossing the thin veil that separates our very different worlds, and yet you believe that I was nothing but a vision?' She leaned forward. *'A deity in a world that does not believe in gods? A monster in a world that gives its own monsters the keys to the kingdom? No, Luke. I'm afraid I am very real, very real indeed.'*

The crack in the ground widened to almost three feet in width and Raven found himself peering down into a ravine, perhaps a mile in depth, with fire and molten rock at the bottom of a wide and open cavity. He looked up at Lisa and Randall but he immediately understood that the scene was meant for him and him alone. Within the flames, crouching down as if inspecting the burned and bloodied souls that lined the ravine floor, sat a black and ominous figure; its tail long, its claws sharp and its eyes as red as blood. It looked up at Raven and smiled, its teeth dripping with rotting flesh and black ash, its scales cracked and split like burnt skin. It reached to him, an arm that somehow closed the mile long distance between the ravine floor and the open hallway of the mansion, and he felt the white hot tip of its razor like claw on his cheek.

'It's time for you to lose something precious to you, Luke.' Molly grinned. *'Something you love more than yourself, something that you cannot live without.'*

A bolt of lightning scorched the earth outside and there was a boom of thunder so loud that it felt like it lifted the house from its very foundations.

He heard a child's voice and looked up to see his son burst through the door from the kitchen hallway and skip across the tiled floor of the reception area as if he didn't have a care in the world. He merrily passed Lisa before she had the notion to scoop him up and proceeded to run towards the open arms of the eagerly welcoming Molly Staker, as if the woman with the wild hair and demonic eyes was as familiar to him as his own mother.

'*Come to me, Harry, that's right.*' Molly's head turned and she glared at Raven, her eyes orange and enflamed. '*Come to Molly, come to me my sweet. I'll take good care of you my child, far better care of you than the two hateful and volatile humans who have had the audacity to call themselves your parents.*' She bent down on her knees and wrapped her arms around the young boy. She peered over Harry's shoulder and winked at his mother, slowly dragging her tongue across her dry and cracked lips.

'That's my *son*!' Lisa, her mouth drawn down in a vengeful sneer, raised the crossbow. 'I'm giving you three seconds to let my boy go, you bitch.' She thrust the weapon in front of her like a pitchfork. 'And then we'll see what this baby can do!'

Raven held up his hands. 'Lisa, no! You might hit Harry! Let me talk to her.'

Lisa growled. 'I'm done talking!'

Raven looked down at the gaping hole in the ground and watched as the black and crooked figure crouching within the flames reached out and started to pull itself up the rock face, its mouth open, its black tongue peeking out from between its dagger like teeth. He looked up at Randall and Lisa but they appeared completely unaware of the monster ascending from the fiery depths, the crack in the earth just metres away from them. Randall was completely focused on Molly and his son.

'Lisa, please.' He glanced at Molly who was cradling his boy in her arms. 'For Harry.'

Lisa's finger rested on the trigger of the crossbow; the bolt aimed at the spot between Molly's eyes. Her own eyes flitted to Raven; her brow furrowed in uncertainty

'Take the shot, Lisa. Do it. Do it now!' Molly was laughing. *'Come on! You want to. You know you do*!' She held Harry out like a toy doll. Raven wondered how the young woman could be so strong. Her arms held Harry as if he were no weight at all. *'You're full of all the threats and all the fight. Come on! Let's see what you've got!'*

Harry was crying now, the ugly voodoo doll held to his cheek like a comforter. Molly was terrifying him.

'Let him go Molly! Just let him go!' Raven implored while keeping one eye on his ex-girlfriend and half an eye on the rapidly approaching demonic beast. 'He's done nothing! He's innocent! If it's me you want then take me!'

Molly threw her head back and laughed, a high pitched mewling laugh like the piercing cackle of a hyena. Lightning flashed across the sky once more, the rain coming down in torrents. *'I don't want you Raven! I have no interest in you! You're nothing to me now, nothing at all! I have something better!'*

'My son? Why?' Raven looked up at Randall who was preparing to make his move from the shadows.

Molly shook Harry like a rag doll. He screamed. *'Because he means everything to you!'*

Raven held out his hands. He peered into the depths and glimpsed the hateful eyes of the rapidly rising deity, its claws gripping the earth like the talons of a velociraptor, its tail whipping from behind it like the thrashing torso of a deadly snake. It was coming for him.

'He does, he does. He is my life, my heart.' Raven stepped forward towards the edge of the smoking split in the earth. 'But if you take him, I will still be here, still alive, still able to come after you.' He shook his head. 'I will never rest, not one minute of one day.' He peered at her from under his heavy brow. 'Not until I have my son.' He growled. 'Or I have my revenge.'

Randall leapt from behind Molly and grabbed her around the shoulders, the gun pushed into the small of her back. 'Molly Staker, I'm placing you under arrest for the murder of …'

Suddenly the gun turned in Randall's hand, his wrist cracking as an unseen force turned the Glock towards his own chest. Randall released Molly and placed his left hand on the grip of the gun, desperately wrestling with the invisible hand that was crushing his bones and compressing his flesh. He screamed out as his trigger finger was violently depressed, several bones in his hand fracturing in the process, and the bullet left the barrel of the gun, whizzed through the short space between it and his body and pierced a hole in his side. He fell backwards.

'Don't fuck with me, Raven!' Molly whirled on him, spittle flying from her mouth. *'I am blessed*!'

Molly's back was to Lisa so she seized the moment. Lisa pulled the trigger of the crossbow and the bolt swiftly and silently left the barrel and tore through the air towards its target's exposed spine. Almost instantly Molly stepped to her left and the bolt whizzed past her and disappeared out of the open front door. She turned and pointed her own gun at Lisa. She smiled. *'Game over, my sweet*!'

Lisa gasped. She had nowhere to go, nowhere to run. She looked up at Raven, her eyes wide and pleading. She mouthed a silent, '*I'm sorry.*'

Without warning a claw hammer came flying through the air from the direction of the entrance, striking Molly on the side of the head with a loud and gruesome thwack. She dropped Harry and fell to the floor, blood pouring from a large gash in her skull.

Billy West stood in the open doorway, grinning. 'I thought you guys might need some help.'

Molly pushed herself up and grabbed the boy once more. She pointed her gun at Billy and fired but he moved with a grace that belied his stocky frame and dived behind the heavy wooden door. The bullet struck the thick mahogany and splinters erupted from it like sharp, brown shrapnel. Molly leapt to her feet and made for the exit just as the demon's claw appeared from the cavernous hole in the ground. Molly laughed as she fled. *'He's coming for you, Raven!'*

Raven saw the black and gigantic crown of the beast rising from the smouldering split in the earth, smelled the burning flesh of a billion lost souls and felt a fear that rippled through his flesh like electricity. He turned, took the gun from the raised hand of the wounded Randall Kipruto and raced after Molly. He had to get to his son.

Molly was quick and had almost made it to her car before Raven exited the building.

He ran to the rear of the vehicle as Molly opened the back door. The rain was pouring from the heavens like a waterfall and he was soaked within seconds.

'Give me my son!'

He raised the Glock and pointed it at her. He had every intention of killing her. If it was a choice between her life and the life of his son then the decision was the easiest he would ever have to make.

Molly looked up at him, almost surprised, and her hair was normal again. It clung to her face, the rain streaming through her thick, dark curls and soaking her tiny frame. Her eyes were back to the dark brown that they were before, her scar subtle but ever present, her freckles scattered across her face like stars in the night sky. She looked like the pained and vulnerable young woman that she was. He saw fear and sorrow in her eyes. And regret.

'Luke, I …' She looked down at the floor.

'It's okay, Molly. It's okay.'

She shook her head. 'It's not.' Her clothes were sodden but Raven could see tears rolling down her soft, white cheeks.

'I can help you.' He put the gun in the waistband of his jeans.

'Not after everything I've done.'

'There are people, Molly. Specialists. They can,' he paused, 'help unpick the pain that you've suffered.'

Molly looked up, faint hope painted on her face and in her eyes. 'They can?'

Raven nodded. 'They can.'

She took a deep, heaving breath. 'My father, he …'

Raven nodded once more. 'I know.'

'I shouldn't have done … those things.'

Raven shook his head slowly. 'No.'

'Teddy knew. He knew that it was wrong. He told me but I wouldn't listen. I *never* listen.' She looked up at the sky. 'I miss him.'

Raven watched the fragile and enigmatic young woman as the tears streamed down her face and her body shook with each heavy sob. Despite everything, he felt sorry for her. She hadn't stood a chance in life. Not really.

Molly looked down at the floor once more, ashamed. 'I want my mum.'

Suddenly Raven felt the fiery breath of an undead beast, heard the growl of eternal hatred, smelt the ash of a million burned cities. He knew, without needing to turn his head, that the devil was on his shoulder.

Molly looked up and Raven saw that the fire had returned. Her hair fanned out like the long, colourful feathers of a courting peacock and her skin was rippling like thrashing waves on the ocean.

'I am the Hawk!'

She raised her gun and pulled the trigger.

****

Lisa came racing out of the building, almost tumbling onto the paved driveway, and saw Molly bundling a body into the back of her car. Harry was running towards his mother and crying, the voodoo doll lying on the floor beside Molly's feet.

'Luke!'

Molly turned and laughed. She raised a hand.

'See you another time, Lisa!' She opened the car door. 'In this life or the next,' she ran a hand tenderly down her scar. 'God will decide.'

As the rain continued to pour down in heavy streams and

another streak of lightning tore across the sky from right to left, Molly Staker got into her car, fired the engine and raced away into the black of night. Like a ghost ship at sea, within a few moments she had evaporated into the air like vapour.

EPILOGUE

'How's Randall now?' Sally West was perched against the kitchen worktop and sipping on a cup of hot coffee. Her husband, Billy, was sitting almost sheepishly at the breakfast bar.

'Making a good recovery.' He smiled. 'It seems that he and the PC assigned to him, Ruby something or other, have really hit it off. From what Lisa tells me, she's practically his live in nurse, tending to his wounds and god knows what else.'

Sally scolded him. 'Billy!' She pointed a finger. 'Now you're jumping to all sorts of conclusions.'

He shrugged.

'I won't forgive you, you know.'

He looked up. 'For what?'

'For getting yourself into all that trouble with that hoodlum Ronny Valentine and his crew.'

He nodded. 'Yeah, I know. You're right.' He breathed a sigh of relief. 'That could have ended badly.' He looked out of the back window. The sun was beaming and the sky was blue. 'For both of us.'

'You're just lucky that Randall put in a good word for you. Otherwise …'

Billy nodded.

Sally sipped on her coffee. 'You're not a crook like your father, Billy West.' She peered at him over the rim of her cup. 'So don't play at being one. It's unbecoming of you.'

Billy knew she was right.

'I spoke to Jane this morning.'

Billy smiled. He knew Sally had missed her friend. 'How is she?'

'Getting there. She's been through a terrible ordeal and the emotional scars will take a long time to heal. I feel so sad for her, for everything.' Sally's eyes glistened with impending tears. 'But at least now it's over.'

There was a silence between them, both of them recalling the vibrant, caring and beautiful young woman who had once lived next door.

'How's Lisa doing?' Sally set her cup down and plunged her hands into the pockets of her loose fitting slacks. Billy thought she looked beautiful in her butterfly patterned halter neck and with her shoulder length dark hair pulled back in a loose bun. He often wondered how he had bagged himself such a gorgeous wife. What good deed had he done in a past life to deserve to have it so good in this one? He knew he needed to cherish her, to look after her.

'As well as to be expected.' He frowned. 'Harry's fine, I went to see them both just yesterday. He's back to playing with his toys and running his mother ragged. But Lisa looked tired.'

'Well, she will. After everything that's happened.'

'She's strong, though.' Billy recalled the image of Lisa holding the crossbow like a warrior princess with blood on her face and a ferocious intensity in her eyes. 'She doesn't

513

take any shit.'

Sally sat down on the stool next to him and placed a hand on his knee. 'Any news on Luke?'

Billy shook his head. 'No, nothing.'

'And ... the girl?'

Billy ran a hand through his beard. 'Disappeared, almost as if she had never existed.'

Sally wrapped her arms around herself as if her body had suddenly become cold. 'The families of those poor victims. I just can't imagine the trauma, the hurt.' She shuddered. 'Nine people you say?'

Billy nodded. 'The cave was a makeshift abattoir alright. Body pieces scattered all over the place, some with slices taken from them as if they were cuts of prime beef.'

Sally put a hand to her mouth. 'Jesus.'

Silence descended once more.

Sally put a hand on Billy's arm and smiled reassuringly. 'They'll find him.'

Billy nodded. 'I hope so. I really do.'

'They will.'

****

Far away, over rolling hills, deep valleys, raging seas and icy mountains, a fire roared and music played. Dark tumbling curls rested upon sleight shoulders and pink lips sipped on hot, steaming liquid.

The earth shuddered as a kitchen knife sliced through raw, pink flesh. The distant sound of a man's voice wafted through the air like incense.

There was a sigh. And a laugh.

About Pale Face and the Raven

When DI Luke Raven is called out to investigate the death of a young woman on Westhampton Common, the violent and bloody scene triggers a clairvoyant ability within him that he struggles to comprehend. Anthony Richards is a young man with a troubled past and a dangerously urgent desire to re-connect with his estranged father, the enigmatic and mysterious Robert Charon. Meanwhile, a cold blooded murderer with a pale face and a ghostly appearance is on the loose in Westhampton, callously controlled by an ancient demon with a thirst for vengeance.

Pale Face and the Raven is available from Amazon.

BV - #0030 - 141021 - C0 - 197/132/29 - PB - 9781912964895 - Matt Lamination